A Woman's Fight

This book is dedicated to all women and men who deserve equality and a voice.

A Woman's Fight

Chapter 1

1840, Pontoise, France

Twelve-year old Maria held her breath, hiding among the folds of the burgundy-colored velvet drape at the end of the hallway leading to Papa's study. She wasn't supposed to witness one of Papa's secret Masonic meetings, but he'd never know if she kept very quiet.

She held her breath as seven men marched down the hallway, right past her, with Papa at the front of the line. They were all dressed in black suits and top hats with odd little white and blue aprons tied around their waists. The aprons were decorated with light blue rosettes that reminded her of the rosette hair ribbons Papa gave her on her last birthday.

After the men entered the study and shut the door, Maria crept down the hallway and knelt with her ear pressed against the door. Soft voices, too quiet to be heard, spoke, and then hard knocks sounded. She clasped her trembling hands together and brought up the image of the study in her mind. It was her favorite place to sneak off to, although she wasn't allowed inside. The room, always comforting, was infused with the honey-sweet smell of Papa's pipe tobacco. Shelves crowded with books stood against three walls, and Papa's great ornate desk sat in the center of the room.

Another knock. It must have come from the wooden gavel she'd seen on the desk. But why did Papa knock? She strained to hear the words that were spoken louder now, but they were strange and didn't make sense. Then Papa's voice rose above the rest. He said something about beauty, wisdom, and liberty.

The next sound she heard was a rousing cry of 'liberty, equality, fraternity'! She knew what each of those words meant. Papa had seen to it that she was schooled by the best tutors, even though girls were rarely given such a good education. *A girl has a brain just as good as any boy*, Papa said over and over again until the words were chiseled into her memory.

So why then did *Maman* say that only men could be Freemasons and that women were never allowed to see or hear a Masonic meeting? She insisted women were not to get involved with such things. But women and men weren't so different. Maria grew up knowing that.

She had to see inside the room, to see what was happening.

She steeled her nerves and carefully placed a nearby chair in front of the door. After a deep breath, she climbed up on her tiptoes and peered through the transom. An armoire blocked most of her view, but what she did see amazed and frightened her, and made her hands shake. Her father was on his knees, his head bowed, a shining sword laid out in front of him. She'd never seen him on his knees.

He raised his hands and said, "This Lodge is opened. Hail to the Great Architect."

Who was the Great Architect? Maria could hardly breathe. She wanted more than anything to be in that room, close to Papa, kneeling with him. He wasn't one to exclude her from anything, so why this? What was so secret that she wasn't allowed inside? If they were discussing liberty and equality, then she wanted to be a part of the discussion. Papa said many times that men and women must be equal, or society would collapse. Yet here he was, participating in a meeting where women were not allowed. It wasn't right.

She stretched a little higher for a better view, but the chair wobbled, and she lost her footing. The chair tipped over and she fell to the ground, landing on her side. She scrambled to her feet and hoped nobody heard the clatter.

A loud, angry-sounding voice called out, "Right Worshipful Master, there is an intruder!"

They'd heard. Maria ran as fast as she could down the hallway to her bedroom and slipped under the bed covers. She'd seen and heard too much and now Papa would be furious. In the dark, she trembled. What would happen to her if they found out that she was the intruder? Would Papa be angry? A moment later, her door opened a few inches, and a stream of light shot in. She squeezed her eyes shut, pretending to be asleep.

Papa's soft voice whispered, "Maria."

She didn't answer.

He whispered again, "Maria, I know it was you. Curiosity is admirable, but not in this instance. I envision that one day women will be initiated into the Brotherhood and will stand as equals to men, but until that time, do not ever listen in again or you will face dire consequences."

A cold chill snaked up her spine. The door closed and she was again plunged into darkness. Dire consequences? What could that mean? The Masonic meeting had to be important, or they wouldn't threaten intruders with dire consequences. Now she really wanted to know what they discussed, and to experience everything Papa and the rest of the Masons did. She'd find a way to break the "men only" rule and make Papa's vision come true. One day, she'd stand with him as a Freemason.

Chapter 2

1870, Paris, France

Maria stood in the Masonic Hall, her hands gripped tightly on the edges of the lectern. The hall was filled to capacity with well-dressed men, watching her, waiting to hear what she had to say. They'd come from all over Paris to hear her speech, or perhaps to see for themselves if a woman could speak intelligently on the subject of equality. They'd find out soon enough. She felt honored to be the only woman invited to speak in the Masonic halls and filled with pride when she received praise for her eloquence. The only thing better would be if she could be a Freemason herself.

She drew in a deep breath and smiled. With all eyes on her, she focused her attention on the speech, her nerves dissipating. "Honored gentlemen, we are heading towards the twentieth century, yet France has fallen into a dreadful state where not all of her citizens are treated equally. These are not the medieval days of ignorance. To allow the mistreatment of anyone should be a criminal offense. A crime is being committed on our shores. Whom do we hold responsible for this crime?" She paused to let them consider her question for a moment. "We must hold ourselves responsible, for we are France, and we should be ashamed of what we allow to happen in our great country. As Freemasons, you are all bound by oath to serve humanity, so I ask you now, what will you do? Will you stand by and watch the poor suffer and die or will you rise up and speak out against this corrupt and cruel government of ours?"

A roar erupted from the crowd. Maria had roused their compassion, her goal. If they truly took their oath seriously, they'd make excellent benefactors to the cause of equality. With the Masons on her side, the government would have to listen. As Papa had always said, a thousand voices were stronger than a single voice.

When the audience settled down, she finished her speech and politely shook hands with the audience members as she made her way through the hall. Outside, rain tumbled down and splattered on the cobblestones. She hurried to a waiting carriage. She never liked to hang around, feeling that an emphatic speech held more impact if it was left ringing in the ears and not spoiled by idle chatter.

Tired, she leaned back against the leather seat as the carriage rolled down the road with the methodical rain pattering on the canopy. She loved the rain because it cleaned and freshened everything, at least it felt that way. If only people's minds could be washed clean so easily.

The carriage stopped at an intersection and Maria wiped the rain-splattered window with her sleeve. There was a sea of umbrellas bobbing up and down as people scurried to or from somewhere, dashing this way and that, trying to keep dry.

As a group of people stepped off the footpath to cross the street, she saw a young, bedraggled woman crouched on the street corner. The woman was drenched from the late afternoon rain, and even from across the street Maria could see she shivered. A small child lay across the woman's lap and a tiny limp arm with pale fingers poked out from beneath a ragged coat sleeve. Not one person stopped to help or offer money.

Maria grasped the sill of the window until her fingers hurt. She had to do something. She jumped out of the old two-wheeled Cabriolet carriage, and ran across the street, holding her hand up to stop the traffic. She stepped around puddles and dodged fast-moving carriages that refused to slow down, her clothing sodden.

When she made it to the woman, Maria extended her hand. "Come with me."

The woman took Maria's hand and cradled her child with her free arm. As they sheltered in an alcove, Maria grabbed the sleeve of a well-dressed man as he passed by. "Do you not see this woman and child? Are you any better than them simply because you have money? Are you blinded by ignorance? Perhaps you could open your purse in the name of humanity rather than spend your precious francs on some trinket in the name of selfishness."

The man freed himself from her grasp and rushed off down the street. Maria straightened her shoulders and adjusted her soaked hat whose feather drooped down over her cheek. She tugged gently on the woman's hand. "*Ma chère*, I will take you somewhere safe and warm."

Blinking the rain from her eyes, the woman cuddled her child close and whispered, "*Madame*, I don't want pity."

The woman was young and barely out of her teenage years. It wasn't pity Maria felt, but concern. She couldn't imagine being a young mother with no money and no hope. How could any woman manage under those circumstances?

"It's *mademoiselle*. I pity the thoughtless men who ignore all but the upper classes, not those less fortunate souls." Maria stepped out into the footpath and blocked the way. She raised her voice to those passing, "Do you find it easier to dismiss a poor woman than sympathize with her plight?"

"*Mademoiselle*, please," the young woman implored, tugging on Maria's sleeve.

Maria apologized, "I did not mean to embarrass you. I have a rental carriage across the street." She pointed to the carriage. "It's warm and dry. If you will allow me, I will take you to a rooming house, not out of pity, but to make up for the lack of kindness in this world. My name is Maria Deraismes."

"I'm Berdine, *Mademoiselle*."

Maria held Berdine's cold hand tightly and when she didn't resist, led her across the street toward the carriage. They lost their footing several times on the slippery cobbles but recovered and continued to the other side.

As they climbed into the carriage, a well-dressed man with a woman hanging onto his arm shouted, "If you feed gutter rats, they'll only breed more gutter rats. You should have let the rain wash away the rubbish."

Ignoring the man, Maria called to the driver standing on the platform at the back, "Phillipe, take us to the rooming house on *rue Callais*, please. The one run by *Monsieur* Abbon."

Berdine sat quietly, her head slumped over her child and her hands trembling. Maria could see in her demeanor that she was ashamed, embarrassed to be the person she was and where she was. It cut into Maria's heart. She wanted to take Berdine in her arms and tell her everything would be all right, but it would be a lie. Nothing would be all right until poverty and social classes were eliminated.

Before long, they arrived at the red brick rooming house. She would have escorted Berdine herself, but the speech had left her weakened with her usual stomach ailment and she had to get home. She spoke as kindly as she could, "Please tell the proprietor, *Monsieur* Abbon, that I ask he give you a room." She took Berdine's hand. It was like ice. "He usually has a pot of stew or soup on the stove. It's not the best, but it will warm you and your baby."

The carriage swayed as Phillipe climbed off the platform and came around to the doorway. He held an umbrella for Berdine. "I'll escort you inside, *Madame*."

Berdine leaned toward Maria and whispered, "I am also a *mademoiselle*. I have no husband."

"It matters not to me, *ma chère*. Now go inside and get your child out of this awful storm. Should you need anything more, let *Monsieur* Abbon know. He's a kind man." Maria tucked a handful of francs into Berdine's palm.

Berdine nodded and stepped from the carriage and huddled beneath the umbrella. Maria rubbed her hands together, wishing she'd worn her gloves, then felt a pang of guilt that she lived in a fine house with plenty of clothes, food and furnishings, and was able to hire a carriage on rainy days, while Berdine had no such luxuries at all. What was money anyway? Paper and coins. How ridiculous to value a thing so inanimate above humanity. Maria did her best to never let money define her. She swore many years ago that she would use her inheritance as a means of survival, not as something to elevate her status. Papa would have wanted it that way as well.

While Maria watched through the misty carriage window, Phillipe took Berdine to the door of the rooming house, returned to his position at the rear of the carriage, and started off again. The carriage rolled along over the cobbled streets, its old springs creaking as the wheels fell into ruts and grooves. They passed couples on their way to the theatre or to some restaurant for a sumptuous meal, their heavy woolen coats and umbrellas keeping them dry. Such a contrast it was. The elite and the destitute living side-by-side, one ignoring the other's plight and simply going about their business as if the poor around them didn't exist.

The damp chill of the night mixed with her wet clothes made Maria tremble. The cold had settled deep into her bones. If only the clouds would part and allow the sun to warm the city, even for a short time.

She was soaked to the skin, which meant there'd be no way to hide that she'd been out in the rain. She dreaded the inevitable fuss that her older sister, Anna, would make when she saw her dripping wet. With a firm, motherly voice, Anna would send her right to bed with a cup of hot tea, clicking her tongue and shaking her head, complaining that the cold would aggravate Maria's childhood stomach ailment. And it had. But Maria didn't want mothering. She wasn't a child anymore.

The carriage stopped.

"*Mademoiselle*, we're here," Phillipe announced as he came around and opened the door, the large black umbrella in his hand. "Allow me to assist you inside."

"Thank you, Phillipe." She climbed out, her legs shaking and her teeth chattering. "I think it's gotten even colder."

"I believe you're right." Holding the umbrella over her, Phillipe walked her up the path to her front door. "Will you need the carriage again tomorrow, *Mademoiselle*?"

She paused under the covered stoop. "No, no, I'll be staying in tomorrow. I have a speech to write for the conference on human rights at the Grand Orient Masonic Lodge. You will attend, won't you?"

"I will certainly do my best to make it. I always look forward to your speeches, such amazingly turned words, better than most men, I'd wager. You write from the heart. Paris will someday be at the forefront of equality, I can feel it. I've been reading some of *Monsieur* Hugo's writing, like you suggested, and I've concluded that you and *Monsieur* Hugo are the saviors of the common people."

"Savior? I hardly compare to a great writer like Victor Hugo, Phillipe. He can spin ordinary words into a masterpiece. I don't measure up to him. I'm sure *Monsieur* Hugo's a far greater humanitarian than me as well. He would probably have taken that woman and child into his home rather than a rooming house."

"*Mademoiselle*, please take no offense, but your home isn't so large that you can take in all the strays of Paris. You should take pride that you do what so many refuse to do. You make a difference to the suffering. You and Victor Hugo. Like I said, the saviors of Paris."

She wanted to change the subject. No one should be called a savior when they were trying to do what was right. It was common decency, not being a savior. "Oh, by the way, I heard that *Monsieur* Hugo is finally out of exile and has returned to Paris."

Phillipe nodded. "Yes, I heard that also. He should never have been forced from France in the first place. Good people are hard to find. Imagine if both of you collaborated on a speech. That would be one talk nobody would soon forget. Two of the best writers in Paris, side by side, speaking from their hearts." He chuckled and shivered, then motioned to the door. "Listen to me prattling on when you should be inside out of this cold rain."

"Nonsense. One more minute in the late afternoon air won't kill me. You bring up an interesting point, Phillipe. What a draw it would be if we could have Victor Hugo's name on the agenda. He's also a Freemason, did you know that?"

Phillipe shook his head. "I didn't. Then surely he'll come to help support you and the Masons. And likely half of Paris will come along as well."

Maria felt a sense of camaraderie with Phillipe because his views about equality and rights mirrored her own. She went out of her way to use his services, even though his carriage wasn't the most comfortable and she had a perfectly good carriage at home. It was better to give him the money when she rented a carriage, rather than give it to the large Parisian Transport Company. Phillipe lived frugally in a one-bedroom apartment, raising four children on his own. He deserved the money more than a transportation giant.

Maria placed her hand on the doorknob, but hesitated. "Would you like to come inside for a moment, to warm up a bit? I'm sure Anna has a pot of tea on the stove."

"I would like to, *Mademoiselle*, but I have more passengers to pick up. It also wouldn't look good for someone like me to be in your house at night."

"Oh, hang decorum! I am fed up with everybody passing judgment on others. You are welcome in my house at any time, day or night. But I do understand if you must get going to pick up another fare. Thank you for the ride." She reached into her purse. There was nothing there. "Oh, dear, Phillipe, I've given all my money to that poor woman. I am so sorry. I'll send the money to your house tomorrow."

"No need to apologize." He tipped his top hat, causing rivulets of water to run from the brim and splash onto the stoop. "I will do my best to make it to the speech."

"I'll see to it that the doorman at the Lodge knows you're my guest. Good night, Phillipe." She opened the door and stepped inside. A rush of warm air enveloped her. She hurried to shut the door behind her to keep out the chill.

She took off her coat in the foyer and hung it on the coat rack, a trickle of water dripping onto the white marble floor. In the fireplace across the room was a huge crackling fire with flames licking their way up the chimney. She crossed the room quickly and sat close to the fireplace, settling into Papa's old worn chair. She warmed her hands, then unbuttoned her shoes and placed them on the brick hearth, wiggling her toes to get the blood flowing.

She watched the split logs burn as fiery embers glowed brightly in a display of red and orange. So many people took simple comforts like a fire for granted. How many people would be cold tonight? She knew Diddier Abbon, a Master Mason, would put Berdine and her child in a room for at least a few days. But then what? Where was she to go after that? The Freemasons would help anyone who needed help and offer what they could, but their charitable funds had thinned over the years with so many falling on hard times. If only they'd let women into their ranks, their donations would double.

"Maria, you're home," Anna said from the kitchen doorway, wiping her hands on her apron. "How long have you been here? I just washed the dishes, but there are a few scones left, and I can put on another pot of tea."

"Later. Come and sit with me for a while."

Anna pulled a chair close and sat down, reaching out to feel Maria's clothes. "You're soaked. You need to get out of those wet clothes."

"I will, in a minute." Maria watched the flames. "Oh, Anna, I can't stand how nobody seems to care about anyone but themselves. Everywhere I go, I see our people in misery. Hungry, starving people. Strangers begging for a crust of bread. This is Paris, not some dried up village in the middle of nowhere. How can the government allow this to happen? How can any of us? We need to do more. I need to do more."

"What do you mean? You already devote all your time writing those blasted essays and making speeches. I hardly see you anymore. With your stomach problems, you can't do much more. You push yourself too hard as it is. You know what the doctor says. Do you want to end up bedridden from exhaustion? I promised Mother on her deathbed that I'd look after you."

"And I appreciate everything you do. It's just that I can't in good conscience sit by and do nothing. I just saw a woman begging on the corner, cradling her baby, soaked to the skin in the rain. You should have seen the spectacle, Anna. Nobody looked at them. It broke my heart."

"Is that how you got wet? You went out in the rain without an umbrella? Did you also dress down the well-to-do as they passed by?"

Maria nodded and smiled. She knew how much Anna hated it when she spoke openly and told off the upper classes. "They deserve a few harsh words now and then to remind them they're human. You know what I was thinking? If women are to be equal, we all need an equal education. Without the same education that men receive, we can never attain what they do. You and I were lucky that *Maman* and Papa insisted on us being schooled. Few girls have that opportunity. You know I'm right."

With a sigh, Anna took Maria's hand. "Yes, you are, but I still think you do too much. Come on, go upstairs and get dried off. I'll steep some tea."

Maria got up but paused before going upstairs. "Phillipe said something to me just now."

"Phillipe always says something. That man's mouth never stops moving."

"He's passionate, that's all. He said that I should collaborate with Victor Hugo."

Anna's brow pinched. "What? Victor Hugo? Collaborate how? I doubt that's a very good idea."

Maria knew very well that Anna worried about Hugo's liberal political views and his many run-ins with the government. "I know exactly what you're thinking. But I've made speeches against the government, and nobody has exiled me from France."

"Not yet."

There was no need to respond. Anna wouldn't listen anyway. Maria headed up to her room. Regardless of what Anna thought, she'd have to find out where Hugo was staying and approach him with the idea very soon. Surely he'd say yes.

Maria took off her wet dress and looked over at her desk. She could write Hugo a letter asking him to stand with her at the conference. She'd mention that it was at the Grand Orient Lodge, and hopefully he'd feel obliged to come and speak to his Masonic brothers, just as Phillipe had speculated.

It seemed hypocritical that she was allowed to speak in the Lodge, but she couldn't attend one of their regular meetings. One day, she'd open the doors of the Lodges to all sexes and prove that women were as upright and charitable as any man. She'd don the strange lambskin apron and wear it proudly. Times had to change. Freemasonry had to change. But before any of that, she had to find where Hugo was staying and make sure he agreed to come to the conference. How could he possibly say no to such an invitation?

Chapter 3

Maria spent the next two days sick in bed from a chill. Even though Anna insisted she rest, she still managed to write and edit her speech for the human rights conference. She chose just the right words to convey her thoughts, which of course would be backed by Victor Hugo, if he showed up.

As usual, Anna tended to her every need. It was almost like having *Maman* back. Anna would have made a good mother, if only her husband hadn't died before she'd been able to conceive a child. Now they had each other. Anna's overprotective nature wasn't all bad though. It meant she cared, and that felt good.

After putting the finishing touches on the last paragraph of the speech, Maria got out of bed and went downstairs to the sitting room. She had to get out of her stuffy bedroom for a while. The morning sun shone brightly through the east-facing bay window, casting a rainbow of color across the carpeted floor. How refreshing it was to see the sun. *La belle lumière du soleil*, the beautiful sunlight, as *Maman* had always said.

Maria sat on the padded bench by the window and looked out at the morning. Everything was wet and fresh. Droplets of water clung to branches and puddles were scattered everywhere.

Anna came down the stairs. "You shouldn't be out of bed yet."

"I'm feeling better. Besides, now that the sun's out, I'd like some fresh air. Come with me into the garden."

"You've finished your speech, then?"

"It's as good as I can make it. Did you manage to track down Victor Hugo for me?"

She'd sent Anna the day before to deliver a message to the hotel where he was reported to be staying. Her message asked Hugo to co-write an article about equality, and included an invitation to the conference.

Anna shrugged and draped a blanket over Maria's shoulders. "No, not really. I went to the hotel, but the desk clerk refused to say whether *Monsieur* Hugo was staying there or not. I left your letter anyway." Anna looked away and mumbled, "Against my better judgment."

Maria frowned. It was disappointing news. "You're my sister, Anna, not my mother. Let me worry about politics."

They walked out to the back garden. Anna picked up a pair of shears from under a seat and cut several rose stems. She put down the shears, shook the water from the rose petals and placed the stems on the seat. "The conference is tomorrow, Maria. Aren't you nervous?"

Picking up a rose, Maria breathed in its scent and smiled. "Inside, yes. On the outside, I hope not. For a woman to gain the respect of men, she must not show any weakness. That's what Papa always told me."

Anna nodded. "He really was revolutionary in his thinking, wasn't he? That's where you get it from. I remember sitting around the dinner table in Pontoise, listening to Father and Mother discuss politics and how absurd it was to exclude women. They never made us feel like lesser people just because we were born female. I miss them terribly."

"So, do I. And I'm proud to be like Papa. You're like him, too, only you refuse to admit it." Maria strolled around the garden, lifting her skirt to stop it dragging in the puddles. She inhaled deeply, enjoying the dewy-fresh scent of the roses and fragrant gardenias, thankful that the cold weather hadn't stopped their blooming. "I wish more people were as open-minded as *Maman* and Papa were."

"Are you talking about me? I *am* open-minded. I just don't want you getting in trouble with the government by associating with the wrong sort of people. If you're not careful, you'll end up in a cold, damp jail cell."

"You're exaggerating, Anna."

"I know why you act like you do. You think you need to do as much as you can before you die. Isn't that it? You think if you don't fix the world, nobody will. But you have a long way to go before the reaper pays you a visit, unless you don't slow down." Anna suddenly turned toward the house. "What's that? Did you hear something?" She took a step toward the house. "There, do you hear it? Someone's knocking on the front door."

They both went inside and hurried through the house. Anna opened the door. On the stoop was Phillipe the carriage driver and the woman, Berdine. Phillipe took off his tattered silk top hat and bowed his head.

"*Mademoiselle* Deraismes, this young lady waved me down. She was looking for you."

Berdine came forward, her eyes cast down. She *was* young, younger than Maria had initially thought. Berdine's child was nowhere to be seen.

Maria motioned inside. "*Bonjour, ma chère.* Won't you come in?"

Without looking up, Berdine whispered, "I wish I could do more than offer my thanks to you, but I have nothing." She quickly wiped her eyes with the back of her hand and continued, "My sweet Adella, my precious darling daughter...she is in heaven now. But her last days were spent in a warm room with hot soup to fill her belly. *Merci, Mademoiselle, merci* for your kindness."

Maria felt her face flush. Her body grew heavy, and her knees shook so violently that she stumbled right into Anna, who held her until she regained her footing. She closed her eyes and saw the child, Adella, clearly in her mind. A tiny bundle in ragged clothing. If only she'd done more. Why hadn't she taken them in herself, or at least taken the child to a physician?

"*Mademoiselle*, are you all, right?" Berdine's voice trembled.

Maria took a deep breath. Her lungs filled quickly with much needed air. She took a step forward and grasped Berdine's hands. "Where is your daughter now?"

"Taken away to the pauper's cemetery, *Mademoiselle*. If there is anything I can do to pay you back for your kindness, I will. I can clean and cook. I'll do anything."

Maria couldn't believe what she heard. Here was a woman who'd just lost a child, and she wanted to work to repay a small offering of charity that didn't even save the child. What an absurdity.

"You owe me nothing, *ma chère*. Please, come in and join us for breakfast. Anna, what do we have?"

Anna wiped a tear and said quietly, "Toasted bread, tea cakes, crepes and jam, milk, tea."

Berdine shook her head and backed away slightly, almost pulling free from Maria's grasp. "No, *Mademoiselle*, I cannot impose on you further."

"It's not an imposition. Now, come inside. Phillipe, you're welcome to come in as well." Maria released Berdine's hands and motioned her inside.

With a quick nod, Phillipe crossed over the threshold. "I have some time before my next fare."

When they were inside, Maria closed the door. "Berdine, you are most welcome in our house. Please come and sit by our fire. And know that I am so very sorry for the loss of your child." Maria escorted Berdine and Phillipe to the chairs in front of the hearth and then went to the kitchen with Anna.

No words were necessary as they placed several cakes on a tray and steeped a pot of soothing chamomile tea. As Maria took out four teacups from the cupboard, she had a thought. What if she brought Berdine along to the conference tomorrow? She could serve as an example of what was occurring every minute in Paris. It would force the audience to look at the face of poverty and feel the grief that Berdine felt.

When the tea had steeped, Maria and Anna went back to the sitting room and served their guests. At first, Berdine hesitated to accept any food, but after Maria insisted, she took a cake and ate it quickly. It was obvious that she was very hungry. Maria could only imagine how dreadful it must be to live in constant need. The fear, the heavy burden of never knowing if death was waiting just around the corner, surely must take its toll on even the hardiest of people.

Before long, Berdine had eaten several cakes and downed two cups of tea, slipped her shoes off, loosened her frayed scarf and stretched her feet toward the fire. Her stockings were old, torn, with holes in the toes. Her young face seemed aged beyond its years. Eyes that were surely once curious or hopeful were now dark and sad, that same ghostly visage that Maria saw everywhere throughout Paris. The same faces were on street corners, in parks, or huddled in doorways. Empty eyes and vacant expressions. They were the faces of despair.

Excuse me for a moment," Maria said.

She went upstairs to her room and found a dress in her wardrobe that she'd long outgrown. It would probably fit Berdine's slight figure perfectly. After folding it and placing it in a box, she paused for a moment and picked up a framed daguerreotype of her parents, their faces staring back at her. *Maman* had once donated her entire collection of dresses and overcoats to a home for destitute women. For months, she'd worn the same dress, never complaining and never asking for more.

Why not follow in those footsteps? Maria grabbed all her clothes off the hangers and tossed them in a pile on her bed. What did she need so many clothes for? Half of them she never even wore. And since Berdine wasn't the only woman struggling for survival, a donation program was exactly what Paris needed. If every well-off woman in Paris gave up just one dress, there'd be enough to clothe all the women in the entire city.

"Anna!" Maria called out. "Come up here! I have an idea."

She'd start a citywide donation program. Even the bourgeoisie and the ostentatiously affluent would likely contribute to make a self-serving show of their excess wealth, and their generosity to the lower classes. Whether or not they truly believed in helping the poor didn't matter, so long as the poor benefited.

Maria went to the cedar chest that contained her shoes and pulled out several pair that were in good shape. After all, what were dresses without shoes? When people embrace one another as equals, Paris would become be a shining beacon of love.

Chapter 4

Before going to bed, Maria made plans with Anna to set up a charity through *L'Association pour le droit des femmes*, the association for the rights of women that her friend Léon Richer had started a year ago. It felt so good that there was finally hope on the horizon for the women of Paris.

When she woke the following day, refreshed and cheerful, even the incessant rain that pattered relentlessly on her bedroom window couldn't dampen her spirits. She sat up in bed and smiled at how sweet and gentle Berdine had looked after she'd fallen asleep on the sofa. At that moment, she was no different from any other person.

It had taken some gentle convincing from both Maria and Anna to get Berdine to agree to stay with them, but eventually she'd relented, perhaps from the sheer exhaustion of objecting. Why did so many people demonize the poor? Social standing certainly didn't make someone more or less of a human being. It made no sense to hate those less fortunate. Of course, she knew part of the reason was to have someone else to blame for society's ills, taking no responsibility upon themselves.

Anna knocked on Maria's bedroom door. "Are you up yet?"

Maria's joy waned a bit when she got out of bed and felt a sharp pain in her stomach. She'd have to hide her discomfort, or Anna would insist she stay in bed and rest. That ailment had plagued her since childhood, and it wasn't going to get better. She'd accepted that, but Anna still mothered her. There was no time for rest, because in a matter of hours she'd be making an important speech in front of an audience of Freemasons, intellectuals, and ordinary citizens.

"I'm up," she called to Anna.

She slipped on her soft-soled house shoes and straightened, feeling confident that her speech would evoke a variety of emotions punctuated, hopefully, with a sense of responsibility to do what was right.

She opened the door and saw Anna standing in the hallway with a large bouquet of flowers. "Léon sent these over for you."

"He did? That's not like him. He doesn't generally fritter away money on such vanities. In fact, he never fritters away money at all."

Anna shrugged. "There's a small note attached."

Maria plucked the folded note from among the stems. She recognized Léon's handwriting. There was only one sentence:

Maria, some beautiful blossoms to beautify your day - Léon

She took the flowers from Anna, marveling at their beauty. There were sprays of lilac, sprigs of deep green fern, and perfect pink roses. Their perfume filled the entire room. Anna turned to go without another word. That wasn't like her.

"My darling sister, please tell me you're not still mad with me. You'll come to the conference, won't you?"

Anna turned with a trace of a smile and took back the flowers. "I'll put these in a vase. Of course I'm coming. Someone has to look after you. In fact, Berdine finally agreed to come as well."

"She did?" Maria was a bit surprised that Berdine had decided to attend because she'd declined rather insistently. She must be curious to see and hear what went on at a conference. Curiosity was always a good thing. Well, usually it was. "I'm glad we'll have her with us. Although I need to make sure she's not made a mockery. She'll be our honored guest."

"Of course. I've already told her that she needn't do anything except stay close to me the entire time you're making your speech. She's very smart, Maria. She has no education, yet she speaks well above her situation in life. I can only imagine what she could accomplish with an education. She's anxious to hear what all the speakers have to say about human rights."

"Wonderful!" Maria followed Anna downstairs to the kitchen and placed the bouquet in a Limoges porcelain vase that had belonged to their grandmother. The value of the vase would probably feed a family for a month. It was such an extravagance, but she couldn't bear to part with it. It was all that was left of her beloved *mémère*.

Before long, Maria felt another twinge. She sat down at the large rough-hewn rustic table that Papa built so many years ago and grasped the edge. As much as she tried, she couldn't hide the pain this time. The doctors—so many of them over the years—could never diagnose what was wrong. Frustrating yes, but also frightening not knowing if it could result into a serious complication and force her to be bedridden.

"Your stomach is bothering you again, isn't it? Every time you have a public appearance your stomach acts up. I've already brewed you up a pot of your medicinal tea with an extra dose of peppermint."

The fact that Anna didn't try to make her cancel the conference meant she'd accepted that her objections fell on deaf ears. Maria smiled to herself and watched her sister pour out a cup and tea and put it on the table. "Thank you."

"Just drink the tea. Oh, and Berdine wanted me to tell you something. Something very personal and private. She almost couldn't bear to tell me."

Maria took a sip of the steaming tea. The peppermint, extra strong, instantly soothed as it went down. "What did she tell you?"

Anna sat down across from Maria. "She was very worried that you might judge her cruelly. I assured her you wouldn't. She was never married, you see, but became pregnant while working as a prostitute. Oh, Maria, my heart goes out to her. I can see in her eyes that she feels degraded and less of a woman. With her baby daughter gone, she has no one. I cried all night for her."

Tears tumbled down Maria's cheeks. She wiped them away but more took their place. "Part of my speech is about stopping the government sanctioning of prostitution. There is no way possible that women will ever be considered respectable members of society when the government still allows and even encourages prostitution. What we need are more jobs and honest ways for women to earn a living. Anyway, I'll make certain that Berdine knows that the past is the past. She's got to know that we move forward and learn from the past, but we don't need to relive all of it."

Maria clearly remembered the words of her wise *Maman: All people are the same under the skin, but it's the outside that they are judged by, right or wrong.* Wise words indeed.

Maman had always been far more outspoken and free-thinking than other women in her circle and had stepped beyond the expectations of a wife and mother. She'd been a strong woman who'd lost her only son and another daughter when they were babies. Maria always suspected that was the reason *Maman* doted on her and Anna. They were given every opportunity, especially an education that was usually reserved for boys.

Living without an education seemed impossible, yet many were forced into that life. There were so many things to learn about. And not just the classics, but modern politics and literature. So many women were missing out on the basics, which gave them a distinct disadvantage in life and opened them up to abuse and a lower position in society.

"Anna, did you ever hear from Victor Hugo? Any word at all?"

"No. Nobody really knows if he's even in Paris. It might have been a rumor that he was. You know how rumors circulate."

Maria sighed. "I supposed I didn't really expect him to show up. And what about Honoré Daumier or Barbey d'Aurevilly? Will they be at the conference?"

"Almost certainly." Anna's mouth turned downward into a small frown. "They'll be there to make a stand against equality. I know it's wrong to hate, but I hate those men."

Maria finished the tea. "Maybe it's not such a grand idea to bring Berdine. She's in a very fragile state, and with Daumier and his gang of misogynists present, I don't think it would be a healthy environment for her."

From the doorway, Berdine spoke in her soft, hesitant voice, "*Mademoiselle*, I look forward to attending. I am seventeen years old and for most of those years, I've heard and experienced things no woman, or man, ever should." She glanced at her fee. "Please, what does *misogynist* mean?"

Anna answered, "A woman-hater. Someone who doesn't respect a woman's right to live as an equal." She got up, poured a cup of black tea and handed it to Berdine.

"Oh. I've met many men like that." Berdine looked, a smile on her lips. "I once heard someone say that to discount either gender is to lose half the population."

Maria smiled, too. It was Léon who'd said that. Where had Berdine heard him? It seemed Anna was right, Berdine was a smart young woman. "Sit down, *ma chère*, and have some breakfast. My friend, Léon, will come by later to take us to the conference. Oh, and Phillipe, the carriage driver you've met, will also be coming to the conference, as well as Anna, of course."

Taking a seat, Berdine sipped the tea and brushed a strand of hair from her eyes. "Then I shall have many friends there."

They ate a satisfying breakfast of eggs and toasted baguette with orange and quince marmalade, and lingered over cups of *café au lait*, chatting for the better part of an hour until it was time to begin dressing for the conference.

With some time to herself, Maria sat at her desk in her room and went over her speech. Her concentration was broken when a flash of lightning lit up the sky outside her window and a booming crash of thunder shook the house. No sunshine today.

"Maria! Léon's here!" Anna called.

Maria slipped on her shoes, straightened out her dress, and joined Berdine, Anna, and Léon in the foyer. Léon, with his deep-set eyes and his hair dripping wet, was a pitiful sight. But when he smiled, he became a beacon. His personality shone through the storm. Anna had on a fine dress and shawl. Berdine, who'd fixed her dark hair in a neat chignon, fit into Maria's old dress as if it were tailored just for her.

Berdine pulled Maria aside. "*Mademoiselle,* while I am more than appreciative for all you've done, I must confess that looking as I do, I no longer appear like a poor street person. No one will recognize me as one of the needy."

"Don't you see, you provide exactly the example you should. Appearance is meaningless. Money or situation does not define a person, but a change in circumstance is a thing that any one of us could fall into. You can rise to any position, provided you're given the opportunity. That's what I want the people to know." Maria gave Berdine a hug.

Léon squeezed some of the rain from his hair, came forward with arms spread wide, and embraced Maria. "Ah, my darling Maria." "I didn't request more rain for today."

"Nor did I. Oh, and the flowers are beautiful, but you shouldn't have spent money on such an extravagance." She pulled free and gave him a kiss on both cheeks. He was more than ten years her senior, but she felt almost as close to him as she did to Anna, like an older brother.

"I would never consider you an extravagance. We probably should get going. I've brought my old Phaeton carriage so there'd be enough room for everyone. And don't worry, I just had the roof fixed."

"Wonderful. Our new friend Berdine will accompany us." Maria pointed to Berdine. "She's staying with us for a while. She recently lost her darling baby girl."

Léon gave Berdine a nod. "I am sorry for your loss. Terribly sorry."

"*Merci, Monsieur*," Berdine said softly.

After a brief pause, Léon motioned everyone outside. Maria stepped from the house into the fresh, crisp air. The wet grass smelled sweet, almost like being in the country on a summer's night. Anna handed her an umbrella, sharing one herself with Berdine, and they all followed Léon to the carriage.

With no doors, it was easy to climb inside the Phaeton without the effort of maneuvering layers of skirts and petticoats through a narrow doorway as with other carriages. Anna and Berdine took the rear seat, while Maria sat in the smaller front seat with Léon.

While in good shape, the carriage indeed was old and the springs creaked under the weight of four passengers. Maria knew that the Phaeton had belonged to Léon's grandfather and went through so many renovations that it was practically rebuilt. There was likely little left of its original self, except perhaps the springs.

Once everyone was settled, Léon shook the reins and the two black mares began their stately stride down the street, splashing in puddles trapped between the cobbles. It wasn't long before the rain soon stopped, and a brilliant rainbow streaked across the Parisian sky.

Maria's stomach tightened when they turned onto *rue Cadet*. Just ahead was the Grand Orient Masonic Lodge, the sponsor of the conference. The Masons were always supportive of anything to do with human rights and equality. She'd a suspicion that it was their way of quietly speaking out against the restrictive government, a way of bringing about change by uniting the people. She loved being involved with them and couldn't wait for the day when she'd wear the apron herself.

Although the Freemasons openly embraced the promotion of charity, morality and ethics, they'd been heavily persecuted by Napoleon Bonaparte because he feared them, believing them to be dissidents. And although they'd regained their status in society after Napoleon, they were still not completely free of distrust. Maria understood why. It was primarily because they met in secret and refused by oath to discuss what went on in their closed Lodge meetings. Very few rulers would be comfortable with large groups of citizens discussing things behind closed doors. But to her, they were friends.

As Léon slowed the carriage, finely attired gentlemen walked toward the Lodge, shaking the rain off umbrellas and top hats as they went inside. Carriages, large and small, lined both sides of the street with their horses and drivers already looking cold and bored.

Léon gave Maria a gentle nudge. "Here we are, my lady. Make sure to give me a copy of your speech so I can quote you in the *Opinion Nationale* tomorrow morning."

She reached into her brocade purse and pulled out all three pages of her speech. "You can have it now. I have it memorized." She'd anticipated that Léon would want to print a portion of the speech in his paper.

"I should have known." Léon slowed the carriage to a halt in front of the Lodge building. "Why don't you all get out here and go inside while I park the carriage."

Maria climbed out first, helping Berdine and Anna from the rear seat. She leaned back in. "Don't be long, Léon."

"I won't. I think I saw a spot just down the street." He jiggled the reins and headed off.

Several men, Freemasons Maria knew, tipped their hats to her as they went up the front walk. She climbed up the steps to the Lodge and waited with Anna and Berdine. She was ready and feeling confident right up until she saw Honoré Daumier and his cohorts Jules Barbey d'Aurevilly and Alexandre Dumas making their way toward the building. Of all the men in Paris, why did they always insist on showing up at her speeches? Life would be so much better if they just stayed home.

Her nerves triggered as Daumier got closer. She always felt intimidated by him and could never shake the uneasy feeling he created in her. He kept his eyes on her as he came up the steps, pausing briefly before going inside.

With a barely perceptible nod of his head, he acknowledged Maria and mumbled, "Waste of time listening to a misguided suffragist."

Maria wasn't about to get baited into an argument. Instead, she forced a gracious smile. "*Monsieur* Daumier, I'm so pleased to see that you're a supporter of human rights. As you may know, all monies collected for admission are for charitable reasons and given to the poor. You may rest easy knowing your money is well spent. Thank you for caring about those less fortunate."

He didn't respond in words but huffed indignantly and strode off through the Lodge doors. Now Maria knew for certain that he'd write a scathing article or draw one of his inflammatory cartoons mocking equality just to get revenge on her. But it was worth it to put him in his place, and it felt good to irritate him.

By the time most of the attendees had gone in, Léon arrived, out of breath. "Hurry inside! There's a rabble heading this way, carrying signs and banners."

Maria peered past him but couldn't see anyone. "What sort of signs and banners? Who are they?"

"No one you'd care to meet. I saw one sign, and that was enough."

Maria's hands shook. There were usually protestors at the various salons and conferences, but judging by Léon's concern, this wasn't an ordinary group. "What did the sign say, Léon?"

"Women belong in the bedroom, not the factories."

Maria felt her cheeks flush hot. It was people like that who undermined progress. She looked over and saw Berdine trembling. "Léon, if it is the last thing I do, I'll make sure women are liberated from degradation and closed-mindedness. It makes me so mad."

"Oh, I know you will, but for now, let's get inside so that mob doesn't distract you from your mission. Your battlefield is the lectern, Maria, not the street."

She nodded and went inside the Lodge with him, winding her way around the throng of men in the foyer—Masons in their ritual aprons and laymen alike—and went into the great hall. Many of the seats were already filled. As master of his own Lodge, Léon withdrew a folded sash embroidered with rosettes and the Masonic square and compasses, from his overcoat pocket and slipped it across his chest, as many other Lodge masters had done. Maria wanted one of those sashes and wanted to wear it right in front of Daumier.

She held tightly to Léon's hand and walked with him to the lectern at the front of the hall. As she took a seat beside the lectern, Léon left her to take his own seat in the audience. She drew in a deep breath and looked out at the crowd, finding Anna and Berdine standing at the rear of the hall. Then she saw Daumier glaring at her from the front row. Her hands shook again. She wiped her forehead with a lace handkerchief and shivered as a chill rose up from within. Daumier grinned with yellowed teeth and took out a sheaf of paper and a small piece of sketching charcoal.

Then, a soft murmuring erupted, growing stronger as heads turned this way and that. Everyone rose from their seats, looking toward the hall entrance. As the crowd parted, Maria saw a somewhat stout man with short white hair and an equally white full beard. His face, distinguished with wrinkles around the eyes and forehead, was familiar. He made his way through the throng, straight up to the lectern. Maria's breath caught in her throat. Victor Hugo had come after all.

Chapter 5

When the Lodge master came to the lectern and shook Hugo's hand, Maria's stomach fluttered. But rather than speak to the audience, Hugo turned to her and smiled.

Softly, he said, "*Mademoiselle* Deraismes, while I have never been able to attend any of your speeches, I am an avid follower of your writings." He took her hand and kissed it. "I am here tonight to offer whatever support I may to the cause of humanitarianism."

The hall crowd grew. Word of Hugo's arrival must have spread. When everyone took their seats again, Maria sought out Léon. There he was, seated in the middle of the room next to Phillipe. She caught Léon's gaze, and he winked.

She shifted her weight slightly in the chair as the master of the Lodge rapped his gavel and addressed the group, "Brothers and visitors, I have the privilege to introduce *Mademoiselle* Maria Deraismes, and her special guest, *Monsieur* Victor Hugo."

Applause filled the room. Maria stood, with Hugo by her side, and approached the lectern as the master stepped aside. Her legs trembled. She held onto the sides of the lectern and smiled. "Good evening and thank you for giving me the opportunity to stand before you, not as a woman, but as an equal. Differences in gender should be cause for celebration, not repression." She moved slightly so Hugo could speak.

He added, "I have spent the better part of my life ashamed and appalled at the French government. That is not something I am proud of. I wish to embrace France and be proud of my country, but not while those less fortunate souls are punished and ignored, forced to live in poverty and die on the street. All citizens deserve, no, all citizens have the basic right to survive and live each day with food and shelter. I promise you, I will again exile myself from France unless we are all freed from tyranny!"

A roar of approval, and disapproval, filled the hall. Hands clapped in agreement or waved about in anger. Maria saw Léon smile and nod. He always enjoyed debate, the more controversial the better. She scanned the crowd and saw Daumier lift his stooped body from his seat.

"*Mademoiselle* Deraismes!" his voice, coarse and angry.

She was taken aback. Why was he addressing her when it was Victor Hugo who'd spoken? "*Monsieur*?"

"You were invited here as a courtesy, *Mademoiselle*. I find it most inappropriate to insult your audience by inviting an exiled criminal to speak out against the leaders of our country. You may discuss your ridiculous opinions in a private salon, but in a Masonic Lodge you must mind your tongue." His ancient eyes narrowed practically to a squint.

She had to maintain focus on him, not let him see any fear or apprehension. "*Monsieur* Daumier, you speak for the Masons? As I understand it, you are not a member of the Masonic Brotherhood." She watched as his expression changed. She'd struck a nerve.

"*Mademoiselle*...it matters not...you...I speak for men everywhere."

He was rattled! How wonderful. She knew he respected the Masons and would never say or do anything to disrespect them. That gave her strength.

"No, *Monsieur*, you can neither speak for all men nor speak for the Masons. Is *Monsieur* Hugo not a man? Do you claim to speak for him as well? Perhaps we should clarify things by asking the master of the Lodge his opinion on the matter." Would Daumier back down or would he continue his verbal assault? No matter what he did, Maria readied herself to stand firm. If he won even a small battle, she'd lose credibility.

The master rose from his seat behind the lectern and moved next to Maria. "Gentlemen and Brothers, this is not an appropriate time to raise semantic objections. *Mademoiselle* Deraismes deserves our attentiveness, not our ridicule. She was invited here as an equal and has the freedom to speak her mind. And as our guest, *Monsieur* Hugo is to be offered the same respect. Please, *Mademoiselle*, continue." He sat back down.

"*Merci*." Maria found Léon again and continued, "I would like to give my thanks and appreciation to *Monsieur* Hugo for taking time from his day to attend this conference. *Monsieur*, would you like to continue?"

Hugo shook his head. "You are the speaker, *Mademoiselle*. I am here at your bidding simply as a show of support. If my infamy brings crowds to listen, then I have accomplished more than I hoped. Please, continue with your talk." He moved away from the lectern and bowed his head.

Maria drew in a deep breath and held it for a few seconds, then let it out slowly. What an incredible honor it was to have Victor Hugo sharing the stage with her. But now she had to make her speech. Everyone, including Hugo, waited.

She cleared her throat and began, "The progression of France as a nation still in recovery from the 1848 revolution can only occur without shortsightedness. All of her people must be received as citizens, equal and with basic rights. No man, woman, or child can be treated as less than an equal. All must be educated together, without prejudice to social standing or gender. To segregate people into classes will remove any progress we've made in the 22 years since the revolution. Without equality, France has accomplished nothing. We must embrace liberty, equality, fraternity!"

She placed her hand over her heart for emphasis. Léon was the first to jump to his feet and applaud, followed soon by almost everyone in the hall. She'd made her point, and they had heard.

Hugo approached and gave her a hug and a kiss on both cheeks. She saw Daumier get out of his chair and vanish into the crowd.

Where had he gone and what was he up to? It wasn't like him to leave before the speech ended. But there wasn't time to worry about his motives. She still had to finish the rest of the speech.

A few minutes passed before the audience settled down and took their seats again, but once they did, Maria completed her speech without further incident. To the sound of applause, she made her way into the foyer with Hugo for a brief customary reception.

It was the sort of evening that should have no end. It felt wonderful being in the same room with so many Masons. Maria could actually feel the energy of the Lodge. She introduced Berdine to Hugo and the other attendees. There was an immediate outpouring of sympathy and amazement at how Berdine carried herself in light of her tragedy. That reaction was what Maria hoped for.

Hugo placed a thick leather-bound book in Berdine's hand and whispered, barely loud enough for Maria to hear even though she was standing right next to him, "Your strength, Berdine, makes me proud to be French." He paused for a moment, stroked his beard and smiled broadly at Maria. "One day we will all realize that women comprise the backbone of humanity. Good evening, *Mademoiselle* Deraismes." He grinned and left.

Maria lifted Berdine's hand and looked at the book. It was Maria's favorite work by Hugo, *Les Misérables,* signed on the cover by Hugo himself. Berdine leaned in close to Maria. "I cannot read, *Mademoiselle.*"

"Then you will have to learn if you're to read *Monsieur* Hugo's book."

Léon, with his drab and slightly threadbare coat over his arm, smiled happily and offered his congratulations. "My dear Maria, what a magnificent speech. You never disappoint. I'll be sure to write a glowing review in my paper tomorrow." He looked around. "Did Victor Hugo leave? I would have liked to shake his hand."

"Yes, he left just now, and he gave Berdine a signed copy of *Les Misérables*. I'm still giddy from being close to him. And can you believe Daumier?"

"Actually, yes. Why does he bother to come to these conferences when he finds them so reprehensible? I think he thrives on the drama he creates. I saw him scurry out of here like a gutter rat, sketch pad in hand. Although I believe his cohorts are still skulking around here somewhere. Oh, Berdine, Anna is waiting out on the front stoop chatting with some friends if you'd care to join her and keep her company. She's never comfortable around large groups. We won't be long."

Berdine nodded and headed to the door, the book clutched to her chest. Maria looked around and saw Alexandre Dumas, Daumier's friend, gathered with a small group, frowning and red-faced. It seemed like Daumier and his cohorts were getting bolder at each meeting. Probably, she surmised, because the ranks of those falling in line with equality were growing. Any progress was good progress, but not in Daumier's eyes. But there was hope, regardless of his drawings and rants, and she still felt energized.

"Léon, I'd like to stop by your office tomorrow to discuss an idea for an article, if that would be all right."

"Of course. It's about time we worked on another joint project." He glanced at his old, scratched pocket watch. "We'd better be leaving now, Maria. It's late and you shouldn't be out in the cold." He took her arm gently and led her through the foyer.

When they were close to the door, she heard angry voices coming from outside. She peered out through the doorway but didn't see Anna or Berdine. "Léon, where's my sister?"

"I told her to wait just outside the door," he shouted above the increasing noise. His face blanched. "The protesters!" He held tightly to Maria's hand.

Maria rushed forward, out of his grasp. "My sister is out there somewhere, Léon."

"Then let's go."

It had gotten dark out, but Maria saw well enough. A large crowd gathered on the street waving banners and clenched fists in the air, shouting and jeering. Many of the Masons yelled back, telling the crowd to disperse. Maria looked around but couldn't see Anna anywhere.

She hurried toward the protesters and pushed through the mob until she came to a clearing. There in the center of the crowd was Anna and Berdine, crouched and huddled together on the cobblestones, shielding their faces as people threw rotten fruit and eggs at them.

"Anna!" Maria screamed above the racket. She ran toward them only to have the mob turn its attention to her and pelt her with tomatoes. One struck her face. Ignoring the sharp sting to her cheek, Maria stood in front of Anna and Berdine, her arms outstretched.

"Stop this at once!" she called out, but the onslaught continued.

Maria sank to her knees after the side of her head was struck with something hard. She felt Anna's arms around her; strong, safe, warm. It was hard to see anything clearly. Shapes and colors were blurred. Then she was lifted and carried away. But she couldn't leave Anna and Berdine. She struggled and tried to speak, but no words came. Where was Anna?

"Maria? Maria, can you hear me?" it was Anna's voice.

"I have you, Maria," now it was Léon who spoke.

"Where's Berdine?" Maria managed to whisper.

"Right here beside me," it was Anna again.

A moment later, Maria's vision cleared and she saw they were near the Phaeton carriage. "What happened, Léon?" He gently put her down on the pavement, supporting her until she had her footing.

"They started throwing rocks and one hit you on the head. Those swine. How are you feeling?"

Anna ran over and wrapped her arms around Maria. "Oh, I'm so glad you're all right. But we have to get home, away from that rabble." She dabbed at Maria's forehead with a handkerchief.

Maria saw a trace of blood on the handkerchief. She pushed Anna's hand away. "Forget about me, how are you and Berdine? Are you hurt? Where is Berdine?"

"Over here, *Mademoiselle*." Berdine came closer, took Maria's hand and kissed it. "No one has ever done anything like that for me before." Her dress was stained and her hair dripped with egg yolk.

Maria doubled over when a sharp pain hit her stomach. "Berdine, not all Parisians are like that mob back there."

"I know that, *Mademoiselle*."

Maria straightened as the pain diminished. "Oh, please call me Maria."

They climbed into the Phaeton, with Maria sitting next to Léon. As soon as everyone was settled, he urged the horses forward with several violent shakes of the reins. He obviously wanted to get away from the scene as fast as possible, but Maria was not about to let the protesters ruin the evening. No one was hurt, and other than a slight bump on the head, she felt uplifted from the lecture.

She watched Léon as he stared straight ahead. His eyes were dark and his nose too large, but he had an inner goodness that made him handsome, nonetheless. It was odd how so few saw his beauty, his integrity, and kindness. The world needed more men like him. With a contented sigh, Maria looked out of the carriage.

"Léon, isn't it a wonderful evening?"

He grunted. "Wonderful? You almost got killed and your sister and Berdine are covered in rotten fruit. You think that's wonderful?"

"Well, perhaps not that part." Maria nudged him. "It could have been worse. At least now I know what my article for your paper will be about."

Léon shook the reins. "I'm starting to think Anna is right in worrying about you. Perhaps you should slow down a bit."

"Nonsense. There's so much to do and if I don't do it, who will?" Her head throbbed and she felt a little lightheaded, but didn't want to worry Léon, so she kept it to herself.

Léon fell quiet as he usually did when he didn't want to argue. Maria closed her eyes and leaned back, listening to the rhythm of the horse hooves clip-clopping over the cobblestones. As brave as she was trying to appear, the truth was that she'd been terrified when faced with the mob. It was instinct, not bravery that made her rush forward.

The carriage slowed. Maria opened her eyes and saw why Anna had gasped. Léon muttered a curse. The house was splattered with the same rotten fruit that covered Anna and Berdine.

Maria straightened up. "*Merde*. Cowards." She turned around and saw Berdine cowering in the back seat. It would be best not to alarm her, so Maria lightened her tone, "What a waste of fruit. So many are hungry and here they are, wasting food."

"Is that all you can say?" Anna said harshly. "They know where we live, Maria, *and* they were waiting for us outside the Lodge."

"I know. But we can't let them know they've scared us. We'll clean up this mess in the morning." Maria stepped from the carriage, but as her feet touched the ground, her legs trembled, and she collapsed. Her head ached and she couldn't catch her breath. Her vision faded to black and muffled voices swirled around her. Then, everything grew quiet.

Chapter 6

A distant sound echoed in Maria's head, but she couldn't quite place it. She listened carefully. It was a clanking sort of noise. She opened her eyes and looked around. She lay in her bed with Léon asleep in the chair beside her, his head lolled to the side. The clanking stopped and Anna came in carrying an empty cloisonné tray.

"Oh, thank God you're awake," she said, sliding the tray onto the dressing table. "I hope I didn't wake you. I dropped the tray and broke the tea pot. My hands are still shaking from you falling and not waking. How are you feeling? How's your head?"

Léon stirred, but didn't wake. Maria reached up and felt a sizable bump on the side of her head. She sat up slowly, still feeling somewhat dizzy. "What happened?"

"You fainted. You were hit by a rock at the Masonic Lodge. Remember? You gave me quite a scare. Berdine went to get Doctor Pouchard."

"I don't think that's necessary, Anna. It's only a bump." Maria probed her head again. Sore, but certainly not bad enough to bring the doctor. "I wish you hadn't sent Berdine out alone at night."

"She insisted. Léon wanted to go with her, but she said she wanted to do something to repay you for your kindness. I would have gone, but I couldn't bring myself to leave you." Anna went to the bedroom door. "I think I hear someone knocking at the front door. That'll be Doctor Pouchard." She gave Maria a look that said *stay in bed* and hurried from the room.

Léon woke, stretched his legs out and yawned. He smiled when he saw Maria looking at him. "So, you're back among us, *Mademoiselle* Deraismes?"

"So it seems. I do have a bit of a headache, but it's not severe enough to stop me working on that article with you."

"What article?" Léon got out of the chair and rolled his head from side to side.

"Don't tease me, Léon. I have some wonderful ideas. I can incorporate what happened at the Lodge into the article, drawing attention to the plight of women in general and then close with Berdine's situation. I won't use her name, of course. Can you bring me some paper?"

"Maria," Léon leaned down and took her hand, squeezing it gently, "We'll work on the article in the morning. You need to rest now."

She was tired, so putting off the article was probably a good idea. "All right. But I'll come to your office tomorrow and then we'll work on the article."

Anna came back in with old Doctor Pouchard. With a wink, Léon released her hand and headed for the door, giving Anna a nod as he left. Pouchard approached the bed, carrying a black leather bag. He didn't look happy.

"So, Maria, I see you haven't heeded my advice and are still gallivanting all over Paris. And this time I hear you were struck by a rock." He clicked his tongue and continued, "If I could tether you to the bed, I would. I made a promise to your mother that I'd look after you. If she only knew how stubborn you are."

Anna chimed in, "She did."

He examined the bump on Maria's head and poked at her stomach until Maria shoved his hands away. He meant well, she knew that, but his constant fussing about her ailment had worn thin. She was well aware of it and didn't need him to remind her there was little he could do.

"Doctor, Anna takes care of me and administers medicinal tea when I need it. I feel quite well and my head hardly hurts at all." She looked over at Anna. "Where is Berdine?"

"Downstairs. She's fine."

With an indignant huff, Pouchard closed his bag and scribbled a note on a small piece of paper. He handed it to Anna and spoke to her, "I wrote down a few herbs I want you to add to the tea. Make sure your sister drinks two cups a day." He glanced at Maria. "Two cups a day, Maria."

Anna folded the paper and put it in her pocket, then escorted Pouchard from the room. Maria slumped back onto her down-filled pillows and wondered what it would be like if she had no home or bed and had to sleep on the street with no doctor to tend to her injuries. What misery it must be to have no help.

She closed her eyes, hoping for dreams of her childhood, a time when everything was carefree and joyous, and days were filled with play. Remembering the happy times provided an escape from the present stresses of life.

When morning came, the bright sun burst through the window and woke her. She felt refreshed. It was another day filled with promise. As she got out of bed, she heard voices downstairs, women's voices. Anna's controlled voice was distinct, but the other voice was shrill, almost piercing. It definitely wasn't soft like Berdine's, yet it was familiar.

Smoothing her hair as much as she could, Maria went to the top of the stairs. Anna was engaged in an argument with someone. But who? Maria went down and immediately recognized Louise Michel, an outspoken fellow feminist who antagonized Anna at every opportunity.

Louise saw Maria and threw her hands in the air. "Oh, my dear Maria! I heard about the bastards attacking you last night. If I'd been there, I would have bashed their cowardly heads in."

Maria stood by Anna. "Then it's a good thing you weren't there. What are you doing here, Louise?"

Louise glared at Anna. "Your sister wouldn't let me up to see you. There's a rally tonight. It's a protest against that donkey Louis-

Napoleon. He does nothing to support the people, so we're trying to gather enough of a crowd to storm the Tuileries Palace. You really must come."

"She's not going anywhere with you, Louise." Anna motioned to the door. "You'd better leave now."

"I only just got here, Anna. Why don't you go and make us a pot of tea so I can talk to Maria without you interrupting."

Maria could almost feel the heat coming off Anna's flushed face. If only Anna would ignore Louise instead of letting her rile her. Louise was like a splinter in her skin.

Even with Louise as a friend, Anna deserved respect in her own home. Maria had to calm the situation. "Louise, I won't be attending the rally. I have work to do with Léon Richer. But why don't you come over in a few days and tell me about the rally. Perhaps I can report on it in the *Opinion Nationale*."

"It would mean a lot more to us if you came along, but I suppose if you can't…"

Anna had her hands on her hips. "Why would my sister go with you? So she can get arrested like you? How many times have you been arrested, Louise? Three, four? You're trouble, and we don't need trouble." Anna took a step forward and pointed at the door again. "Please leave."

"My arrests are testament to my accomplishments, Anna. They are badges of honor."

"Then you must have enough badges to cover your entire body." Anna spun around and strode to the kitchen.

Maria sighed. "Louise, I do wish you and Anna would learn to tolerate one another."

"Oh, it's good for her to have an adversary. I really do have to be going, though. I wish you'd reconsider about the rally."

"Just be careful, and don't get arrested." Maria walked her to the door. "Remember, come around in a few days. I'll try to send Anna on an errand or something."

Louise smiled, winked, and practically skipped down the foot path. It made Maria smile. Louise's passion was fueled by her protests and debates. That was precisely why they'd become friends. Maria couldn't do as much physically as she'd like, so she lived vicariously through Louise, giving her support when she could.

"Good, she's gone," Anna said from the kitchen doorway. "You shouldn't associate with her. She's far too free with her tongue, especially about the Emperor. I can almost guarantee that she'll get herself arrested again at the rally. It'll serve her right, too."

"She's done a lot to bring attention to the plight of women, Anna. She's not a bad person."

"I should have known you'd defend her."

Someone banged on the door. Then Léon's voice called out from the front stoop, "Maria! Anna! Open the door!"

Maria let him in. "The door was unlocked, Léon. You're always welcome to come in on your own. Did you see Louise? She just left."

"Yes, I did, but it's not Louise I'm here about. I just overheard some policemen talking. It's bad news."

Maria glanced at Anna and then back to Léon. "Bad news? As if getting pelted by rotten fruit wasn't bad enough. Now what's going on?"

He came in and closed the door behind him. "It's far more serious than a bunch of protesters. We are *all* about to suffer because of Louis-Napoleon. He declared war on Prussia."

Chapter 7

Maria and Léon sat in front of the fireplace, discussing what war would mean to Paris, while Anna and Berdine busied themselves by tidying up the house. Having Léon around for comfort at such a time was a blessing. How could Louis-Napoleon be so arrogant as to declare war against Chancellor Bismarck without considering what it would do to France? War wouldn't accomplish anything, yet apparently Louis-Napoleon thought it would.

Léon got up and stoked the fire with an iron poker. "I'm sick about this."

Maria nodded. "So am I. Has everyone gone mad?"

"I think perhaps they have. I knew it would only be a matter of time before Louis-Napoleon decided to act against Bismarck, but I didn't think it would be so soon."

Maria stared at the flames. "Neither did I. Why did he have to declare all-out war? It's so extreme. This will rip France apart, supporters against denouncers. Bankrupt the country and make everything worse."

Léon nodded thoughtfully and placed the poker back in the stand. "You know, Maria, the Chancellor is a very powerful man, and with Prussia pulling together as a nation, I think it's time to bring up the issue of arming all of France's citizens. Our army is weak, but if all French men and women stand together, we might stand a chance. Wouldn't that unite us all?"

Léon was beginning to sound like Louise. Louise had petitioned numerous times to change the law to allow women to arm themselves. It hadn't made much sense during peacetime, but now the government might listen.

"As much as I hate the thought, you make a good point. You know my feelings on violence, but if all French people stood together as citizens, we'd present a united force against Prussia. Ending the war quickly is all I care about. Oh, but I detest the whole idea of war."

Léon sat down beside her and said, "Would you be willing to host a salon right here where we can present this idea publicly?"

Would that be a good idea? It couldn't hurt, could it? "I suppose so. When?"

"The day after tomorrow will work. I'd like you to make a speech, if it wouldn't be too much trouble. I'll even ask my Masonic brothers to spread the word. Oh, I forgot about Anna. Should we consult with her first? After all, it's her house, too."

"No need. She'll be more than willing to help."

They chatted a bit longer about the issues of war and finished off a pot of tea Anna brought out. Maria's head spun with ideas. Even though she feared war, the excitement about the opportunity it would provide for women to be declared equal citizens, fighting for their country alongside the militia, made it an important thing to do. Was it wrong to think like that? People were going to die and here she was turning it into a platform for propaganda.

Léon paced back and forth in front of the fireplace. "How about if I write an article about how foolish it is not to include women in the fight against Prussian subjugation, both on the battlefield and off? I'll do a summary of your last speech and tie it all together. What do you think?"

Maria agreed. "Another wonderful idea. It's sad to think the only way to bring about equality is during wartime."

A knock on the front door.

Maria got up. "Now who could that be?"

Léon followed her to the door and stood by her side as she opened it. The Prefect of police, Joseph-Marie Piétri, stood on the doorstep with his hands in his pockets. He had a stern and serious look that was amplified by the severity of his stiff uniform. He wore a white shirt beneath a snug fitting dark blue, gold-buttoned jacket cut at the waist, with slim trousers tucked neatly into knee-high riding boots. His eyes were fixed on hers. This was not a friendly visit.

"Forgive the intrusion, *Mademoiselle*, but I have come to inform you that all households in Paris are under a strict curfew. I am sure you must have heard about the declaration of war."

Maria stood stunned. A curfew? That would certainly throw Paris into turmoil. Parisians were not fond of staying in at night. There hadn't been a citywide curfew since the revolution. She motioned to Léon. "*Monsieur* Richer told me about the war. Do you bring any further news?"

"None that I am prepared to disclose at this time. Please be sure to remain inside once the sun has set. You are only free to move about during the daylight hours."

Léon stepped forward. "*Monsieur* Piétri, surely there's no danger just yet. Why is there a curfew now?"

Piétri stared with cold eyes and placed a foot inside the house. He peered around, as if looking for something, then returned his gaze to Léon. "Exactly what is your purpose here, *Monsieur*? A man, alone, in an unmarried woman's house is cause for scandal."

How dare he imply that Léon was anything other than a gentleman? Maria had heard of the rumors that occasionally circulated around Paris where several men, including Daumier, hinted that there were improprieties occurring whenever she had a man over to her house. She pretended outwardly to ignore the rumblings, but privately, it bothered her. Why couldn't they just leave her alone?

She moved in front of Piétri to block his view. "Sir, my home is always open to friends, and *Monsieur* Richer as one of them. I have many friends and colleagues, men *and* women, and I do not discriminate them by gender. Now, please allow me to shut the door to keep out the cold."

He didn't move. Piétri wasn't giving up. "*Mademoiselle*, I believe I saw Louise Michel scurrying away from your house. You haven't been hosting rebellious talk against the government, have you?"

"Excuse me? Who comes in and out of my house is my business, *Monsieur*. Now, if you have no other news..."

The right side of his lip curled up in a half smile. "*Mademoiselle*, I meant no offense or disrespect. I have to admit to being curious about the sort of woman who is supported by Freemasons and argues for an equal state, all while remaining polite and refined, unlike Louise Michel." He glanced outside and lowered his voice, "I admire you and your cause, *Mademoiselle*, but if I said so publicly, I would be scorned by my subordinates. My job is to quell uprisings and rebellions, and to do so on neutral footing. I'm not supposed to take sides."

Did that mean he believed in equality? Maria had only seen the Prefect once before at one of Louise's demonstrations and he was anything but supportive. In fact, he'd threatened to arrest Louise. Maria watched him and noticed a slight change in his demeanor. He wasn't as stiff, a bit more relaxed perhaps.

She kept her voice low and asked, "Why have you really come here tonight, *Monsieur*?"

"I have my men going door to door to inform the citizens of the curfew, but when I saw Louise Michel leave and *Monsieur* Richer arrive, I thought it best to come to you myself. I did not think it wise to run the risk of having rumors spread by my men. As I said, I admire you. However, that said, I would suggest that *Monsieur* Richer leave at once to avoid any further suspicion or gossip about anti-government gatherings. He's a Mason and most non-Masonic government officials believe the Masons are anything but benign."

Léon took a step forward. "Thank you for the personal treatment, and I appreciate your discretion. The last thing I want is to be the cause of damage to *Mademoiselle* Deraismes's good name."

"Then we are both in agreement." Piétri dipped his head and spun around, again looking stiff and authoritative. Maria watched as he strode to the roadway where he had a horse tied to the fencepost. He was a stout man, yet once his foot was in the stirrup, he pulled himself into the saddle with ease.

Léon slipped on his overcoat and went directly to his carriage. He waved to Maria as he got in, but before his driver could move, one of the officers down the street shouted, "Prefect! Prefect! There's a disturbance at the Tuileries!"

Piétri dug his heels into his horse, urging it into a canter, and rode toward the officer. Maria saw Piétri speak to several of his men at the end of the street and then take off at a gallop. It surely couldn't be Louise causing trouble, because she said she'd be at the rally in the evening.

Léon peered out from his carriage, watching Piétri one minute and Maria the next. It looked like he was torn between leaving or coming back inside.

To make his decision easier, Maria motioned him back into the house. He only hesitated for a moment before hurrying up the path. He mumbled, "Well, at least Piétri's gone."

They went inside and Maria sat down on the sofa. "But that doesn't change the fact that many people are going to die in a stupid war."

"It's out of our hands, Maria. We're powerless to stop the war, and I'm including my Masonic brothers in that sentiment. We do what we can, but you know that's never enough."

"Then I'll do something. I can't just sit here." Maria turned when she heard the stairs creak. Berdine was halfway down, wrapped in a woolen blanket. "Please don't think I was listening in on your conversation, but I heard what that policeman said. What will happen to us now? Are the Prussian's going to storm Paris?"

Maria got up and went over to Berdine. "The curfew is only a precaution. There've been no reports of violence or of troops storming anyone. Come and sit by the fire. Where's Anna?"

"She's outside in the rear garden, pruning the roses, I think. Do you want me to get her?"

Maria shook her head. "No, no. Gardening relaxes her and if it keeps her mind off the war, then I'd rather her continue gardening."

They all startled at the sound of horse hooves and men shouting out on the street. Maria went to the window. Two officers on horseback rode fast past the house.

When the rear door in the kitchen slammed, Maria expected to see Anna come in with an armful of roses, but instead, Louise was in the doorway. "Louise? What are you doing here?"

"Good afternoon...again." She smiled and brushed some loose strands of hair from her face. She breathed hard, her cheeks were a rosy blush.

Maria abandoned the window. "How did you get in here? Isn't Anna out back in the garden?"

With a shrug, Louise nodded to Léon and Berdine, then sat down on the sofa. "You won't believe what just happened. I walked near the palace on my way home when I heard shouting. I got a little closer and saw a group of men all cursing the name of Louis-Napoleon. Obviously men of good taste. I kept my distance, though, since I only like to associate with my own group of liberators, you know." She giggled. "Anyway, the police came and one of the bastards saw me hiding near some trees. He must have thought I was involved because he ran after me. He was a great fat goat, so I got away from him. But wouldn't you know, he went and called for two other goats, on horseback no less! I ended up here. I sneaked through your garden and found your back door unlocked. I thought I'd hide here for a few hours."

Maria stared at Louise. It was audacious of her to assume she could stay. If Piétri had seen her, he might not be as understanding as before. Then again, she couldn't very well throw Louise out. Maria looked over at Léon and then back to Louise. "If you weren't with those men at the Tuileries, then why did you run? As a rule, innocent people don't run."

"You think I shouldn't have run, with my reputation? I told you, I wasn't involved. You'll just have to trust me." Louise sat up straight. "You're my friend, Maria, I'd never do anything to hurt you. So, who's your guest?" She pointed at Berdine.

"This is Berdine. Berdine, this is an acquaintance of mine. Louise, are you sure you didn't see Anna in the garden?"

"Well, I might have. I just didn't see the point in letting her know I was here."

"That's because you knew I'd tell you to get out!" Anna shouted from the kitchen doorway.

Louise folded her arms across her chest. "I'll only leave if Maria tells me to. I need stay here because if I get arrested now, I won't be able to attend the rally tonight, now will I?"

Maria sighed, and Anna bit her lip. There was no way Anna and Louise would ever see eye to eye. As always, Maria got caught in the middle.

"I'm sorry, Louise, but I agree with Anna. You really should leave. But go straight home this time."

"Are you letting your sister's contempt for me cloud your judgment? She hates me because I'm outspoken. But it takes the loudest voices to be heard. I'm only asking to stay for a few hours."

With a groan, Maria acquiesced. "All right. You can stay here, but only for a couple of hours. I'm sorry, Anna, but I can't put her out."

Léon added, "We should all sit down and hold a civilized conversation and put our petty grievances aside. This absurd war will affect each one of us and we'll need to plan how best to deal with it."

Louise smiled and lifted her feet onto the table in front of the sofa. "What an outstanding idea, Léon. Oh, Anna, could you fetch me a cup of tea? I take sugar and cream."

"Get it yourself." Anna stomped all the way up the stairs, calling over her shoulder, "You'd better not be here when I come down."

Berdine quickly followed after Anna. Maria glanced at Louise, who stifled a grin.

"Louise, this house belongs to Anna as much as it does to me. Please show her the same respect you do me."

After a short pause, Louise mumbled, "I'm sorry. I'll apologize next time I see her, which hopefully won't be for some time."

Léon pointed to the kitchen and cleared his throat. "Why don't I make some tea? Let's move into the kitchen where we can have a more intimate conversation without bothering Anna."

Following Léon, Maria and Louise sat down at the kitchen table. Léon went to the stove and picked up the teapot but dropped it again when the door flew open and one of Piétri's officers barged in with his gun drawn.

"*Mademoiselle* Michel, you are under arrest. And *Mademoiselle* Deraismes, you are held responsible for sheltering a criminal."

Maria looked over at Léon. "Remind me to keep that blasted door locked."

Chapter 8

Maria watched helplessly as shackles were placed on Louise's wrists and ankles and she was escorted out the front door. Maria followed and did her best to explain to the officer that Louise wasn't involved in the demonstration at the Tuileries, but he wouldn't listen to reason. The cold air bit into Maria and she shivered uncontrollably.

She covered her ears when the officer steadily blew on a whistle until three other policemen rode up to the house, as if they were trained dogs responding to their master's call. The officer explained the situation to one of the men and ordered him to ride off and bring Piétri. The officer held onto the shackles, treating Louise like a hardened criminal. Maria couldn't think of anything to say. Even Léon didn't seem to know what to do.

Anna and Berdine came outside as well. Anna draped a heavy woolen coat over Maria's shoulders, shooting glaring looks at Louise and mumbling under her breath that Louise was nothing but trouble.

Pressing up close to Maria, Léon said quietly, "You should not be out in the cold. They have no legitimate cause to hold you for anything. Louise, on the other hand, might not be able to defend herself so easily. Her past behavior will certainly play into this accusation. I also have a feeling that they want to make an example of her, whether she really was involved in the disturbance or not."

Louise screamed as the officer tried to push her forward toward an approaching police wagon. She struggled and spat at the officers.

"I did nothing, you miserable bastards! You followed me because I'm a woman!"

Behind the wagon was Piétri on horseback, trotting along with a sour expression. If Louise could only mind her mouth, she might stand a chance of convincing him of her innocence. Once jailed, it would be hard, if not impossible, for her to get out. Louise should know that, she'd seen plenty of her friends locked away.

Maria turned to Léon. "We can't let them take her. I believe her. I don't think she did anything."

"Neither do I. Not this time at least. Let me see what I can do." Léon strode to the Prefect. "Prefect Piétri, may I have a word?"

If Léon could persuade Piétri to let Louise go home, then maybe she'd learn her lesson and stay out of the public eye for a while. Louise continued struggling, but she'd stopped cursing and spitting. Perhaps there really was a chance she'd behave.

After a brief conversation with Léon and his officers, Piétri urged his horse forward to Maria. What had his officers said to him? Did he believe them, or Léon?

Piétri looked down at Maria. He was far more imposing on horseback. "*Mademoiselle* Deraismes, I understand from my men that you have been harboring a suspected criminal. And I hear from *Monsieur* Richer that you are innocent. What am I supposed to think about this apparent contradiction?"

Before Maria could speak, Louise pulled free from the officer and stomped over to Piétri's horse. "I am not a criminal! I was walking near the palace when one of your stupid lumbering officers decided to chase me instead of the real offenders. Who went after the men? Nobody I'd wager. Far easier to chase down an innocent woman, *n'est ce pas?*"

Why couldn't she be quiet? Piétri stiffened and glared down at Louise with unblinking eyes. She was too outspoken for her own good and may have ruined any chance of him letting her go.

The officer grabbed her by the shackles and dragged her backward, away from Piétri, which made Louise start again with the cursing. Piétri slid off his horse and motioned for Léon and Maria to follow him a short distance away from his officers.

Piétri stopped and kept his voice in a whisper, "I thought I'd told you to go straight home, *Monsieur*. And you, *Mademoiselle,* what have you to say for yourself? If Louise Michel truly is guilty of instigating government dissention, then harboring her is a crime."

Maria spoke before Léon could, "*Monsieur* Richer was worried for our safety, so he remained to make certain we would be all right. As for Louise, she told me she was on her way home and simply passed by the palace. She said she knew nothing about the demonstration. I truly believe her when she says she was not involved."

Piétri looked back at Louise, then shook his head slowly. "*Mademoiselle* Michel has been arrested before and she's been run off for throwing bottles at the police during a suffragist demonstration. And she was almost arrested a while back for attempting to incite a riot. She's the most volatile female I've ever encountered, yet you say she's innocent. I don't see how her presence at the Tuileries could be coincidental."

It seemed as if Piétri had already made up his mind. Maria hated seeing Louise bound and struggling, and although Louise certainly was not meek, she still made a pitiful spectacle in shackles.

"*Monsieur* Piétri I believe what Louise told me." She had to make him believe Louise hadn't been looking for trouble. The problem was, Louise was not one to back down, even to the police. "I know how...passionate she is, but in this case, I honestly do not believe she did anything wrong. She ran because she knew your men would assume her guilt. Can you blame her?"

Piétri eyed Maria. "It would have been better if she'd have stayed at the palace. I think that perhaps I should bring you into the station for questioning as well to get everything on record."

Louise evidently couldn't hold her tongue any longer. "You're a ridiculous excuse for a man, Piétri, if you refuse to believe Maria. Go ahead and run me in, only leave Maria alone. She is an honest woman who doesn't deserve your maltreatment."

Piétri glared at Louise and then brought his attention back to Maria. He spoke so quietly that she could barely hear him, "You would do well to distance yourself from personalities like Louise Michel. I can only do so much for you if you insist on becoming entangled with her ilk."

"She's a friend. Would you turn your back on a friend in need? I'm well aware of her reputation and infractions with the law. But since you have no proof that she was involved with the demonstrators, on what charge can you arrest her?"

Piétri kept his voice hushed, "*Mademoiselle,* you're a respectable woman, so I shall give you the benefit of the doubt. However, I'll need to make a show with Louise Michel and take her in. She'll be released in the morning for lack of evidence. At least she won't get into any more trouble tonight." He turned around and faced his officers. "Take *Mademoiselle* Michel to the station house and lock her up."

He spun around and strode to his horse. Without looking back, he rode off down the street. His men hastily shoved Louise, who was screaming obscenities, into the wagon and followed after him. Maria waited on the footpath until the wagon turned a corner and vanished.

Léon came over to Maria. "You tried."

"He knows they can't prove she did anything wrong so he's going to release her in the morning. It's all so stupid. He's taking her in just to keep her out of trouble for the rest of the night."

"Can't blame him for that." Léon smirked. "Maybe it'll have some impact on her."

"I doubt it." Maria shivered. She couldn't feel her toes any longer. "We should go inside before we freeze to death. I thought this blasted weather was warming."

Anna waved to her from the doorway. "Come inside."

Walking arm-in-arm with Léon, Maria said quietly, "I think perhaps now that Louise is unable, I should attend the rally tonight so I can write a first-hand essay on what I see."

"You're beginning to sound like Louise. You need to keep away from her and her rallies. Besides, I'm sure Piétri will be patrolling there."

"I'll be an observer, not a participator. How can I write on a subject unless I'm actually there? I can't stay separated from the people. I need to be involved. And that reminds me, what about the Freemasons? Why aren't they doing anything? If they'd let women in, there'd be thousands more members and we'd all protest at the steps of the palace."

"Oh, don't bring the Masons into this mess with Louise. I'm not so certain this is the right time for you to be involved with Masonry or with rebellion. I heard what Piétri said. He can only protect you to a degree. You push him and he'll arrest you, too."

"That's what I'm talking about. If women were Masons, we'd all have the protection of the Brotherhood. Besides, this is the perfect time to push. France is at war with Prussia and the people are at war with inequality. Louise's rally should stir up the people. That's what we need."

"I suppose I should come with you then, but not as a representative member of the Masons. For now, though, I want you to get inside and lock the back door so no more intruders can get in. I'd better be getting home myself before Piétri comes back. I don't want to give him any more reason to accuse us of improprieties."

"I don't care what he thinks. Let them all think what they like."

"Hmm, I'd rather not be the cause of salacious talk." Léon dipped his head and went to his carriage.

Maria turned and walked to Anna who held the door open. Maria embraced her and gave her a kiss on the cheek.

"Why don't you go to the country for a while, Anna? You can rest and get away from the city."

Anna closed the door once they were inside. "You're not getting rid of me so easily, little sister. I can take Louise's taunts. I'd rather stay here with you. You know the real reason I came to live with you? When I was married to Hipolyte, I felt safe. But when he died, I couldn't bear to be alone. I never told you this, but every time the house creaked, or the wind blew a bough against the window, I would cower in the wardrobe for hours. Without Hipolyte, I felt lost. I don't like being alone. You're my family, Maria and I need you as much as you need me. So, I'm here now and I'm not leaving. I will stand by you and support you. Now, what are we going to do to help France move into the future?"

At that moment, Maria saw her sister in a different light. Anna had a newfound strength rising up from the depths where it had been suppressed for so long. With Anna by her side, Maria knew she'd accomplish more than she could on her own.

She smiled. "We'll do everything we can, Anna. You and me together. And Berdine, of course. This is a woman's country as much as it's a man's country. We must stand strong."

Anna nodded. "I'll be right beside you all the way. But I will not support any of Louise's antics. I don't think her style of rabble-rousing is effective. At least not in the long run. Especially with the war looming. Everyone will have had enough of fighting and her antagonism will drive them away." She slid the door lock in place.

Maria squeezed Anna's hand. "What do you think *Maman* and Papa would say if they could see us plotting to change the country?"

"Father would give us that look of his. You remember, the one where he'd stare down his nose without a word. I never could tell if he was angry or agreeing with something I said." Anna laughed.

"He probably didn't know what to say. He was outnumbered in a houseful of women!" Maria chuckled but then doubled over when a sharp pain pinched her stomach.

Anna put her arm around her shoulder. "Come on, I'll make your medicinal tea and then you should go straight to bed."

They went to the kitchen and Maria sat down. She really wanted to attend the rally, but she didn't quite feel up to it now. "I think you're right. I *am* tired."

Anna took a tin of herbs from the shelf over the stove. "I'm worried about what this war will do to Paris. I wish we could all sleep until it's over."

"So do I. But wishing it away isn't very realistic, is it? I have such a dreadful feeling that this war won't end well for anyone."

Chapter 9

Over the next few months, Maria watched helplessly as Paris turned into an encampment for French soldiers. Outside of the city, Prussian troops gathered and created turmoil where provisions were reduced or cut off all together. Food supplies diminished and the citizens grew increasingly worried with each new day. She and Anna had managed to stockpile an ample supply of food before it became scarce and willingly shared what they had with those in need, although it would eventually run out.

The Deraismes household had been converted into an ambulance service base for the transportation and care of the wounded, with Maria and Anna running the operation day and night. Berdine moved into a small apartment with several other women and devoted her time to the *L'Association pour le droit des femmes*, collecting and processing donations. On September 1, Louis-Napoleon surrendered and was captured at Sedan, in the northeast of France. He was exiled to England in shame.

As if the situation wasn't dire enough, on September 6th, news came that Jules Favre, the new vice president of the French government under General Trochu, declared that France would not relinquish any territory 'nor a stone of her fortresses' to Prussia. His statement so angered Bismarck that the war intensified and Prussia's grasp on Paris tightened.

Exhausted, Maria fell into bed at night fully clothed. Thankfully, in mid-November, as the autumn temperature dropped and icy winds whipped through the city, she had a brief respite from the onslaught of injured.

At the kitchen table, she warmed her hands around a hot cup of tea and picked at a slice of stale bread. "I simply have no appetite, Anna."

"You must eat. You've already sacrificed sleep, your writing, and money, please don't add food to that list."

"It's not that I don't want to eat, it's just that my stomach won't allow it. This war is drawing the spirit right out of France, and out of me, too."

Maria stared into the cup and wondered how long men could continue battling over borders. They were too stubborn and too arrogant to talk about a truce. People died for nothing. Only yesterday, she'd seen an old man and woman, huddled together by the side of the road, dead from starvation or the cold.

Anna continued, "Don't talk like that. You know there's been talk of peace. Once they sign an armistice, everything will return to normal. The wounded will heal, supplies will be brought in, and we can pick up where we left off." Anna cleared away the dishes from the table and draped a blanket over Maria's shoulders. "I almost forgot to tell you, Léon stopped by today with some news."

Shrugging off the blanket, Maria stared at her sister. "What news?"

"He said that there was to be another meeting of the Freemasons tonight. He'd like you to come and present a speech about your feelings on feminism and the war."

"Really? When did he stop by?" Maria was more than ready to increase her involvement with the Masons. They seemed like the only people willing to take action against the government.

"You were resting upstairs. I didn't want to bother you."

"I wish you had. I can't prepare a speech that fast."

"Yes, you can. I know it and Léon knows it."

There was no arguing with Anna, or Léon for that matter. In an unfortunate twist of fate, the war had provided a platform for feminism, for women to be involved in government. Leave it to Léon to recognize that fact.

Maria went back to her bedroom to develop a speech. She'd write it about how women, being refused an equal education, were unable to participate in the political arena, and how different the war and negotiations might be if level-headed women were allowed to contribute.

She sat down at her desk and looked at the gilt-framed daguerreotype of her parents. "Oh, Papa, why can't everyone be like you and *Maman* were? I see it every day, women treated as less than men. It makes me sick. I've worked so hard for equality, but I don't think I'm making a difference." She took the frame and held it to her chest. "And now Léon wants me to make another speech. I've already made so many speeches, yet nothing has changed. I wish you were here. You always knew exactly what to say to give me encouragement."

When her melancholy eased, she put the frame back on the desk, took a deep breath and picked up her pen. As thoughts formed in her mind, her excitement grew. It was as if her ideas were being fed to her. She glanced at the photograph again and smiled. Papa was still with her, in spirit.

It had been so long since she'd spoken publicly, but she had plenty to say. Only a month ago, against Anna's wishes, she and Louise had rallied for women to be more actively involved in negotiations with the Prussians, but they were ignored and almost arrested. That incident only spurred Maria on, making her more determined than ever to get involved with public demonstrations.

"Maria! Maria, come downstairs!" Anna called. "Léon's here."

Maria looked through the window at the darkening evening sky. She'd been working all day and had lost track of time. Looking in the mirror, she smoothed out her dress, the only formal dress she'd kept. Dark green, with a green and gold embroidered bodice.

She picked up her speech and skimmed through it. She'd crafted several points of discussion, good points that were sure to bring about a meaningful discussion. With the speech in hand, she went to the top of the stairs and saw Léon standing at the bottom.

She smiled. "I'm glad you're here. I'd like you to listen to my speech and give me an honest critique."

He dashed up the stairs and took her by the arm, walking with her to the bottom. "Oh, dear, I'm afraid there's no time to rehearse your speech. I've come as your official escort and have my carriage outside. We'll need to leave right away."

Maria hesitated. "I'm glad you'll be my escort, but why the rush?"

"It's after dark. The curfew. I'd like to get off the streets as soon as possible. The Masonic Hall has been under scrutiny lately. I think the government believes we're subversives plotting a coup."

"Aren't you?" Maria smirked.

"Of course not. Masons are not politically motivated." He tried to suppress a smirk of his own. "However, we can't help it if some of the brothers disagree with our government."

"Some of the brothers?"

"Perhaps a vast majority, but you know what I mean. We're sworn to uphold the laws of our country, but when the well-fed pampered bourgeoisie are wrong, well..." He winked and opened the front door.

Anna handed Maria her coat and gave her a hug. "Good luck, little sister, although I know you don't need it."

"Anna, why don't you come, too. The Masons won't mind, will they Léon?"

"Not at all. My brothers have nothing against women, except when it comes to admitting them into the Brotherhood. Seems a bit antiquated and contradictory, doesn't it?"

"Well, then, if nobody minds, I'd love to come." Anna looked down at her plain brown dress. "Oh, dear, should I go dressed like this? This isn't very formal."

Maria nudged Léon. "She looks beautiful, doesn't she? In fact, she outshines me."

"You're both as lovely as a garden full of flowers. Now, come on, or we'll be late."

They went quickly to the carriage and settled into the seats, chatting about the increasing Prussian pressure on France and the progress toward armistice. As they neared the Masonic Hall, Maria saw Daumier, with his slightly slumped shoulders and forceful gait, going inside.

"Maria, don't worry about him." Léon took her hand. "He's been relatively quiet since the war started. What a pity he wasn't exiled along with Louis-Napoleon."

Everyone laughed and Maria instantly felt better. Daumier was only one man. A man who'd become famous for drawing silly *Bas Bleu* cartoons, showing feminists as unattractive and ignorant with their everyday *bas bleu*, or blue stockings, showing beneath their skirts. He showed them gathered in poor country homes in informal salons and mocked them by hinting that they were so uncouth that they didn't care if they exposed their undergarments. In the past he'd successfully elicited scorn of any feminist woman by projecting them as ugly, unfeminine and ill mannered, casting them in a light that devalued them and put them on the fringe of decent society. But that was then. Times were different now.

The hall wasn't nearly as crowded as it had been before the war, but there were still many men, and to Maria's surprise, several women, gathered in small conversational groups.

"Léon, I wasn't expecting to see women attending."

He smiled. "That's why I wanted you to come. I wanted it to be a surprise. Some of the Mason's wives have been pressuring their husbands for more equality in the household. That one over there," he pointed to a well-attired lady wearing a large multi-colored plumed hat, "She told her husband that she doesn't want to be left at home when the Lodge holds speeches or presentations. She must have convinced him, because there she is, looking rather proud of herself if I do say so."

Maria could scarcely believe it. Perhaps the war hadn't dulled the desire to stand equally as citizens after all. The seats filled quickly, but the Lodge master had the front row reserved for his special guests. He escorted Maria to the lectern while Léon and Anna took their seats in the front row. Three women, the one with the plumed hat and two others in dresses equally splendid, sat next to Léon. The women each sat up straight, looking dignified, and smiled broadly at Maria.

When the seats were mostly filled, the master quieted the audience. "Brothers, honored guests and ladies, again we have the privilege of presenting *Mademoiselle* Maria Deraismes as a guest speaker. *Mademoiselle*." He stepped away from the podium.

Maria noticed Daumier several rows behind the women. It looked like he'd started sketching a drawing. So single-minded in his loathing. When a disturbance interrupted the silence, Maria looked away from Daumier and saw Louise squeezing past several men at the doors to the hall. All heads turned as she hurried to the front row and took the last seat next to the women.

When again it fell quiet, Maria began, "Women and the democracy. If the politicians remain obstinate in their blindness and continue to refuse women the rights of every human and social being, they will advance nothing, slow everything, and compromise the future."

Mixed applause rose amid general muttering, but when Daumier stood, a hush settled over the hall. He leaned forward and pointed a gnarled finger toward Maria.

"*Mademoiselle*, you criticize a government you know nothing about. Women are more suited to affairs of the household, not affairs of the state."

At that moment, the women in the front row all stood and hiked their skirts to their knees. Each was wearing heavy, blue stockings...their *bas bleu*. From the lectern, Maria had a view of the entire audience. There were those who were shocked and appalled at the women's audacity, and then there were those who smiled and applauded at their rebelliousness.

Daumier fumed, his face ember-red. "When women act out in public in such a manner, it is no wonder they cannot be taken seriously. Sit down and retain some of your diminishing dignity!"

Anna and Leon looked at Maria. What did they expect her to say? Did they think she was privy to the women's outburst? As much as she hated to admit it, Daumier had a good point. This was not the venue to stage a demonstration, but if she told the women to sit down, she'd lose their trust and appear a traitor. She touched the gavel on the lectern. It looked just like the one Papa had on his desk in Pontoise. She grasped it tightly and rapped it several times.

"May I have your attention?"

Everyone sat, except for the women who'd now lowered their skirts, and Daumier. He wiped his forehead, his chest heaving. He was working hard to control his temper.

The Lodge master stepped in front of the lectern. "Please, settle down and give your attention to *Mademoiselle* Deraismes. Interruptions and outbursts will not be tolerated." When the Lodge grew quiet, the master stepped aside and relinquished the floor to Maria.

Her nerves were jangled, and her hands trembled. She needed a familiar face. Her eyes went right to the front row where Léon smiled, giving off his warmth and encouragement.

With a deep breath, she began, "We are here to discuss the war with Prussia, and the war with inequality. Both deserve our immediate, and uninterrupted, attention."

The women in the front row glanced around, bowed to Maria and took their seats. Daumier sank slowly into his chair, like a cobra coiling down into its basket. Order restored; Maria continued her speech without any further objections. At the conclusion, the gracious crowd gave her a standing ovation. The applause raised her spirits.

Once in the foyer, Leon and Anna chatted together, while Maria found herself among a group of men who started debating her views on the war. She was not in the mood to listen to them prattle on about why women should not be involved in politics and tried to think of a way to escape without insulting them. As their words became heated, someone took her by the hand and pulled her away. It had to be Léon coming to her rescue. He always seemed to know when she needed help. She turned to thank him and saw that it wasn't Léon. It was Daumier, tightening his grip on her hand.

Chapter 10

Daumier continued to pull Maria through the Masonic Hall's foyer and into a small meeting room off to the side. He released her. She wanted to call for help, but would anyone hear with all the chatter in the foyer? And what if Daumier only wanted to talk in private? She might be overreacting. She felt a drop of perspiration drip down the side of her face.

Once inside the room, Daumier closed the door and turned to her, his eyes intense and his cheeks burning red. "*Mademoiselle* while I appreciate your candor and intelligent manner of speech, I feel I should offer you a precautionary warning."

Maria and backed away. What was he talking about? She'd been thrust into a vulnerable position, but she'd have to stay calm and in control or he'd pick up on her fear.

"What is it you want, *Monsieur*? Please let me return to my friends."

"In a moment. I heard that you had been mixed up in a street fray many months ago and was struck with a rock. Whoever threw that rock must not like outspoken women. Paris can be a dangerous place to live, no? You are trembling. Are you afraid? You do not think I would harm you, do you?" He moved closer, stale pipe smoke on his breath. "I should warn you that there are those in Paris who are concerned with the political climate and do not wish to have a horde of militant feminists running about creating distraction from the real work at hand. The security of Paris is on everyone's mind right now. You should watch your step and take care that you do not end up a casualty."

What a terrible threat, and in private, too, so no one could overhear. There was nothing to say. She breathed in slowly through her mouth and exhaled through her nose to calm down. It worked, and her nerves calmed.

He continued, "Have you nothing to say in your defense, *Mademoiselle*? Am I to take this as an admission of guilt, that you and your willful followers are aware of the trouble you cause? Paris must concentrate on the war, not on a rebellious mob of *bas bleu*."

Enough. Maria summoned her strength. "*Monsieur*, you continue to harangue me at every opportunity. Why? Because I believe that all people in France, men and women, be treated as citizens? You cannot halt progress."

His eyes widened and his mouth gaped. Had he expected her to cower and bend to his will? His expression changed slightly, a trace softer, and his face lost its redness. "*Mademoiselle* Deraismes, you are a well-educated and well-spoken woman, that, I cannot deny. Your mind and your wit equal that of a man, however, I am set in my beliefs and no one, not you or your colleagues, will ever change my mind. If you do not cease your speeches and inciteful rhetoric, then I shall be forced to take more aggressive action. The government is in turmoil, *Mademoiselle*, and the *bas bleu* cause nothing but trouble." He stared at her but instantly backed away when the doorknob turned.

Léon stuck his head in and flung the door wide open when he saw Daumier. "Maria, are you all right?"

Daumier huffed. "Of course she is, imbecile. Do you take me for a scoundrel?"

Léon came into the room, staring at Daumier, and said loudly, "In response to your question, *Monsieur* Daumier, yes, I do take you for a scoundrel. A well-positioned scoundrel, but a scoundrel, nonetheless. Come on, Maria, there's someone I'd like you to meet."

Maria edged away from Daumier. What a relief it was to get away from him. She left with Léon and went back to the foyer, tempted to look back and see if Daumier followed, but she didn't want him to see her nervousness.

She kept her voice in a hushed tone, "I'm glad you came in when you did, Léon. I wasn't sure what he might have done. Why can't he stick to his artwork and leave us alone? With his artistic talent, he could do so much, but he lets hate rule his world."

"He's a pretentious man with a very high opinion of himself."

Maria stifled a smile. "You shouldn't say things like that. He has a lot of important friends. What if someone overheard you?"

"I wouldn't care. Ah, there's the man I want to introduce you to. His name is Georges Martin." He led her to a small gathering of men. "Georges, this is Maria Deraismes."

Georges smiled. "I am very honored to finally meet you, *Mademoiselle*. I have attended many of your speeches and read every one of your essays."

Georges, young, well groomed, and wearing a small lapel pin of a caduceus, the staff and entwined snake. Maria knew that the caduceus was the symbol of the god Hermes and the medical profession, which meant Georges must be a physician.

She nodded her head slightly. "Are you a supporter of equal rights, *Monsieur* Martin?"

"My personal views are that all people are on this earth to serve one another, and to discount any one of them simply because of gender or economic position is an insult to the Creator."

"Your views are my own, *Monsieur*."

"Call me Georges."

Léon gave Georges a pat on the back. "Georges and I are putting together a petition to allow women into the Brotherhood, although Georges still hasn't taken the oath yet. He's made it known that he won't join until women are allowed in. But I'm working diligently to get him to do so before that day comes. Easier to work from the inside, I always say."

Maria watched Léon to see if he was serious about petitioning the Masons. He'd tried several times to persuade the Freemasons to permit women, but his requests were always dismissed. Now it seemed he'd found an ally to help with his efforts, although since Georges wasn't a Mason, his assistance might not carry much weight.

Maria gave Léon a wink. "I think that's a wonderful idea. If there's anything I can do, please let me know. I'd love to make a personal plea."

Léon smiled broadly and exchanged glances with Georges. "Georges and I are standing united with a handful of like-minded Masons. This is perfect timing to get our petition some serious attention. The war has the country in a state of agitation and in a mindset ready for change. Every brother in the Lodge stands on equal footing. No one person is better than another. True equality rules the Lodge."

Maria had never understood why women were excluded from the fraternity and spirituality of Freemasonry. Papa had never given a reason, other than saying that's how it had always been. But if it was true what Léon said about everyone being equal in the Lodge, then it was pure hypocrisy not to let women be part of the organization.

She looked around at the men who were gradually leaving the foyer. "And if the Masons say no?"

With a shrug, Léon whispered, "Then we will try again later. You know me, I don't give up so easily. Now, I also want you to write an essay pointing out all the pertinent facts about anti-feminist ideals you've discussed over the years. Be sure to make special note of citizenship and rights. Oh, and don't forget to bring up education. Freemasonry fully supports all citizens receiving an equal education. We detest repression. I want to include your essay with our petition."

Maria drew in a breath, overwhelmed that one of her essays would become an official part of a Masonic meeting. It would have to be precise and heartfelt, but not with too much emotion. What an opportunity! Anna would probably want to help, too.

Maria let out her breath and smiled. "You know I'll do what I can to get women into the Lodge."

"I know." Léon returned the smile and gave Georges another pat on the back. "Well, I'd better get Maria home."

Georges dipped his head. "It was indeed a great pleasure and honor to meet you, *Mademoiselle*. I look forward to working with you on this endeavor."

"The feeling is mutual, *Monsieur* Martin."

Léon motioned to the door. "It's late, Maria, we'd best be going before we get picked up for violating the curfew. Where's Anna?"

Maria looked around and saw the women from the front row of the meeting hall off to one side chatting. "I'll go and see if she's over there." She headed toward the women, but before she got too close, she heard Louise's loud laugh.

"They kept me in jail for nearly two months this time!"

Maria found her in the center of the circle of women. "Louise, when were you arrested?"

"Oh, a couple of months ago. They came and got us at the *Hôtel de Ville*."

"I hadn't heard about that. No wonder I haven't seen you around. What happened?"

"We were simply requesting to receive arms so we could stand against the Prussians. The government apparently didn't agree with our request." Louise laughed again. "Perhaps I stole a few guns."

How she found stealing guns and a jail sentence funny was beyond all reasoning. Maria glanced around. "Louise, have you seen Anna?"

Turning around in a circle, Louise looked around in mock concern. "Oh, dear, has she run off? What a pity."

"Please, Louise, I need to find her."

"Well, she's around somewhere. I saw her just a few moments ago with Léon."

"I was just with him. Did you happen to notice if she went outside for fresh air?"

Louise's mood darkened. "I told you I don't know where she is. You're her sister, not me." She turned back to her friends.

Louise had changed. She was more belligerent and ruder. Could jail have made her that way? No matter, there wasn't time to worry about Louise's personality. Anna had to be waiting outside in the cold to escape the stuffiness and noise in the foyer and get away from Louise.

Maria pulled open the door and peered outside. The chilled air rushed in, and a few flakes of snow drifted through the doorway. She gathered her coat around her and stepped out. Several men from the meeting headed off home on foot or in carriages, but Anna wasn't anywhere to be seen.

"Anna!" Maria called out. Léon's carriage was close, so she hurried over to it and found Anna huddled inside under a pile of blankets with only her head poking out. "Anna! I've been looking for you."

"Sorry, but if I had to stay in the same vicinity as Louise for one moment more, I swear to you, I'd have been forced to violence."

"That's a horrible thing to say." Maria almost laughed because Louise had said something very similar once about Anna, only not in such polite terms. They were more alike than either of them cared to acknowledge. "Aren't you cold?"

"Not under all these blankets. Are you ready to go?"

"As soon as Léon says his goodbyes." Maria climbed in beside Anna. It was almost like they were little girls again, hiding beneath the bed clothes, pretending they were explorers in a cave somewhere.

A minute later, Léon climbed into the carriage. "I see you found your elusive sister."

He got in and shook the reins. As the horse clip-clopped down the road, the snowflakes came down at a faster rate. It would be

Christmas soon, and although there wasn't much to celebrate during a time of war, it was still a time to spend with family and friends. Maybe there would be an armistice before the new year, maybe a new beginning for France, and maybe the Masons would accept women. Maria sighed. There were so many uncertainties. What Paris needed was peace and healing. But how could anything heal while the citizens were ignored, and the government did as it pleased? What they needed was a new government.

Chapter 11

1871, Paris

The cold of winter kept Maria mostly at home. Christmas had come and gone amidst talk of a peace treaty, and while Léon and Georges attempted to place their proposal for women to be admitted into the Masonic Brotherhood, more pressing matters overrode their attempt.

Now the end of January, winter held Paris in its firm grasp. It broke Maria's heart to see how the poor were hit the hardest. War caused even further depletion of the already meager food supplies, leaving little for charitable donations. Maria and Anna did what they could by giving away their extra blankets and coats, but once they were gone, there was nothing left to give.

Anna had been sick for a week with a terrible bout of coughing, and even though she insisted she was well enough to move about the house, Maria banished her to bed. Caring for her sister became the most important thing in Maria's life. Because the house wasn't very warm due to a lack of firewood or coal, she gave her blankets to Anna so she'd get better. Without blankets, Maria slept in her coat.

As the wind howled outside and the snow sifted down from the clouds, Maria took Anna's lunch upstairs and placed the tray on the nightstand. Anna sat up, looking better than she had in days.

"I've brought you a nice bowl of chicken soup. It's the last of the chicken, so you'd better eat it all."

Anna looked over at the soup. "You have it. I'm not hungry." She coughed a few times and lay down.

"Nonsense. I already ate, so unless you want it to go to waste, then I'd suggest you eat it." That was a lie. Maria hadn't eaten yet, but it was more important for Anna to regain her strength. "I'm not leaving until you finish every last drop."

Anna settled into her blankets and eyed the soup. "I know you haven't been looking after yourself. Your skin is pale and your eyes have lost their sparkle."

"That's because it's the middle of winter and Paris is still under siege. It's not because I didn't eat a bowl of chicken soup."

With a long sigh that ended in a cough, Anna sat up again. Maria placed the tray across Anna's lap and handed her the spoon, then waited until she started on the soup. Maria felt Anna's forehead and was pleased that it felt much cooler than the day before.

Maria went into the hallway when she heard an urgent knocking on the front door, and hurried downstairs. She peeked through the curtains—a newly acquired habit—to see who was there. She'd always opened the door without looking, but not anymore. There was no telling anymore who might try to get in. To her complete surprise, it was Daumier. He had something in his arms, but she couldn't see what. Again he knocked.

"*Mademoiselle* Deraismes!" he shouted.

What could he want? There was no one else in the house but Anna. What if he intended harm? Quickly, Maria picked up an iron poker she kept beside the door and held it at her side, then opened the door a crack. Daumier stood back, stomping his feet in the snow, but as soon as he saw Maria, he pushed forward and tried to force his way inside. She leaned against the door, but when she saw what he clutched in his arms, she gasped. A small child wrapped in a moth-eaten blanket lay motionless.

Maria opened the door wide. "Oh, good heavens! Please, come in."

He strode forward and turned in a circle, as if looking for something. "Where shall I put him?"

"Here, on the sofa. Who is he?" Maria shut the door. "Lay him down carefully."

Daumier, gentle in his actions, took great care to position the child on a pillow while keeping the blanket snug around the small body.

"I do not know who he is. I drove by down the street a bit when I saw him curled up and near-frozen curled against a building's wall. He cannot be more than four or five. Who permits a child out in weather like this?"

Maria sat beside the child and placed her hand on his forehead. He was cold and his cheeks were burned red from the freezing temperature, but he was alive. His tiny chest rose and fell in slow breaths.

"You don't even know his name or where his parents might be?"

Daumier shook his head and brushed some snow from his overcoat. He knelt down on the floor beside the sofa. "I did not know what else to do, and you were so close by." Then, as a sort of afterthought, "I heard how you help the wounded soldiers and thought you could help this boy."

"I consider it my duty to help anyone in need. You did the right thing, *Monsieur*. We still have some provisions, which is more than I can say for most of the people. Will you stay with him while I go and get my coat to cover him?"

Daumier nodded and felt the boy's cheek with the back of his hand. "How could his mother leave him in the cold?"

Was it a rhetorical question, or did he really want to know? Maria rushed upstairs to her bed and grabbed her woolen coat, then rushed back downstairs. "*Monsieur*, could you stoke the fire? Perhaps we can move the sofa closer to the hearth."

Daumier stood. "I will move it, *Mademoiselle*. You make some hot tea."

He remained abrasive, but his behavior wasn't important at the moment. Maria placed her coat over the child and went to the kitchen. She'd seen so many children die from the cold and starvation, but she didn't want to tell Daumier that the boy looked as if he might not make it through the day. Instead, she went about boiling the water.

Peeking from the kitchen doorway, she watched as Daumier slowly pushed the sofa across the floor. How odd seeing him act so humanely. Completely out of character, but a welcome sight.

When the water boiled, Maria steeped the tea and brought the pot and a cup into the sitting room. "Is he warming up?"

"Perhaps a little. Do you have any warm clothing for him? His shirt and trousers are torn and wet."

"Nothing that would fit him, I'm afraid, but I can find something. Keep him covered and try to get him to sip the tea. We'll need to warm him from the inside and make sure his fingers and toes are not burned from the snow."

Daumier looked up for a moment before returning his focus back to the child. Maria put the teapot and cup on the floor near the fire and went upstairs to Anna's room. Anna, half out of bed, asked, "Who was at the door? I couldn't hear a thing."

"Daumier."

"What!" Anna stood up. "Are you all right? Do you need any help?"

"No, no, it's nothing like that. He came here with a small boy he found in the snow. I've never seen him like this. He's worried about the little boy, Anna."

"Is the boy a relation of his?"

"No. He says he doesn't know him. That boy doesn't look well. His skin is cold and his body is weak, there's no fight left. I have to wonder if he was trying to scrounge food and became lost in the storm. His parents must be beside themselves."

"Unless he's an orphan. This war has created many orphans." Anna wrapped a blanket around her shoulders. "Could be his parents abandoned him because they couldn't afford to feed him. You'll need my help."

"You stay in bed. There's nothing more you can do for him. It'll do no good for you to make yourself worse." Maria helped Anna lie back down.

She went to the wardrobe and found a thick nightshirt, far too big for the small boy, but at least it would keep him warm.

Halfway downstairs, she stopped. Daumier sat on the floor in front of the fireplace, cradling the little boy and rocking him back and forth, humming some song. She took another step, which creaked. Daumier looked up and gave a fleeting smile.

Softly, he whispered, "He awoke and looked at me. He seems to be sleeping now. He will be all right."

Maria made her way to the child and knelt down and felt his cheek. Icy cold. "Here, let me take him and dress him in these dry clothes."

Daumier relinquished the little boy, then warmed his hands by the fire. Maria gently placed the child on the carpet and uncovered him. The boy's clothes were a threadbare pair of trousers and a thin shirt that had more holes than actual shirt. Worst of all was the realization that the little boy's heart had stopped beating. He'd died in Daumier's arms.

Chapter 12

Maria sat alone on the floor with the child. Once it sank in that the boy died, Daumier flew into a rage and stormed from the house. It wasn't clear whether he was angry at the child dying or that Maria was unable to save him. After gently wrapping the little boy's body in the coat, Maria left him and went upstairs.

Anna sat up in bed, her brown knotted. "Maria, how's the child?"

The heartbreak caught up with Maria and she wept. She sat on the bed with Anna and embraced her. "He didn't survive. I knew he wouldn't, I just knew it. How could this happen? We don't even know who he is."

"Where's Daumier?"

Wiping her tears, Maria motioned outside. "He left. You should have seen him."

"What do you mean?" Anna smoothed Maria's hair with her fingertips.

"He was tender. But when he found out the little boy died...well, he left in a fury. I feel sorry for him, Anna."

"The boy or Daumier?"

"You know I mean Daumier."

Ann huffed. "Don't be ridiculous. He doesn't deserve your sympathy."

"Oh, Anna. We're all from the same stock. I have to admit, though, that I never thought of Daumier as having a kind heart. He's so full of hate, yet there seems to be a remnant of empathy deep down. Not at all what I expected." Maria got off the bed and went to the window. A trace of sunshine shone down from a gap in the clouds, making the snow glisten, but everything remained cold and frozen. Daumier's footprints went down the front path to the street. It was impossible to see where they went from there.

Anna threw off the covers and got out of bed. She sat in a chair by the window and picked up a hand mirror from the dressing table. "I look terrible. I want to go out today. I don't want to think of death anymore. I've been cooped up inside too long. I want to see Paris before it's too late."

"Too late? Too late for what?"

"This war has ripped our country apart. I need to see the Paris that I remember before everything is destroyed."

It wasn't like Anna to be so resigned. Maria shook her head. "You're not well yet. It's too cold out. Maybe by the end of the week, if you're better. Besides, I have to contact the doctor so he can remove that poor child downstairs."

"I'm the older sister, Maria. If I want to go out, I'll go out." Anna replaced the mirror and went to her wardrobe. "We can go to the doctor's house together and let him know about the little boy."

Maria sighed. She knew there was no arguing with her sister once she'd made up her mind. "All right, but you'll need to dress warmly." She left Anna to get dressed and went downstairs to sit beside the little boy. His small body lay motionless. Such a young life cut short because of the war.

She waited in front of the fire until Anna came down and knelt next to her and whispered, "He's so small. Do you want to leave him in your coat?"

"Yes. He deserves a warm coat. He's just one more unnamed victim of this war." Maria got to her feet. "We should try to find his parents."

Unfortunately, there likely wasn't much hope in finding the child's home, if he even had one. The orphanages were overcrowded with children that many were turned away. Those parents who couldn't afford to feed their families left their youngest children, the ones who couldn't work or beg, out in the cold to be picked up by the authorities. It could be that this little boy had been one of the disposable children. It was hard to imagine how anyone could be so desperate to do that to their own child, but it happened more and more.

Anna handed Maria another coat, not nearly as warm as the one wrapped around the child and opened the door. Looking back, she whispered, "Why do you suppose Daumier brought him here?"

"He said it was because he knew we helped the soldiers, but I think there was more to it than that. I think he was afraid to go any-where else."

"Why?"

"I don't believe he wanted anyone to see him like that. He knew I'd never use his empathy against him, but others surely would."

Anna stepped outside. "Oh, it is cold. You're talking about Louise, aren't you? She'd announce it to everyone and make Daumier a laughingstock. For once, I think I'd agree with her."

"No, I wasn't talking about Louise. Besides, she was arrested last month and as far as I know, she's still in jail. I meant Léon. You know how he's always looking for a new way to discredit the misogynists." Maria closed the door behind them and placed her arm around An-na's shoulders. "Are you sure you're up to taking a walk?"

"It's only a few houses away." Anna coughed a few times and leaned into Maria. "Just don't treat me like an invalid. You're the one who's been suffering more with your stomach, so if anyone needs pampering, it's you."

Maria ignored the comment and looked up at the sky. More clouds had moved in, threatening to snow again. The tracks from Daumier's carriage were visible in the soft snow. It must be a chal-lenge to live life as an angry, disillusioned man. Why was it so hard for him to accept change and embrace the benefits that an equal so-ciety would bring?

They were almost to the doctor's house when Maria's foot slipped on some ice and she fell, landing on her side. A sharp pain shot through her body. Anna quickly bent down and offered her hand just as a carriage rolled by. Daumier looked out the side window. He made no attempt to stop the carriage and even turned away. Maria watched as the carriage continued down the street. Perhaps he really was a heartless man after all.

Anna helped her to her feet and clicked her tongue. "Did you see that? How can you defend such a hateful man? If he had even an inkling of a soul, he would have stopped to see if you were all right."

There was nothing to say in response. Maria had expected him to stop, to at least offer some help, but instead he'd turned a blind eye. Where had his compassion gone? Within a few minutes, he'd reverted from a sensitive man to his abhorrent self.

She took a moment to recover, her side hurting and a nasty bruise probably forming. It certainly wasn't turning out to be a good day. They continued to the doctor's and went inside. Heat from inside greeted them. Maria unbuttoned her coat right away. "Hello, Dr. Pouchard, are you in?"

A voice from the rear of the house called out, "Who's that? I'll be right there!"

A moment later, Pouchard appeared, wiping his hands on an apron. "Ah, Maria. You don't have an appointment today. Are you ill again? Or is it, Anna? What are you doing out of bed, Anna?"

Maria shook her head. "No, no, this is not about either of us. I have some terrible business I need help with."

Pouchard removed his apron and walked over to the fireplace. "Oh, dear, it's quite warm in here, isn't it? I was in the back room and it's always so cold. I must have built up the fire a bit too much." He prodded the logs with a poker. "So how can I help the Deraismes sisters?"

Maria spoke, "I have a little boy at home. He was found in the snow and unfortunately didn't survive. Can you come and handle things?"

Pouchard threw up his hands. "For the love of God! How many more children have to die before this blasted war ends? Where did you find him?"

"It wasn't me. It was Honoré Daumier. He brought the boy to me."

Anna started coughing. The doctor quickly led her to a chair and hovered over her. "I told you not to get out of bed. Maria, you brought her out in the cold. Shame on both of you."

After a moment, Anna recovered enough to wave the doctor away. "I'm fine, Doctor Pouchard. It's that little child we need to think about."

Even though Pouchard seemed a bit hesitant, he grabbed his coat off the hook by the door and picked up his medical bag, probably out of habit, but Maria wasn't about to argue the fact. Anna and Maria followed him outside. He trudged through the snow, never looking back to see if they were there. He went directly to the house and opened the door. By the time Anna and Maria made it, he was already crouched near the boy's body.

He didn't look up, but mumbled, "He can't be more than five or six years old. An orphan by the looks of him. Malnourished, too." He covered the body again and whispered, "He's better off."

How sad to hear a doctor say such a thing. Why did no one stop to help the boy? Could it be that the people of Paris had no more compassion left in their hearts?

Pouchard picked up the child, cradling him in his arms. "I want you two to stay inside now. I'll take care of this little dear. Anna, go straight up to bed, and Maria, stop trying to save the world. I've told you before that all the strain you put on yourself will make your condition worse. You'll see, one day you'll be bedridden if you don't slow yourself down."

Maria touched the wrapped child as the doctor passed. "Thank you, Doctor Pouchard."

"You'll do as I say?"

"Of course." Maria opened the door. "Thank you again."

After he left, Maria went upstairs to her bedroom and sat down at her desk. So many thoughts ran through her head. An essay poured out of her about the horrors of war and the consequences to Parisians. She wrote about orphans and fatherless children, women in dire need of help, yet getting none. She tucked it into her pocket and hurried downstairs. Anna clanked around in the kitchen.

"Anna! I'm going out for a while."

"But you told Doctor Pouchard—"

"I told him what he wanted to hear. Besides, you promised to go right to bed. I'll be back shortly."

Before Anna could raise any objections, Maria hurried from the house. Léon lived quite a distance away, but if she got to the main street and managed to find a taxicab, she'd get there must faster. Surely Léon would support her in bringing to light the plight of the poor. Maybe a march in the streets would get the attention of the government.

Turning onto *Place du Carrousel* near the Tuileries, Maria saw a crowd of people milling about in the street. They were happy, smiling and patting one another on the back. For the life of her she couldn't imagine what could have happened to bring about such cheer. She worked her way a bit closer. A woman and a man were in the midst of an animated conversation. She moved even closer to hear what they said.

The man held the woman's hand, and it looked like he had tears in his eyes. He said, "This is a day I shall remember for the rest of my life."

What day? Something had obviously transpired, but what? Maria came up next to the couple. "Excuse me, *Monsieur*, but has happened?"

He looked at Maria. "Oh, *Madame*, have you not heard?"

"Heard what?"

"The war has ended!"

Chapter 13

The war had ended. It sounded too good to be true. As Maria stood there shivering in the snow, more and more people began to emerge from their homes and gathered around in the street near the gardens. It seemed like she'd been standing there forever when a voice called out, "Maria! Maria!"

She turned. It was Léon, coming from near the Tuileries palace across the street, and he was smiling. He rushed over and threw his arms around her. The news must be true, or he wouldn't be so excited. "Léon, am I dreaming?"

"No, you're not. War is over."

"So, an armistice was signed?"

"Well, yes, but…"

Maria pulled away and looked into his eyes. There was something about his tone. It must be the terms of the armistice that had him a bit hesitant. "All right, tell me the details."

"It's cold out here and you're half frozen. Why don't we go to my house? I have my carriage just around the corner."

Maria readily agreed. "I was on my way to see you anyway."

The ride to Léon's was short, yet because he wouldn't divulge anything, it seemed to take forever. Finally, they arrived and once inside, he motioned to a comfy old chair with down feathers protruding from tears in the seams. "Please sit." He sat opposite in a rocking chair and drew in a deep breath. "Favre signed an armistice with Prussia."

"You already said that. But there's a lot more, isn't there?"

"There certainly is. Favre agreed to pay Prussia 200 million francs and another five billion as war recompense, and hand over most of our forts and armaments."

Maria's heart sank. That meant surrender, not a mutual armistice. "How is this going to change things?"

He shrugged. "At least the war is over. According to what I heard, Adolphe Thiers, the statesman, made it a condition of the armistice that France be governed by a National Assembly."

"What exactly does that mean? Are we at peace or not?"

Léon sighed heavily. "We are. However, I can feel a spreading tension throughout the city already. I don't think this celebration is going to last. We're in for a change."

"Why do you say that? What are you thinking, Léon?"

"I also heard that Thiers is allowing Prussia, or shall we say the new German Empire, to parade through our streets in a victory march."

"What? I can't believe this. How could any Frenchman allow such a thing? I suppose I should be happy that there won't be any more killing, but I'm worried."

"You're right to worry. Once the excitement wanes, the people will realize the humiliation."

"You're worried about a civil war?"

"Well, I don't know about that, but I am concerned that there might be an uprising of some sort."

It was disheartening to think that the end of the war might not bring about peace after all. Paris had once been such a strong and beautiful city, but now it was reduced to rampant poverty, disease and death. The people no longer believed in, nor trusted, the government. And now to allow a victory parade?

"Léon, I want to do something, host a public salon perhaps, to see if we can rally the people together to force the government to see we need help, not a German parade. What of the Masons? How do they feel about all of this?"

"There's an emergency meeting tomorrow. I've been working with Georges Martin, you remember him, and I was planning to bring up the subject of women initiates again, but I think this new armistice will be all the brothers will want to talk about. Especially since I've heard that the new government is going to be made up of *monarchists."*

As if things weren't bad enough. Monarchists would try to suppress the people even more and eliminate the competition. France wouldn't be much better off than during the war. The poor would get no help from the government and issues of equality would be discarded permanently. How could this happen? Everything was turned upside down. Instead of peace and rights for everyone, there would be worsened hardship. It wasn't fair. A few powerful men were ruining the country. It had to stop. Maria got up and paced around the sitting room.

"Léon, I've had enough. I'm going to climb the Arc de Triomphe and scream at the top of my lungs for equal rights! They have to listen. *Thiers* has to listen."

"Don't get all riled up." Léon blocked her way and made her stop walking. "You're not going to do anything. We need to take things slowly and see what happens."

Of course he was right, but it would be very hard to sit back and wait. "Fine, but I want to write a strong article for your paper. I want to make a public announcement disclosing the violations to basic human rights. The Bourgeois have to be force-fed this information, or they'll never understand."

"You'd better watch yourself. You'll upset Daumier and his supporters even more."

"I have a feeling Daumier won't be so hostile toward me anymore."

"What makes you so confident of that?"

She paused. "We had an...encounter. At my house."

"What! You and Daumier?"

"Oh, it's nothing like that."

Maria explained about the little boy as Léon listened attentively. When she finished, he went to the window and looked out. Without turning, he said, "That's one of the saddest tales I've heard in a long time. I never would have thought Daumier could act so humanely. Maria, one of the things on tomorrow's agenda, if we get past discussing the armistice, is how Daumier, Jules Barbey d'Aurevilly and Alexandre Dumas have joined forces. They are calling on all of the Masons who are sympathetic to their cause to refuse admittance to women."

"Why? Why would they care what the Masons do?"

Léon turned around and faced her. "Because they see the Masonic Order as having influence in governmental decisions. As I'm sure you know, many government officials are in the Order. Once the Brotherhood reiterates their stand on refusing to recognize women as equals, then their influence will trickle throughout the new government, again placing women in a lower status than men. At least that's what Daumier and his followers believe. They think women are too sympathetic and would undermine the monarchists."

Maria clenched her jaw out of frustration. To use an independent organization for their own selfish goals was beyond disgraceful. Daumier would stop at nothing to get his way. His hatred of equality made him an incredibly ugly man. The tenderness he'd shown with the child deceived her for a while. This was a man who lived only to see his own aspirations and beliefs transpire. Maria knew what she had to do. To topple the anti-feminists, she'd have to bring down Daumier and his cohorts. France had to have a government that truly represented all of the people as citizens or France would fall.

Chapter 14

Léon drove Maria home past crowds of people spilling onto the roadway, celebrating. Their faces were happy, and they embraced one another with tears of joy. Apparently, nobody had taken the time to consider whether the new government would truly bring peace or not. Maria knew all they cared about was that the war was over. Who could really blame them? After all, it had been many months of bloodshed and hardship.

After thanking Léon, she hurried inside to tell Anna the news, but as soon as she stepped over the threshold, she knew Anna had already heard. With a smile, Anna handed Maria a cup of tea. "How wonderful is this day? It feels like a weight has been removed from my shoulders." Anna stared at Maria. "Why is it that you don't look as happy as I feel? What's wrong?"

"I spoke with Léon. Things may not be as good as they appear right now."

"What are you talking about? The war's over. How can that *not* be good?" Anna took Maria's coat.

"The Prussian army is going to march through the streets of Paris to show their victory. Our new government is made up of those old monarchists who want nothing more than promote themselves into positions of power regardless of the cost to France. We will still be oppressed. It makes me sick."

Anna sat down and shook her head. "I should have known it was too good to be true. All I want is to live in a peaceful society where no one is left out. Is that so much to ask?"

Maria felt the same. It shouldn't be too much to want peace. "We need to march through the Tuileries to the palace. We have to show them that they cannot hold us down any longer, that the people of France are strong and won't lie down like dogs. I'm going to gather together the largest, angriest mob I can. We'll show those monarchists that we want a say in our own government."

Anna jumped up and embraced her sister. "I'll help you! We've been polite far too long now."

Pulling back, Maria looked into Anna's eyes. "I should probably mention that Louise will be released from jail soon. She'll definitely want to lead her own group of supporters."

"Now that I didn't need to hear. Can't we march without her?"

"We could, but her followers will likely double our numbers. We need to make an impact, Anna. The only way to do that is to rally as many people as we can."

They went to the kitchen and began preparing dinner. Anna banged pots and mumbled to herself. She obviously wasn't pleased about the concept of joining forces with Louise, but she never said a harsh word until she ladled out two bowls of broth and sat at the table.

Anna dipped a chunk of stale bread into her soup and said, "Anything that involves Louise is bound to end in trouble. This is a bad idea."

"We *want* to stir up trouble. That's the whole point. We need to stand as a united force to show that we can't be ignored."

"You'll end up in jail, just like Louise. Sometimes I think that's what you want."

Maybe Anna was right. The thought had occurred to Maria a time or two. An arrest would lend legitimacy to her standing as a fighter of rights. Then again, jail would also give her a negative reputation among the bourgeoisie. She got up and went around the table to Anna. "There has never been a Deraismes in jail, and I'm not about to break that tradition."

"Good. Now finish your broth. At least with the war ending, we should be able to get supplies soon. I can't wait to have a sumptuous dinner of roast chicken and potatoes."

"So, your appetite is back?" Maria smiled and kissed Anna on the forehead. "Your fever's down, too."

"I do feel much better. If only the city could heal as well as me."

They finished their meager supper and went to bed early, since there didn't seem much point in staying up and worrying about the impending trouble. But when Maria got under the covers, she couldn't sleep. It was too quiet, unsettling. The people had all moved back indoors and the streets were silent. She slipped out of bed and sat by the window. The yellow light from the street's lamps illuminated the snowflakes floating to the ground. It looked peaceful and beautiful.

But Paris would not be peaceful yet. There'd been a brief break in the tension, yet with news of a monarchist government, the tension would soon return.

In the distance, a thin layer of clouds veiled the moon. She'd always taken comfort from the moon, but now it stayed hidden, as if ashamed to shine down on the city. She dropped the curtain back and closed her eyes. Everything was so overwhelming. Maybe it would be best to prioritize the most urgent matters. She went to her desk, took out a sheet of paper, and wrote:

1. Tend to the wounded.
2. Assure food and material supplies can come to the city.
3. Organize the march.
4. Stop the misogynists.
5. Initiate women into Freemasonry.

A lot to do. She glanced at the pendulum clock on the wall. Seven in the evening. Léon would still be up.

It didn't take her long to get dressed. She sneaked around quietly, making sure the floorboards didn't creak, grabbed her coat off the rack downstairs, and hurried outside. A blast of freezing wind slammed into her. She tugged up her collar and kept her head down as she slogged through the snow drifts.

She kept going and just when she didn't think she could take another step, she arrived at Léon's house. There were no lights on. She pounded several times on the door. He had to be home. It wasn't like him to go to bed so early, unless exhaustion claimed him. She knocked a few more times, her fingers numb and her teeth chattering.

She stomped her frozen feet. Eventually, he answered the door. His hair was disheveled and his clothes were rumpled. "Were you sleeping, Léon?"

He peered outside, looking one way and then the other. "I'd fallen asleep in the chair. You didn't walk here, did you?"

"Yes, now will you let me in or am I to stand out here all night?"

"*Mon dieu!* You are one determined woman. Come in and tell me what's on your mind."

Warmth filled the house, although there weren't more than a few embers burning in the fireplace. "Léon, I was thinking about what we can do and came up with some main points we can start on." She pulled out her list and handed it to him.

Reading through it, he looked up after a moment and smiled. "I like it. Exactly why did you come running over here, though? You could have shown this to me tomorrow."

"True, but we'll need to work on number five before your meeting tomorrow."

"The Masons, eh? What about one through four?"

"Well, it won't hurt if we scramble them up a bit. I'm planning to tackle them all, but perhaps not in sequence. I'm going to stop by the hospital in the morning to see if there is anything I can do for the wounded soldiers, then I'll provide what help I can to see that supplies are once again brought into the city. Once that's all taken care of, you can help me plan our march."

Léon studied the list again. He showed her the paper and pointed to number four on her list. "It seems like you're avoiding this one. How is it you're intending to rid the world of stodgy old misogynists?"

"I don't know yet. But it'll come to me. I believe if women can become Freemasons, it will lead France into become a country of equality. Which means we need to press the matter with the Masons. Their influence might drive equality forward." Maria fanned her face. She felt flushed. "I think I need to sit down."

Hurrying to help her to the sofa, Léon made sure she was comfortable before he said anything. "You should not have come out in the cold. I'm going to call for the doctor."

"You'll do no such thing. I have an appointment next week. I've just over exerted myself, that's all. I'm short of breath from walking through the snow. Now, shall we put our heads together and see what we can come up with? I want to speak at your meeting tomorrow."

"You weren't invited, Maria."

"I don't care. I can be a guest."

"Only topics on the agenda can be discussed. This isn't a regular meeting, it's an emergency meeting. Only Freemasons in good standing can attend."

"If I were a man, I'd be able to speak my mind." Maria got off the sofa. "This division between men and women, rich and poor must stop. If I want to be a Freemason or a politician, then I should be allowed to be one. If I want to vote or run a business, then I should have that right. And if I want to enjoy basic rights, then by God, I will! They are rights, not privileges."

"Sit down, Maria. I'm your friend, remember? Don't get mad at me. I'm just telling you the structure of our meetings. I'm not acting as Lodge master at this meeting. I can't even bring up a topic that's not on the agenda. But..." his voice trailed off.

She sat back down and loosened her coat. "But what, Léon?"

"But, we always have a break during the meeting as a sort of open forum. This might be the time to bring up the issue of women initiates. However, you still wouldn't be allowed in the Lodge."

"Then you'll have to act as my voice."

Léon smiled and waved the list in the air. "Write me your thoughts and I will gladly speak for you."

"Wonderful! You have no idea how grateful I am. I am so fortunate to have a friend like you."

They discussed what to say for over an hour, drawing up logical arguments why women should be included in the Brotherhood and why the Freemasons would be better off with women among their ranks. If the Masons accepted women, then it would be easier to get women acknowledged as equal citizens. It would be a beginning.

After they finished, they celebrated with a glass of wine that Léon had put aside for a special occasion. They sat and watched the dying embers in the hearth until a furious banging on the door broke the peace. Léon jumped up. He headed to the door and mumbled, "Who could that be? I hope that's not Anna out in the cold looking for you."

"No, she was asleep when I left. Be careful. It might be a thief looking for money."

"No thief would be silly enough to try and rob me, I have nothing. And I'm fairly certain thieves don't knock." He opened the door and was pushed aside as three large men shoved their way in.

Maria got up and backed away. The men were well dressed and looked important, not at all like the many ruffians running rampant through Paris. The largest of the three dragged Léon to the sofa and forced him down. Another stood at the door, while the other circled around the room.

The large man near Léon leaned down and asked, "You're up late, *Monsieur*. Busy writing your inflammatory articles?"

Maria couldn't catch her breath and felt faint. She took another step backward, but the man near the door pointed directly at her and growled, "Stop right where you are, *Mademoiselle*."

Léon worked his way off the sofa and faced the men. "What is it you want here? Who are you? I have no money, if that's what you're looking for."

The large man let out a gruff laugh. "It is not money we come for, *Monsieur* Richer. Consider this a warning. There will be law and order in France now. People like you, *Monsieur*, will become extinct."

Maria wanted to run to Léon. He'd been threatened for writing the truth. If people couldn't speak their minds to expose the problems in the world, then how would anything every change? She drew in a deep breath and moved toward Léon.

As calmly as she could, she said, "Please, we were doing nothing here but talking. We are friends and were discussing the end of the war. Is that wrong?"

"Shut up!" The large man puffed out his chest and clenched his fists. Within a heartbeat, he lunged at Maria and slapped her across the face. "You will learn your place, woman!"

She stumbled backward. What had just happened? Her cheek stung. She'd been assaulted. How could something like that happen? Léon ran to her and stood in front of her. He looked around frantically. Then he suddenly left Maria and ran to the desk, pulled open the top drawer and brought out a revolver. He pointed it at the large man and rolled back the hammer.

Chapter 15

Maria watched over Léon's shoulder as he gripped the gun tightly in his hand. He stood his ground, with his hand steady and his face red with anger. The intruders moved together and headed to the door. She prayed Léon wouldn't fire the gun.

The large man looked at Léon and smirked. "This is not over, *Monsieur*. You'll pay for this."

All three of the men rushed out the door and disappeared into the night. Maria's entire body trembled so badly that she sat in the nearest chair, her hands clasped to stop them shaking. Léon slammed the door shut and locked it.

He hurried to her. "Are you all right?"

"I think so. What was all that about? What's going on? Oh, Léon, I was so afraid when you brought out that gun."

Léon gently lifted her face and touched her cheek. "I am so sorry for this. Let me get you a damp cloth for your cheek."

"No, no, I'll be fine. It's not your fault. You did nothing wrong. Is this what we have to look forward to now?"

"I hope not."

They sat together and had another glass of wine to settle their nerves. When the clock struck eleven, Maria jumped up. "Anna! I've left her alone. What if those men went to our house? I have to go home."

"All right, all right, but you're certainly not going alone. Let me get the carriage. Just stay here and I'll bring it around front." He hurried off through the back door, leaving Maria alone.

She sat back down and leaned forward, resting her head in her hands. The possibility of peace and restoration of Paris was so fleeting. Léon was right about the new government. It was as oppressive, in not more so, than the last one. How would anything change if those in charge continued to bully the people? It became clear now that citizens were going to have to seize control and make the changes themselves.

But how could she charge into a battle with the government when she felt ill most of the time? It wasn't fair. Maybe she needed to rest a bit, have a good meal, and build up her strength. The war, after all, had been very taxing on everyone, and she certainly felt the effects.

After a few minutes, Léon came in and escorted her to the carriage, a small, open two-wheeled Cariole, far better than walking. He shook the reins and urged the single horse into a trot. On the way, they passed by several people running through the streets looking terrified. Had the same men paid them a visit? How could this happen in Paris? Léon drove slowly and rounded the corner to her street but suddenly pulled on the reins and brought the carriage to a halt. Maria peered ahead and saw a man's body lying in the middle of the road.

"Who is it, Léon? Is he dead?"

"You stay here, and I'll go find out." He climbed out and knelt down beside the body.

Maria couldn't see much from her seat, so she gathered her skirts and stepped outside the carriage. Léon rolled the body over and leaned down. The streetlights only illuminated small triangular areas of the road, not enough to see the man clearly. She moved closer to see if she recognized the poor soul. After a few steps forward, she stopped. It was Louis-Nicolas Dardelle, one of the more rebellious members of Louise's group. Judging by the blood on his face, he'd been beaten quite severely.

Léon turned around. "Maria! Get back in the carriage."

"Who did this, Léon?"

"I don't know. He's breathing, but he's taken quite a beating, and it looks as if he has a broken nose."

"Well, we can't leave him here. Let's take him to Doctor Pouchard."

Léon hesitated for a moment before he stood and glanced toward the carriage. "How, Maria? I only have enough room for two. It's not safe to leave you here or send you alone with Dardelle. Whoever did this to him might still be around. You wouldn't be safe in either instance."

Maria shivered, chilled to the bone, both from the cold and from the scene before her. There was no way she'd be able to walk the rest of the way home. "Take him. I'll wait over there in the shadows." Without giving Léon, a chance to disagree, she hurried on trembling legs and pressed her body against an icy brick wall. No one would see her hidden in the dark unless they passed right by her.

It took Léon a few seconds of angry mumbling before he dragged Dardelle's body toward the carriage. He struggled but managed to get Dardelle into the seat. Maria heard a sound and looked around only to see a cat scrounging amongst a pile of rubbish. When she turned back around, Léon stood right beside her.

He took her by the arm. "Hurry and get into the carriage. Don't worry about me, I won't be far behind."

She wanted to argue, but the chill that had settled in her body made her accept. He helped her into the Cariole and led the horse down the road for a moment before handing her the reins and falling in behind the carriage.

Maria jiggled the reins to keep the horse moving and looked behind. Léon was nowhere to be seen. As she drove through the streets, she worried that he'd be found and beaten or arrested if the men who broke into his house found him. Surely, he could have squeezed into the carriage. She would have made room. Why didn't she insist?

She'd almost made it to the doctor's house when four men jumped out from behind some bushes and blocked her way. One of the men held a club and slapped it into his hand to be intimidating.

Maria steered the horse to the other side of the road, but the group moved as well. There was no telling what they were capable of, so she shook the reins forcefully and urged the horse forward.

Before she got very far, the lead man rushed forward and grabbed the bridle, bringing the carriage to a halt beneath a street-lamp. He stared at Maria as another man came around and peered into the carriage.

"Who's that you've got there?"

Maria drew in a deep breath. "He's an injured man. I need to get him to a doctor."

"And what are you doing out at night?"

Maria shook the reins, but the horse couldn't move. "This man needs help. Move aside!"

The other men in the group moved to surround the carriage, but they stopped when the closest man called out, "It's Dardelle!"

The man with the club approached and climbed half into the carriage, causing it to lean in his direction. "What happened?" He lifted Dardelle's chin and examined his face. "Nose looks broken."

The men gathered on the side of the carriage where Dardelle sat slumped and whispered to one another. Maria listened as they speculated on who might have assaulted Dardelle until she was asked again what happened.

She explained, "I was on my way home when I came upon *Monsieur* Dardelle in the middle of the street."

"And you lifted him all by yourself? I find that hard to believe, *Mademoiselle* Deraismes."

"You know my name?" She looked closer at the man with the club. His face wasn't familiar. "From where you know me, *Monsieur*?"

"I am a friend of Louise Michel. I have also had the pleasure of attending several of your speeches in the past."

"*Monsieur* Dardelle is hurt badly. I really must get him some help." If they'd let go of the horse, she wouldn't feel so vulnerable. Her cheek still hurt from the slap she'd received and was a constant reminder that it was not safe to be out, even with friends of Louise.

"Yes, yes, of course. Where will you take him?"

"Dr. Pouchard is on the next street over. He's my physician."

"We will escort you, *Mademoiselle*. My name's Jean." He waved to his cohorts and then hung onto the side of the carriage, one foot positioned on the small step beneath the doorway. "Let's get moving, *Mademoiselle*."

Maria gave the reins a forceful shake. The men walked along both sides of the carriage. The flimsy Cariole rocked toward Jean's side, feeling like it was about to topple over. Maria held onto the reins with one hand and grabbed a rail near her doorway with the other. She looked out into the dark, searching for any sign of Léon, but saw nothing. Hopefully he'd already made it to the doctor's. But what if he'd been stopped by the self-appointed guardians of the new government? She glanced over at Dardelle and saw his arm twitch.

"Jean, I think *Monsieur* Dardelle is waking up."

"How far to the doctor, *Mademoiselle*?"

"Only perhaps a quarter mile."

Jean nodded, peering around. "I will not be able to accompany you all the way, *Mademoiselle*. The streets are not safe for anyone, especially those of us who are willing to fight the government and restore Paris to a city where *everyone* can live in peace and safety."

They continued in silence for a while, but the quiet was unnerving. The men walking beside the carriage began to dissipate into the night. Only Jean remained. They must have known they were almost at Pouchard's house.

In a whisper, she said to Jean, "Doctor Pouchard's house is the fifth one down on the right, with a wrought iron gate."

Jean nodded slowly and checked Dardelle again. Then, unexpectedly, he jumped off the carriage step and vanished. It had been a small comfort having the men around, but with them gone, she'd have to get Dardelle to Pouchard's herself. Where was Léon? She was all alone. *Maman* counseled her many times that the best person to rely on was yourself.

Giving the reins a sharp shake, she hurried the horse along. Dardelle moaned and reached his hand toward his face.

"No, don't touch," Maria said softly, pushing his hand away. "You might have a broken nose."

He groaned again. One eye blinked opened, the other remained swollen shut. He coughed. "Who are you? Where am I?"

"My name's Maria and I'm taking you to a doctor. We're almost there."

"No, no, no. Let me out here."

"*Monsieur* Dardelle, Doctor Pouchard is a man I trust. He's my own personal physician."

"Who are you?"

"Maria Deraismes."

"Ah, *Mademoiselle.* Of all the people in Paris, I'm glad it was you who found me."

"We're almost there. Hold on a moment longer."

Dardelle made an unsteady nod and fell silent. The sound of the horse's hooves as they clip-clopped over a cleared patch of cobbles broke through the night. She pulled back on the reins to slow the horse and reduce the noise. Pouchard's house lay ahead. She edged to the side of the road outside of the house just as a figure moved from within the shadows across the street.

Chapter 16

Maria steadied her nerves, waiting for an attack. Should she run into Pouchard's house or stay with Dardelle? Who was it hiding across the street? If it was Léon, he'd have already dashed out to help. She waited in the carriage and gently placed her hand on Dardelle's shoulder.

"*Monsieur*, please keep quiet. There's someone moving about across the street."

In a whisper, he replied, "Get inside, *Mademoiselle*. I shall be fine."

"I'm not about to leave you out here by yourself." She peered into the dark, but couldn't find any sign of the person in the shadows. Only Jean's friends knew where they were going, so who could it be skulking around in the dark? "Come with me, *Monsieur* Dardelle." She took hold of his hand and tugged. "You have to get out. I can't lift you by myself."

Dardelle groaned and reached for the handrail. He pulled himself up from his slumped position and groaned louder.

Maria climbed out and came around his side. His legs trembled, but with her help, he managed to get out and stumble his way up Pouchard's path. They were within a few steps of the front door when the sound of heavy footsteps made Maria stop and turn. The same large man who'd barged into Léon's house stood with clenched fists. He must have been waiting outside Léon's and then followed the carriage.

The man glared. The light shining through Pouchard's front window cast a yellow tinge over the man, giving him a waxy appearance. Maria managed to edge Dardelle a bit closer to the door.

"Stop right there!" ordered the wax-faced man.

Maria fumbled for the doorknob. If she could get the door open, there might be a chance to make it to safety. Her fingers touched the brass knob a moment before the door opened.

Léon's voice called out from the doorway. "Maria, come inside quickly!" He took charge by assisting her with Dardelle, then slammed and locked the door as soon as they were inside. "What took you so long? I was about to come looking for you. I took a quicker way through back gardens and parks, but I thought you'd still be here faster than me. I should have stayed with you and walked alongside."

"No, no, this worked out far better, Léon. If you hadn't already been here, I don't know what I would have done. Some friends of *Monsieur* Dardelle caused a delay."

Doctor Pouchard hurried to help with Dardelle, and with Léon's help, got him to a bed in an examination room. Furious banging on the door went unanswered. Pouchard brought a lamp closer to his patient and motioned toward the front door. "Somebody makes that idiot stop. I can't conduct an exam with all that racket."

Léon placed his arm around Maria. "I locked the door, he can't come in unless he breaks it down. Doctor Pouchard, would you please have a look at *Mademoiselle* Deraismes? She was struck across the face by the man outside."

With a wild wave of his hands, Pouchard shook his head. "What is this world coming to?" He leaned in closer to Dardelle. "Someone certainly was serious in their attempt to do you harm, weren't they?"

Dardelle probed his face. "Those curs! Wait until I'm able to see with both eyes! I'll hunt them down and—"

"You'll do nothing of the sort." Pouchard clicked his tongue. "You'll stay here until you're well and then you'll fall in step with this new government. You'll obey their tyrannical laws or you'll die. I can see that already. Tell me I'm wrong."

Maria stepped out of the examination room and looked toward the door. The banging had stopped. She couldn't tell if the assailant had gone or if he was waiting for someone to leave, ready to pounce like a cat after a mouse. Perhaps he would be brazen enough to kick in the door regardless of if it was locked or not. Her underclothes were damp with perspiration, and she felt lightheaded. She would much rather be sitting at home with Anna, in front of the fireplace sipping tea, not a care in the world. But that wasn't possible now.

"Maria," Léon took her by the arm, "Come and sit down. I should never have left you."

"I need to rest for a bit to collect myself." She went with Léon to a chair in the sitting room. "You don't need to wait with me. Go and see how Dardelle is doing."

"No. I left you before and you could have been arrested, or worse, killed. I'm staying by your side this time. How are you feeling? Be honest because I'll know if you're lying."

She shrugged. She actually felt a little better, perhaps because the knocking had stopped. "I'm fine, but I'm worried about Anna. Those men are so aggressive. They could be capable of about anything."

Léon placed his hand on Maria's shoulder. "Then I'll go and make sure that no one has bothered her. You wait right here and rest."

"I can't let you go out. That man is after you. I'll go myself."

"He assaulted you once. I'll be damned if I'll let that happen again. I can run to your house and back before you have time to sing *Sur le Pont d'Avignon*." He headed off toward the rear of the house.

Maria got up, still dizzy, and gripped the chair. Léon left through the back door before she could stop him. He should have waited for a while to make sure the man hadn't gone around back. If something happened to Léon, she'd never forgive herself. Of course, if Anna was in trouble, she'd feel just as guilty.

She sat down again and picked up a journal she found on an end table to fan her face, but when she caught a glimpse of the title, she abandoned the idea of a makeshift fan. The journal, *Le Droit des Femmes*—women's rights—was Léon's journal. Pouchard had always been a supporter of equal rights, but for him to keep a copy of *Le Droit des Femmes* in his sitting room was unexpected. Most people were not so open about their beliefs, especially those beliefs centered on the government being corrupt in nature. She tucked the journal behind the chair cushion so Pouchard wouldn't get into any trouble, should any officials barge in.

She looked around the room. Decorating the walls were portraits of Pouchard's deceased wife, lovely paintings of landscapes, and his framed medical diploma. She'd known him most of her adult life and certainly knew him to be the sort of man who was not afraid to speak his mind, and frequently he did exactly that. That's why she respected him and counted him as a friend, as well as her doctor.

She pulled out the journal from behind the cushion. If he felt comfortable displaying his rebellious side, then why try to stop him. Yet he'd told Dardelle to go along with the new government. Could it be that Pouchard grew tired of seeing all the death and fighting? After all, his sworn oath was to heal those in need.

Getting off the chair, she wandered around the room and glanced above the fireplace at the mantle clock. An hour had passed. Where could Léon be?

"Excuse me, Maria." Pouchard stood in the doorway.

"Yes? How's Dardelle?"

"I did what I could for his nose and put some salve on his cuts. He'll need to rest for a few days. I slipped him some medicine, so he'll sleep. The idiot wanted to leave and track down the men who beat him."

"That sounds like him. I certainly appreciate your help." Maria motioned to the clock. "Léon went to check on Anna to make sure she was safe. He's been gone too long."

"I've heard that these men behind the new government are threatening anyone who stands against the monarchists. It doesn't surprise me to see *Monsieur* Dardelle as a victim. There will be more, I'm certain of that."

Maria winced as a sharp pain stabbed at her stomach. Right away, Pouchard led her to the sofa. "My stomach has been hurting more than usual. I thought it was because of all the worry and that I haven't had much rest lately, but I think it's just my old illness getting worse."

"Didn't I warn you about that? I told you to ease back on your speeches and public appearances."

"How can I? Paris needs help and *I* need to do what I can."

"I think you've exceeded what you can do. Lie back and relax for a moment and let me get you some medicine for your stomach." He hurried from the room.

Maria checked the clock again. It would not have taken Léon long to get to her house and back. Something must have happened. She got up again and went to the back door, and placed her hand on the knob, but hesitated. It would be safer in the carriage. She turned and bumped into Pouchard.

"I told you to wait in the sitting room, Maria. You'll never get better if you keep running around."

"You're a fine one to talk. I saw *Le Droit des Femmes* lying out on the table for all to see. You believe in freedom and equality, yet you tell your patients to get in line with the new government."

Pouchard thrust a small vial toward her. "Drink this."

She did as he said. The medicine was strong and bitter, but she knew it would help. He gave him back the vial. "Well? What do you have to say for yourself?"

"You expect me to defend my words? Well, I won't. We don't live in a utopia, Maria. In fact, from what I've seen and heard, we are standing on the precipice of a near-dictatorship. I hate the maltreatment of the poor and I hate Paris for becoming what it is."

She'd never seen him so angry. His face blushed red and his hands shook. Like most people, he was conflicted inside. Part of him wanted to be a good citizen and obey the laws, but the more humanitarian part of him simply couldn't. It was the same with all her close friends and associates. Nobody wanted to disobey the government, but they'd been left no choice. Even when the war ended, that small glimmer of hope, it turned out that things hadn't changed after all.

At the sound of the doorknob turning, Maria and Pouchard both startled. Maria stepped back. They glanced at each other. No words were necessary. They were both praying it was Léon. The knob rattled and Maria realized the door was locked.

She edged close and whispered, "Léon?"

"Yes it's me. Open the blasted door. Hurry!" He sounded out of breath.

Pouchard dashed forward and opened the door. Léon rushed in with Anna partially covered by his coat. When he stepped into the light, Maria gasped. His face was scratched and bleeding. She embraced Anna and closed the door quickly. "Léon, what happened?"

Anna answered, "It was horrible. Léon came to make sure I was all right. He said you were worried about me. I assured him there was no danger and told him to go back to you. Then, as he left, a mob of men set upon him. I saw it from the window. I called out to him and he managed to get inside, but the men didn't leave. They threw rocks at the house and were shouting all sorts of terrible things. We managed to sneak out the back but had to take the long way around to get here."

Pouchard examined Léon's face, but Léon pushed him away. "It's not bad, Doctor Pouchard. I fell into a rose bush. It's nothing more than a few scratches from some angry thorns." He shook his head. "They'd followed me, Maria. Anyone around me is in danger. I've got to get away from here."

Maria embraced him. "But where will you go? There's nowhere safe anymore."

"My Lodge is safe. In an emergency situation such as this, all Masons are to gather in their respective Lodges. Don't worry about me. Doctor Pouchard, it doesn't look as though you're a target of their ire, so you should all be relatively safe here…for now anyway. As soon as morning comes, I'll come back."

Pouchard nodded. "Why don't you let me clean off those scratches first?"

"No, it's not necessary. I need to get to the Lodge. Maria, Anna, be careful and stay away from the windows." Léon pressed his ear against the door, opened it, and rushed out.

Dardelle's deep voice rasped behind everyone, "Was that Léon Richer?" He leaned against the wall.

Raising his voice, Pouchard turned. "*Monsieur* Dardelle! Get back in bed. Doesn't anyone listen to me?"

With a throaty grunt, Dardelle said, "I can't sleep the entire revolution away, now can I?"

Anna gasped. "Revolution?"

Maria took her hand and held it tightly.

Dardelle smiled, although his swollen and bruised face only allowed half of his mouth to turn up. "You see my face, *Madame*? This was an invitation to a revolution, and I've accepted that invitation. The people of France do not have to tolerate such behavior." He lowered his voice, and Maria detected a sparkle in his open eye. "The soldiers haven't had time to remove the wartime cannons from the streets. I intend to capture those cannons. Armaments for the people. Armaments for the revolution."

Maria watched Dardelle's expression. He meant every word. The fight would continue, only this time it would be against France.

Chapter 17

After Dardelle's announcement, Pouchard escorted him back to the examination room with a few strong words about listening to a doctor, while Maria and Anna went to the sitting room. Anna paced and Maria sat and tried not to let the pain in her stomach show. The night passed slowly, and Maria's eyes grew heavy, but she dared not close them. She had to stay awake in case Dardelle brought trouble.

To stop from falling asleep, she struck up a conversation with her sister. "Those men showed no compunction in attacking Léon and Dardelle. That means they'll care even less about the common man on the street."

Anna frowned. "I know. I was thinking the exact same thing. I'm really scared. And then when Dardelle said that about the cannons I about screamed. We should get out of Paris and go to Pontoise for a while."

"I can't leave. I won't leave, Anna. Running away and hiding in the country won't accomplish anything. We need to do what we can to support the people. Our strength will give them strength."

Anna flopped onto the sofa beside Maria. "Then maybe I'll just go on my own. I can feel the tension on the streets. How can you not be afraid?"

"I didn't say I wasn't afraid. But do you honestly think you can escape what's going on by running off to Pontoise?" Maria got up and went to Pouchard's kitchen.

She needed time alone to collect her thoughts. Even though it was late, a pot of clear broth sat warming on the stove. She ladled herself a small bowlful and sat down at the table. Noticing a stack of paper at the far end of the table, she took a sheet and found a pencil on the counter.

Time to get some articles in the papers and bring the people together in a non-confrontational way. Violence wouldn't help matters, but Dardelle's plan to seize the military cannons was designed to be confrontational. If the people could begin peaceful protests, then perhaps the government would listen, before it was too late.

She sipped on the broth and nibbled on a piece of bread, jotting down her opening paragraph, but Dardelle interrupted, "*Mademoiselle* Deraismes, I never thanked you for helping me." He strolled into the kitchen and leaned against the wall near the stove.

"Léon picked you up. I only drove you here. When you said you were going to capture the cannons, you weren't serious, were you? Please tell me you wouldn't really place the cannons into the hands of revolutionaries."

"Call me Louis. I will do nothing until we are further provoked by those government monkeys."

"What do you mean by 'further provoked'?"

"We plan to get our hands on the cannons and move them into strategic positions around the city. If the government refuses to issue proclamations of civil rights to all citizens, then we shall react to their provocation." He sat and glanced at the paper in front of Maria. "What's that you're working on, if I may ask?"

"Just an essay for *Le Droit des Femmes*. You're familiar with it?"

"Richer's journal? Of course. I've also read everything you've ever written in it. That's why I know you would rather seek a peaceful resolution to France's surrender to Prussia. But, *Mademoiselle*, you must realize that our own government does not seek peace among the lower classes. They have all but declared war on us."

Dardelle's words rang true. Only a few days old, the surrender had already spurred dissatisfaction among the people. "Louis, what will happen if you move the cannons? What are your intentions? Do you intend to fire upon our own people?"

"The Bourgeois are not our people. True Frenchmen support French citizens, all of them. What I'm seeing is that the upper classes want to keep their positions as overlords to the rest of us."

Maria didn't respond. What was the point? He'd made up his mind. He wasn't wrong, but preparing for a citywide attack wouldn't end well for anyone. She didn't want to banter any more with him. His ideals were too radical. If she ignored him, he'd leave once he saw that she wasn't an attentive audience. At least she hoped he would. She went back to her writing.

"Well, *Mademoiselle* Deraismes, it seems you're somewhat of a hypocrite."

She pushed back her chair and stared at him. "How dare you say such a thing. I've suffered verbal and physical attacks from Honoré Daumier and his cohorts, but I haven't let that deter me. Léon and I were attacked by a government-promoting ruffian, and I fight each and every day for equality. Just because I don't agree with blasting the streets of Paris with cannon balls doesn't mean I will not fight to free France from tyranny."

Dardelle sat without speaking. It felt good to put him in his place. She watched him, a pitiful site with his injured face, but he still struck an imposing figure. His lip curled upward in a half-smile, and he bowed his head. "I apologize to you, *Mademoiselle*. I did not mean to offend you. It's just that I'm so used to dealing with men who say one thing and then go and do another. I know how much you and your sister have done over the years, and I would never intentionally do anything to dishonor you."

Well, that was unexpected. Maria forced a slight smile. "Thank you. You'd better get back to your bed before Doctor Pouchard sees that you're up and straps you to the bed frame."

With a wink of his good eye, Dardelle limped off to his room. Alone again, she finished the broth and returned to her writing. She didn't get very far before her mind wandered and she thought of Léon. He'd said all the Freemasons were gathering in their Lodges. But what did that really mean? Why were they supposed to meet there? For what purpose? Could they have influence over the government? If there were Masons among the leaders, they would be able to change things. Then again, nothing had been done about the previous government. Why didn't the Masons do something? Perhaps they couldn't. It didn't seem likely that men with a Masonic mindset would ignore inequity among the citizens, which could mean they didn't have the influence she'd hoped. If only the government was run like a Lodge, each man equal once he crossed the threshold of the Lodge, then reason and equality would rule.

When someone cleared their throat, Maria looked up. Anna stood in the kitchen doorway. "Can I come in?"

Maria motioned to the chair beside her. "I can make you a pot of tea if you'd like."

Anna shook her head and sat. "You're my sister, so I'll stay in Paris with you no matter what. I love you, Maria, and I promised Mother I'd look after you."

Their mother had always expected Anna to be the responsible one. Ever since Maria's childhood stomach illness, Anna had been placed in charge of making sure younger sister was safe. It didn't seem fair, but Anna never once complained. Even now she stuck to her role as big sister.

"I love you, too, Anna, but you forget that I'm also a grown woman. I'm not a child anymore. Your responsibility for me ended when I grew up."

With a heavy sigh, Anna got up and went to the stove. "It doesn't matter, I'm the eldest. Maybe I will have a bit of tea after all." She found Pouchard's tea container and set about brewing a pot.

They sat together and worked on the essay until they could no longer concentrate. Pouchard showed them to a room where they could spend the night and then went to bed himself. Sometime during the night, Maria woke as she heard Pouchard's front door creak open and then click closed. She lay still. Had someone come into the house, or did someone leave?

Not wanting to disturb Anna, she crept quietly from the room and tiptoed through the house, listening for footsteps or voices. An eerie stillness permeated the entire house. The only sound, someone snoring, probably Pouchard. She peeked into the examination room. Empty. It had to be Dardelle who'd been sneaking about. But why would he slip out in the middle of the night?

She continued through the house to the front door. Unlocked. How thoughtless of Dardelle not to even bother thinking about the safety of the other occupants. His thoughts were likely focused on securing the cannons. He could label his violence as a rebellion, but it still had the bitter taste of war. She locked the door.

Logic and compassion were needed to transform a battle-torn country like France. The trick was getting the message to the public. She peered through the gauzy curtain covering the front window. No moon, only darkness periodically punctuated by the yellow light of the streetlamps. The night used to feel welcoming, the quiet lending itself to calm, but now, the dark felt frightening.

She shivered and went back up to bed and slipped under the covers. She couldn't sleep. Would Léon still be at his Lodge at such an hour? How exciting it would be to sit in the Lodge, discussing the coming events with men from all walks of life, nobody taking on a superior quality. The Lodge must be the closest thing to a utopian society. She opened her eyes and sat up.

How liberating it would be if Masonic ideals were applied to society outside of the Lodge. From what Léon always said, Masons were to act 'on the square', being the best person possible. She had to become a Mason to give her position in the world more credibility. A woman Mason would garner attention, and her actions would surely serve as a model for citizenry, instilling the idea of equality among all. She lay down and settled onto the pillow. Perhaps the morning wouldn't be so bad after all.

Chapter 18

Maria woke to a city in turmoil. The National Guard had tried unsuccessfully to collect the cannons that were scattered throughout Paris, but groups of rebellious citizens managed to get to them first. The cannons were placed at strategic locations in many of the working-class neighborhoods, defending the people against the government's thugs. Dardelle had carried his plan to fruition, just as he said he would.

With a light breakfast of bread and tea, Maria and Anna sat in Pouchard's waiting room, not sure if it was safe enough to go home. There'd been no word from Léon. All of the news had been delivered from the local constables. Even though the day was lovely, clear and sunny, the usual flurry of activity was nowhere to be seen. Nobody ventured outside.

Someone knocked on the front door. Pouchard leaned into the waiting room. "Ladies, stay here."

Maria stood and listened carefully when he opened the door and heard an exchange of voices too hushed to understand. A moment later, Louise Michel rushed into the room. She threw her arms wide open and embraced Maria.

"Maria Deraismes! I'd heard you were hiding out here." She backed away and gave Anna a cursory glance.

Right away, Anna defended, "We're not hiding. Who told you that? Why aren't you in jail?"

"Got out. Just in time, too, by the looks of things. And Louis Dardelle told me."

Maria looked over at Anna and then back to Louise. "What do you mean by the looks of things? How bad is it out there?"

"Oh, I'd say we're about where we should be. Dardelle is going to take over the city. We'll soon be freed from our captors!"

Anna scowled.

Maria stared. "Captors? Aren't you exaggerating just a bit?"

With a smirk, Louise folded her arms across her chest. "No. We're armed now. Once we have Paris, we'll take over the rest of France. Free the people. We can't lose."

Louise's words meant she'd already joined the rebellion, believing the common people could take control of Paris. With her hot temper and defiance, she was bound to get into trouble.

Maria sat. Her stomach tightened. Anna must have sensed her discomfort, because she reached over and placed her hand over Maria's.

Softly, Anna asked, "Are you feeling all right?"

"I'll be fine. Louise, if you get involved with Dardelle, you'll either be arrested again or killed."

Pouchard barged into the sitting room. "Prefect Piétri's coming up the path."

Maria rose with Anna, but Louise ducked behind the sofa. She whispered from her hiding place, "Don't bring him in here. He's been trying to get me back in jail since I got out."

Anna shook her head and rolled her eyes. "Oh, yes, and I suppose you're completely innocent of any suspicion he might have."

The last thing they needed right now was to fight among themselves. Maria placed her finger to her lips. "Shush. What do you think he wants, Doctor Pouchard?"

Pouchard shrugged. "I'm not sure, but I'll go and find out." He hurried from the room and returned a few minutes later. "He knows you and Anna are here, but he asked only to speak to you, Maria. He's alone."

"All right. He's a reasonable man, surely no harm can come from talking to him." Maria gave Anna a reassuring smile and went to the front foyer.

Piétri stood with his hands behind his back, looking closely at a portrait on the wall. He must have heard her approach, because he turned around and dipped his head slightly. "*Mademoiselle* De-raismes."

"Good morning, Prefect. I understand you were asking for me?"

"Yes. While some of my men have been informing local residents of the illegal activities that had transpired early this morning, I wanted to personally convey my assurance that order will be restored shortly." He bowed his head again.

"May I ask how you knew I was here?"

He glanced around and opened his mouth like he was about to say something, but didn't say a word. He looked nervous, or perhaps he wasn't sure that he really could restore order. Pointing to the portrait he'd been examining, he mumbled, "Handsome woman."

Pouchard walked up beside Maria. "Yes, that's my wife. What exactly is it that you want, Prefect?"

Piétri looked down at the floor and stared at his boots. "I've been ordered to conduct a search of the premises, *Monsieur*." He looked up. "I must look for any evidence of sympathy toward those who do not favor the government."

"What? Preposterous! I won't allow you to set foot in my home." Pouchard blocked Piétri. "Under whose orders do you proclaim this ridiculousness?"

"Adolph Thiers, our Provisional Government Chief Executive."

So now Thiers had an official title. He'd traded France to Bismarck for that title. Such a politically minded man was not what France needed. He'd already divided Paris and was forcing the citizens to take sides. If news of the rebels standing against Thiers spread the districts and outside of the city, the country would certainly be dragged into another conflict, French against French.

"Excuse me," Maria stepped forward. "Since you asked for me, does this mean you are to search my home next?"

Piétri came further into the foyer. "Please listen. I'm fully aware of what I'll find in this house and in yours, *Mademoiselle*. For this reason, I volunteered to do the job myself. I wanted to let you know, *Mademoiselle*, that you must go home as soon as possible so it doesn't appear you and Doctor Pouchard are collaborating together."

Relaxing his posture, Pouchard seemed to study Piétri for a moment. "I don't understand."

"Doctor Pouchard, I know you attend *Mademoiselle* Deraismes' speeches, subscribe to *Le Droit des Femmes* and have Louis-Nicolas Dardelle in one of your examination rooms. Trust me when I say that I hold no ill feelings toward those desiring equal rights and better conditions for all classes of people. I do, however, believe in upholding the law. For this reason, I must order you to turn Dardelle over to me."

Dardelle had to have known he'd be hunted down and that's why he chose to escape in the middle of the night. But was it to protect himself or Pouchard? Piétri, Thiers, and Dardelle were like boys in a schoolyard, each fighting for their position in a hierarchy. Their mindset centered on winning, whatever it took. Maria knew it was up to women to save men from themselves.

"Dardelle left last night." Maria pointed toward the examination room. "I heard him leave."

Piétri stared at Maria. He didn't blink and it felt like he was gauging whether or not she told the truth. Finally, he nodded. "I'll have to search the house anyway to make sure he's not hiding."

Pouchard stepped aside, his lips pressed together, and his arms crossed. He didn't say a word.

As Piétri walked down the hallway toward the examination room, Maria hoped he wouldn't find Louise hiding in the sitting room. Hiding made her look guilty, whether or not she'd collaborated with Dardelle. Maria and Pouchard followed behind Piétri. He went into each room, but didn't bother to search very thoroughly. When he came to the sitting room, he saw Anna and nodded politely. He didn't go all the way in.

He finished his brief search after a few minutes and ended up back in the foyer. "Well, I'm terribly sorry to have disturbed you, Doctor Pouchard. *Mademoiselle*, please get home right away. Even small groups of people suspected of disagreeing with the government will be watched." He turned and left.

Pouchard locked the door and then burst out laughing. "So now I'm lumped in there with Dardelle!"

"You think this is funny? Thiers can ruin you."

"I'd like to see him try." Pouchard stopped laughing. "I am a physician. My oath is to treat those in need, not to go around stirring up a rebellion. Now, while I hope these brave rebels succeed in toppling Thiers, I'll do nothing openly to help them. I shall continue to doctor the wounds of both sides of this new conflict, regardless of their standing on the matter."

Pouchard didn't usually advertise his opinion, but now it seemed he didn't care. He was a good man who followed his conscience, although wasn't taking potential trouble seriously enough. Maria to Anna in the sitting room. Louise sat beside Anna on the sofa, neither talking, but they also weren't arguing or sniping at one another. Could it be that they'd found a way to tolerate each other?

Anna stood and motioned to Louise. "Maria, do you know what she just told me? She said that several destitute families were rounded up last night and put in prison."

Maria shook her head. "For what?" Who would arrest entire families? Louise must be wrong. "Were they protesting or did they commit some crime?"

Louise flung her legs onto a table in front of the sofa. Her worn boots thumped against the surface. "No. Their only crime is being poor. I thought maybe you could speak to your Freemason friends and see if they can do anything. I know they're a charitable bunch that hold a bit of sway with some of the officials."

"Charitable, yes, but they're not miracle workers, Louise. Have you seen Dardelle? He was in terrible shape when we found him."

"He's all right. In fact, his condition only serves to emphasize our plight. He's been moving around since early this morning, showing the people what they have to look forward to."

Anna sat on the edge of the sofa. "I knew things were bad, but I had no idea how bad. Why is Thiers doing this?"

Maria had no answer. Nobody could see into another man's mind or soul. Thiers must believe he knew the way to restore Paris. Surely he wouldn't condone the vicious behavior happening in his name. A leader wouldn't allow such things to continue, at least not in good conscience.

Apparently, Louise also wanted an answer to Anna's question, because she cleared her throat and stood with hands on hips. "You don't have any insight, do you, Maria? You know in your heart that we have to fight against this injustice. You know what's right. Admit it and join us."

Louise wasn't wrong. The people had to make a stand, but using violent tactics would only further incense the government. Louise and Dardelle had a way of rallying the people, but Maria knew better than to get swept up in the fury of passion. Her father had always made both Anna and her take a step back from a situation before plunging into it. She had to do that now. But explaining this to Louise without sounding like she didn't support the fight for freedom wouldn't be easy.

She looked into Louise's eyes. Her determination was cause for admiration. "Louise, I want to gather more substantial facts before I commit myself to openly joining your group. I can tell you this, though, I will never support a government that embraces prejudice and suppression of the lower classes. I will, as always, avail myself to you in whatever capacity I can. I'm going to meet with Léon as soon as I can and find out what he knows about the situation."

With a huff, Louise rose her voice, "So basically you're going to sit around and do nothing? We need to act now, Maria." She glanced at Anna, as if seeking support from her. "Did you forget what I said about the poor families being thrown into prison? Women, children. There was no cause for that. They don't care who they abuse. It's only going to get worse, Maria. The longer we stand by and do nothing, the more people will be hurt and imprisoned. Will you stand with us or not?"

Louise wasn't going to understand anything but immediate action. But this was not the time to react out of emotion. Maria agreed with her father's philosophy; assess the situation before reacting. "I'm with you in spirit, Louise. I will never stop fighting for what's right. I simply can't commit to joining with you yet."

Louise relaxed her posture and looked as if she'd just lost a loved one—eyes cast down, shoulders slumped. "Then Dardelle was wrong."

Maria watched Louise carefully. Was this a new ploy of hers to garner allegiance? "What are you talking about?"

"He said he believed you would stand beside us all the way to victory. He was wrong." Louise frowned, turned abruptly and left the room. The front door slammed a moment later.

Anna blurted out, "Are you really going to do nothing, Maria? You heard Louise, entire families are in danger. Thiers wants to rid Paris of the poor."

"We need to see where all of this is heading first, before we make any blatant overtones. We're in a very precarious position."

"Well, I will give whatever I can." Anna strode from the sitting room. "Louise! Wait for me!"

"Anna! Wait!" Maria followed but stopped at the closed door. Was she wrong for not immediately joining up with Louise and Dardelle? Perhaps it was time to make the hard choice and do what was right.

Chapter 19

Maria sat by the front window in Pouchard's house, lamenting how both Anna and Louise thought she'd turned her back on them. They were wrong, or were they? Maybe she *was* too afraid to pit herself against the government. No, that wasn't true. She believed that injustice demanded defeat at any cost, yet what had she done to achieve that? *Maman* had always said that everyone should live by the Latin phrase *acta non verba*, action, not words. But she'd only accomplished the last part of that phrase.

Anna hadn't returned by late afternoon, so Maria grabbed her coat and went outside, gazing up at the sunny, cloudless sky. Even a lovely day couldn't bring cheer to the unusual silence pervading the city. She shivered. Maybe Anna had gone home. With their house close by, Maria buttoned up her coat and went as fast as she could down the street. Before long, her legs ached, but she pressed on and hurried inside.

"Anna? Anna, are you here?"

Silence. If Anna had gone with Louise, she was playing with fire. She should know better. Or maybe Anna had the right idea. *Acta non verba.* The usual warm and inviting hearth was nothing but cold gray ash, making the house bleak. An uneasy feeling crept through her. She had to find Anna and Louise and set things straight.

Where would Louise be? She'd certainly avoid going anywhere Piétri might look. She couldn't leave Paris without a departure authorization from the National Guard, leaving her stuck within the city boundaries. She was the president of the Montmartre Women's Vigilance Committee, but would she go back to such an obvious place as their meeting hall? That would be one of the first places the police would look. Then again, Louise always did as she pleased, but this time, she had Anna with her.

Maria set her mind on going to Montmartre. Now she had to find a way to get there without arousing suspicion from the police. Léon knew the city and would surely know how to get to Montmartre secretly, and since she wanted to see him anyway regarding what the Masons had discussed the night before, she might as well find him. She went outside and walked to the end of the street where there were generally a few Hanson cabs in the area, but this time there was nothing. Not a cab, carriage, or pedestrian. Léon's house was too far away to walk, but how else could she contact him?

She turned to go home as someone called her name. "Maria Deraismes? Is that you?"

Turning, she saw a young man in a fine suit coming out of a house across the street. She was sure she'd seen him somewhere before, with Léon, but what was his name? Ah, yes. He was the physician she'd met at the Lodge after her speech, Georges Martin.

"Good afternoon, *Monsieur* Martin."

He came across the street. "Oh, *Mademoiselle*, you shouldn't be out. As I'm sure you know, the climate here is quite unsettled, and I'm not talking about the weather."

"Yes, I know, but I need to find Léon Richer."

"Really? Then follow me." Georges motioned with his head to the house he'd just come from. "I was on my way home."

"So that's not your house?"

"No. Some of us have been, well, discussing the future of Paris. Come on, let's get you in where you'll be safe."

How sad to think that the same streets she'd grown up walking were no longer safe. Georges took her by the elbow and escorted her to the house. As soon as he opened the door, a rush of warm air came out, bringing with it the scent of fresh bread, an instant feeling of welcome. They walked through the house to a back room where soft voices chatted.

"Gentlemen, look who I found," Georges announced as they stepped into the room.

Léon jumped up from a chair looking frightened. "Maria! Are you all right?"

"I'm fine. I was about to set off to find you."

Georges spoke up, "I found her on the corner, alone. I didn't feel it was safe for her, so I brought her here."

Maria spoke to Léon, "I was hoping to catch a hansom cab. There were no policemen around. I was in no danger. Besides, Anna has gone off with Louise and I need to find her. I think they went to Montmartre."

Léon nodded to the other men in the room. "Excuse me, brothers, but I should speak to *Mademoiselle* Deraismes." He crossed the room. "Let's go somewhere a bit more private, Maria."

When they got to a different room decorated with tapestries, Léon shut the door. "What were you thinking? I wouldn't have left you at Pouchard's if I'd have thought you'd go gallivanting all over Paris. Have you forgotten already that visit from Thiers' ruffians?"

"Of course I haven't forgotten. Look, Louise spoke about destitute families who were thrown into prison for no apparent reason. She managed to get Anna of all people on her side. I told her that I didn't want to act or take sides until I found out more and then Anna stormed off after Louise. She's not at home. I need to do something, be more like Louise. I can't allow families to suffer while I sit in my nice house, sipping tea and eating a hot meal every day."

"Maria, I've seen your ice box. It's empty. The war was hard on everyone, not just the working class and the destitute. The best thing you can do to help is to keep the people informed and work at convincing Thiers that he has to create a government that works for everyone. You can do that, I know you can."

Léon believed in her so much, but his faith and flattery didn't make her feel any more useful. "I want to make a difference like Victor Hugo does. Or even like Louise or Dardelle. They act, they don't just stand back and watch. I don't want more killing, and I don't want to see my country in ruin."

Léon took her hands in his. "You're a magnificent young woman and each word you write and every sentence you speak gives credence to our cause. Not everyone can be a reckless revolutionary."

"But shouldn't I stand with my brothers and sisters? I have to follow through on the words I speak."

"You lead by example, Maria. People see you and they listen. You're a charismatic woman, that's your strong point. You're more like Hugo than you know. We all have to take our strengths as they are. We're not all meant to die on the battlefield."

Maria paced around the room. She knew that in her present health, there was no way she could stand among Louise's friends in a physical fight. But regardless, she had to find Anna and make sure she wasn't in any trouble. The thought of Anna involved with Louise's radical tactics frightened her. "Can you help me look for Anna?"

Léon flashed a smile and nodded. "Of course. Give me a minute and I'll get my coat and take you home. Then we'll go and find her first thing in the morning."

"On the way home, perhaps you could tell me what went on at your Lodge last night."

He smiled again but shook his head. "You know I can't disclose anything that happens in the Lodge. But, when you're a Mason yourself, you'll be privy to everything and I'm sure you'll by master of your own Lodge soon enough."

She sighed and felt a glimmer of hope. Did that mean the Lodge had agreed to initiate women? Even if it didn't, Léon had succeeded in calming her down like he always did. His gentle nature was one of her favorite things about him. Now if they could find Anna and convince her to come back home before another revolution started, all would be well.

Chapter 20

Maria and Léon spent most of the following day getting to Montmartre, hiding in alleyways, staying in the shadows, and taking less-used streets. But finally, they found Anna. She'd taken refuge with Louise and her gang of confidants, hiding from the National Guard as they began a sweep of the area to arrest rebels. It was by pure chance that Léon had recognized one of Dardelle's followers sitting on a brick wall, although it had taken some persuasion on Léon's part to get the man to take them to Louise.

There were more than twenty men, women, and children, in addition to Anna and Louise, crowded into the basement of an abandoned shop. The people were half-starved and had evidently been hiding from the roving thugs of the Thiers government for some time. Anna worked side-by-side with Louise, comforting the children and aiding the ill. Louise excelled in that capacity and poured out her compassion. Feeding the hungry and helping anyone who asked for help was the main purpose of the Women's Vigilance Committee. Maria now regretted not finding Berdine and bringing her along.

Maria and Léon stayed in the basement sanctuary for two days, purchasing or scrounging what food they could for the refugees. By the end of the second day, she had to leave because a Guardsman on the street recognized her. The man called her by name and ordered her to leave Montmartre. She had to go or risk drawing attention to Louise and Dardelle.

She explained to Louise that she wouldn't be able to help anymore due to her notoriety around the city, and although disappointed, Louise understood. Anna decided to go with Maria and as luck would have it, they found one of the few hansom cabs still operating. The clip-clop of the horse's hooves over the cobbles rang out in the silence.

When they got home, Anna went inside, and Maria asked the cab driver to take her a few miles away where Berdine had a room in an apartment shared with several other women. She paid the driver and asked if he could pick her up in an hour. She found the apartment and knocked on the door. A tall woman answered and ushered her inside with a welcoming smile. The apartment, while small, was comfortable and cozy, with a warm hearth and the smell of bread coming from the kitchen. Maria found Berdine fanning a loaf of bread with her apron. What joy and relief it was to find her well.

"*Mademoiselle*, it's wonderful to see you," Berdine embraced Maria. "Please say you'll stay and have some tea, bread, and jam. I made the bread."

"Please call me Maria. Of course I'll stay. I wanted to see if you'd heard the latest news about what's happening."

Berdine's shoulders drooped. "We've heard some. This is why we mostly stay inside these days. We still manage to distribute the scant donations we receive through the *L'Association pour le droit des femmes*. But the donations are getting fewer and fewer."

"Sadly, it's not going to get any better." Maria sat at the table while Berdine and her friends brewed tea and smeared a layer of jam over a thick slice of bread, sliding a plate in front of her.

They chatted about current events and how the National Guard now controlled the city. After an hour, Maria looked out the window and saw the hansom cab waiting on the street.

"I need to go now, Berdine, but please feel free to come for a visit any time, providing it's safe to do so."

She nodded and smiled. "I will. Take care of yourself, Maria."

With a slice of bread wrapped in a thin towel that Berdine insist she take for Anna, Maria gave her a parting hug and hurried to the waiting cab. On the drive home, the cab stopped briefly when two young men dashed out and charged across the street, followed by three National Guardsmen. By the time she got home, a feeling of relief washed over Maria. She'd felt vulnerable being outside, her house now more of a sanctuary than ever before.

Over the next several months, matters didn't improve and in fact became worse. The government refused to relax its stranglehold over the working classes and small skirmishes broke out all over the city. Maria made several speeches in public forums and at the Masonic Lodges, but each meeting ended by being cut short by the National Guard who broke up the gathering. By March of 1871, tensions were high and the strain between Thiers' rule and the non-bourgeoisie reached a breaking point.

One evening, Maria stood by Léon at the lectern of his Lodge and prepared for her next speech, while Anna took a seat near the front. The audience consisted of men and women of every imaginable station, a good thing, but she shuddered when she saw both Louise and Dardelle at the back of the hall. The authorities certainly would notice them.

As the crowd settled, Léon leaned close to Maria and whispered, "I think we're in for an exciting night. I've heard it rumored that Dardelle is planning to announce the results of the election."

Maria looked out over the crowd. Word had spread that the Paris election had only garnered a little over two hundred thousand votes, mostly from the working-class neighborhoods, since the majority of bourgeoisie had already fled the city. Everyone already knew the expected outcome. It would favor a more socialist sort of government, one that would promote equal education and more feminist-minded subjects like equal property ownership and paternal responsibility for abandoned women with children. It had the makings of a grand new rule that could bring about peace, finally. If only Thiers would recognize the election and what the people wanted.

"Léon, I don't want my speech to be overshadowed by the announcement. I want people to fully comprehend the points I make."

"I know. The Lodge master forbade Dardelle from speaking inside the Lodge. He'll have to wait until the meeting is over."

"Good. It's not that I don't want him to make the announcement, but sharing the space with Dardelle will be distracting and my message might not be heard."

"You have nothing to fear. All eyes and ears will be focused on you." He smiled.

Maria cleared her throat and took the lectern when Léon stepped aside. "Good evening. We are on the eve of a new beginning. I am not talking of elections or battles won or lost, but something far greater. Humanity has withstood amazing trials and has always persevered, but tonight, in this room, we have an example of equality. Look around you. Men and women are seated together, not segregated by gender or class. What I see as I gaze out is what I should see every day as I go about my business. There can be no separation because there *is* no separation." The crowd applauded and she continued when the noise subsided, "Education is the key to any progressive society. If any one group of people is denied an adequate education, the society will eventually falter and fail."

It only took a few more minutes to finish the short speech, but it was received with rousing applause and cheers. Maria couldn't stop smiling because she knew in her heart that a new era had arrived. The audience slowly filtered from the room, but instead of the usual gathering in the foyer, everyone ended up outside the Lodge. She and Anna stayed close to Léon, while Louise and Dardelle climbed atop a low wall.

Several National Guardsmen watched from across the street. They didn't move in. Were they waiting to act until after the announcement? As Dardelle raised his hands, a hush fell over the crowd.

His injuries from the assault had long since healed, but he had a permanent limp as a result of the beating. It gave him a sort of sympathetic edge that the people really embraced. If Thiers knew how he'd actually helped Dardelle, he'd be mortified.

Dardelle seemed to look at every person in the crowd, a tactic Maria knew he used often to make everyone feel like he was speaking to them personally. "I know you're all anxious to hear the results of our election!"

The frenzied crowd cheered and shouted to the point where Maria covered her ears. Anna pressed in close, but neither she nor Maria took their eyes off Dardelle.

He waited patiently until it grew quiet again. "As *Mademoiselle* Deraismes said moments ago, we are on the verge of a new era! The people have spoken! We have elected a new city government!"

The resulting noise and stamping feet made the ground tremble. Hats flew into the air, backs were slapped enthusiastically and men and women were united as one. Maria looked across the street. The National Guardsmen were still there, only they were grinning. Why? They hesitated for a moment before stepping onto the road and crossing toward the crowd.

Immediately, Dardelle noticed them, cupped his hands around his mouth and shouted, "Stop right there! This is a peaceful gathering!"

The crowd turned in unison. The National Guardsmen stopped, removed their caps and threw them to the ground. Next, they removed their rifles off their shoulders and lay them on the road. Dardelle climbed off the wall and approached them. The crowd quieted. Not a whisper was heard. Maria could hardly breathe. Could they really be surrendering, giving up the fight to suppress the people?

One of the Guardsmen nodded to Dardelle. "We offer our weapons, and our services, to the new government."

Were they being truthful or was it a guise to get close to Dardelle? There were no other Guardsmen hanging about, no one waiting to rush out and attack. Nobody moved, except for Dardelle. He picked up the guns and handed them to a man behind him, then he spread his arms wide and embraced the Guardsman. "Welcome, brothers!"

Maria grabbed Anna's hand. What an incredible day! Léon reached his arm around her waist. He had to yell to be heard, "Maria! Can you believe it? Even the enforcers are coming over to our side."

She nodded. Anna cheered and waved along with the crowd, caught up in the joyous mood. Dardelle got back onto the wall next to Louise, took her hand, and raised both of their hands in a victorious salute. The people showed no sign of dispersing, so Maria nudged Léon. "I'd like to get home. I'm tired." In truth, the noise gave her a headache. "But I won't soon forget this night."

"All right, we should go." He guided Anna and Maria through the crowd. They made it to the Cariole carriage and climbed in.

Looking back, Maria saw a larger group of National Guardsmen marching toward the crowd. They were in two rows of five men each and had their rifles pointed forward. These were obviously not men who were ready to abandon Thiers yet. Léon jostled the reins furiously and clicked his tongue to get the horse moving. Anna turned around as well and mumbled that she hoped Louise would get away.

At the sound of gunfire, the horse startled and took off at a run. With the jerking of the carriage and the scattering of the crowd, Maria couldn't see either Louise or Dardelle. She prayed that the National Guard hadn't shot them. Their attack was unprovoked. No one created a dissension and other than the few rifles that had been surrendered, everyone was unarmed. The sound of more shots echoed off the buildings and panic ensued. People ran in every direction, screaming and cursing.

When the carriage came to an abrupt stop, Maria spun around. Léon slumped forward with the reins gripped in his hand. "Maria," his voice was raspy. "Take the reins."

"Léon, were you shot?" She grabbed the reins.

"Yes." He leaned back. Blood stained the front of his coat.

"Where were you hit?" Maria handed the reins to Anna. She unbuttoned his coat. A small wound. From her days treating wounded soldiers, she knew it looked like an exit wound. She felt around the back and found a small tear in the middle of his coat.

"It hurts, Maria. I can't breathe."

"I think the bullet went right through. Hold on, Léon. Stay awake." Taking the reins from Anna, Maria slapped them up and down. "Move!" She turned to Anna. "Keep him talking, don't let him fall unconscious."

Of all people, how could Léon get shot? It must have been an errant bullet. Léon, bent forward again, moaned. Taking a quick glance, Maria saw a bullet hole through the back of his seat. She shook the reins harder. Even with the horse at a run, it would take too long to get to Pouchard's, but she didn't know of any other doctors in the area.

Léon sat up awkwardly. "Maria..." His head rolled to the side.

"Léon? Léon!" Maria pulled back on the reins.

Anna felt his forehead and lifted an eyelid. "He's unconscious, Maria. He's losing too much blood. We have to do something."

Maria steered the carriage over to the curb beneath a streetlamp. "Help me get his coat off. We can press it against the wound to stop the flow of blood. Oh, Anna, how could this have happened?"

Working quickly, Anna managed to remove the coat. She folded it and held it against Léon's chest as he slumped forward again. Maria could now see the entry wound in his back more clearly. It wasn't bleeding much at all, so she left it alone. She faced forward again but felt the blood drain from her face. Honoré Daumier held the horse's bridle. This, she did not need.

Chapter 21

Maria's hands trembled as she gripped the reins and Daumier locked eyes with hers. His face, stern, and his breath left streams of smoky plumes, giving him the look of a snorting dragon. Maria handed the reins to Anna and got down from the carriage. She stayed near the door, ready to climb back up.

"*Monsieur* Daumier, I'm on my way to a doctor's office. It's an urgent matter. Léon Richer has been shot."

Daumier continued to hold the bridle but moved around to the side more and peered into the carriage. "Shot? How?"

"A vicious attack by the National Guard at the Masonic Temple."

"Why?"

"I don't know. Louis-Nicolas Dardelle announced the results of the election, so perhaps Thiers' men didn't want the results known. Please, I have to get Léon some help."

"You know, *Mademoiselle*, if you and your friends had not pushed the government into action with your inflammatory ideas and ridiculous election against the government, then perhaps none of this would have happened."

Was he really placing blame away from the real culprits? How could he in good conscience do that? Maria walked closer to Daumier. "You haven't seen what I have. You haven't knelt beside a starving child or held a dying woman because she couldn't afford medicine. And you weren't there when the National Guard opened fire on a group of unarmed men and women. Now let go of the horse."

Daumier lowered his eyes. "I have seen a child die, do you not remember? It is the fault of the parents, not the children. If children are starving, then it should be a priority to get them food."

"With all due respect, Honoré, that's exactly what the Women's Vigilance Committee, the Freemasons, and every other believer in basic human rights is trying to do. We're not just sitting around in our *bas bleu* plotting how to dismantle men's dominion over the world."

"Maria!" Anna called out. "We've got to hurry!"

"Let go, *Monsieur*." Maria grasped the bridle and pulled the horse's head toward her.

Daumier let go. He looked at Léon again and then back at Maria. "There is a doctor not far from here. Number 12 *rue Saint-Antoine*. Down the street, turn left and continue to *rue Saint-Antoine*. Number 12 is on the corner." He glanced around and stepped onto the footpath.

Maria hurried into the carriage and got moving right away, nodding to Daumier as she passed. She turned left where he said, but there were no streetlamps at all, making it impossible to see much at all. If not for the lights in the surrounding houses, she'd be driving blind. The quiet and the darkness were unsettling. At any moment, she expected someone to jump out. Every now and then Léon let out a moan as the carriage wheels slipped between the cobbles or hit a rut. She couldn't read the street signs and slowed the horse to a walk, peering into the night.

"Anna, can you see where we are? Where's *rue Saint-Antoine*?"

"I don't know. Your eyes are better than mine."

"I think there's a crossroads up ahead. That has to be it. How's Léon?" Maria leaned out of the carriage for a better look at the street ahead. She saw the small street sign but couldn't read the name on it. She grunted in frustration, got out, and ran to the sign, which thankfully declared it was indeed *rue Saint-Antoine*. She looked at the closest house. Number 14. That meant number 12 had to be on the same side, but on the other corner, through the intersection. Waving to Anna, she motioned to the house.

Maria ran to the front door of and banged several times. It took a moment before a man—old, with gray hair and a matching beard—answered. He walked with a cane and wore small eyeglasses perched near the tip of his nose. "Can I help you?"

"Are you a doctor? I have a wounded man in the carriage." Maria pointed to the street.

"Yes, I'm Doctor Kellermeister. What's that you said about a wounded man?"

"He was shot. Quite by accident, I assure you. Please, he's bleeding badly."

"Well, you'd better bring him in quickly then. How did you find me? I've been retired for years." The old doctor held open the door and peered at Anna as she got out and tried to pull Léon from his seat. "Oh, dear. Is it only you two women?"

Maria nodded. "Yes, but we can manage."

"I have a border staying with me. I'll get him to help. Just a moment." He went in and called out, "Alexandre! Come down here! I need your help."

A tall, distinguished gentleman with smoky-brown hair, dressed in a well-made suit came down the stairs. "What is it? What's wrong?"

"This lady needs some assistance with an injured man. He's received a gunshot wound."

Alexandre stepped outside. "Didn't I tell you there would be shooting in the streets? Thiers is a tyrant and he's destroying France."

Kellermeister clicked his tongue and waved his arms about. "That's enough of that talk. Go and help the ladies carry that man into my study. You can put him on the sofa. I'll go and get my medical bag."

Maria went with Alexandre and introduced herself as he lifted Léon, "We got caught in the fray when the National Guard descended on an unarmed group of our friends at the Masonic Lodge."

Even though Alexandre had to be at least in his mid-fifties and somewhat gangly, he heaved Léon onto his shoulder with ease and walked slowly to the house. "That must have been the noise I heard. I told Doctor Kellermeister that is sounded like gunfire, but he never wants to hear anything ill about Thiers."

Maria and Anna followed Alexandre to the study. Anna stood beside Maria and asked, "Are you a doctor as well?"

Alexandre gently lay Léon down. "Me? Oh, no. I'm a writer and a poet. Hardly any use to anyone, I'm afraid." Alexandre placed a pillow under Léon's head and lifted the coat from his stomach. "It looks like he's lost a lot of blood, but his breathing is regular, and it doesn't seem that he's coughed up any blood, which is a good sign." He glanced at Maria. "You don't happen to be Maria Deraismes, do you?"

How could he have guessed that? She'd have remembered a distinct man like him. His hair, full and wavy, a thin beard outlining his jaw line, and eyes that were gentle yet fiery at the same time. No, she'd never seen him before. "Yes, I'm Maria Deraismes, and this is my sister, Anna."

"I knew it!" He covered Léon with a blanket and went over to a large chest, pulled out a clean sheet and removed Léon's bloody shirt. "Here, keep this sheet on the wound until the doctor gets back. Ah, yes, you were making a speech at the Masonic Lodge tonight, weren't you?"

Léon's skin around the wound was dark with bruising, but the bleeding had eased to a slow ooze. Maria held the sheet against his stomach but must have pushed too hard because he groaned. "I'm sorry, Léon. Are you awake?"

He opened his eyes and stared right at her. "Is that you, Maria? What happened?"

Maria smiled and looked up at Anna and then back to Léon. "I was so worried about you. A bullet came through the carriage and hit you in the back."

He closed his eyes again and moved his hand under his back. "What? I don't remember that."

Maria moved his hand away. "Just lie still. You're at a doctor's office."

Alexandre knelt beside the sofa. "I'm Alexandre Weill. We'll need to clean the wound and stitch you up, but from what I can see, it looks as if you were very lucky and the bullet didn't hit anything vital."

Alexandre Weill? Maria certainly knew the name. She'd read his articles and essays for years. But for a writer, he seemed to know an awful lot about medicine. "How do you know so much about wounds, *Monsieur* Weill?"

"I don't really. I helped Doctor Kellermeister during the war. We've only just got the house looking like a house again and not a hospital. Excuse me while I go and help him find his equipment." Alexandre got up. "Like I said, we've only just put everything away and he probably can't find a thing."

When Alexandre left, Léon opened his eyes again. "Did I hear right? Is that Alexandre Weill?"

"Yes." Maria sat on the edge of the sofa and felt Léon's forehead. "I didn't even know he was still in Paris."

"Neither did I. Ouch, don't lean on my ribs like that."

"I'm not leaning, I'm applying pressure to stop the bleeding."

"So the bullet came out the front?" He tried to sit up but winced and lay back down.

"Stop moving, Léon. Yes, it came out the front, but I don't think it hit anything vital. At least I hope not. It looks like it came out between your ribs on the right." Maria peeked under the sheet. The bleeding had stopped completely.

He gave a pained laugh. "What an ironic situation. I went through the war without a scratch only to get shot on the street during peacetime."

Anna stood over the sofa and shook her head disapprovingly. "Léon, you shouldn't joke. You could have been killed."

"I'm still alive, Anna, and for that, I'm eternally grateful. Let me laugh if I want. However, that bullet has left my gut stinging like it was jabbed by a red-hot poker."

Doctor Kellermeister and Alexandre came back into the room. Maria stepped aside as the doctor went right to Léon and examined him thoroughly, much to Léon's discomfort. After a few minutes, the doctor, with Alexandre's help, sewed the wounds, applied some salve, and wrapped a large white bandage around Léon's abdomen. Maria watched as Alexandre worked efficiently, as if he'd been doing it his whole life. She'd also learned to treat and sew wounds during the war and felt a strange kinship to him.

When they finished, Doctor Kellermeister gave Léon a pat on the arm. "Now, you'll need to stay here for a few days. Even though the bullet isn't a worry, you could have internal bleeding. I'll have to watch you carefully. I think the bullet cracked a rib, too. I only want you getting up if you need to relieve yourself, otherwise, you're to lie still."

Maria smiled at Léon. "I'll make sure he does what you say, Doctor."

Léon objected, "Have I no say in this at all?"

"No, Léon, you don't." Maria pulled up the blanket. "Besides, you could use a few days' rest."

"Léon?" Alexandre clapped his hands together. "Of course. You're Léon Richer. What an honor to meet you, sir. I can't believe I'm in the same room with the Deraismes sisters *and* Léon Richer. This isn't quite how I'd envisioned us ever meeting, however."

Léon tried to sit up again, but Maria pushed him down. He frowned and looked at Alexandre. "It's nice to meet you, *Monsieur* Weill. I'd rise and greet you properly, but my nurse here won't let me."

Alexandre shook his head. "No, no, Doctor Kellermeister said to rest, and that's exactly what you should do. So, tell me exactly what happened back at the Lodge."

They all talked about the speech, Dardelle's announcement, and the shooting until Léon couldn't keep his eyes open anymore. Kellermeister came into the room, checked on his patient and sat in a rocking chair by the hearth. He rocked back and forth and took out a pipe from his pocket.

With the unlit pipe in his mouth, he turned to Maria. "I overheard you say that Louis-Nicolas Dardelle said that *his* government was elected."

By his tone, Kellermeister didn't sound like he agreed with the election results or Dardelle. Maria watched Alexandre to see if he had any reaction, but his expression hadn't changed at all. She faced Kellermeister. "It's not Dardelle's government, Doctor Kellermeister. It's a government for the people. It's a restorative government. A change in the leadership is imperative if France is to recover and progress forward. Basic human rights have been lacking for so long now, as you surely must know."

Kellermeister eased out of his chair and slipped the pipe back into his pocket. "A country cannot cater only to women and the poor while ignoring the rights and privileges of wealthy men."

Maria stared. What was he talking about? Was he really against helping the downtrodden? She saw something in him that reminded her of Daumier, which made sense. Daumier knew where Kellermeister lived. They had to be friends. A couple of old misogynists who cared little about the poor.

"Doctor Kellermeister," she said, controlling her temper as best she could, "It is a shame that your personal opinions cloud your judgment when it comes to issues of equal rights, but I do hope, for your own sake, that you will try earnestly to support our new system of leadership. People, whether from a working-class background or of the bourgeoisie, are all equally deserving of food, shelter, and education. We share this planet and not one man, woman, or child should be denied the right to live and thrive."

Kellermeister drew in a breath and puffed out his chest. "Ah, yes, you promote equal education for all people, don't you? And just what is a prostitute or laundry maid to do with an education? Would knowing how to read and write make the prostitute a better whore or the laundry maid clean clothes in a more efficient manner?"

How insulting could one man be? Kellermeister was even more offensive than Daumier. The familiar pang returned to Maria's stomach, but she was too mad to care. "You're a doctor. You care for the ill and infirm. You've seen what starvation and poor living conditions do to the human body. How can you stand there and say the wealthy deserve more? How can you accept that women should be whores or maids? If everyone received the same education, then everyone would have the same opportunities and not be forced into drudgery and dangerous occupations."

Kellermeister walked to the doorway and turned around. "I will treat anyone who is in need of medical care, but I also have the need of the occasional whore or maid. Without them, my house would be a mess and my loins would ache. Each serves a purpose." He continued out of the room without another word.

As Maria stood, hands trembling, too shocked to say a thing, Alexandre approached. "I am so very sorry, *Mademoiselle*. Doctor Kellermeister is a stubborn man who speaks his mind. Please don't think his views are my own."

"You live under his roof. I hope his poisoned tongue doesn't infect your own." Maria sat back down near Léon.

"No, it does not. In fact, I rather enjoy taunting him at every opportunity. I've told him that not only do I support a new revolutionary government, but I also support initiating women into the

Masonic brotherhood." Alexandre laughed. "That last one just about gave him a stroke. He's an old Mason with archaic ideals."

Alexandre's laughter was infectious, and Maria found herself smiling. Her anger subsided. "Why do you stay with such a man?"

"Well," he started.

Anna sat in Kellermeister's rocking chair, squinted her eyes, and growled, "All women belong on their backs while the men run the country."

Maria broke out in laughter, only to stop when Léon groaned. "All right, we need to be quiet. I don't want Léon disturbed. He has to rest." She tucked in the blanket and stood. "Perhaps we should go into another room."

They walked down the hall to a smaller room lined with bookshelves packed with volume upon volume. On one of the shelves were a golden Freemasons square and compasses, arranged with the square on top of the open compasses, just like the Masonic symbol for the brotherhood. As a Mason, it was hard to believe that Kellermeister would condone abuse of the lower classes. How could he practice equality in the Lodge, and then persecute those beneath him? Perhaps Alexandre stayed with him to try to change his mind. She should learn more about Alexandre and his motives for being in close quarters with such a hypocrite. She also felt a deep stirring inside, an attraction to Alexandre. It had been a long time since she'd felt like that. He intrigued her and she wanted to know everything about him.

Chapter 22

After talking with Alexandre past midnight, Maria and Anna were shown to a bedroom next to his. There were two small beds and by the decorations and wallpaper, it looked as if it had been a room for children, a charming room with an ambiance of innocence.

They took off their dresses, leaving on their underclothes.

Anna climbed into one of the beds and sighed heavily. "I like Alexandre. He's intelligent, charismatic, and funny. He reminds me of Father when we were young."

"Yes, he does, but he's a lot more handsome than Father." Maria smiled. "Doctor Kellermeister, on the other hand, reminds me a bit too much of Daumier. How could a Freemason tolerate and even support poverty and inequality? He's mad."

"I think he's so dedicated to his wealthy lifestyle that he can't stand the idea of change. He likes being at the top of society."

Maria slipped under the covers. "You know, this makes me more determined to infiltrate the ranks of the Masons and infuse their old-fashioned views with a dose of feminine rationality."

"I love your determination. You'll make an excellent Mason. And I do believe you'll undo the Kellermeister-Masons."

Maria blew out the lamp on the nightstand. She waited until Anna's breathing settled into a regular pattern, wrapped a blanket around her shoulders, and slipped out to check on Léon. He snored softly on the sofa and didn't seem to be in pain. She tucked his blanket around him to make sure he was warm enough and then curled up in the chair next to him.

She looked around the dim room. The curtains were heavy and dark, the lamps were plain and functional, and the stale stench of pipe tobacco permeated everything. What an uncomfortable and uninviting place. She didn't fit in a room like that.

There was no doubt in her mind that she had to do what she could to tear down the invisible walls that separated men and women. But how? Marches, petitions, and speeches were all well and good, yet the impact wasn't being made. Men like Daumier and Kellermeister stuck to their ideals and were so determined to undermine progress that they were like a festering disease.

What do you do with a disease? You cure it. There were things that Daumier and Kellermeister had in common. They were both bent on keeping women in their place. What exactly did they believe was a woman's place? Remaining uneducated? Yes. Catering to a husband? Yes. But it was more. They truly believed that women were not capable of standing as equals. It was likely they even thought a woman's brain was not the same as a man's. Fools, all of them.

Maybe she'd been going about it the wrong way. Once a disease had taken hold and infected every part of the body, there may not be a cure. In that case, it would be logical, and beneficial to the uninfected, to prevent further spread. Stopping the disease of misogyny would mean showing people that women were indeed capable of doing the work of men. An excellent start would be to get women into the Masonic brotherhood. Penetrating the ranks of a purely male dominated order would send a message heard far and wide. That would be the impact she needed.

Feeling hopeful, she closed her eyes and drifted off to a fitful sleep. She woke several times when Léon groaned or stirred and checked to make sure he was all right. At last, the morning arrived. The sunshine streamed in through a gap in the curtain and shone right in her face, leaving no possibility of going back to sleep. She headed back upstairs and got into bed but lay awake thinking of the future of Paris.

Once Anna woke, Maria went downstairs, but halfway to the sitting room, she heard Léon's voice. He spoke clearly as if nothing was wrong. His voice sounded as strong as usual.

She stepped into the room. He sat propped by pillows, having a conversation with Alexandre. She listened for a few moments, curious about what topic they were discussing.

Léon said, "I wonder if the bullet that struck me was really an accident. I mean, after all, I was blatantly threatened in my own home."

Alexandre replied, "But if they fired on you knowingly, they could have just as easily hit Maria or Anna."

Maria went into the room. She didn't want to hear more. "It seems you're feeling better."

He rubbed the bandage and shrugged. "Well, Doctor Kellermeister changed the dressing and gave me an unpleasant potion to drink and said I'm already healing nicely."

"What, in one day? Nonsense." Maria sat on the sofa beside him. Kellermeister was probably as poor a physician as he was a human being. She lifted an edge of the bandage but couldn't see much at all. "I'll have a look myself a bit later on."

"You needn't bother, Maria, the doctor already said the bullet missed my lung and that I should be up and around in no time."

"We'll see about that." Maria found a bowl of hot soup next to Léon. "Is this for you? I don't think you should eat or drink anything but water just yet."

"It's just broth. Doctor Kellermeister said—"

Maria pushed the bowl away. "If Kellermeister told you to drink a cup of hemlock, would you do it?"

"Maria, what's the matter? You're never so vitriolic toward a host, at least not so early in the morning."

Alexandre put down a book and spoke up, "She has every reason to be caustic, Léon. I'm afraid Doctor Kellermeister and *Mademoiselle* Deraismes had a disagreement last night. To my thinking, however, I give the win to the lady."

Not only was Alexandre a gentleman, but intelligent as well. Maria felt a flutter inside. After helping Léon with his broth, she went for a stroll with Alexandre around Kellermeister's garden. They wandered around where fragrant blossoms and leafy shrubs were carefully placed according to height and color, and talked about politics, liberty, and Paris. The weather had warmed, and the scent of early blooming roses provided a delightful atmosphere. She hadn't felt so calm and happy in a long time, nor had she felt so at ease with a man she'd just met.

Over the next couple of days, she and Anna tended to Léon and avoided Kellermeister as much as possible. As often as she could, Maria sneaked off with Alexandre for animated conversations about the government and Dardelle. Having a like-minded man around made the days pass quickly.

She sat with Léon as he stretched his arms above his head, his exercise prescribed by Kellermeister. "Léon, you're able to walk and move around on your own now. It's time for me and Anna to return home. But if you need me to stay, I will."

Léon ended his exercise and took her hands in his. "Are you sure it's me you want to stay for? I've seen you around Alexandre. He makes you happy."

She gently tugged her hands free. "That he does, but it's you I'm concerned about."

"Kellermeister should let me go home any day now anyway. "He flashed a sly smile. "But perhaps you can stay on here with Alexandre."

She nudged him. "Stop it."

"Or perhaps Alexandre could rent a room in your house rather than stay here." His smile returned.

"Léon! You are incorrigible." Maria stood and gave him a kiss on top of his head. "You've been a good patient."

The following day they all sat around the hearth with Alexandre when Kellermeister came home from an errand. He sat in his rocking chair and shook his head sadly. "It's official. There are now almost a hundred installed men to make up a Communal Council at the *Hôtel de Ville*. Paris is now governed as a socialist Commune."

Léon leaned forward, holding his side. "Commune? There's really a Commune?"

Maria couldn't believe it. A commune established an administrative center in Paris. Exactly what they needed.

With a sour look, Kellermeister continued, "*Monsieur* Richer, you appear to think a socialist leadership in Paris will put an end to all of the troubles. I assure you, it won't. Revolutionaries never win."

Maria couldn't help herself. "What about the American Revolution? They fought against British rule and won. When there are wrongs sanctioned by the government, *Monsieur*, sometimes a revolution is necessary."

"*Mademoiselle*, are you promoting dissension? I thought you were against hostilities." Kellermeister smirked as if he'd caught her in a lie.

His smugness irritated her, but it didn't matter what he thought. He was only one man. Maria smiled as graciously as she could. "Doctor, violence rarely accomplishes what the perpetrator of the violence intends. However, that said, if it takes a battle to obtain liberty, then perhaps in some instances violent outbreaks can indeed be condoned."

"Then you concede that Adolph Thiers is correct in waging battle against the revolutionaries of this Commune."

"Not at all. He stands for maintaining a monarchical society that encourages the mistreatment of the people who are the very backbone of this country. That, Doctor Kellermeister, simply does not make sense."

Kellermeister opened his mouth to talk, but nothing came out. He was speechless. He walked to the window and peered out. "I've had your carriage brought around. *Monsieur* Richer, you may return home. You must stay off your feet as much as possible and those stitches will need to be removed in another two or three days. Any physician can snip them out."

Léon eased up to his feet. "I thank you with the utmost sincerity, Doctor Kellermeister. Without your help, I'd likely be dead."

Kellermeister nodded abruptly and left the room. Anna mocked him by striding around the room with her head hanging down and her hands clasped behind her back.

With a shrug, Alexandre whispered, "Léon, and ladies, I suppose those are your walking papers, so to speak. I apologize for the Doctor's manners. He's been retired and somewhat removed from society for a number of years now."

Maria would miss her talks with Alexandre. His eyes, warm and friendly, gazed into hers. His wit and charm were unparalleled and even Léon couldn't match his intelligence. She'd have to invite him to her next speech.

They all went out to the waiting carriage where Alexandre helped Léon up, making sure he was comfortable in the seat before he turned to Maria. "It has truly been an honor to spend time with you, and your lovely sister. I shall value these past few days and keep the memories in a special place in my heart." He nodded to Anna but turned his focus back to Maria.

The sentiment was sweet, and Maria felt her cheeks flush. She was behaving like a silly schoolgirl. When they were all seated and Alexandre handed the reins to Anna, Maria had a sinking feeling in her stomach. It wasn't the usual pain, but a sort of ache. She'd felt the same ache at her parents' funerals and when Anna left the household after marrying Hipolyte. She stared straight ahead and nudged Anna to get the horse moving.

She didn't turn back. She couldn't. It would make it that much harder to leave if she saw Alexandre standing on the street. Nobody said a word as they drove slowly in the late morning sunshine, passing quiet houses with thin plumes of smoke trailing from the chimneys.

No people ventured outside. No children played and no women pushed laughing babies in their prams. Only the sound of the horse's hooves on the road broke through the silence.

She had the sense that Alexandre remained on the street, watching, and when she turned around in her seat, he was indeed there. He waved and she saw his smile even halfway down the street. She waved back and felt an elbow jab into her ribs.

Léon gave her an overly melodramatic frown. "If I were a jealous man, I'd say you prefer his company to mine."

"Rubbish, Léon. It's just that he's an interesting man with fresh views, not unlike your own."

He laughed, grabbed his side, but continued to laugh. "You're such a liar, Maria Deraismes. It's not just his opinions on human rights that you're enamored with."

Anna laughed along with Léon, finally blurting out, "I thought you said he reminds you of Father?"

"Maybe he does, in some ways, and maybe he doesn't in others." Maria turned away and looked out to the side. She wanted to look out the back window to catch a final glimpse of Alexandre, but if she did, she'd never hear the end of it.

When they were almost home, Léon pointed to a kiosk on a street corner. "Anna, stop. Maria, would you mind getting out and reading that poster?"

She climbed out and looked at the poster plastered on the kiosk. A bold title read, 'Meeting at *Hôtel de Ville*, Montmartre 2 April Midday'. Below, the text defined the extent of the meeting, a gathering of the local citizens to discuss how best to create an equal education system, how to raise funds for widows and orphans, and how to rebuild areas of Paris that were ruined during the war. Maria got back into the carriage, excited to read that progress was in the works.

"Léon, there's a meeting tomorrow at the *Hôtel de Ville* to discuss how to proceed with the new government."

He touched his bandaged abdomen and looked at the kiosk. "Tomorrow? Couldn't they have the decency to wait another week?" He sighed. "Well, my friends, I think we should go."

Anna shook her head firmly. "You're in no condition to go, Léon."

"Maybe not, but it's important I go. I have a paper to run and if I don't publish the latest information, how will the people know what's going on?"

Placing her arm around his shoulder, Maria gave him a gentle squeeze. "I'll go. I'll take notes on what's said and give you a full report."

Anna gave the reins a shake and continued down the street. "Then it's settled. I'll stay with you, Léon, and Maria will get the news. But I don't think you should go alone, Maria."

Maria's first thought was to invite Alexandre, but how would that look? It would be better to go alone or find another friend. Maybe Alexandre would be there anyway and then they could bump into each other. Of course, it really was nobody's business who she associated with or even if she went to the meeting alone. "I'll go there by myself. I'd rather not have anyone around to distract me."

Anna and Léon exchanged a look that annoyed her. She knew they were thinking she was talking about Alexandre. Anna stopped the carriage in front of the house. Maria helped Léon inside while Anna took the carriage around back. Once inside, Léon went straight to the sofa and lay down with a grunt and a moan.

"Do you need anything, Léon? Would you like some tea or perhaps something to eat?"

"No, no, don't fuss. I need to rest for a few minutes. I'll be able to go home soon and then I'll be out of your hair. Didn't you tell me you'd written an essay? Perhaps I could read that."

"I'd forgotten about that." She went to the desk drawer and took out the essay she'd written before the shooting incident. She skimmed it quickly and was amazed to see how appropriate it was. She'd written about equal education and recognizing women's rights. "Here it is."

The day passed peacefully. Léon read the essay and spent his time editing it, while Anna and Maria got the household back in order after their absence. Maria couldn't wait to attend the Montmartre meeting the next day, mixing with crowds of people all anxious to hear what the Commune government had in store. Even better was the idea that the people, the Communards as they'd become know, themselves would be part of the decision making. Paris was on the forefront of setting an example for the rest of the world, and that left her breathless.

In the evening, she collected what she'd need for the meeting—paper and sharpened pencils placed in a leather bag—and picked out appropriate clothes to wear. She was tempted to put on an old pair of *bas bleu* Louise had given her as a joke but thought better of it. No point in purposely stirring up trouble, although it would be funny.

Léon planned to dedicate an entire publication to the meeting, and for that reason, she had to take thorough notes. Sleep didn't come and since she didn't want to bother Anna or Léon, she sat in the garden under the moonlight, the cool air chilling her to the point where she wrapped herself in a blanket lying on the bench. A veil of cloud moved in, obscuring the moon. Even so, it gave her comfort. *Maman* used to recite an old nursery rhyme about the moon. She tried to remember how it went.

> *When the sun travels down to end the day,*
> *The moon rises up to guide the way,*
> *The dark of night is nothing to fear,*
> *So long as gentle moon is near.*

She hadn't thought of that rhyme since she was a little girl. It got her through many frightening times at bedtime when shadows seemed to create monsters and frightening mythological creatures on the walls. And now, even hidden by the clouds, that gentle moon looked down. She sat for a while longer, gazing at the moonlit clouds, listening to some beetle or other insect crawl through the leafy litter beneath the trees. When her eyes grew heavy, she went inside and got into bed. The Commune was a godsend, and Thiers was bound to fall.

Chapter 23

In the morning, Maria dressed and prepared to head off to Montmartre before anyone else had woken. She made a simple breakfast of eggs and toast, enough for Anna and Léon as well. The smell of cooking must have woken Léon, because he shuffled, slightly bent over, into the kitchen and sniffed the air.

"You'd better watch out, Maria, I could get used to this." He sat down holding his side and reached for the teapot on the table.

"You look like you're feeling better." She slid a plate of toast his way. "I'm glad to see you up and around."

"I'm still a bit sore, but that horrid medicine Kellermeister gave me seems to be working. Are you sure you'll be all right today? I don't mind telling you that I'm more than a little concerned with you going alone."

"How long have you known me? I'm capable of looking after myself. I don't intend to dally after the meeting. In fact, I'll rush back and tell you all about it. This is the beginning of the healing that Paris has needed for so long." She had a good feeling about the meeting and Léon's needless worry wouldn't dampen her spirit. "It's progress."

He smeared some jam on the toast and took a bite. "Of course it's progress, but I'm not sure Thiers is going to accept Paris under a Commune rule. If he did, he'd have all of the other cities crying out for reform. He doesn't want equality. He wants a monarchy where he's at the top of the heap sitting upon a golden throne."

Taking a seat beside Léon, Maria sipped on chamomile tea. She'd purposely been trying not to think of Thiers and here was Léon forcing her to do just that. "Why don't we give the Commune a chance?"

He lifted his teacup to his lips, but didn't drink right away. "I didn't mean to sound negative. It's just that we keep getting a little glimmer of hope only to have it snatched away again. Maybe I'm getting too pessimistic."

From the doorway, Anna said, "It's good to keep a thread of pessimism, that way you don't get too disappointed when everything unravels."

Léon motioned to the chair opposite. "Spoken like a true optimist. Please sit down and enjoy this delightful breakfast your sister prepared."

Anna eyed Maria. "You look absolutely serene this morning, Maria. Are you sure you'll be all right going alone?"

"You sound like Léon. I'll be fine. There'll be a lot of people there. There's always safety in numbers. Now, if you'll eat your breakfast, I'll clean up the kitchen and then I'll be off." It would take a while to drive to Montmartre, but the ride would give her time to contemplate about how things would soon change. She didn't want to get her hopes raised, but the Commune would erase all the ill deeds of the monarchy. These were certainly exciting times.

After everyone had their fill, Anna helped wash the dishes, occasionally voicing her concerns. Maria checked on Léon one last time before leaving. Satisfied he'd be all right, she slipped into her coat and went out to the small carriage house in rear of the main house. She got the horse ready for the trip, and climbed into the carriage, shook the reins, and looked up at the window as both Anna and Léon waved.

Last night's clouds had cleared away, leaving a brilliant blue sky. She leaned back as the mare started off down the lane. Several people strolled down the street or drove along in their carriages. Even if they weren't going to the same place, it was nice to know that the streets were again alive with humanity.

The sunshine warmed the day and after about an hour, Maria unbuttoned her coat and let it drape loosely. The closer she got to Montmartre, the more crowded the streets became. Word had evidently spread quickly about the meeting. A small group of men climbed into a carriage saw her and waved. They were some of the Freemasons she'd met at her various speeches. She waved back.

Hopefully there would be a lot of women at the event as well. If she'd only known about it earlier, she could have spread the word. Ah, but then that's exactly what Louise would likely have already done.

Maria felt well, a good sign since her stomach hadn't bothered her all day. In fact, she felt better than she had in a long time. As she neared the *Hôtel de Ville*, she looked around at the throngs of people milling about. A man to one side looked like Alexandre, but when he turned, she saw it wasn't him after all. Alexandre probably didn't even know about the meeting. With luck, Kellermeister hadn't heard either.

She steered the carriage to a spot along the street just past the *Hôtel de Ville* and sat for a while. The people around her were a glorious mix. Men and women chatted amiably, some dressed in fancy clothes and some in rags. It didn't seem to matter on this day. Then, as if by providence, Alexandre crossed the street toward her. He smiled and tipped his hat.

"Maria! How wonderful to see you here. I'd hoped you'd make it. I have to warn you, Doctor Kellermeister is around here somewhere. He's set on finding a fundamental mistake in the Commune." He extended his hand and helped her down.

She held his warm hand in hers. His grip, strong and powerful, yet not so much that it hurt. "I only hope not too many of the monarchists are attending. Shall we go inside?" Even when her feet touched the ground, Alexandre continued to hold her hand. He only released his grip when they stepped over the threshold of the *Hôtel de Ville*.

He asked, "How is *Monsieur* Richer?"

"He's doing well. He would have loved to come himself if he was able."

"And your sister?"

"Also well. She's minding Léon to make sure he doesn't try to do too much too soon. Why didn't you tell us about this meeting before we left Doctor Kellermeister's house?"

"I didn't know about it. The Commune officials have been meeting in secret and only announced the meeting yesterday to avoid giving Thiers advance warning. I've heard rumors that Thiers is preparing his Versailles troops to march on Paris."

Maria couldn't believe what she'd heard. Her heart sank. "Where did you hear that?"

"From Kellermeister. I told you it was only a rumor. There might be no truth in it at all."

"Then again, there might."

They walked through the foyer and proceeded to the central meeting hall. The capacity crowd was divided. The Communards stood to one side, while the other side of the hall had the monarchists, who frowned and tossed nasty epithets at the Communards. And right in the middle of the monarchists were Daumier and his friends, arguing with several women proudly displaying their *bas bleu* with skirts apparently shortened just for the occasion.

Maria stayed at Alexandre's side as he worked his way through the crowd toward the front of the room. She stopped when she heard her name called out, looked around, but didn't see who'd addressed her. Then a woman's voice, unmistakably Louise's, yelled louder, "Maria! Maria! Over here!"

"Alexandre, let's go over there."

They headed toward Louise, which wasn't easy because of the boisterous group surrounding her. When they got close, Louise shouted, "Maria! Make a path for my dear friend!" The people separated so they could get through, and when they did, Maria noticed Dardelle standing nearby.

He turned around and winked. "*Mademoiselle* Deraismes, I'm very glad you found out about our meeting. We will be discussing many things of interest to you. Who's your friend?"

"This is Alexandre Weill, a fellow writer."

"How fabulous. If I'm not mistaken, you've written papers on society's ills, haven't you, *monsieur*?" Dardelle didn't wait for an answer when a man tugged on his sleeve and told him it was time to begin. "Excuse me, won't you? We have to start now." He made his way to the lectern and rapped a gavel several times.

Louise waved a red flag in the air and made an incredibly loud whistle. She'd said the color red was the new symbol for the Commune. The room came to order, except for Daumier. Barely visible among the multitudes of bodies, Maria managed to see him whispering to one of his friends. As soon as Dardelle began to speak, Daumier and his friends rushed from the hall. What was he up to? He probably didn't want to be seen at a meeting sponsored by the Commune. It would do him good to listen to what the people really wanted and expected from their government. What a coward to run off so he wouldn't have to face the demise of his antiquated ideas.

Maria turned her attention away from Daumier and listened to Dardelle. He gestured to the crowd. "You are all citizens of France and are now equal in the eyes of the Paris Commune!"

Thunderous applause filled the room. Along with Louise, several other people waved red flags. To see them publicly declare they were loyal Communards gave Maria a chill. To be so blatant could be dangerous if Alexandre was right about Thiers launching a campaign against the Commune. But Louise wouldn't be Louise is she weren't making a spectacle for the betterment of humanity.

The disorganized meeting went on for an inordinate amount of time, with people yelling out at will what they wanted to see from the Commune. Maria strained to hear among the shouting, clapping, and whistling, but when the sound of gunfire rang loud outside, the rowdiness stopped immediately. With the ear-splitting crack of an-other shot, the audience began to move and push and shove one an-other toward the exit. Shouts and curses ensued. Women, crushed in the crowd, cried out for help. One man fell and couldn't get up be-cause everyone simply stepped over him. Maria couldn't move, the throng of people made it impossible.

She looked around for a way out and saw several men who'd been standing beside Dardelle take him by the arms and escort him quick-ly to a doorway behind the lectern. He may have planned his escape ahead of time.

Louise grabbed Maria's hand and gave her a tug. "You've got to get out of here."

A barrage of gunshots rang out and then screams came from out-side. People inside continued to push and shove, shouting and plead-ing for help.

Alexandre looked around frantically. "Maria, follow me! I saw which way Dardelle went."

Maria nodded. Anything would be better than getting trapped inside the building. It had to be Thiers' troops outside. How could they dare shoot at people when there was no war? And Daumier, he must have known about it and left before the assault began.

Louise pointed behind the lectern. "There's a back door. Go quickly."

Maria held onto her hand. "I know, I saw it. Aren't you coming? You can't stay here."

"Of course I can. This is where I'm supposed to be. We knew they were coming. We've built up barricades across some of the streets. Oh, you should see it, Maria. A group of your Mason friends built one of the barricades on the *rue de Rivoli*. And on the *rue de Gaubourg*, women tossed mattresses from the windows of a factory to make a barricade! We've got hundreds of barricades made up of everything we can get our hands on. And as we're standing here,

Communards are closing more barricades around those bastard soldiers right now. They'll be trapped!"

Maria stared in disbelief. Barricades blocked the streets? On the way to the *Hôtel de Ville*, there hadn't been any barricades. She hadn't any trouble getting around. The streets were all open and accessible. "Louise, I didn't see anything blocking the roads. I think you're wrong. Come with us. You shouldn't stay here."

"Maria, the barricades are blocking the routes out of the city. We found out which way Thiers' troops were coming and we left it open. Ha! We have them now!" Louise tied her red flag around her waist. "You have to go. I wear the red sash of a Communard and if you're too close to me, you could get mixed up in the fray and get hurt."

If she left, she'd be abandoning Louise and the citizens who came with their hearts full of hope. If Louise and Dardelle knew the troops were coming, how could they in good conscience let so many people walk into a battle? These were ordinary men and women. Nobody had come prepared to fight for their lives.

An explosion outside shook the building and made the audience panic even more. A man's voice yelled out *we're done for now!* A woman screamed *help us!* The crowd closed in, moving to the center of the room, pressing together in total fear, frantic eyes wide with terror.

Alexandre took off his coat and placed it over Maria's shoulders. "We need to go now, Maria!"

It was a terrible decision to make, but the drive for survival forced Maria to follow Alexandre. They made it to the lectern a moment before a group of uniformed soldiers barged into the hall and fired shots into the ceiling. A shower of plaster rained down over the people. Maria wanted to make it all stop, but how could she? She had no magic words that would drive the soldiers away.

Alexandre found the back door, but it was locked. He began kicking and bashing it with his shoulder. The soldiers moved further into the hall, striking at the people with the butts of their rifles. Men and women fell and screamed, trying to scramble to safety. One woman, hit on the head, was left lying on the floor, bleeding and getting trampled.

Maria gasped at the sight before her. Could it be a dream? Maybe she'd wake up any moment, tucked in her warm bed. When a bullet slammed into the wall beside the door, she knew she stood in a living nightmare, not a fanciful dream. Alexandre managed to break the lock by striking the door with his foot. He shoved Maria through. She stepped out into the fresh air and sunshine. The door closed behind her. She reached for Alexandre, but he wasn't there.

Chapter 24

Maria stumbled forward a few steps behind the *Hôtel de Ville*. The sounds from the front were even louder now that she was outside. Several carriages without drivers or passengers were parked nearby. Were the passengers still inside the building? And what of Alexandre? *He* was still inside! She pushed on the door, but it wouldn't open. Alexandre must have blocked it to stop her going back in.

A stab of pain in her stomach made her double over. Of all the times for her stomach to hurt. There was no way to make it to her carriage. She could get in one of the other carriages and leave, but then someone else would be stranded. Her head spun. She wanted to be home with Anna and Léon. A breeze drifted in and with it, the distinct metallic smell of blood. Her stomach roiled.

"*Mademoiselle* Deraismes!" shouted a man's voice.

She turned, her vision too blurry to see who called out. She blinked a few times. Piétri and several National Guardsmen had come around behind the building. They held rifles. Maria swayed, about to faint. Someone took her by the arm. Where were they taking her?

Then Piétri's voice grew close, "You'll be all right. I know of a safe place."

Nowhere in Montmartre was safe. What was he talking about? Slowly, her vision cleared. The National Guardsmen took her into a building. She resisted. "No! Let go of me."

Piétri spoke again, "It's all right. These men are with me. They're not Thiers' men. Many of the National Guard have laid down their guns in support of the Commune."

Did that mean Piétri stood with the Communards? A group of people were huddled together inside the building, looking frightened and confused. There were more National Guardsmen among them. Piétri told the truth.

Maria drew in a deep breath. "*Monsieur* Piétri, I have friends inside the *Hôtel de Ville*."

"We all do, *Mademoiselle*. Please wait here." He left her in the middle of the room and hurried back outside with his Guardsmen.

Not one person in the room said a thing. After a few minutes passed, Piétri returned with two more people. He brought them next to Maria and went back out again. A woman grabbed Maria's coat sleeve and gazed around with the most pleading and desperate eyes Maria had ever seen.

In a trembling voice, the woman whispered, "Should we wait here? Those soldiers out there are killing innocent people. I saw a young man shot in the head. Half his head was gone. There's blood everywhere. Everywhere."

Maria didn't know what to say. What advice could she give? She pried the woman's hand off her arm and forced herself to remain calm. "Stay here. It's safe in here. There's nothing you can do outside."

Maria went to the door and listened. There weren't as many gunshots, although the heartbreaking sound of agonized crying and screaming filled the air. She opened the door a crack and peeked out in time to see a soldier shoot a woman in the chest. The woman collapsed to her knees, her wide eyes staring at Maria until she fell over and lay still. The woman had a red sash around her waist, like Louise's. Could that have made her a target? And what of Louise? She might already be dead.

Among the fallen people were several soldiers, bloodied and beaten. There was no way to know if they were dead or not. She watched and let the images imprint on her brain. This was a day she wanted to remember. Every horrific and gruesome detail was important. Then, rising up above the racket, a woman's voice wailed, a different cry from the rest. It betrayed an awful loss. Maria stepped outside and looked for the woman. Most of the Communards had made a sort of human barricade in front of the *Hôtel de Ville*, standing with their arms looped together, but a few scattered people still fought with the soldiers. The woman was not at the barricade, nor was she behind it. The wailing continued.

Maria stepped further away from the door. There she was! Her hands, stained red with blood. But that wasn't the worst sight. The woman knelt beside two children. Maria had to get to the woman to help. She crept close enough to see a little boy and a little girl with bloodied clothing, lying on their backs, staring with dead eyes at their mother. Maria couldn't feel her legs. Dazed, she stumbled forward and took the woman by the back of her coat, dragging her backward.

Resisting, the woman clawed at the air and cried out for her children. Ignoring her pleas, Maria got a better grip on the hysterical woman and pulled her away. A moment later, Piétri appeared and hoisted the woman over his shoulder. Maria followed them to the building and hurried inside. The people who were quiet before now started fussing and weeping. They took the woman when Piétri put her down and led her to a corner. It seemed as if they knew her.

Maria looked at Piétri when he came up beside her. He shook his head sadly. "What did you think you could do out there? You could have gotten yourself killed."

"That woman's children...why?"

"Because, Mademoiselle, a Communard is a Communard. Thiers doesn't care if his mighty Versailles troops shoot children. All he cares about is putting an end to the Commune, and he'll do whatever it takes to accomplish his goal."

"Well, I care. We can't hide in here and let even more people die. Have you seen my friend, the man I was with? Tall—"

"It's a madhouse out there, *Mademoiselle*, I can't even find half of my own men. Everyone here knew the risk when they came, even your friend, I'm sure. I would suggest you get used to the idea of staying here for a while. Once the barricades are closed up, the troops will have nowhere to go. They are well-armed, we're not. It's going to be a long fight."

"I can't stay here. I have to get home to my sister." How had a simple meeting turned into a full-scale battle? It certainly seemed like Dardelle had an escape route planned, which meant he was willing to sacrifice the very people who supported him. She'd never have expected a man like Dardelle to be cold-hearted. And because of the attack, Alexandre was missing.

Piétri placed his hand on her shoulder. "I understand your concern and frustration, but we need to stand strong to show Thiers that he can't throw a handful of soldiers at us and send us running."

He was right about that. Any sign of weakness so early in the establishment of the Commune would give Thiers hope. They had to resist with all their might. The woman in the corner sobbed and the group around her wept as well.

When Piétri headed to the door again, Maria rushed after him. "Wait! Can you look for my friend? He's tall, grayish-brown wavy hair and a beard framing his face."

"There must be a hundred men out there who fit that description."

"Will you at least look? His name is Alexandre."

"I'll do my best, but only if you promise not to go back outside again."

"I will, if you bring those little children in here to their mother. I know she'd prefer it if she was with them."

Piétri glanced at the woman and gave a sharp nod, then vanished through the door. Maria found a place to sit so she could lean against the wall. Her stomach burned and the taste of bile coated her throat. She closed her eyes, but all she saw where the dead bodies strew outside of the *Hôtel de Ville* and soldiers aiming their rifles at the running Communards. As soon as she was home again, she'd have Léon dedicate an entire publication to Montmartre. That is, if she ever got back home.

The commotion outside quieted down and after a short while, Piétri returned with the two dead children wrapped in dirty overcoats. He gently lay them down near the woman. Through her tears, she thanked him and cradled her children. Maria shut her eyes and concentrated on making the pain in her stomach go away.

"*Mademoiselle* Deraismes." Piétri sat down beside her. "I could not find the gentleman you were inquiring about. But you should take it as a comfort that I also did not find anyone matching his description among the dead. Perhaps he managed to get away."

"Perhaps he did." The only way for him to be safe was if the soldiers hadn't stormed inside the *Hôtel de Ville*. "I appreciate you looking."

"Are you feeling all right? You look very pale."

Maria nodded. "I'm very tired. Listen. I haven't heard any more shooting. Do you think the troops have moved off?"

"The last I saw, they were gathering together down the street. I don't know what for. I wish now the barricades hadn't been placed. I would rather the soldiers leave Montmartre and return to Versailles."

"I'm sure everyone here echoes those sentiments. But I doubt they'd leave on their own even if they could."

Piétri got up and glanced around the room. "I'd better take another look outside."

"Please be careful."

With a nod, he reached into his coat pocket and brought out a piece of folded cloth. "Here, take this. You look like you need some nourishment."

Maria took the cloth and unfolded it. Two small pieces of crusty bread lay inside. She tried to hand it back, but he pushed her hand away, turned, and hurried through the doorway. She looked over at the people huddled around the woman and her deceased children. They needed the bread more than she did.

She struggled to get up, because each time she moved, pain coursed through her body. She needed her medicine. After a few tries, she managed to stand. The people watched her as she approached. It was an uncomfortable feeling, like they expected her to say some words of wisdom. She had none.

"Please, take this and share it." She gave the bread to the nearest woman. "The Prefect of police, *Monsieur* Piétri, said we may be here for a while."

A bearded man in filthy torn clothes pulled a red handkerchief from his pocket and waved it in the air. He looked vaguely familiar. "We are Communards, *Mademoiselle*. We are prepared to resist the tyrants for as long as it takes. Didn't I see you with Louise Michel?"

Maria had seen the man near Louise inside the *Hôtel de Ville*. "Yes. Do you know where she is? I lost sight of her during the confusion."

"As did I. You're Maria Deraismes, aren't you?"

"Yes."

"Louise speaks of you often." He tied the red handkerchief around his arm.

Maria nodded. "She's an amazing woman. I only hope she made it to safety."

The sharp crack of a single shot rang out. It sounded like it was right outside the door. A moment later, Piétri stumbled inside and held the door open while three young men charged in. Piétri clutched his chest and shoved the door closed. The three men with him leaned against the door as Piétri collapsed. Maria ran to him. His breathing came in strained and rattling gasps. His eyes were glassy. She'd seen many dying men with the same look during the war.

"*Monsieur* Piétri," she whispered, gently taking his hand away and checking the wound in his chest. A fatal wound.

In a voice that sounded more like air escaping from a bellows, he declared, "This is it for me, *Mademoiselle*. Keep these people safe."

Maria took a shirt one of the men handed to her and held it against the wound. Piétri groaned but didn't put up any resistance. She knew he was too weak to do anything. There was no doubt he'd soon die. From the amount of blood, he'd probably been shot in the heart. She wanted to say so much to him, to thank him for rescuing her, and the woman and her children.

"*Monsieur. Monsieur?*" Maria watched as his eyelids slowly closed and a final exhalation of air escaped his lips. He'd spent his last moments on earth saving the people he served. Maria clutched his hand and hoped he knew how much his sacrifice meant.

Chapter 25

Once things quieted down, Maria crept out of the building, staying close. Reports drifted in that Montmartre had been bathed in blood during the attempted siege, with the Communards fighting bravely until the soldiers mounted a retreat. Surviving Communards said that the Versailles soldiers were unprepared to deal with the street barricades and opposition and ended up retreating. During their retreat, they had opened fire on the men and women hiding behind the barricades. The blood of Communards stained the cobblestones and dying bodies lay unattended as the remaining people scattered and the troops tore down the abandoned barricades.

Maria retched as the stench of death swirled around her. Corpses were strewn everywhere, the wounded, crying out for help or moaning in agony. She wandered around, half dazed, helping anyone she could. She tore at her dress, using the fabric to bind bleeding wounds. With no more wounded in need of care, she staggered to her carriage. Bullet holes pierced the leather seats, and one wheel had been damaged, but the mare was unhurt.

She had to get away. In desperation, she unhitched the horse and climbed onto her back. She'd only ever ridden bareback once while in the country as a young girl, but she needed to make sure Anna and Léon were all right. She started out upright but soon lay forward with her arms wrapped around the horse's neck. The skittish horse startled at every noise and jerked its head around, which caused Maria to slide and almost fall off. The streets were filled with incensed people guarding the remaining barricades, yet she was allowed through the blockades without question and was even given a hero's welcome as she passed.

There goes one of our brave freedom fighters! they'd shout. Or they'd start applauding. She realized that it must have been obvious by her disheveled appearance that she'd been in the Montmartre attack. But all that mattered at the moment was getting home. It took an eternity until she made it to her street. Several people milled about, engaged in conversation. Were they Communards or monarchist supporters? She couldn't tell. They saw her and stopped talking as she went by. Then she saw Anna outside the house, looking up and down the street.

"Maria!" she screamed, running toward the horse.

The mare realized home was near because she raised her head and trotted. Anna helped Maria down and together they took the horse to the stable out back. They were at the rear door of the house when Maria stopped and fell into Anna's arms, the weight of the world pressing her down.

"It was so horrible, Anna. Even the Prefect, Piétri, was murdered. When the troops finally left, everyone wandered about, too shocked to speak. I saw men collecting the dead and women comforted each other. I did what I could, but—"

Anna opened the door. "Shhh...we'll talk later." The welcoming smell of fresh bread wafted out, yet it only reminded Maria of the bread Piétri had given to her. How many more people would be sacrificed at the hands of Thiers?

Anna took Maria's hand and gave it a squeeze. "You're home now. It's over. I've made some bread and stew. You must be half-starved. Why don't you go inside and see Léon? He's been so worried about you."

"I want to sit with him and tell him everything I saw. You know, when the soldiers were retreating, I prayed they wouldn't storm the rest of the city. I kept imagining that you and Léon were under siege and there was nothing I could do. And Alexandre...he's missing. He saved me."

They walked into the kitchen and Anna pulled out a chair. "Don't think about it anymore. You're home now. Sit down for a few minutes and have something to eat and I'll let Léon know you're home safe." Anna ladled some stew into a bowl, placed it in front of Maria and quickly left.

Staring at the stew, Maria pushed it away. She couldn't eat while so many people were going without. She looked around the kitchen at all the pots and pans and utensils. Whole families shared a single room and didn't even have a kitchen. And here they were, two single women without children, who had so much. Everything they took for granted was a luxury to those who had nothing. She leaned on her elbows and rested her head in her hands. Women were forced to sell their bodies and children were reduced to begging in the streets just to get enough money to buy a stale loaf of bread or rotten vegetables.

"Maria?"

She looked up and saw Léon standing in the doorway. "Oh, Léon!" She got up and went to him, and gave him a hug, making sure not to hold him too tightly. "How are you feeling? You look well."

"I'm healing, but are you? You look like you spent a day in hell." He sat down at the table, wincing slightly. "I'm curious about what happened, but you don't have to tell me anything if you don't want to."

"You need to know. Everyone needs to know. I want to sketch out what I saw."

"Really? You haven't drawn in years." He pushed the stew toward her. "Eat. You'll do no one any good if you die of starvation."

She moved the stew around with a fork and speared a potato. She had to draw the carnage at Montmartre. Ever since Doctor Pouchard said she should give up the exertion of painting and drawing due to her ailment, she hadn't picked up any charcoal or paintbrushes, but now she had the motivation and urgency to sketch the horror. If she could write and make speeches and live through an unwarranted attack from the Versailles troops, then she could certainly make a few drawings.

While she ate a few bites of Anna's stew, she told Léon, in as much detail as she could, everything that happened. He was rapt, shaking his head and slapping his hand on the table after every few words. When she finished, poor Léon looked pale and sick. He was such a gentle soul, and the killing hit him hard. He sat and stared at Maria.

He didn't say anything. Who could blame him for being shocked beyond words. Anyone else would have dissolved into a puddle of tears, but Léon had to be planning how to describe the incident for *Le Droit des Femmes*.

She leaned back and watched him carefully. "Perhaps I shouldn't have gone into as much detail."

"No, it's the detail I want. I can't believe you were right there. I don't want you ever going anywhere alone until Thiers gives up on his absurd attempts to win back Paris."

At the moment, she didn't feel like she ever wanted to leave the house. Searching for Alexandre would be the only reason she'd venture away. He couldn't be dead. It didn't feel like he was dead. Somehow, she could always feel in her heart when someone close had died, and her heart wasn't mourning for Alexandre. It ached for everyone else who'd been injured or killed, but not for Alexandre. Perhaps it was wishful thinking. They had so much more to talk about, so many unfinished discussions.

"Léon, do you remember what I said about Dardelle escaping?"

"Of course. I still find it hard to believe that he ran off and left you and all of those people trapped."

"So do I, but the more I think about it, the more I don't think he willingly left. There were two men who grabbed him by the arms and got him out of the *Hôtel de Ville*. Louise was left behind. I doubt Dardelle would leave her."

"You're right about that. They're so close they might as well be joined at the hip. So what's your opinion of what happened?"

"I'm not really sure. Perhaps they were Thiers' men." Maria looked into Léon's eyes. They weren't as bright as usual. "Oh, I'm sorry, Léon, you should be lying down. I've been blabbering on and not giving any thought to your injury."

"I told you I was fine. I need you to write down all that you told me. We'll get an issue out right away. Is there any way you can find out if Louise survived? I'd love to have her write something as well."

"I'll try. If she's alive, she might know what happened to Dardelle. She didn't seem overly concerned when it happened."

After spending a few more minutes finalizing plans for the *Le Droits des Femmes*, they went to the sitting room where Anna made up the sofa where Léon had been sleeping. Once he settled down again, Maria sat near him to make sure he rested and didn't get back up.

The evening wore on and the subject of Montmartre was never raised again. They played a few games of cards, ate the remainder of the stew and went to bed. Each time Maria fell asleep, she woke to the images of Alexandre or Piétri or the poor children in the street. Tomorrow she'd try to find out more information about Alexandre's whereabouts. Perhaps it would be worth making a trip to Doctor Kellermeister's, not that she fancied the idea of meeting him again.

She got out of bed and looked out the window. Paris slept. To anyone who'd been sheltered from the political climate, Paris would seem to be a quiet and peaceful city. But the truth was hidden by the night. By the light of dawn, the city would again be under Thiers' thumb. The problem with the Commune was that they weren't organized. Unless they could come together as a cohesive group, they wouldn't stand a chance against professional troops. The poorly constructed barricades were evidence of that.

She yawned, finally feeling tired, and climbed into bed. She knew what had to be done. Once Léon had healed enough to travel, they'd arrange another dinner meeting and invite the leaders of the

Commune. If they were all together in one room, then they'd be able to organize a plan of action to maintain the government and keep Thiers out of Paris. The Commune was essential to the future of all citizens, especially the women of Paris. When men and women finally stood together, France would be able to move toward a more perfect existence. Now she had to find a way to make it happen.

Chapter 26

During the few weeks after the attack at the *Hôtel de Ville*, the streets of Paris became a maze of barricaded dead ends. Although no one had seen either Louise or Dardelle, gossip placed them together in a secret hideout somewhere in the city. The same gossip claimed that Dardelle had been rushed out of the *Hôtel de Ville* to a safe location to assure his survival because he planned an attack on the Tuileries Palace. No one seemed able to confirm it for certain, which left more questions than answers. Even worse for Maria was the fact that nobody seemed to know anything about Alexandre. And although Doctor Kellermeister denied any knowledge, Maria had a feeling that he knew more than he disclosed.

The remaining bourgeoisie had locked themselves up in their homes, while the working-class people marched around the neighborhoods in vigilante groups, hunting for any National Guard soldiers or bourgeoisie who didn't support the Commune. Maria heard a story about two wealthy property owners who refused to allow a group of Communards access to their buildings and were arrested, put on trial, and found guilty of a traitorous act. There was no news of what happened after that, and Maria didn't want to know. Roving bands were not the answer and would only draw contempt to the Commune.

On the positive side, there'd been another meeting where an equal education system was discussed so that girls would be given the same schooling as boys. The issue of state sponsored prostitution was raised and after a very short discussion, the Council passed a law to eliminate government involvement in prostitution. Paris was beginning to progress toward equality. With April waning, there hadn't been any further attacks by the Versailles troops, which may have been the reason Maria's stomach pain had eased.

Léon's wound healed so well that he'd been able to go back to his own house and had already published an issue of *Le Droit des Femmes*, although he'd made the decision to rename the paper *L'Avenir des Femmes*, the future of women. An appropriate name if ever there was one.

When one of Léon's assistants dropped off the latest copy of the paper, Maria sat in the rear garden to read it. She hadn't realized she'd been outside so long until Anna came out with a light lunch and a pot of tea. She placed the tray next to Maria and poured. She flicked the paper with her finger. "Am I going to like the issue?"

"Oh, most definitely. Léon has outdone himself this time. He's managed to get some of the most influential writers to contribute. Even Victor Hugo wrote a short article. This is Léon's crowning glory. It's almost too good to be true. Imagine, Anna, a system of government that will treat everyone the same. I'm so proud to be a living part of this revolution. I only wish it could be obtained peacefully."

"So do I. But as things are going smoothly, I'll overlook the bad part of the Commune. You're well, even your appetite is back. I couldn't ask for more."

"Let's do something today. I want to celebrate. Just you and me. I'd like to walk through the Tuileries gardens or take a boat ride down the Seine. I want to enjoy life." Maria got up and motioned to the flowers all around her. "Life is happening right now, Anna, and we should revel in it!"

"My goodness, you are happy, aren't you?" Anna took a sip of tea and giggled.

Maria turned her face to the sun. "Yes, and it feels wonderful. I haven't needed to take any medicine in days, and I have the energy of a sixteen-year-old girl." She'd spent so much time worrying about politics and tending to the physical and mental concerns of everyone, that she'd forgotten how good it was to be alive.

They ate their lunch and chatted about the changes that were occurring before their eyes. Time seemed to stand still, and the garden felt like paradise. For some time, they sat and watched birds flit from branch to branch and honeybees buzz from flower to flower. The beauty of the garden reminded Maria of when she and Anna were young girls growing up away from the noise and dissonance of the city. Once the barricades were removed, they'd go back to their house in Pontoise and relax in the quiet solitude of the country.

Anna got up. "Maria, did you hear something?"

"No."

"It sounded like a knock on the door."

Maria put down her tea. Her heart raced, like it did every time someone came to the house. For weeks she'd been waiting for word about Alexandre. As much as she wanted to know his fate, she'd rather not ever find out if he'd been killed at Montmartre. Living in blissful ignorance made things easier. "Maybe it's Léon."

Anna shrugged. "He rarely knocks. There's only one way to find out though."

Together they went to see. Anna opened the door and Maria gasped. Daumier stood on the doorstep. What could he possibly want? He looked nervous, glancing around and kneading his hands together. Maria's first instinct was the slam the door shut, but curiosity got the better of her.

"*Mademoiselle* and *Madame*, I apologize for the intrusion. I know we have never exactly seen eye-to-eye on matters of feminism, but I must now ask you for help." He kept glancing around and even took a tentative step forward. "Please, may I come inside?"

Anna turned to Maria. "I'd rather see *Monsieur* Daumier in the gutter, but it's up to you, Maria."

What an awful turn of events. Of all the people to be standing on the stoop. Looking at his miserable face brought back the memories of how he'd threatened her and jeered at the many protests and demonstrations. Then again, his eyes betrayed him, showing fear, insecurity, or sadness, reminding her of the time when he cradled the dead child during the war. He wasn't a man to be trusted, yet if he genuinely needed help, who was she to deny him?

"Come in, *Monsieur*." Maria opened the door further and stood aside.

He hurried in and immediately took off his hat, clutching it in his hands. "I appreciate your kindness, *Mademoiselle*. I really do."

Anna locked the door and faced Daumier. "What exactly is it you want, *Monsieur*?"

He lowered his eyes and fussed with the brim of his hat before speaking. "My house was vandalized. Windows broken, paint splashed over my door. And there was a note nailed to my fence post out front."

It wasn't like he didn't deserve to receive a dose of the same treatment he'd given others, but Maria tried to always rise above pettiness. She extended her hand to take his hat. "Anyone in need of help is welcome here, *Monsieur*. Is it your intention to hide out here? We have no room."

He gave her his hat and looked around. "Well, no. I thought we could make an exchange of sorts. If you can help me find a way out of Paris, I could give you information you have been seeking."

What information did he know? Could it be about Thiers? "All right, I'll see what I can do, but as you know, the streets are sealed quite well with barricades. I could perhaps try to get you past as a merchant leaving the city to get supplies. How good an actor are you, *Monsieur*?"

"You do not even want to know what information I have first?"

"Of course I do, but your safety is more important."

Daumier sighed and rubbed his temples. "I have news about your friend, Alexandre Weill."

By the look on Daumier's face, it wasn't good news. When Maria tried to speak, no words came out. She cleared her throat and tried again, "And? Where is he?"

"He was arrested as he fled from Montmartre. He is in Versailles."

Maria stared at Daumier. He'd delivered the most horrible information next to saying Alexandre had died. Then again, Daumier wasn't above lying to get what he wanted. "What makes you certain—?"

"I am telling you the truth, *Mademoiselle*. I know you have your doubts, but all I can do is tell you that I heard about Alexandre Weill from Doctor Kellermeister. He received a message from a cousin of his who lives near Versailles. Weill is to stand trial as a traitor to the government."

"But he's not a traitor."

"It is not me who needs to be convinced. They will want to make an example of him to drive fear into the hearts of those Communards."

"*Monsieur, I* am a Communard." Maria's heart sank. They wouldn't let Alexandre go, not if they were going to use him to show the people what would happen if they continued to support the Commune.

"Be that as it may, the matter still stands that your friend is a prisoner. Now, I have upheld my end of our bargain. How soon can you get me out of Paris?"

"I'm not sure. Let me investigate and get back to you. Can you return home?"

"No. I dare not. I am staying with Doctor Kellermeister. Nobody has bothered him."

"Fine. I'll be sure to get a message to you as soon as I can arrange something." In a way, she felt sorry for Daumier. True, he was getting a taste of what it was like to be the persecuted minority, but no one should ever have to live like that, not even him.

Maria opened the door and waited. Daumier took the hint and left. As he went down the front path, he kept looking around. Would his fear make him realize that his beliefs were at the heart of his predicament? She locked the door and peered out the window.

Anna made a disgusted little sound. "Maria, how could you volunteer to help that man?"

"Would you have denied a man in help?"

"He's not a man. He's despicable."

"Oh, stop it. He's a human being. We should lead the people into this new era by showing them how to treat everyone, even an enemy."

"Why? Daumier will turn his back on you as soon as he's out of Paris. He did it once before to you after you helped him with that dead child, he'll do it again."

"He might, but he'll know the Communards are honorable people." Maria sighed. She knew in her heart that Daumier was too set in his ways to change, his humanity lay concealed behind a shroud of ignorance. Only now and then did his better side show through. If only he'd tear through that shroud.

Anna shook her head. "I wish I could be as certain as you that he can think in a rational and humane manner."

Maria ignored Anna and went to her room to figure out how to make Daumier into a merchant. Although he was well known, his face wasn't. It wouldn't be too difficult to get one of the regular merchants to pass him off as an assistant. That would take care of Daumier, but what of Alexandre? Poor Alexandre, locked up in a filthy jail cell. What if he'd been hurt during the attack? Would they get him medical attention or leave him injured and in pain? What was their ultimate plan for him? Daumier said they were going to make an example of him. That could only mean one thing. Death.

She would need help freeing Alexandre, and that meant asking Léon for his assistance. If he could get his Masonic brothers to stand with him, perhaps they could convince Thiers' men not to hurt Alexandre by pleading mercy. "Anna! I'm going to visit Léon!" Maria called down. She changed her clothes and found Anna waiting near the door.

"I'm coming, too. I'm tired of being cooped up in this house."

Having Anna along would ease the loneliness Maria often felt, even if they didn't always agree. With both of them working together, they got the mare hitched to the carriage quickly and set off to Léon's. The lovely warm weather brought out the children who ran and laughed up and down the streets. Hearing their playful giggles brought a smile to Maria.

Between the nice weather and the children's laughter, Maria's head cleared and ideas flowed in. By the time they got to Léon's house, she already knew exactly what angle to present to the Masons. While Alexandre wasn't a Mason himself, his beliefs and writings were highly thought of within Masonic circles. If Alexandre wasn't freed, then Thiers would run the risk of being jeered by the Masonic brotherhood. Since many officials on Thiers' staff were likely Masons, it would be detrimental for him to create a rift between them. Now, if she could only convince the Masons to make a public plea for Alexandre's release. It would be so much easier to talk to the Masons *as* a Mason, rather than an outsider, or profane, as they called those who were not initiated. Profane indeed. It was profane not to allow women the same privilege.

While Anna tied the horse to a post outside of Léon's house, Maria looked down at her dress and imagined a pure white lambskin Masonic apron tied around her waist. The one Léon wore had blue rosettes of silk, indicating he was a Master Mason. Every Mason wore his apron with dignity. Maria closed her eyes and imagined standing in a Lodge as a Freemason. No gender, no social standing, just a Freemason.

"Maria? Come on. I saw Léon looking through the window."

A moment later, Léon threw open the door and motioned them in. "Quickly!" he shouted.

They hurried into the house and right away saw several men pacing around in the hallway. Léon slammed the door. Maria recognized most of the men. They were Masons. They must be holding an impromptu meeting of some sort.

Maria spoke softly, "I didn't mean to barge in on something, Léon." The last thing she ever wanted to do was interfere in his personal business.

He shook his head and flashed a smile. "No, no, I'm not angry with you. Sorry for sounding abrupt, but you shouldn't be outside right now. We've received news that Thiers is planning another assault on the city, but we don't know when. His troops have been capturing as many Communards as they can. Every time someone leaves the city boundary, there's a soldier right there. At last count we've lost more than twenty men and women."

Maria thought of Daumier. If she managed to get him out of the city, he could be arrested as a Communard. "How can they have soldiers waiting? They can't know which route someone will take. I know the merchants use a different route every day."

"That's what we're discussing. Thiers has effectively shut off our supplies again. The city will run out of food soon. He's trying to starve us into submission."

What a cruel thing to do to his own people. It was bad enough when the Prussian army had the city surrounded, but for Thiers to try the same tactic was unforgiveable. It also meant that he'd probably be unwilling to listen to the Masons. There was so much more at stake now.

"Léon, you remember what I told you about Alexandre Weill?"

"Ah, that you lost track of him at Montmartre? Yes, I remember. What about him?"

"I think he might have been taken as a prisoner in Versailles."

"What makes you think that? Not that I'm surprised, but I'm curious how you would know that. We've only now found out about Thiers' plan."

"Someone told me." Maria glanced at Anna. Anna pursed her lips as if she tried desperately not to open her mouth.

Léon noticed. He stared right at Anna. "Seems like your sister is holding her tongue. What have you done, Maria?"

"I haven't done anything. Anna disagrees with a decision I made, that's all."

"It's Daumier!" Anna blurted. "She's agreed to help him. It makes my stomach sick."

Léon turned and faced Maria. "You're helping Daumier?"

Why was it so difficult for everyone to believe that compassion held more importance than hatred? How ridiculous that she had to defend her actions. "A man asked for help in exchange for information that nobody else has been able to get for me. I see no harm in that."

"All right, all right, don't get upset." Léon pointed to the men. "Why don't you sit in with us? We're taking a bit of a break from the discussion. Before I call the men back to order, what exactly did you come here for? What do you need from me?"

She pulled him aside so the other men couldn't hear. "I want you to make a plea to your Masonic brothers. Can you see if there's anything they can do to get Alexandre and the rest of the prisoners released?"

"Maria, that's what we're talking about. If Thiers really is planning an attack, then we're hoping to make a bargain of some sort. If he releases the prisoners, perhaps we'll ask the Commune Council to agree on a meeting with his representatives."

Someone jumped into the conversation, "He won't agree to that." It was Georges Martin. "I've told you before, Léon, Thiers doesn't care about the lives of a few Communards. He cares about power. That's the whole reason he took those people. He's dangling them over our heads. He knows the power of a threat."

"Then what would you suggest, *Monsieur* Martin?" Maria hoped he had a solution.

Georges looked at the ground. "I don't have an answer. I don't have a military mind, I'm afraid."

Léon clicked his tongue. "Listen to us. We sound like a bunch of school children squabbling over who's right and who's wrong. We need to band together now more than ever." He clapped his hands to get the attention of the men. "Gentlemen! Shall we retire back to the sitting room?"

The men nodded and headed back to the room. Léon escorted Maria and Anna to a small sofa and sat nearby. Several open bottles of wine sat on a table and numerous sheets of paper were strewn next to them. One man with a large, bushy mustache and matching eyebrows was apparently the scribe. He was perched on the edge of a chair with some paper balanced on his knee and a pencil clutched in his hand. As the men discussed the likelihood of another attack from the Versailles troops, Maria listened and tried to glean something useful that could help Alexandre.

The discussion went on for hours. The more they talked about the impact of an attack, the more Maria knew how selfish her thoughts had been. She'd only been thinking of her own feelings and how she wanted Alexandre back. But if troops invaded the city, then hundreds or thousands of men, women, and children would be hurt or even killed. Asking the Freemasons to make a plea to Thiers for the release of a few prisoners didn't sound feasible anymore. Thiers wouldn't let any of the prisoners go. He had the upper hand, and begging would only make him realize he held all the cards.

She'd seen the results of Thiers' actions and he certainly didn't appear to be the sort of man who'd treat people fairly. He was a monarchist through and through. Power and political standing overshadowed any humanity he might once have had. The only way to gain release of prisoners was to make a formal petition through the Freemasons. If all the Lodges in Paris signed, Thiers would realize they supported the Commune and prove how the Commune could be organized and united. With that knowledge, he might begin to see how he'd face resistance to any further attacks.

"Léon, may I speak?" Maria stood without waiting for an answer. The men stopped their arguing and turned their attention to her. "I know most of you and I know there was an emergency meeting of the Freemasons to discuss Thiers and the Commune. I would like to know if you could ask your respective Lodges to sign petitions for the release of the prisoners they've recently taken. We all know they are nothing more than merchants and in one case, a writer and poet. If we can get a petition to Thiers, perhaps he'll actually listen and release them."

One man stood and nodded in agreement. "*Mademoiselle* Deraismes, you are absolutely correct in that the people they arrested were not active Communards, and in fact, several of them were not all that supportive of the new government. The problem we face now will be to make Thiers see his error without making him look like the idiot he is."

Maria understood the point perfectly. The ego of most men generally got in the way of reason and common sense. It would indeed be a challenge to make Thiers believe it was his idea to let the prisoners go. And if anyone could do it, Léon could. He had an innate ability to manipulate words in such a way that he could make anyone believe anything. Léon was truly a treasure.

Léon's voice interrupted her thoughts, "Maria, are you listening?"

Everyone looked at her. "I'm sorry, I was lost in thought."

He continued, "We were just discussing how you need to be the one to make your case to the Grand Lodge. We'll set up another meeting where you can speak directly to the masters of each Lodge." He winked. "Your speeches are always well received, so they'll listen."

What an opportunity! She'd have to make it the best persuasive speech ever. "I'd be honored, Léon. However, if I were a Freemason, I could speak as a fellow Mason, rather than as a profane."

He smiled. "One step at a time. But I have absolutely no doubt that one day you'll wear the apron and open the doors for all women."

She hoped his words would come true, and once Alexandre was back in Paris, she'd continue her push for equality among the Lodges. The success of the Commune would assure equal rights, so the time was right...finally. But first, protect Parisians, especially women.

Chapter 27

After a few days, Maria readied herself to speak to the Lodges. She sat in the garden going over her notes until it became too warm to concentrate. Usually cool and rainy in May, the heat was unusual. She collected her papers and got up to go inside, but before she took a step, she heard a sound and a voice.

Daumier stepped from behind the shadow of a myrtle tree near the rear gate. He'd managed to sneak into the garden somehow. "*Mademoiselle*, have you managed to find me passage out of Paris?"

"*Monsieur*, creeping around isn't the way to enlist my charity."

"You do not understand. I am being followed wherever I go. There is no telling what these people might do if they find me."

"These people? I'm one of 'these people' and they are my friends. I'd suggest you choose your words and references carefully, lest you insult the only person in Paris apparently willing to help you."

"Yes, yes, well it is difficult when I have to keep looking over my shoulder."

Maria really wanted to scold him and tell him that he was now experiencing what Louise, Dardelle, and every other citizen fighting for peace and equality felt. Serves him right to suffer a little. It would do him good to stay in Paris and see first-hand how a government working for the betterment of society operated. "I don't think there's anything I can do for you. Each time someone leaves Paris, they're arrested by Thiers' troops."

"I know that, but there must be something you can do. These people...the Communards trust you."

"You know what else they trust in? Liberty, morality, and equality. If you don't believe in any of those, I won't help you. But if you learn to accept these tenets, then perhaps the Communards would be more tolerant of a bourgeois misogynist like you."

She watched as Daumier balled up his fists. His face reddened and his eye twitched. She'd never been quite so blunt with him before, and it didn't look like he handled it very well. Even now, his stubbornness took center stage. Couldn't he see the changes coming in the world? He'd need to accept the Commune or suffer the consequences.

He took a step backward and lowered his eyes. "I am what I am, *Mademoiselle*."

He'd expressed the first honest thing he'd ever said, yet the admission was nothing more than an affirmation that he had no intention of altering his way of thinking. "Then there isn't anything I can do. Please leave my home." She turned to go.

He dashed forward and grabbed her arm, not hard, but with a sense of desperation. "But what will happen to me? Where am I to go? Nowhere is safe."

She shook her arm free. "Don't ever touch me again. The entire city of Paris is safe for anyone who is open and willing to find a better way of life for all citizens. You're feeling what regular citizens are feeling, fear and hopelessness. Paris will soon be a city of freedom and equality. If you can't support that, then you will have to live elsewhere. Now, get out." She turned and headed for the rear door of the house. It felt liberating to walk away having the last word.

She went straight inside without turning around and locked the door behind her. She pressed her ear to the door, but there were no sounds coming from the garden. Whether he'd left or was he still there, skulking around, it didn't matter. She had her speech to think about and didn't need the distraction of Daumier on her mind. He'd be all right. For all of his bluster, his fears were likely exaggerated. The Communards wouldn't hunt down someone like him, they'd ignore him. The new Commune would grow up around him and block him out like a tree blocking the sun from a sapling. The sapling would struggle fruitlessly and eventually shrivel away like a long-forgotten weed.

With Anna away visiting a friend, the house was still and quiet. She filled the kettle with water, but before she could put it on the stove, someone knocked on the door. It couldn't be Daumier and Anna wouldn't knock. She wasn't expecting anyone.

She made it half-way to the door when a voice called out, "Maria? Maria, are you at home?"

Alexandre!

Could it really be him? How had he gotten away from prison? She opened the door and instantly smiled. He looked bedraggled and thinner, but it was Alexandre, nonetheless. "Oh, please come inside and tell me everything."

He stepped over the threshold, his gait weak and unsteady, yet he found the strength to embrace her tightly. "I didn't think I'd ever see you again," he whispered.

She held onto him, not wanting to let go in case he disappeared again. "Please, sit down and let me get you something to eat."

"That would be nice. They barely fed us at the prison." He sat down on the sofa and sighed heavily.

She prepared a pot of tea and heated up chicken soup that Anna made, peering into the sitting room every few minutes to make sure he hadn't vanished. As soon as the soup and tea were warm enough, she hurried to the sofa and placed a tray on the table in front of him.

He picked up the bowl of soup right away and sipped it quickly. "Maria, I was so relieved when I heard that you'd made it safely back home after the attack. Every time I thought I couldn't go on for another minute, I brought up the image of you."

"So tell me, why were you arrested? You'd done nothing wrong. Did they tell you? And why were you released?"

He swallowed more soup and shook his head sadly. "Ah, being in the wrong place and that was good enough for them. According to their thinking, they captured me at an official Commune meeting, which evidently made me guilty of subverting Thiers."

As he finished the soup, his expression became darker, and Maria knew there was more to his story. Being imprisoned took the spark out of him.

He placed the empty bowl on the table and leaned back. "Many of the people who were captured along with me were not so fortunate. Anyone who had a red scarf or banner on them were tortured. It didn't matter if they were children, women or men, they received the same treatment. I shared a cell with a young man who was taken away and beaten every day, and each day he refused to tell them anything."

How could Thiers allow such treatment of people? She shuddered. "What were they after?" Torture was used when the aggressor needed information and had nowhere else to turn. Which meant Thiers wasn't having any luck finding what he needed about the Commune Council.

Alexandre sipped the tea. "They were specifically after Dardelle. They knew who I was and didn't bother torturing me. They wanted information about when and how Dardelle planned to destroy the Tuileries palace. I presume they got the information they were looking for since they let us all go late last night. We stayed together for a while, but then everyone began to scatter and head off to their homes."

"And you came straight here to me?"

"How could I not? After seeing the monarchists in action, I could not go back to living with one of them. Can you help me find an affordable room?

"No need. You'll stay here. My home is your home. You can stay as long as you want. I'll make up the spare room. I'm so grateful you weren't hurt."

After talking for a while longer, Maria brought him another bowl of soup and the last of a baguette and then got him settled into the small guest room upstairs. Having him close would be wonderful. They'd be able to talk at their leisure about politics and women's rights and get to know each other much better. Hopefully Anna wouldn't mind having a man around for a while.

For the next few days, they exchanged ideas about Thiers, Freemasonry, and the future of Paris. She read him some of her old speeches and he listened attentively. Being with him gave her the comfort she'd been missing, and their discussions provided enlightenment as well. He filled the gaps in her heart that had been there since the Prussian war. His insight into all matters gave her a fresh outlook and she felt a connection to him that was hard to explain.

On Sunday morning, Maria accompanied Alexandre in her carriage to meet up with Léon in the Tuileries gardens to hear a declaration from the Commune Council on the implementation of a new set of rights for women. She wanted to run into Louise to congratulate her and find out more about how she'd officially joined with the restructured Commune-sponsored National Guard, proudly displaying the red sash of a Communard around her waist. Louise had become known as the Red Virgin of Montmartre for her continued involvement in meetings at the *Hôtel de Ville*.

After parking the carriage along the street near the Tuileries, Maria climbed out and stood for a moment, taking in the excitement. Léon stood in a large with his Masonic brothers, but as soon as he saw her, he waved and hurried over. There was no sign of Louise.

Alexandre took Maria's hand. "I believe we're in for an interesting day."

Léon stopped in front of Maria and pointed to a wooden plinth that had been erected. "Maria! Look what we've done just for you."

What did he mean? "Excuse me?" She glanced at Alexandre to see if he had any idea what Léon meant.

Alexandre shrugged. "Sorry, I'm as confused as you are."

Léon broke into a huge smile. "That platform is for your speech. There are a lot of Masons here who are anxious to hear your reasons for initiating women."

"But I thought this was supposed to be a council meeting."

"It is, but your speech will come first. You're the opening speaker." Léon reached his arm around her shoulder. "We're still waiting for more people, so why don't we go for a walk?"

Alexandre excused himself, which left Maria and Léon alone. They strolled through the gardens as birds chirped and swooped from tree to tree. They sat on a bench under a shade tree.

She held his hand in hers. "Léon, what do you think Thiers will try next? He's already arrested and tortured innocent people. Does he hope to ingratiate himself with the people by releasing the prisoners? I'm glad he did, but what's his next move?"

"I've heard a number of things. One is that he's given up and is accepting of the Commune, which I doubt very seriously, and another is that he's about to break through the city gates, which seems more likely. Every time I hear one thing, it's contradicted by another. I've stopped listening to gossip."

"I have this ill feeling that something is about to happen. Like Paris is sitting beneath the Sword of Damocles."

"Try not to worry. You'll upset your stomach again. That reminds me, how are you doing? You look better than I've seen in a long time. And I can see that you've been taking good care of Alexandre."

"I do feel well, but I get tired easily. Perhaps I'm getting too old for all of this aggravation. But Alexandre is an absolute joy to have around. He lost a lot of weight in prison, so I've been fattening him up. Oh, have you seen Louise? I was hoping she'd be here."

"I heard the same thing. I was hoping Dardelle would come. I want to know if the rumors are true that he's still planning to destroy the palace." Léon smirked. "Not that I'm condoning such radical behavior, of course, but what a message that would send!" He clapped his hands. "A much-needed message."

Maria turned and looked over at the sprawling palace. While the point of destroying the palace would certainly be felt by Thiers, damaging such a magnificent building would be a tragedy. How odd to be in agreement with the militant Communards and be against their behavior at the same time.

A faint breeze blew in and picked up some dry leaves, lifting them upward in a spiral. Maria watched the playful leaves, effortless in their ascent, rising higher and higher until they dropped back to earth. How like humans they were. People wanted to be lifted out of their earthly bondage, yet they continued to do things that kept them fixed in an imperfect world.

"Maria! Léon!" Louise shouted.

From across the gardens, Louise waved and ran toward Maria, her skirt, colored by a brilliant red sash around her waist, swished as she moved. She wore a red scarf tied around her hair. Louise had taken on the visage of the Red Virgin, even if the last part was only a symbolic part of the title.

Maria stood. "Louise, I've missed you."

Throwing her arms around Maria, Louise laughed. "Well, I have to keep myself out of trouble and out of the view of spying eyes. You know there are spies everywhere, don't you? I wouldn't be surprised if Thiers' men are around here somewhere. Perhaps they're hiding up in the trees or down in the sewers." She laughed again and turned to Léon. "I've been reading your paper. You're doing an excellent job at keeping the people informed."

"We each do what we can. So, Louise, is Dardelle planning to make an appearance?" Léon glanced around. "I don't see him."

Louise gave a casual shrug. "He'll either be here or he won't."

Maria watched Léon and knew he was irritated, or maybe embarrassed, at Louise's dismissive remark. She knew very well what Dardelle had planned. Maria looked for Alexandre. He waited with a small group of people, stifling a yawn. He turned around and made eye contact with her. She'd couldn't help but smile at his pitiful expression. His eyes implored her to rescue him.

Maria cleared her throat. "If you'll excuse me, I have to go and say hello to someone."

Léon gave her a look. "Well, don't say 'hello' for too long. You have a speech to make in a few minutes."

"I'll be right over there." Maria pointed to Alexandre and nodded to Louise, then hurried away before Léon could offer any more snide remarks. The people greeted her with smiles. "I'm terribly sorry to interrupt, but I need to borrow *Monsieur* Weill."

With a relieved look, Alexandre excused himself and took Maria's hand, leading her toward a bench. "You're an angel, Maria. I am so tired of listening to complaints with no suggestion of resolution. You'd think that if they aren't happy with their lives, they could at least have some idea of how to solve their misery."

"Don't be too critical of them, Alexandre. They've lived their entire lives with an oppressive government. They can't verbalize conditions they've never had. The world is opening up for them, but they've never known anything except subjugation."

"Are you saying you'd like to go and listen to them?"

"Oh, well, I would, you know I would, but I have to make my speech shortly and I'm afraid I wouldn't be able to get away." She turned away so he wouldn't see her laugh.

He did and he laughed as well. Seeing him happy made Maria's heart happy. They sat on the bench and watched the crowd gather, more people filtering in from the streets. No words were necessary. Before long, Léon came over and motioned to the plinth.

"All right, *Mademoiselle* Deraismes, you have work to do." He turned his attention to Alexandre. "You, sir, can come with me to the front of the queue."

As they worked their way through the growing crowd, Maria noticed how Léon still favored the side where he'd been wounded. She'd been so caught up in the excitement that she hadn't noticed it at first. Léon was her best friend and colleague, and yet she'd all but ignored him. He found a spot for Alexandre right in front of the plinth and took Maria around the back and up the steps.

"Léon, are you sure you're well enough to be here?" she whispered.

"Even if I were on my death bed, I'd be here to listen to you. Now, make me proud to be a Communard and a Mason."

She stood on the plinth and let her eyes drift over the crowd. So many people. When Léon clapped his hands a few times, the people quieted down. He gave Maria a brief embrace and stepped down. Her knees trembled and her stomach fluttered. The warm sun felt good on her face. She took a deep breath and bowed her head to her audience. These were the people she loved and who deserved to be loved.

She drew a deep breath and spoke loudly and clearly, "Greetings, my friends." She paused while the crowd cheered and applauded. How happy they looked. It was like being among a large, loving family. "I am so pleased to have the opportunity to speak to you today. On this beautiful day, I'd like to address the topic of education. How often has a man or woman suffered from lack of education? The answer is all around us. Without a sufficient education where the basics are taught, jobs are limited. Men can only be laborers or servants and women, perhaps the most downcast within our society, are reduced to serving the bourgeois as their maids or prostitutes." The crowd erupted, with the women screaming the loudest. Alexandre smiled, and that gave her encouragement. She continued, "Life is meant to be enjoyed, not endured. What reasons could the bourgeoisie possibly have for denying education to the masses? Oppression, repression, and subjugation!" She had to raise her voice over the shouts, "They thought that by keeping us uneducated, we would mind our place. Well, I say we are minding our place. We are Communards and we are Paris!"

What a thrill to stand among the people, bathed in shouts of 'liberty, equality, fraternity'. At that moment, Paris was free from the obstacles of prejudice and class differentiation. They were equal. Men, women, rich, poor, it didn't matter. Next, she'd address the subject of allowing women into the brotherhood.

Léon approached the platform, but didn't get far before three National Guardsmen rode right toward the crowd shouting. Their words were swallowed up in the noise from the exuberant celebration, but as they got closer, Maria saw that they were pointing behind them. The people fell silent. Léon dashed up the steps of the plinth and stood next to her.

One of the soldiers shouted again, "The western gate has been breached! The troops are in the city!"

Another soldier added, "They're slaughtering anyone they can get their hands on!"

No one spoke for a few moments. A terrible silence fell over the gardens. Maria felt Léon's hand clasp her own. He said, "We need to get away from here. They'll come right to the Tuileries."

In an instant, the crowd scattered. Alexandre joined Maria on the platform while Louise did her best to herd the people from the area. The National Guardsmen turned and rode back toward the west. Maria couldn't believe how brave they were to ride right into the conflict. She knew in her heart that she'd never see any of them again. They wouldn't stand a chance against the army.

Alexandre motioned behind the platform. "Look!"

Dardelle marched through the gardens with an entire army of his own. Maria couldn't count how many people, but there must have been a hundred men and women carrying whatever they could use as weapons. Some had shovels, some had guns. He must have known the gate would be breached.

As they stepped down off the platform, Maria said to Léon, "He looks like he's prepared for battle."

"Yes, he does. I wonder if he has his own spies and already heard that the troops got through."

"I was wondering that myself."

The running people must have noticed Dardelle because they stopped and slowly came back. Louise waved her red scarf as she went to Dardelle. Together, they climbed up to the platform. Their army of citizens surrounded them. Maria's head spun. This new battle was bound to end up much worse than the Montmartre attack. So many people would die for liberty or fighting against it. Such a waste of human life.

Dardelle waited until he had everyone's attention, then he began, "Our enemy is invading our precious city. Many of our brothers and sisters have already been cut down in the streets."

His words were used to incite the people, and it worked. They hung on every word. He wanted an all-out battle. He declared war on Thiers. He wasn't wrong in wanting to rid Paris of the monarchist government, but his methods would only bring more death and misery.

Léon tapped her on the shoulder. "Maria, let's not be here when the army arrives."

Maria nodded and turned to Alexandre. "Léon makes a very good point. We should go home and make sure Anna's all right, then lock all the doors and pray this nonsense ends with the troops retreating like they did before."

While Dardelle continued to excite the crowd with his rhetoric, Maria, Alexandre, and Léon made their way through the gardens. Part of her wanted to stay and listen to the rest of Dardelle's ranting, but the other part wanted to get home and hide from the viciousness of the ensuing confrontation. What an awful thing to once again have wounded people littering the streets, seeking aid, or dying where they fell. Children would cry for their mothers and fathers who had fallen, and women would weep for their sons and daughters. Just the thought of it made Maria sick. She needed to stop and catch her breath.

Léon noticed her distress. "Maria, are you all right?"

How could she answer a question like that? No, she wasn't all right, nothing was all right. Paris was in trouble. "How can Dardelle think he can win against professional soldiers? He's outmatched on all fronts. Can we stop for a moment?"

"Of course. There's a low wall over there you can sit down on. Alexandre, can you keep a sharp eye out for any sign of undesirables?"

Alexandre nodded and stood guard as Léon sat beside Maria. Looking down the street one way and then the other, Alexandre said, "I see several people coming this way from the west." In an instant, he strode off toward them.

Sick or not, Maria was not about to let Alexandre head right into a band of Thiers' men. "Come on, Léon, we can't wait here. Alexandre, come back!"

Léon squinted. "My eyes may not be as good as Alexandre's, but I can see those aren't soldiers. He'll be fine."

"I don't care. They might mistake him for a bourgeoisie. He was captured once and I'm not about to let him get caught again, even by Communards."

Moving quickly took its toll and Maria's stomach ached. She refused to slow and hurried as fast as she could. Alexandre wasn't far ahead, but as she closed in on him, she noticed the men he was approaching weren't soldiers *or* Communards. It was Daumier and his friends, with Daumier leading the group. He looked confident, unafraid. So different from the last time she saw him. He was no longer scared to be in public. Something had shifted his way.

Maria called out to Alexandre, "Be careful! I see Daumier."

He turned and called back, "I see him, too. Maybe we should continue on our way home. I don't think we have anything to worry about from him."

Maria wasn't so sure. As Daumier got closer, she noticed something in the distance behind him. What was it? It was dark, like a shadow, yet there were no clouds in the sky to create shadows. She peered intently. The dark mass moved. This was not a shadow at all, but a company of soldiers. Daumier felt brave only because he had armed men at his back.

Léon and Alexandre stood beside Maria. The rhythm of the soldiers' footsteps became audible as they drew closer. They blocked the way to Maria's house. When Daumier got close, he held up his hand to stop his friends.

He walked to Maria and pointed behind him. "*Mademoiselle* Deraismes, I know you tried to help me and although you and I have not agreed on many, many issues, I am now in a position to help you if you allow me to."

Should she believe him? It was Daumier, after all. "What are you offering, *Monsieur*?"

"Those soldiers are heading to the Tuileries and are ridding the streets of anyone they encounter. They are not discerning. Come with us. You will be safe. Our faces are well known to Thiers and his officers. Anyone with us will not be harmed."

"Exactly what are you offering, *Monsieur*?"

"All people not supporting the Commune must gather at the *Hôtel des Invalides*."

How fitting. Napoleon Bonaparte's tomb lay at the *Hôtel des Invalides*. But how could she go there when her fellow Communards were dying in the streets? She wasn't a coward, she couldn't abandon her brothers and sisters. Besides, she had Anna to think about. The only thing to do would be to go back to the Tuileries.

She couldn't speak for Alexandre or Léon, but she had a good idea what they would say. "Thank you, *Monsieur*, for the kind offer, but I must refuse. I cannot in good conscience leave the fight. Paris must be free from tyranny, and I wish to stand with those who risk their lives for that freedom. Perhaps *Monsieur* Richer or *Monsieur* Weill will accept your offer."

Léon cleared his throat. "I have no intention of going anywhere. *Monsieur* Daumier, I would suggest you go ahead to the *Hôtel* before the Communards find you. And Maria, in case you've forgotten, I also fight against tyranny."

Then it was Alexandre's turn. "I, too, will remain here where perhaps I can do some good."

Daumier looked insulted. "Fine. I try to extend a small modicum of sanity, and my repayment is stupidity." He motioned to his friends, and they resumed their stride.

The soldiers were closer, and the occasional shout or scream could be heard as they did who knows what to a citizen along the way. Maria wanted to run. Any open house would provide a hiding place until the soldiers were gone. But she couldn't run and hide. Her conscious wouldn't allow her to. She needed to be with the people she believed in. They had to stand together or Paris would fall.

She watched Léon and Alexandre. They were both so dedicated. Both so driven to help the cause. She loved them both. But love wouldn't keep the soldiers away. "We have to go back to the Tuileries. But first, I need to make sure Anna will be all right."

Léon threw his hands in the air. "And how exactly should we do that? Your house is right in the path of those soldiers. She'll be fine, so long as she stays locked in the house."

"Léon, if Anna hears the troops marching by, she might come out to investigate. They might assume she came out to confront them. I know a way to get to her." She turned around and called to Daumier, "*Monsieur*!"

He spun around. "Have you changed your mind?"

"Not quite. Would you be willing to go to my house and bring my sister to me?"

He seemed to be considering it for a moment. "Why should I do that?"

"Because I'm asking you to. My sister is all alone and the soldiers will be marching right by our house."

Daumier glanced at his friends and then looked back toward the soldiers. "They will be here soon. I would be risking my allegiance to protect a Communard." He turned his attention to Maria. "I suppose your sister has done nothing wrong. It would not be fair for her to suffer at the hands of overzealous soldiers, *n'est-ce-pas*?

Maria nodded. Daumier whispered spoke to his group of friends and they all took off together toward the soldiers. It wasn't only Daumier risking his life and reputation, it was all of the men who'd for years mocked and derided women. Were they simply perpetuating their misogynistic ways in protecting a woman who they deemed incapable of defending herself, or were they genuinely feeling a sense of civility? Whatever their reason, they were going to help. Maria wanted to call out and say 'thank you', but it would have been inappropriate, and might have made them change their mind. Accepting their generosity quietly was probably the best thing.

After a few minutes of watching the soldiers get close enough to see the banners they waved, Léon tapped Maria on the shoulder. "It's time to get you away from here. You're too well known among the monarchists. I'll hide around here until Daumier returns with Anna."

While Maria knew Léon worried about her, it didn't sound like him to treat her any differently than anyone else. "I'm not going anywhere. It's bad enough that I was too much of a coward to go to Anna myself. I'm certainly not about to run and cower after sending Daumier to get her. I should have gone and taken the risk upon myself. You'd treat me differently if I were a man."

"Nonsense." Léon frowned and turned to Alexandre. "See if you can talk any sense into her, would you?"

Alexandre shook his head. "She already has enough sense. Besides, she's right where she needs to be. Daumier owed her a favor, plus it was a logical decision to send him. There's no point in taking unnecessary risks."

Léon's face blushed red and Maria knew he was working hard at controlling his temper. He exhaled heavily. "You're both being ridiculous. If Maria were a man, I would also insist that she get out of harm's way. This has nothing to do with her being a woman. She's sick, Alexandre. I worry about her because she's ill and should not be exposed to the stress of armed murderers marauding through the city. Now, Maria, as a friend, I ask you to please seek shelter somewhere safe."

How could she have made such an incorrect assumption about his motives? She'd known him for so long and he'd never, ever treated her as anything other than an equal. His concern focused on her health, not her femininity. "While I appreciate your concern, I will stay here with you and Alexandre. But I'm telling you, if Daumier doesn't come back with my sister soon, I *will* go and get her myself."

Instead of getting mad, Léon smiled. "I would expect nothing less. I only hoped that for once I could influence you to think about yourself first." He paused and then added, "I don't know what I was thinking."

Time passed and the soldiers came closer, but when the marching stopped for a while, an eerie quiet descended. From what she could see, several groups of soldiers branched out and headed down side streets. Then screaming came. Terrified, frantic screaming. People fled their homes and ran down the street in the opposite direction to the soldier, waving their arms wildly. Where was Daumier? She couldn't see him among the people. Gunshots and wails echoed through the streets.

She stared into the crowd, but they were still too far away to see any faces clearly. "Léon, I have to find Anna."

"No, you don't. Look there." Léon pointed to an alleyway.

Daumier and his friends were crowded together, peeking out from the alley. In between them was Anna, looking frightened, but otherwise unhurt. Why didn't they come out onto the street? The soldiers were too far away, and too busy, to notice them. Maria turned around to see where Daumier was looking. A small mixed-gender band of Communard National Guard were approaching, moving toward the soldiers. Maria held her breath. Anna was right in the middle, between the soldiers and the Communards. With all the noise, Maria hadn't heard anyone coming from the opposite direction. She saw a flash of red clothing. Louise marched along with the Communards.

If the National Guard didn't know Daumier, perhaps they would assume he was a Communard. If so, then Anna would be all right.

Alexandre took Maria's hand and squeezed it gently. "We'll be all right now. Those Guards will help us and I'm sure they'll let Daumier through."

"I hope you're right, Alexandre." Maria waved to Anna and motioned her to come forward.

Anna didn't get more than a few steps out of the alley when the Guards picked up their pace and one of them shouted, "It's that dog Honoré Daumier!" They raised their guns and fired.

Chapter 28

With the acrid smell of gunpowder hanging in the air, Maria ran out in between Daumier's group and the Guard. Thankfully the Guard had fired above everyone's head, presumably as a warning. Louise saw her and shouted for them to stop shooting. Maria's head throbbed from the noise of the Guards, Anna's screaming, and the sporadic gunfire from the soldiers.

The Guards evidently trusted Louise enough to do as she said and lowered their weapons. Maria halted where she was. With her legs trembling so much, she didn't think she could move even if she wanted to. A moment later, Anna ran to her side, and Alexandre and Léon escorted Daumier and his friends behind the line of Guards.

Anna practically dragged Maria near to Louise and then rebuked her, "Maria, what did you think you were doing? You could have been killed."

She was about to answer when Louise raised her gun in the air and shouted, "We're all about to be killed, Anna! Didn't you know that? It's far better to be dead than live under the rule of idiots! We will fight for liberty and equality, or die!" She charged off down the street, followed by the Guards. They all joined in her battle cry of 'liberty and equality', shouting with such verve and spirit that Maria thought her head would burst from the sound.

Daumier spoke next, "I never envisioned such murderously inclined people in all my life."

Maria faced him. "They are trying to protect the liberties they deserve."

He shook his head and motioned all around. "I mean everyone, *Mademoiselle*. Not just your Communards, but Thiers' troops as well. I am sickened by this confrontation. Why could things not remain as they were? Why is it that no one is ever content?"

"Because, *Monsieur*, there was no equality within the working class. It's the working people who build and create the world. Paris was built on the backs of those who toil night and day for a pittance. Why should the poor starve and why should women be trapped in a world where their voices are silenced simply because they were born women? Only an equal society will breed contentment, *Monsieur*."

He didn't respond. Instead, they all watched as Louise and her Guard ran straight into the soldiers. Every now and then, a glimpse of her red scarf let them know she'd stayed alive amid gunfire and shouts. What a helpless feeling to see brave men and women fighting for their rights with all they had and not being able to do anything to help. This was a true instance where gender didn't matter.

Alexandre took Maria's hand. "We should go. We can't help anyone like this. We need to warn as many people as we can."

Maria nodded. The citizens would be afraid and uninformed. Blind ignorance created discord and if people came out into the open to witness the battle, they'd be in the line of fire. She squeezed Alexandre's hand. "We can knock on doors and tell everyone we meet that the soldiers are coming toward the Tuileries. Léon, take Anna and I will go with Alexandre. *Monsieur* Daumier, thank you so much for saving my sister."

Daumier gave a slight nod and strode off with his friends. While bringing Anna wouldn't erase the bad deeds of Daumier and his followers, Maria was happy to see them make their way to safety. There had already been too much killing on both sides. Perhaps Daumier needed to see the effects of repression to soften his heart and see the world more clearly.

Léon and Anna walked quickly down one side of the street, while Alexandre and Maria went down the other, shouting and banging on doors. Many of the houses were already empty, but there were also still plenty of elderly people or women with young children hiding in their homes. Some stayed and refused to move, but others willingly came along, hoping to get out of Paris or hear news of loved ones fighting with the Guard.

When they arrived back at the Tuileries, Dardelle and his followers were gone. Where did he go? He certainly hadn't led his followers *toward* the soldiers. Louise took it upon herself to lead the National Guard to confront the troops, but Dardelle wasn't with them. Each time trouble erupted, he seemed to vanish, only to reappear again later.

Maria turned to Léon. "Since the fight is no longer here, should we wait and see what happens?"

"I don't see why not. I sort of figured Dardelle would mount his attack from the Tuileries, but I guess I had it wrong. If the troops know he's gone, they might not come here after all." Léon shrugged. "We must have collected a hundred people along the way. I'd hate to be wrong and find the troops still charging through the city right to us."

Maria dreaded the same thing. If the soldiers did come, the people would have been safer locked inside their houses. Stay or go, hide or fight. Being responsible for so many wasn't an easy task. She saw a young woman huddled among the throng with two very small children, a boy and a girl, clinging to her skirt.

Maria went over to the woman to offer encouraging words. As the woman looked up, Maria gasped out loud. "Berdine! I had no idea you were here. Last I heard, you'd taken a group of women to the south."

A huge smile lit up Berdine's face. "Oh, *Mademoiselle*...I mean Maria. I'd only returned a few days ago. I was about to find you when this happened. I've heard a lot of people have their faith that the cannons at Montmartre will save us all."

"The cannons? Well, thank heaven you're safe. And who are these little children?"

Berdine's smile faded. "Their parents were killed at Montmartre."

"Oh. But at least they have you now." Maria crouched down and wiped the children's dirty faces with her skirt. "You two stay close to Berdine."

Anna came over and led Berdine and the children away from the milling crowd. Maria wasn't sure what to do next. Everyone wandered about, confused. They hadn't fled after the Montmartre massacre. Did that mean they believed Dardelle's cannons up on Montmartre could hold off Thiers' troops? Could they be so optimistic? The troops weren't even bothering with Montmartre anymore.

"Maria," Léon whispered. "Look over there." He pointed to Berdine.

She'd rounded up other women and children and collected them together in a large group. She went from one woman to the other, offering a quick comforting embrace before hurrying to someone else. Such compassion was rare. "Léon, I have an idea." Maria went over to the women and children.

Papa had always said that the key to organization was good leadership. The Commune was a prime example of poor leadership with a disorganized group of men who hadn't the ability to rally the people into a cohesive group. It struggled, even in the early stages, to accomplish anything. This had to be why Thiers was able to break through the gates so easily. The people needed a charismatic leader.

She drew in a deep breath and spoke to the women, "May I have your attention, please?" They all turned and looked at her as Berdine shushed them. "As women, we've been told our entire lives that we're not good enough to have the same rights as men. We've been told that we're undeserving of a good education and that we must acquiesce to a man's wishes. Well, I'm telling you now that those are lies. We are all made in the same way. Men and women equally have legs and arms and brains, and desires and ambitions. If we want to accomplish something, we need to do it ourselves without relying on anyone else. We need action, not words. *Acta non verba*!" A cheer rose up, but not only from the women. Everyone had been listening. A moment later, the people began to chant '*acta non verba*.' What a glorious sound to ring in a new independence and strength among the people.

Alexandre came over and took Maria's hand. "So what now, Maria? You've got their attention and support, but what do you intend to do with them?"

"We will march to the *Hôtel des Invalides* and seek refuge from the fighting."

"Refuge? What are you talking about?" Alexandre released her hand, his brow furrowed. "That's where the monarchists are, you remember that don't you? Daumier said so. They will not receive Communards."

Maria drew in a breath to steel her nerves. "Sanctuary at the *Hôtel* should be shared by both monarchists and Communards."

Léon cleared his throat. "Maria, you're treading on dangerous ground."

She ignored both men. If she could get Daumier to convince the other monarchists to accept them, it would be a calm entry into the *Hôtel*. If he didn't, they would have to force their way inside and show him and the others that all Parisians needed a safe haven. "We are unarmed and not hostile. Surely the monarchists will see that."

Alexandre looked over the entire group. "I doubt they will."

Maria addressed the group again, "We must all find shelter so no one else becomes a casualty of the invading monarchists. We will go to the *Hôtel des Invalides*!"

Not one person stepped forward to object. She knew they were desperate and needed a leader. She turned and headed off toward the *Hôtel*. With each step, she could feel her nerves getting worse. What was she doing? It would be risky enough to go alone, but with a hundred people, it was madness. She had the feeling of leading lambs to the slaughter. But these weren't lambs, these were the people of

Paris, and they needed help. She straightened up and took long, confident strides to disguise her nervousness. They continued, crossing the bridge over the Seine, picking up a few more stragglers along the way, until the *Hôtel's* golden church dome could be seen in the distance. They'd walked almost two miles under the constant threat of attack, and it took its toll on Maria. Her entire body ached from exhaustion.

The sound of so many footsteps marching behind her raised her hopes. They'd be allowed in, she could feel it. No one would be so hard-hearted that they'd turn away their own people. With aching feet, she pressed on, leading her group right up the long footpath to the *Hôtel*. It was a grand structure with incredible architecture, built back in the seventeenth century. Papa told her about it during one of his late-night history lessons.

She'd been spellbound at Papa's knee as he explained that the architects, *Liberal Bruant and Jules Hardouin-Mansart,* created a complex of buildings in support of injured soldiers. It stood as a multi-floor hospital and a sort of retirement barracks for soldiers in need of housing. Later, the church with its magnificent golden dome was constructed.

The dome shone in the sunlight. Imagine, soldiers having their own dedicated church so they wouldn't have to make their way through the streets, many missing limbs or struggling with crutches. Charity had always been part of France's history. The entire *Hôtel* complex of buildings and courtyards was built as a charitable contribution to the country's veterans. She glanced back at the group behind her. How could anyone refuse to admit these people?

Her feet ached and when she thought she couldn't take another step, Léon and Alexandre flanked her and each placed an arm around her shoulders. She had all the support she needed.

They continued through the ornate main gate and up the footpath, the massive *Hôtel* stretching out before them. Any other time,

Maria would have admired the sumptuous gardens of neatly trimmed trees and shrubs, but not today. Her focus remained on the task at hand.

A bit short of the tall double doors, someone yelled from a second story window above, "Halt! If you do not remove yourselves from the property immediately, we will open fire!"

Surely they weren't serious? They probably didn't even have any arms. But it wouldn't be wise to test them.

Behind her, Berdine called out, "Maria, I saw a rifle. Are they really going to shoot us?"

Maria wasn't sure if they'd shoot or not. They couldn't shoot everyone, but even the loss of one soul would be too many. "Berdine, keep the people back while I negotiate."

Alexandre spoke up, "Negotiate?"

"Let me try. Make sure everyone is protected from gunfire, should they attack. Keep them back." Maria stepped forward and peered at the window. A shadowy figure hid behind a sheer curtain. She'd have to rely on the man's sense of decency.

She called out, "*Monsieur*, I have with me a group of people seeking shelter. We only wish to come inside where we will all be safe from the soldiers. There has been too much killing already."

"Why would you come here? Leave. You're not welcome." A rifle appeared in full view, pointing downward.

Maria's knees trembled so much, she thought she'd topple over. "We are not leaving. I have women and children with me. Will you turn them away to die in the streets?"

The man didn't speak, but the rifle continued to point directly at Maria. Her heart pounded. If the man pulled the trigger, it would only take the blink of an eye for the bullet to rip into her body. What would it feel like? Would she die before it hurt? If she died, what would happen to the rest of the people?

The man pushed the curtain aside and leaned out of the window with the rifle gripped in his hand. He was young, clean shaven, with a ruffled white shirt opened at the collar. He stared down at her with anger in his eyes. "I told you to leave. I don't want to hear about the plight of some Commune-loving *bas bleu*. Move along. If women want to be equal to men, then let them die like men."

She stood firm, no flinching, no retreating. Many times, *Maman* would say if women retreated in the face of adversity, they would never get ahead in the world. Maria could not retreat. She planted her feet squarely on the pavement, ready for whatever might happen.

"Maria," Léon and Alexandre whispered together.

She raised her hand to let them know she didn't need their help. At least she didn't think she did. To the man in the window, she called, "If you're looking for someone to accept responsibility, then keep your weapon aimed at me and let these people pass through the doorway to safety. I will accept any retribution you feel necessary, provided you allow your fellow citizens here the same rights as you to remain alive."

The man didn't move. His red-faced hatred bore into her. She could actually feel his loathing. But when the door flung open and Daumier stepped out, the intensity of the moment broke. Daumier looked at the crowd and then brought his attention to Maria.

"I knew that was you, *Mademoiselle* Deraismes. Who else but a stubborn woman with compassion for the wretched of society would dare challenge a man with a gun?"

"*Monsieur* Daumier, these are not the wretched, they are as deserving as anyone. They are men and women and *children*." She stressed the word 'children', knowing where Daumier's sympathy lay. She turned and motioned to Berdine. "Berdine, bring some of the children forward, quickly."

Daumier's demeanor instantly softened at the sight of the children. His shoulders stooped even more, and his brow pinched tightly. He looked back at Maria. "I suppose it's not the fault of children who their parents are."

Without anyone telling her to, a little blonde-headed girl, barefoot and wearing a ragged dress, wandered up to Daumier and took his hand in hers. He didn't shake her off but rather tightened his grip around her tiny hand. Sadness, true sadness, showed in his eyes.

Maria took a tentative step forward. "*Monsieur*, may we come inside? The soldiers are not far behind."

He shrugged and went back inside, still holding onto the little girl's hand. Maria stood to the side and motioned the people into the building. She glanced up and saw the man with the gun had left. Alexandre and Léon stood beside her while Anna and Berdine herded the children. A burst of gunfire not far away startled the group. Maria waved urgently to get the people inside. After the last person entered, Maria crossed the threshold to safety.

Alexandre closed the door behind them. "Maria, if I hadn't seen it for myself, I would never have believed it."

Looking around at the relieved faces surrounding her, Maria took a deep breath. Quietly, she whispered, "I need to sit down. My legs are trembling so badly."

Alexandre smiled and found a chair by the door. "Sit down, then. Do you always have to make sure everyone else is safe before you think of yourself?"

Léon answered, "Yes, she does."

Maria sat and took another deep breath. "I've done nothing. Daumier made the choice to let us in. Thankfully he isn't about to stand by and let children die. He may not have the same consideration or compassion for adults, but his love of children has saved us all. Perhaps one day he'll recognize the goodness inside him."

"I can't wait for that day," Anna mumbled.

Opposite the front door was a huge window spanning the entire height of the corridor, looking out over a large center courtyard.

Maria saw the golden church dome across the way. She'd never set foot in any part of the *Hôtel* or the church but always wanted to. Now inside, it felt cold, simply a hiding place that didn't allow for time to admire the architecture or ponder the craftsmanship or even to visit Napoleon's tomb, which lay directly beneath the dome. It had become a functional sanctuary, nothing more.

After a time, Daumier appeared and went right to Maria. "*Mademoiselle,* there is food and water in one of the storerooms down the hall. There is ample room for everyone here, but I must warn you that many of the men here will not be as understanding. I would suggest you and your cohorts do nothing to create further tension."

Maria nodded. "We will stay right here. And thank you for the food."

Daumier shrugged and spoke softly, as if he didn't want to be overheard, "It is not much. Just some bread, fruit, and vegetables. There are some buckets of water, and I believe a few bottles of wine still intact. It was all we had time to gather, but there's enough for all of us. If anyone tries to prevent you taking any, tell them to see me." He turned and shuffled away.

Maria watched him go. He made it seem painful to extend even a little courtesy. Suddenly, a loud explosion shook the building, and the children screamed. In an instant, the people closest to the door stood with their backs against it. Was it cannon fire? Who would fire a cannon so close? Surely the troops wouldn't attack the *Hôtel*. Daumier said it was where the monarchists and their supporters were told to gather. She found Anna and Berdine.

The echo from the boom quieted, but gunfire soon followed. The sound of breaking glass came from upstairs as the windows must have shattered. Children screamed, and men and women cursed in anger and frustration. Maria embraced Anna. Were they never safe? Had Daumier lied? But if he did, he would be condemning himself along with the people.

Then a voice from outside shouted, "In the name of the true government of Paris, the Commune National Guard orders you to surrender!"

Chapter 29

Maria stared at the door. Nobody knew what to do. Someone had to let the Guard know that Communards and innocent people took shelter inside. Maria started toward Alexandre but stopped when several shots rang out from upstairs. The monarchists were shooting at the Guard.

From behind, Léon took hold of Maria and led her away from the door. He pointed to the ceiling. "How do I get upstairs? I've never been here before."

"Neither have I. Let's find a staircase and tell those idiots upstairs to stop firing. We also need someone to tell the Guard that Communards are inside." Maria waved to Alexandre. "Can you make sure the children are safe? Léon and I are going to get upstairs and try to convince the monarchists and the Guard to stop shooting. But I don't think it's safe to open the doors and make our plea."

Alexandre shook his head. "No, I think they'll charge in if we do. They won't know who's a Communard and who isn't. Be careful and keep your head low. Remember, they aren't expecting any of us to be in here. They'll shoot first before finding out who's who."

With Léon, Maria ran down the corridor and found a marble staircase leading to the upper floors. They headed up to the second floor but stopped and crouched when a more gunshots came from the *Hôtel* were met with return fire from outside. A moment later, all went quiet. Hurrying toward the room where the gunshots came from, before the Guard stormed in, Maria and Léon shouted to stop shooting.

When they finally found the right room, the one right above the front door, Maria peeked inside. The shooter lay dead. She didn't even know the man's name and there he was, with the top of his head missing. His fingers were still wrapped around the trigger of his rifle and his bloodied eyes stared at the ceiling.

She turned away. "When will the killing end? I will never get used to the sight of death."

Léon moved her to a chair and wiped his eyes. "I know him," he said softly, pointing to the dead man on the floor. He used to come to my Lodge, but I haven't seen him in several years. His name is Jean. *Was* Jean. Stay here, away from the window. I don't want to see you move." He stepped over the body and boldly went to the window. He wasn't even hiding.

"Stop your attack!" he shouted, "There are women and children inside!"

From outside, a man called back, "Monarchist women produce monarchist children, and monarchist children grow up to be monarchist adults! Therefore, they are equally to blame for the state of Paris! We must cut the head from the monarchist serpent!"

Léon now leaned out of the window and yelled louder, "There are both Communards and monarchists in here! Will you kill us all?"

"If you help the monarchists, then you are also part of the serpent!"

"Unreasonable swine," Léon mumbled, then shouted again, "Go and hunt somewhere else before you murder innocent people. If you shoot innocent people, then you are no better than Thiers."

Maria got up and stood beside Léon. She shouted, "Listen to him. We came here for shelter, to find safety from Thiers' troops. Haven't enough people died already? Must you keep killing until there is no one left?"

The man replied, "Then send out the monarchist cowards who hide behind women and children."

Léon pulled Maria away from the window. "I swear to you, Maria, the people of Paris haven't learned a thing. Must it always be an eye for an eye with them?"

"Let me try again." She waved her hands to get the Guard's attention. "Listen to me. As Communards, we support a free government.

We must lead by showing an example of what we believe in. Equal treatment for all people. Law breakers must be held for a legal trial and receive the same treatment whether they are a Communard or monarchist. Put your guns away!"

The Guard kept his gun pointed at Maria. After a tense pause, the rest of the Guards began muttering amongst themselves until finally they all lowered their weapons. The leader stepped forward and spoke, "You must be the fiery *Mademoiselle* Maria Deraismes."

"I am. And who are you?"

"A friend. You speak wisely, *Mademoiselle*. Will you allow us to come in and round up the monarchists?"

"Only if you leave your weapons outside."

"Absolutely not, *Mademoiselle*. We were shot at once, you don't think we'll walk in unarmed, do you?"

"Why not leave the monarchists here with us? They're not going anywhere. You should patrol the streets and protect the citizens who weren't fortunate enough to make it here."

Léon tapped her on the shoulder. "All right, you've spoken your mind. Now get away from the window."

"*Mademoiselle*! A moment longer, please."

"You see, Léon, they're willing to negotiate." She leaned back out the window. The Guard had scattered toward the road, leaving only the leader remaining beneath the window. Maria felt Léon's breath on her neck. He wasn't about to leave her side. She called back, "Are we in agreement, *Monsieur*?"

The Guardsman replied, "*Mademoiselle*, keep your people inside. The troops are approaching down the road. I hope you know what you're doing by protecting monarchists." He took off at a run to join the rest of the Guard.

Léon pulled her away from the window and grunted. "If they can't hold off the soldiers, we might be in for some trouble."

"Some trouble? I think we're in for more than a bit of trouble. We need to find somewhere safe for the people. I remember my father telling me that during the storming of the Bastille, the mob broke into a huge underground armory that is on the grounds somewhere. I don't know if it's still an armory, but with any luck, the room will be large enough for us all to fit."

"Then we'll be trapped like rats."

"Not necessarily. Papa said the armory can be secured from inside and the door is then impenetrable."

"Against guns?"

"Well, I don't know, he didn't say. But we have to try. It might be the only safe place. Any ideas where it might be?" Maria found a large rag and covered the dead man's face. As soon as she placed the rag, blood soaked right through.

Léon knelt and touched the man on the shoulder, then looked around. "I've never been in the military, so how would I know where an armory would be?"

"Stop complaining and help me find it. From what my father used to tell me of battlements, armories were well protected by heavy, reinforced doors. If we find a door like that, we'll find the armory. And it's probably underground."

"I don't like the sound of that. What if the door's locked?"

Maria shot Léon a sharp look. She didn't need any more negative thinking. They went back downstairs and told Alexandre and Anna to keep the people as calm as possible and to make sure absolutely no one went outside.

Maria hurried down a staircase, through several corridors set out in a grid-like pattern and searched for a door different from the others. She passed by room after room, some with narrow doors too flimsy to contain an armory and others partially open. She peered into every open room and found offices or libraries or multi-bed chambers. But no armories.

She went to find Léon before continuing her search further into the complex, turned down another corridor, and ran right into him as he was searching for her. He said he found a door strengthened with metal supports all around the edges and across the center.

He explained, "The door wasn't locked, but it opened to a steep staircase. Too dark to see. We need a lantern or a candle."

They searched for a light source in the nearby rooms, but when they met up with the monarchists gathered in a larger room, they could go no further.

A grizzled old man with greasy gray hair and a permanent frown etched on his face pointed a small gun at Léon. "Don't come any further. Go back the way you came. Unlike *Monsieur* Daumier, I am not in agreement with Communards sharing our safe refuge. Go!"

Maria stepped forward. She no longer felt afraid, but angry and fed up. Her cheeks burned, her head throbbed, and her stomach ached, but it gave her that much more incentive to push ahead. How incredibly ridiculous that even in such desperate and dangerous times, the battle between classes and politics still persisted. She moved in front of Léon. "In the name of humanity, lay down your weapon and allow us to protect the less fortunate. You have money and power, *Monsieur*, but that means nothing during war."

"We shall see, *Mademoiselle*. In such situations throughout history, it has always been the weak who've perished and the strong who survive. I, *Mademoiselle*, am strong."

Holding her head high, Maria refused to back down. "We have justice and morality on our side, *Monsieur*. Perhaps we are the downtrodden, but our fortitude gives us strength."

"Enough!" came a sharp voice. Maria turned and saw Daumier coming up behind her. "There has been enough killing and violence to last a lifetime. What does it matter if these scraggly refugees take shelter here? There is enough room for all of us to avoid one another.

Mademoiselle Deraismes, you certainly seem to attract conflict wherever you go."

Maria saw a slight smile appear on Daumier's lips. Without another word, he turned and headed away. A moment later, the old man also left. Maria let out a long breath. "Oh, Léon, I'm getting too old for all this squabbling."

Léon wiped his brow with the back of his hand. "*You're* getting too old? I was about to faint. Either you're getting braver or I'm getting more cowardly. Each time you confront someone with a gun, and it seems to be an increasing trend with you, my heart stops. I think it'll stop for good soon."

Maria winked at him. "If your heart ever stops beating, the world will end. How can the world continue without you? Now, my dearest friend, we need to find a lamp. If we don't get those people to safety soon—"

"Yes, I know. Why don't you go back to Anna while I head down into the depths and make sure it really is the armory? There must be an old torch or lamp down there somewhere."

Maria shook her head. "But it's as dark as night down there, Léon. You'll fall and kill yourself."

"Better to succumb to clumsiness than a bourgeois bullet." He headed off toward the door. "Don't worry about me, just keep the people calm. I won't be long."

She waited until he disappeared down the corridor before going back to Anna and Alexandre. Anna and Berdine had the children gathered together, telling them a story while Alexandre stood guard near them.

Anna looked up and smiled, but Maria knew it was only for the children's benefit. "Maria, have you found somewhere for us to go?" Her voice sounded nervous.

Maria smiled at the children. "You're doing a fine job, Anna. Léon's gone to find the armory and make sure it's safe."

"Well I hope we'll all be able to fit down there."

"Anna, can I see you for a minute?" Maria motioned for her to follow a short distance from the children, and lowered her voice, "We might still have trouble from the monarchists. You may not believe this, but Daumier just saved us. Unfortunately, they don't all support Daumier's humanity. The sooner we get into the armory, the better. Can you tell Alexandre to inform the rest of the people?"

Léon came rushing toward them. "I found a couple of oil lamps. And it is the armory, but it's been abandoned. There are stacks of old crates marked 'munitions'. It's quite large down there, but it's filled with rats. I'm not entirely sure if it would be better to stay up here and take our chances with the monarchists and troops or go downstairs."

When a loud cannon blast shook the foundation, Maria flinched and took Anna's hand. "We'll go below."

They rounded up everyone and headed down the worn concrete steps into the near-dark armory. The lamps were small and only illuminated a portion of the space. Maria tried to remain calm, but the armory with its strong smell of water-soaked concrete was overpowering and her stomach roiled. Alexandre came to her and held onto her hand, squeezing it gently.

Anna dragged an old stool over and motioned for Maria to sit. "Léon and I can handle things. You've done enough."

In no position to argue, Maria sat. "We'll need someone to act as a guard and remain at the top of the stairs."

Anna looked around. "I'll see if Léon will do that. You rest and I'll make sure everyone is as comfortable as possible. Alexandre, stay with her and make sure she doesn't get up."

Alexandre nodded and stood beside Maria. She watched helplessly as Anna scurried about getting everyone downstairs and settled. The scant light filtering from the corridor showed Léon standing at the landing near the door. He called down once everyone had made it safely and said there was no way to lock the door from the inside. The lock had apparently been broken and never repaired. Probably why it had been abandoned as an armory.

Even underground she could hear the sound of cannons and gunfire. She had to distract herself. She got up, with Alexandre staying close by, and went to one of the munitions crates. As expected, empty. Alexandre opened other crates, all with the same result. Couldn't there be at least one weapon that had been long forgotten?

Maria wandered around, making sure everyone was as comfortable as possible, while Alexandre regaled the children with fanciful stories of castles and dragons. Anna and Berdine did their best to braid the little girls' hair. But when Léon called down from the landing for everyone to be quiet, a cold chill hit Maria. She could see the outline of Léon's body. The way he crouched, stiff and intently listening at the door, she knew the troops must have entered the *Hôtel*. If the monarchists disclosed Communards were hiding, they'd be found and arrested for sure. Or worse. Tiptoeing toward the staircase, Maria waved at Léon.

In a whisper, he said, "I think Thiers' men have stormed through the doors."

Maria stepped carefully and made her way up the stairs. "Do you think they'll check down here?"

Léon shook his head. He whispered, "I don't think so. I think they're leaving."

With her ear to the door, Maria listened to distant, echoing voices that became fainter and fainter. She exhaled and leaned into Léon. "I'm so tired. I want to go home."

Léon kissed her on the cheek. "Not much longer."

Once the commotion outside settled down and the voices vanished, Maria left Léon to go and help Anna, but didn't get more than two steps down when one of the children screamed out, causing the other children to cry in fear. Anna reacted and grabbed the child, a little red-haired girl.

Anna looked up to Maria. "She's been bitten on the leg by a rat!"

The little girl continued to cry hysterically and try as she might, Anna couldn't calm her. Maria hurried down the remaining steps and examined the girl's leg where a trace of blood stained her thread-bare stockings. Before she could do anything more, someone began banging on the door. Léon leaned against it, his eyes wide with fear. Alexandre dashed up the steps while Maria moved in front of the women and children and waited.

Chapter 30

Maria watched helplessly as the door creaked open, and try as they may, Léon and Alexandre couldn't hold their position and were shoved out of the way. Two looming figures barged in and stood on the landing. Léon and Alexandre scrambled to get up and hurry down the stairs, almost falling over one another. They stood with Maria, blocking the rest of the people. Léon, his eyes narrowed and his jaw set, was more angry than frightened.

Softly, Maria asked, "Léon, can you see who they are?"

He kept his eyes on the men. "It's Alexandre Dumas and Jules Barbey. Daumier's wretched cohorts. They heard the child."

"At least they're not Thiers' men. Maybe we can reason with them." Maria turned to Anna. "How's the child?"

Anna shrugged. "I don't know. She's stopped crying at least. But I don't think this is exactly the time to discuss this."

"Give her to me, quickly." Maria took the child, cradled her, and stepped forward. "There are children down here. Surely you won't harm innocent children."

Barbey and Dumas didn't move. Maria rocked the little girl and got a little closer to the staircase. The men were silhouetted so she couldn't see their faces clearly, but when another figure came up behind them, she knew right away who it was. The stooped shoulders and shuffling footsteps gave away that it was Daumier. He edged in between his friends and held up a lantern. Now she could see all of their faces clearly.

Daumier spoke, "*Mademoiselle*, the troops have moved off. We told them that there were no Communards here." He made his way slowly down the steps about halfway. "Is that child injured? I heard crying."

Maria nodded. "Yes, she was bitten by a rat."

"Then I would suggest you come out of this awful place at once."

Léon grabbed Maria's arm. "I'm not so sure we can trust him."

"I think we can, Léon." Maria looked into Daumier's eyes and saw a glimmer of the same compassion she'd seen when he held the dead little boy by the fireplace. "*Monsieur* Daumier, is it really safe?"

Now he looked offended. "I said it was." He turned around abruptly, climbed up the stairs and left with Barbey.

Dumas drew in a breath. "Mademoiselle, my good friend Victor Hugo has spoken fondly of you. I will assist in ushering you and your friends to safety. I stand here as a staunch opponent to the monarchists." He dipped his head and left.

The heavy weight that had been pressing Maria down lifted. If Daumier and his friends were willing to help, perhaps things were looking up.

Léon went to the foot of the stairs. "I'll go up first." He vanished through the doorway.

Maria nuzzled the little girl and then handed her back to Anna. If Daumier and Dumas were indeed telling the truth, then they'd be able to get out of the rat-infested armory. But where would they go? The streets would still be crawling with armed troops. "Anna, you wait here, I'm going up top to see what's taking Léon so long."

Alexandre shook his head. "I don't think that's a wise decision, Maria."

Anna placed her hands on Maria's shoulders. "I agree. Stay here. What if Daumier lied and the soldiers are waiting for us. We'll be captured and tortured."

Maria hesitated. Leave it to Anna to come right out and speak her mind. "I promise I won't get myself arrested."

Before Anna could complain further, Maria grabbed the slimy handrail and pulled herself up the steep steps, holding up her skirt as best she could so she wouldn't trip. Her legs shook and the effort made her stomach cramp, but she made it to the top and peeked out the door.

All was quiet. Where had Léon gone? Venturing further, Maria listened and detected distant voices and a sound that could have been footsteps. She inched closer toward the main entrance of the *Hôtel* where the voices were clearer. Why did she let Léon leave? If he'd been captured, she'd never forgive herself.

She looked out a window and saw Léon halfway down the front walkway. But he wasn't alone. He was among a group of men who milled around outside. She recognized several men. They weren't soldiers, but Freemasons. As the group walked up path toward the building, she realized Georges Martin stood with Léon. When they were close, she opened the door.

Léon ran forward. "Maria! Everything is going to be all right. I don't know how my Masonic brothers knew we were in here, but they did."

"What about the troops? We all heard the cannon fire."

With a light laugh, Léon pointed to the men. "You'll hear no more. Half of the troops are also Masons. When my brothers banded together and marched through the streets, the soldiers abandoned their cannons and moved aside." He laughed again. "We have an escort to the Grand Orient Lodge."

He threw his arms around her. His warm embrace made her feel safe. She closed her eyes and allowed herself to melt into the security of his arms. When he relaxed his hold, she opened her eyes again. "Léon, did you see Daumier or Barbey?"

He pulled back and looked into her eyes. "No. There's no sign of them. I can tell you this, though, the next time I see Daumier, I intend to thank him for not telling the troops we were in the armory."

Maria nodded. She thought the exact same thing. "But what are we to do in the Grand Orient? I know it's a large temple, but can we all fit?"

Georges Martin came up beside Léon. "There's plenty of room. Have no worries about that." He took Maria's hand and kissed it gently. "It's very nice to see you again, *Mademoiselle*, however, I do wish the circumstances were a bit different."

She smiled. He was as charming as ever. "Yes, I can't say any of this has been an enjoyable experience. Oh, no, I forgot all about the little injured girl. She was bitten by a rat. She needs medical care right away."

Georges glanced at Léon. "I'll have a look at her."

Léon nodded. "You and Georges go and bring the people out." He turned and walked down the path toward the group of men.

She led the way to the armory. Alexandre waited at the top of the stairs with the little girl in his arms. Anna came up behind him.

Anna sighed heavily. "Where have you been? I was so worried when you didn't come back. Tell me what's going on." She looked at Georges. "Oh, hello again, *Monsieur...*"

He bowed his head slightly. "Georges Martin, *Madame*."

Anna frowned. "Maria, what's happened? I don't like being un-informed."

Georges examined the little girls' leg. "This needs to be cleaned and dressed, but she shouldn't suffer any adverse consequences." He headed downstairs, calling out that everyone should follow him out of the armory.

Maria took Anna's hand. "I came back as soon as I could. Léon ran into a gathering of his Masonic brothers. They've come to escort us to the Grand Orient."

"You think that'll be safe from Thiers?"

"I hope so. Surely no one would dare attack the Grand Orient." Maria's head spun and she had to steady herself by grabbing onto the door. Alexandre handed the little girl to Anna and was there in a heartbeat to support Maria.

Anna felt Maria's forehead. "You're feverish. I knew all of this would make you sick. You do too much. Come and sit down. There's a chair over there." Anna pointed down the hall.

Alexandre led Maria to the chair. "If there's anything I can do, let me know."

After sitting, she glanced around, but her eyes wouldn't focus. It was horrible being so weak and helpless. She leaned forward, feeling faint. "Is there any water?"

"I'll find some," Anna said, leaving at once.

Maria didn't have the strength to talk. Blackness crept in from the corners of her eyes. She could hear the little girl sobbing, but soon it became muffled, and Maria felt her body sliding off the chair.

Chapter 31

Maria's head throbbed and she felt sick. She opened her eyes but only saw a brick wall. Slowly, she looked the other way and realized she was in a small room. The furnishings weren't familiar. Then she noticed a small plaque above the door. Squinting, she made out the outline of the Masonic symbol of the square and compasses. She must be in the Grand Orient Lodge. If that was the case, how much time had passed? Was everyone safe?

The door opened and Anna came in straight to the bedside. "Oh, Maria, you're awake."

Maria forced herself up on her elbows. "I don't feel well at all. My head hurts terribly and I feel sick. Please tell me you got all of the people away from the *Hôtel*. And where's the little girl? And Berdine, and Alexandre? Where's Léon?"

Anna smoothed Maria's hair and pulled up a blanket. "Lie down. You need to stay quiet and rest. Everyone is fine. We're all safe. Now that you're awake, I'll get the doctor, Georges Martin, to come back and check on you again. He said you're suffering from exhaustion."

"I'm sure I'll be fine once I rest some more. Can you ask Léon to come here?"

"I'll do nothing of the sort. You're to get some more sleep. That's what Doctor Martin said."

"I don't care what he said. If you don't bring Léon, I'll go and find him myself." Maria knew she was in no condition to get out of bed, but hopefully Anna would believe her. Léon would tell her the unvarnished truth without dodging around the facts.

In a huff, Anna spun around and stomped to the door. Without turning, she mumbled, "Don't blame me if you don't get well."

After Anna left, Maria closed her eyes and tried to think of something as a distraction from her pain. Even though they'd managed to save a few people, there were still so many outside the protective walls of the Grand Orient. Someone would have to get word out that there was a sanctuary available. And then, once the troops left Paris, the city would be in need of restructuring. That meant the time would be ripe for demanding equal education and worker's rights. Times were changing, but she knew enough not to be delusional to hope for too much too quickly.

The door opened and Léon came in. "You look terrible."

"Well, thank you for your honesty, Léon, but I think you could have softened your observation a little."

He smiled and shook his head. "Then you would have known I was holding back. I believe in honesty, you know that. Georges is on his way up." He went to the bedside and felt her forehead. "You're a very sick woman, my friend."

"That much I know already. Tell me, how are the people? The children?"

"Everyone's being cared for. Anyone who's sick is receiving the attention they need and there's food in their stomachs."

Maria scooted up onto the pillows. "And the soldiers?"

"Still roaming through the streets arresting anyone they can, at least the ones not fighting back."

"And those who are fighting back?"

"I don't think it's necessary to say more about that. Maria, we've all done what we can. Paris is too dangerous right now to venture out. And look at you. You've put everything into this blasted battle of wills."

She sat up fully now. "Don't you dare diminish what's happening as a mere battle of wills. This is war, Léon. War against common sense, war against the working classes, and war against humanity. Do you disagree?"

He looked down at the ground and sighed heavily. "No, of course not. You know me better than that. I had no intention of diminishing anything. I'm worried about you, that's all."

Lying back down, Maria reached out and took his hand. "I'm sorry." Of all the people to lash out at, Léon deserved it the least.

She lay quietly, with Léon's hand in hers until a knock on the door broke the silence. Georges came into the room and nodded at Léon.

Georges glanced at Maria with a gentle smile. "Well, you gave me quite a scare. I'm pleased to see that you're awake. I have some medicine for you, but I had to wait until you were awake before giving it to you."

Léon excused himself without a word. Georges conducted a cursory examination, probing her abdomen, feeling her forehead, checking her eyes. She focused on the square and compasses above the doorway. With the Mason's belief in the tenets of freedom and equality, they would help make Paris a city that other countries could admire and hopefully emulate.

"Maria, drink this tonic." Georges handed her a small vial.

She took a sip. Terrible tasting and bitter, as most medicine was, but Georges wasn't about to move until she swallowed the entire thing. With little choice, she drank it down. To her surprise, it had an immediate effect, like the smoothest silk coating the inside of her stomach. A minute later, her headache eased, and she had her energy back.

"You're to rest now." Georges tucked the blanket around her and left.

She lay still and listened to voices outside the room. First, Léon spoke softly, and then another voice rose above his. It sounded like Georges. Were they arguing? After a few moments, the voices faded away and Maria's eyelids grew heavy. He'd slipped her a sleeping potion in the medicine. She didn't want to fall asleep. She still had so much to do.

If the Freemasons would agree to publicly support *L'Association pour le droit des femmes*, then it could be used as a platform from which to launch a more forceful plea for equal rights. What a perfect idea. Feeling relaxed, she let her body sink into the soft mattress. Her mind didn't focus on any one thing.

A knock jolted her awake. The door opened and Léon came into the room. "Maria, I'm sorry to wake you."

"What is it," her voice was dry, raspy.

"I've been speaking with my fellow Masons and we're all in agreement that this attack by Thiers might be the opportunity we've all been waiting for."

"Opportunity?" Maria swallowed and cleared her throat. "Are you talking about standing firm against the government?" Hopefully he'd gathered enough supporters to make a difference.

"We've been working all night collecting the names of the injured and displaced, including those who were killed. At least the ones we know about. We'll make a petition to Thiers with all the names listed. He'll have to pay attention to our plight."

Maria nodded. This was exactly what they needed. The Communards failed to keep the troops from invading the city because they were disorganized and ill-prepared, but with additional support, they'd present a united front that couldn't be ignored. Maria looked around. "What time is it?"

"Morning. Anna will be up in a minute with some breakfast. Oh, and Alexandre's been asking about you. Seems he's quite worried." Léon winked.

"Stop it. He's a friend, that's all. Besides, I feel much better." She pulled down the covers and swung her legs out of bed. "Now get out so I can make myself a bit more presentable."

"Georges said you were to stay in bed. You need to rest."

"I've been resting." A sudden pain in her stomach made her double over and groan. Apparently, the medicine only offered temporary relief.

"There, I told you." Léon rushed over and helped her back into the bed. "Lie still and I'll bring Georges right up." He hurried away, returning a moment later with Georges.

After a brief examination, Georges shook his head. Maria knew right away that her condition was more dire than she'd thought. She hoped she would outgrow it. During her childhood, she'd sometimes be in bed for months at a time.

Léon must have noticed her mood because he sat on the edge of the bed and held her hand. He whispered, "You'll be fine. Women like you can never be stopped by some silly illness. As soon as you're feeling better, we'll publish some more articles and..."

Maria felt a warm tear drop onto her hand. Did Léon know something? Was Georges hiding the seriousness of her illness? "Georges, how bad is it?"

"You're very weak. Your stomach appears to be inflamed and your abdomen is distended. You need bed rest for an extended period of time, Maria. If you don't follow my orders, you could die from damage to your organs. Oh, and a better climate wouldn't hurt."

"Have you told my sister?"

"No, I thought that's something you'd want to do."

Maria waited until he left and then looked at Léon. "What am I going to do? I hate this damned illness."

"Don't be so hard on yourself. It's not like you have any control over it." Léon stood and paced around the room. "I feel responsible, Maria."

"For what?"

"For your condition. I always seem to push those I care about the hardest."

Maria hating seeing Léon think he'd done wrong by her. As he paced, she saw his brow pinched with worry. "Oh, Léon, this stupid illness has plagued me long before I ever met you. You've kept me going this long. You never let me feel sorry for myself." She reached out for him as he passed, grasping his sleeve. "Come and sit with me for a while."

They sat together, talking about the first time they met and about their first collaborative article on feminism. Maria didn't want to stop the intimacy of the moment. Eventually, Anna came into the room and interrupted, motioning for Léon to leave the room. Reluctantly, he did, and Anna sat down on the bed.

She adjusted the blankets and fussed with the pillows. "Are you feeling any better?"

Maria nodded and forced a little smile. There was no sense in worrying Anna too much. "The medicine Georges gave me has helped a lot. Léon and I were talking, and we've decided to take a small respite from the cause until the government settles down."

Anna stared. "What? You, take a break? I don't believe it."

"We'll come back even stronger, with full support from the Freemasons. We just need to...organize things first. Perhaps you and I can leave the city for a while. What do you think of that?"

"Are you serious or just toying with me? I've wanted to get away from Paris since this war started, you know that."

Maria smiled. No one could ask for a better sister. "Of course I'm serious. What about Brittany? We haven't been there since we were children. The weather should be nice and warm this time of year."

"Brittany? I *love* Brittany. The weather will do you good, too. When are you planning to leave?"

"Well, not until we take care of our charges. They need somewhere to go where they'll be safe from Thiers troops."

Anna's mood darkened. "As much as I want to leave, we won't be permitted out of the city. Thiers has every route blocked. It's far too dangerous to step outside, let alone try to leave altogether. Besides, you're too weak to be sneaking around."

Maria sighed and closed her eyes. Maybe it had been a dream to run away to Brittany where there was no war and no killing. Ah, but the thought of peace and warm sunshine made it a lovely dream. With her eyes still closed, she heard Anna get up and leave. Getting Anna and as many of the women and children out of Paris, and out of harm's way, was every bit as important as leaving for health reasons. There had to be a way out past the soldiers. Léon said half of the troops were Masons themselves. If the Masons requested safe passage for the women and children, then it might be possible. A plea for charity and mercy. But would the soldiers really let them pass?

She sat up, ignoring the pain, and found a pen and a few sheets of paper on a bedside table. The plea would have to be heartfelt. Oh, if only she were a Mason, then her words would carry more weight. She thought for a moment, then wrote.

The Grand Orient of Paris requests safe transit from Paris for refugee citizens. In the name of the Great Architect, allow this document to represent the spirit of mercy.

Satisfied, she lay back down. Hopefully she hadn't overstepped her bounds by using the term Great Architect, the Masonic representation of the Creator. If she could get signatures from the higher-ranking Masons, there might be a chance of getting the most desperate to safety. If she had to leave the city for her health, then she'd take the women and children with her.

Chapter 32

Maria jumped at a strange noise out in the hallway. She sat up and right away noticed very little pain in her stomach. What a relief. She climbed out of bed and made her way to the door. The sound was a clattering of some sort, almost like dishes. She opened the door and peeked out. The hallway had people rushing to and fro. Some were carrying small crates while others held armfuls of clothing.

She stepped out of the room and tapped the closest person on the shoulder. "Excuse me, what's going on?"

The young man stopped and smiled. "Ah, *Mademoiselle*, I'm sorry if we were too noisy."

"Please don't worry about me. Why is everyone running about? Has something happened?"

Léon appeared from among the people and rushed up to Maria. "You're a genius!"

Maria stared at him. "What are you talking about?"

He laughed and moved aside as a couple of children scampered by. "I went to check on you and found that note you'd written. I took the liberty of showing it to my brothers and we're all in agreement. We're in the process of arranging for a march to Versailles."

"Versailles?" Of all the places, why would Léon pick Versailles? Was he expecting Thiers himself to stand aside and let the masses pass from the city? It would be far easier to slip out where the route was guarded by only a few soldiers that were hopefully Masons.

"Don't give me that look, Maria. A united force presents a difficult target. All the world is watching Paris to see what happens. As you know very well, most countries don't agree with us Communards and think of us as violent rebels, but they surely wouldn't condone Thiers murdering a group of women and children fleeing the city. And with a platoon of Freemasons at their side, the world's Masons will rally their support."

"How will the world know what's going on, Léon? Thiers wouldn't dare let it out that his soldiers killed innocent people."

"No, he wouldn't. But with my brothers leading, not a single bullet could be fired by a fellow Mason. If a soldier who isn't a Mason fires, then he'd have hell to pay from any Masons standing with him. Word would leak out, I can guarantee that. This is your idea, Maria."

"Perhaps it was my *idea*, but you certainly made it a possibility. Do you think it'll work?"

Léon flashed a slight smile. "Of course it'll work. And even better, the Lodge had crates of donated items in the basement that were to be distributed after the war, so we're packing everything. We have blankets, clothing, and household items. The people might be displaced from their homes, but at least they'll have some comforts."

His exuberance was contagious. With supplies, the people could manage for a while until they were able to return to the city. Being away from the repression and killing would surely give them the solace they so sorely needed. Maria lay down and enjoyed a quiet moment with Léon. He sat right beside her, holding her hand, without saying a word. After a time, Anna hurried in with Berdine close behind.

Both women smiled and nodded to Léon. Anna took Maria's other hand. "Everyone is almost ready to leave. Are you well enough? If not, I'll stay with you. Alexandre said he'd stay by your bedside, but I told him that's my place."

Maria sat up. "Don't worry about me. How is the little girl who was bitten by the rat?"

Hanging back a bit, Berdine said, "She's fine, but I need to keep the wound clean. Maria, I'm afraid. I've never been treated well by the bourgeoisie. They won't allow me, or any of the other lower-class citizens to leave the city. They'll want to make an example of us, just like they always do when anything goes wrong. It's the way things have always been."

Maria threw back the covers and got out of bed. "We have the support of the Grand Orient, Berdine. If the soldiers attack or harass us in any way, they'll have the Freemasons rising up in defense. Many prominent and powerful citizens are Masons. I don't think that's something they'd want."

Léon nodded. "At least that's what we're relying on."

Berdine physically relaxed. Maria found it hard to imagine that an intelligent young woman like her had lived in fear all her life, ignored and belittled like she didn't matter.

Maria motioned to the clock on the wall. "We need to get moving. The sooner we leave the city, the better for everyone. I'll stay right beside you, Berdine. You need not worry about a thing. Everyone here today is equal."

Reaching into a fabric sack, Berdine took out her autographed copy of *Les Miserables*. "I want you to have this, Maria. I think *Monsieur* Hugo meant to give it to you all along."

"It's *Monsieur* Hugo's book to do with as he pleases. He gave it to you."

"But I can't even read the words. It's of no use to me."

Maria pointed to the fabric bag. "Put the book back. It's yours. Like I told you before, you now must learn to read. On the pages of that book are words so meaningful that it would be a crime if you did not read each and every one."

"Then I will learn to read and love every second of it." Berdine smiled.

Those were words Maria would hold in her heart. They left the room and headed to the main entrance. Maria stayed close to Berdine and held onto Léon's arm for support. Men, women, and children worked together collecting supplies, regardless of their gender, age, or position in life, exhibiting a perfect example of humanity at its finest. Thiers, Daumier, and every other human should see how people could come together for the greater good. Maybe their eyes would finally be opened. There was no issue of gender or inequality at all. Everyone *was* equal at that moment.

Maria sighed. "I hate war, Léon. I hate war and I hate injustice."

"You know I echo that sentiment. I'll continue to fight the ignorant until they listen."

Léon told the truth. He'd never give up. He complemented her own stubbornness. If she'd had a brother, she would have wanted him to be just like Léon.

They followed the last of the people outside. The sun warmed the day, but it couldn't distract her from the seriousness of what they were about to do. As a group, they started down the street toward the Seine once again. But this time, crossing the river might be difficult if the soldiers had it under their watch. Alexandre walked with her for a while, keeping her distracted with talk about the history of Paris.

But before long, Maria started to slow down. The exertion took her breath away. How would she make it all the way to Versailles? She'd slow the entire group and jeopardize everything.

Léon took her hand and gave it a squeeze. "What would you say to acquiring a carriage?"

Maria shook her hand free. More than anything, she wanted to walk alongside the people to show her camaraderie. "Léon, I'm not so infirm that I can't march with my brothers and sisters. My whole life has been spent trying to give aid and support to those who truly need it. I'm not about to stop now."

"Out of everyone you know, don't you think I'm the most familiar with how your mind works and how you live your life? I understand how you lead through example, but there comes a time when you also must admit to your limitations."

He had her best interests at heart, but it was hard to hear.

"I suppose a carriage isn't the worst idea you've had." She smirked.

As soon as the words left her mouth, an explosion shattered the still morning air. The people instinctively ducked down and glanced around, terrified. A moment later, a cannonball struck a building not far from where they were. Bricks and dust flew into the air, crashing down onto the roadway. Women screamed and children cried.

Léon helped Maria, Anna, and Berdine to a stone wall where they crouched for protection as Alexandre and Georges Martin dashed around to make sure everyone was all right. When the dust settled, gunfire started. Bullets cracked overhead and struck windows. Then came the unmistakable sound of footsteps and the metallic clanking of soldiers as they strode down the street with swords and guns.

The group of Masons quickly stripped off their overcoats to display their colorful sashes and Masonic aprons. They stood, surrounding the people, and waited. Only a few seconds passed before two orderly rows of soldiers paraded toward them.

Maria tried to get up, but Léon stopped her by pushing her down. It didn't feel right cowering to the side while everyone else, including Alexandre, was so exposed in the roadway. The soldiers marched closer and then spread into a blockade across the street. Their captain stepped forward, his rifle raised. Maria could barely catch her breath. Beside her, Anna was softly moaning. From inside the protective circle, children's cries rose.

The captain kept his rifle raised when he spoke, "Disband immediately or you will all be arrested."

The Grand Orient Lodge master left the group and approached the soldier. "We have women and children here. We are going to take them out of the city so they'll be safe."

The response was terse, filled with anger, "Disband immediately!"

Without a word, the Masons lined up opposite the soldiers, but this only caused the troops to take their weapons in hand and point them toward the group. Maria struggled to get away from Léon and stumbled on shaky legs among the people. They were her people and she couldn't abandon them. Alexandre embraced her. Distant cannon fire mixed with the crying. Berdine rushed to Maria's side and took her hand. They would pass through the city as one or die as one.

The captain again shouted, "Disband!"

But the Masons stood firm. The master of the Lodge shouted louder, "You will let us pass!"

The heavy tension hung in the air as if a blanket covered the city. Gunfire took the place of cannons. How many people were still being slaughtered by Thiers' fury? How much devastation did he want? Berdine had her eyes cast down, as if expecting the worst.

In a whisper, Maria said, "Berdine, I won't let anything happen to you." Leaving Berdine and Alexandre, Maria pushed her way through the people and found the Lodge master. "*Monsieur*, we need to get moving. We need shelter."

He turned and stared at her. "*Mademoiselle*, we're being held at gunpoint. Perhaps you should stay with the rest of the women and leave negotiations to the men."

How dare he suggest that men alone had to protect women. She took a few steps forward and moved out in front of the master. Her knees shook and her head spun, but she had to stand firm and at least give the appearance of strength and fortitude.

She held her hands out to show she had no weapon. "Lower your guns and allow us to pass. We are unarmed. These people are not involved in this battle between the bourgeoisie and the Commune Council. They are innocent working families who deserve to live."

She waited as the captain looked her up and down. Could he be considering her plea? After a few moments, he laughed and glanced around at his men, but he kept his rifle raised when he spoke. "If I'm not mistaken, you are Maria Deraismes, the outspoken friend to all the wretched and suffering. I don't think you need the protection of the Masons, but rather, they should promote you as their leader!" He laughed louder and motioned Maria forward.

She trembled so much now that she could barely remaining standing. She didn't want to die or feel a bullet rip through her body. Léon called out to her, but she kept her eyes on the captain. She took a tentative step toward him with her head held high. Hopefully she appeared in better condition than she felt.

"Sir, whether people are called Freemasons, Communards, or bourgeoisie, we are humanity. We are the working class, the employers, the educators. Status is meaningless in the struggle for survival. And survival is all we desire. Allow us passage so we can continue to live our lives."

The captain didn't move his eyes off her, staring, studying her. If something didn't happen soon, she'd collapse. She was vaguely aware of Anna's voice calling out to her, but the words were indecipherable. No matter what she yelled, Maria would not back down.

Then quite unexpectedly, the captain lowered his rifle and motioned for Maria to approach further. He said softly, "*Mademoiselle*, while I admire your bravery and brashness, I cannot simply commit a dereliction of duty. I hope you understand. I cannot allow you, or anyone in your group, to pass from the city."

"Then you will have to shoot us down like rats in the street if you will deny us our God-given rights to survival." She couldn't stand any longer. Her entire body felt liquid and she fell to her knees.

Chapter 33

Maria heard Anna's voice first, then Léon's, faint, but distinguishable. She opened her eyes to a uniform looming over her, and as her vision cleared, she realized it was the troop captain. Her nervousness got the better of her again.

He knelt beside her. "*Mademoiselle* Deraismes? Are you all right?"

"I believe so. I don't know what came over me." A leader had to be strong. "I'm fine now. It's the heat of the day, that's all." She graciously accepted his hand and stood up.

She nodded. "It's getting late, sir, we need to continue to Versailles. Have you no conscience, no feelings at all. These are innocent people who've been caught in this dreadful battle. If you allow them to pass by, I will stay in their stead."

He took a few steps back, with his rifle at his side. "You really would sacrifice yourself, wouldn't you?" He blew out a long breath. "You are a troublesome woman, *Mademoiselle*." He motioned to his soldiers. "Continue the march down the street, weapons ready!"

"Does this mean you'll let us proceed?"

The captain winked. "It seems that way." He nodded to her and followed after his men, calling to her over his shoulder, "You'd better hurry. I cannot wait to tell my four sisters that I met the great Maria Deraismes. They quote you in their sleep!"

Maria stood alone, not believing what she heard.

Léon came, shaking his head. "How many times must you scare the life out of me?"

"Perhaps this will be the last time." She turned around. "Anna, can you and Berdine watch over the children?"

Anna nodded. "Of course. But I think we should rest for a while first. You're weak and your face is terribly pale. I'm your sister, I can tell you're not feeling well."

"Nonsense. I've been standing here resting for the last ten minutes." Maria forced a smile. "We need to get moving if we're to get to Versailles before dark. *Then* we can relax."

They moved as a tight group through the streets, mile after mile, without encountering anyone else. The sun, low in the sky, caused the air temperature to drop to a refreshing coolness. Versailles wasn't too much further. Once at the palace, she'd rest for a while before making preparations to meet with Thiers. She had to convince him that the Communards were be law-abiding people and deserved to receive fair and equal treatment. If he listened, he'd recall the troops and stop his attack.

Berdine smiled at Maria. Her entire demeanor had changed to a young woman less intimidated, stronger, and with a will to survive. She motioned with her head to a group of children. "Maria, because of you, these children will live. You pulled us all from the fires of hell. A simple 'thank you' is hardly good enough."

"There are no thanks necessary. Live well and get educated. It's inherent that we all have the right to live in this world. No one should ever be able to take that away."

Berdine's eyes teared as she nodded and went back to the children. It warmed Maria's heart to see her embracing a new sense of hope. Hope that the future would be better than her past. Alexandre slipped his arm around her waist.

"You are the only woman I have ever met who can illumine the minds of everyone you meet."

"Oh, Alexandre, no one person can accomplish our goal. It takes the combined effort of all of us."

"Very true, but you've succeeded in rallying this mismatched group from the beginning. I commend you for that." He gave her a quick kiss on the cheek and then dropped back among the people.

Maria's cheek flushed where his lips had touched. Surrounding her were so many wonderful people, and she cared for each one of them. They continued on, trudging through the streets until they came to the outer perimeter of the town of Versailles. They'd quite literally been walking all day. For so long they'd gone without seeing another soul, but suddenly they were thrust into a flurry of activity all around, even though it was early evening. Merchants hawked their goods, and the mouth-watering aroma of fresh baguettes hung in the air. Under the lamplight, three small children ran across the darkened road kicking a ball between them, as if the terror in Paris didn't exist at all.

How could these people, so close to the brutality, not even care? Maria wanted them to understand what was happening to their fellow countrymen only a matter of miles away.

Léon whispered, "We can't say or do anything to these people, or we'll be arrested for sure as Communard spies. You cannot step up to give one of your rallying speeches right now. We have to find Thiers' personal guard and hope they'll listen."

"Are you now a mind reader? How did you know I wanted to get the word out about the horror in Paris? These people live in ignorance."

"Yes, I'm a mind reader when it comes to you. I know you want to shout from the rooftops that Paris is under siege. But you can't."

Maria shot him a scowl. He knew her too well. Versailles had become isolated and shielded from the terror, full of people who were not on her side. She should not have brought her people to a place where they had nowhere to hide. "I think I may have made a mistake, Léon. I've dragged all of these people for miles and miles, and for what? Am I really so arrogant that I thought Thiers would personally meet with me and give shelter to us? We're exposed. Word will spread that we're here. What was I thinking? Why didn't you stop me?"

Léon huffed. "Stop you? Stopping you would be as impossible as stopping a flood with a bucket."

"Point taken. I can be stubborn at times."

She tried very hard to do the best thing and doubting only served to detract from her plans. She had to show strength, and if that didn't work, she'd throw herself at Thiers' feet and beg for mercy.

Continuing their march, they approached the grounds of the Versailles palace. The only time she'd ever visited the magnificent gardens surrounding the opulent palace was years ago, when she was perhaps thirteen or fourteen and they'd taken a family trip to Versailles to visit her mother's cousin whose name she'd now forgotten. It had been a wonderful holiday filled with big family dinners and strolls around the palace gardens. The smell of flowers had been overwhelming. Roses, gardenias, and exotic vines and flowers she'd never seen before, in a rainbow of colors.

She'd hated to leave and had cried all the way home. Papa regaled her with the story of how Louis XIV chose his hunting lodge as a template for the opulent palace with gardens spreading out in all direction. In 1682, he officially moved his court to the palace to rule France as an absolute dictator.

Now the palace was again being used for military purposes. Wilhelm, the Prussian king, had recently been declared the new German Emperor in the hall of mirrors in the palace. What an insult to have him stand in France as a figurative conqueror. The palace, once a source of beauty, now served as a reminder that tyranny still raised its ugly head in France.

She walked faster, anxious to see the gardens again, but with the people behind her trudging along, she slowed again, not wanting to get too far ahead. The palace wasn't visible yet, but the huge expanse of bright green grass surrounded on all sides by trees, a veritable forest of trees, came into view. The faint scent of flowery perfume began to fill the air. She stopped walking too suddenly and Léon bumped into her from behind. She'd been lost in her daydream.

"Léon, we should stop for some food before we make it to the palace." She pointed to a *boulangerie* with a delicious array of baked goods displayed in the window. "Maybe even a few sweet pastries for the younger children. I've brought all the money I had on hand."

He nodded in agreement. "Well, I've very little money with me, but you shouldn't be the only one to contribute. I'll take up a collection from my Masonic brothers." Without waiting for a response, he dashed off to the Masons, calling out 'money for the widow's trunk'.

The men reached into their pockets and handed whatever change they had to Léon without hesitation. The 'widow's trunk' she knew, was their term for charitable collections to be dispersed to those in need. Before long he had both hands full of money. Laughing, he came back to Maria. "We've plenty now."

Together they went into the *boulangerie*, bright lamps burning, throwing shadows on the walls, and waited until the proprietor finished up with a customer. Bread and beautifully decorated pastries were displayed in glass cases.

Maria whispered into Léon's ear, "I feel odd in here. We've escaped a bloody battle and now here we are buying sweets. There are so many in Paris starving. I wish we could feed them all."

Léon smiled. "Right now, these people with us need food."

She agreed. If she had the ability, she'd buy everything in the bakery and distribute it among all of the citizens so no one had to go without. Her stomach growled. She couldn't remember the last time she'd eaten. "Let's get as much as we can. But I'll make a pledge right now that as soon as I can get back to Paris, I'm going to set up a food line outside my house for the hungry."

Léon gave her a kiss on the cheek. "And I'll advertise it in my paper."

The proprietor cleared his throat and pointed to the door. "Are you with that rabble outside?"

Maria glanced out the window at her friends, her neighbors, her fellow Parisians. She was proud to be with them. "We would like some of your delicious baguettes and pastries, please. It's rather cold out and getting late and the children are quite hungry."

With a toss of his head, the proprietor pointed again at the door. "I do not serve dirty red Communards. Get out of my establishment."

Maria felt Léon's hand on her arm, gently urging her to leave. She pulled back until Léon let go. She placed a handful of coins on the counter. "Sir, we have money. Isn't money the same no matter who passes it? Isn't one stomach the same as another, needing to be filled equally? I stand before you not as a Communard, not as a Parisian, but as a human being. Those people out there are human beings. Labels do nothing but alter perception. We are all the same under the skin."

The proprietor frowned and came from behind the counter. "I have a respectable shop here and I'll not have the likes of you cause me trouble. Get out now or I'll call for the police."

What would the harm be in selling bread to the hungry? No one would even know. Was the man so intimidated by Thiers' troops that he was afraid he'd lose his business if he was seen helping the downtrodden of Paris?

She'd have to be more persuasive. "Sir, those people out there are not subversives, they are simply trying to escape the dangers of Paris. Surely you won't turn your back on those less fortunate than yourself. You have a bakery filled with food and we have money to buy that food. Your business is to sell these goods."

The proprietor went to the window and looked out, wiped his hands on his apron, and stepped outside. Back and forth he walked in front of his shop, all the while keeping his eyes on the group milling around in the street.

Maria glanced at Léon. "At least he seems to be considering it."

But she was wrong. The proprietor whistled loudly and called out. "Some help here! Communards! Communards! Communards in Versailles!"

Léon rushed out ahead of Maria. She followed and went right to Anna and Berdine. The Masons circled around the group with Alexandre helping to keep everyone else in the middle. Again, the children started to cry. What unimaginable turmoil they had to endure. The proprietor kept shouting until a small contingent of soldiers rode to the shop.

One of the soldiers pushed up the brim of his hat and stared down, his eyes squinting in the yellow streetlamp light. "Here now, what's the racket?"

The proprietor waved his arms wildly. "This rabble...spies! Come to steal from me they did!"

Maria pushed her way in between Georges and another Mason. "That's not at all true. We simply wished to get away from the fighting. These people need protection from the violence. We have money to buy bread."

The soldier dismounted in a fluid motion, his feet touching the ground gracefully, and approached Maria. "And who are you to speak for this ragged mob?"

"Maria Deraismes. A friend of the people and proud citizen of France."

He scrutinized her, looking her up and down. He motioned for the Masons to part and then moved in among the group. Maria could do nothing but watch as he strolled about, slowly walking past each person, his boot heels clicking on the cobblestones. He seemed to pay particular attention to the women.

Without warning, he suddenly withdrew his sidearm from its holster and pressed the gun barrel to Berdine's forehead. "This one wears the red sash of a Communard!" he shouted.

Maria took a step forward, but another soldier restrained her. The red sash he was talking about was simply an old red scarf Berdine had wrapped around her shoulders for warmth. She had no coat. At the time, Maria hadn't even considered the color. Now though, she wished she had. Berdine's eyes were wide and the children around her held tightly to her skirt, screaming and weeping.

"Stop!" Maria shouted above the noise. "She's no more Communard than you. It's cold and she used that scarf to keep out the chill. Look at her. Look into her eyes. She's a harmless woman, a mother. She's not—"

"*Ta gueule*, shut your filthy mouth!" the soldier shouted viciously. He grabbed Berdine by the hair, keeping the gun to her head, and dragged her into the open. He tossed her to the ground and stood over her. The children ran to her, but the solider slapped one little boy across the face, knocking him down. The other children ran back to the safety of the crowd. When Berdine screamed, he slapped her as well and ordered her to shut up.

Maria's heart pounded and sweat dripped down her face. She had to do something, but what? She was only one person against Thiers' ruthless army. Two more soldiers dismounted and quickly placed shackles around Berdine's ankles and wrists, then dragged her off. The Masons linked arms and began closing in the circle around the people, trapping the soldiers inside, chanting 'liberty, equality, fraternity'. Maria pulled away from the soldier restraining her and started to run toward Berdine but was quickly caught again.

The soldier's fierce grip hurt her arm. Before she knew what happened, she was on the ground, on her back, and heavy iron shackles were locked around her wrists. She looked up and saw Alexandre with a wooden club in his hand come up behind the soldier. He brought the club down the moment the soldier turned. It missed the soldier's head and struck him instead on the shoulder. In an instant, the soldier withdrew a gun and fired. Alexandre stumbled backward with blood dripping down the side of his face. He tumbled to the ground.

"Alexandre!" Maria screamed.

The soldier fired a bullet into the air and shouted for the Masons to let him through. When they refused, he fired a shot at the nearest man who grunted and flew backward. Maria struggled, but the soldier had her firmly. The Masonic chain broke when the injured man fell, which allowed more soldiers to ride straight through the line, trampling anyone in their way. They dismounted and roughly forced Maria toward the palace.

"Let me go! I have done nothing..." A hand clasped her mouth shut. Her heart thumped and she felt sick, her stomach a hard painful knot. She heard Léon shouting and Anna wailing but missing was Alexandre's voice.

Chapter 34

Maria struggled, dragged between two soldiers through the streets away from the sweet-smelling gardens of the palace, and forced into an ominous two-story brick building. The heavy metallic door swung open on squealing hinges, and she was taken inside. It smelled strongly of urine. She twisted and tried to wriggle free but couldn't.

The wretched place had only scant light coming from the occasional oil lamp hanging on the slippery-looking walls. The soldiers let go and prodded her forward to walk down a long, arched corridor. Shaking, she couldn't lift her feet and ended up shuffling and stumbling, but the soldiers offered no help at all. Near the end of the corridor, voices, whimpering voices begging for mercy, rose up, their pleas echoing off the walls.

She stopped at the end, dazed, but received the butt of a rifle in her back. So this was Thiers' prison. What a horrible place. No windows, fresh air, and no light. The suffocating mustiness made it feel like the building would crush the life out of her.

"Please," her voice came out in a faint whisper, "You can't do this. I've done nothing." With her throat parched, the shackles on her wrists cutting into her skin, and the stench, she almost vomited. She needed to breathe fresh air, to taste clear, cold water.

"Move." The soldier jabbed her in the back again with the rifle.

Trickles of perspiration dripped down her face. She did as she was told and continued down another corridor to open metal door, tarnished with a cage-like window in the middle. The voices were louder now, all around her, echoing. How many people were locked up in such a horrible prison? A man in the cell across from her banged on the door and cursed. Was he a criminal or a Communard? Did it matter? All were the same in Thiers' eyes.

The soldier shoved her inside the cell and slammed the door behind her. The ear-splitting sound of clanking metal rang in her ears.

The only light in the cell filtered in from the corridor. She stretched her arms and when her fingers touched the cold, slimy-damp brick walls, she recoiled. Mildew and wet mortar permeated the small cell. Her stomach tightened and bile rose in her throat.

She leaned over, resisting the urge to vomit. Perhaps worse than being imprisoned was the fact that she hadn't a clue what was happening outside with Léon, Anna, or Alexandre. He'd been shot, but had he been killed? And what of everyone else? The Masons, Berdine, and the children.

She moved toward the door, her outstretched hands groping in the darkness. She pressed her ear against it but could hear nothing but the frightened and angry prisoners all around her. It didn't seem possible that they'd lock her away without a trial or a hearing to discuss the charges. Then again, Thiers was obviously not a reasonable man. Was this her fate? Trapped and imprisoned like an animal?

With the air so stale and thick, she could hardly draw breath. Desperate, she put her nose and mouth as close to the gaps around the cage window as she could and inhaled, sucking in slightly fresher air, but not by much.

It didn't take long for her eyes to adjust to the blackness of the cell, and she could make out the walls and a shape in one corner that could be a cot. What could she have done differently to avoid capture? Probably nothing, and she'd do the exact same thing again if she had to. If the Communards had been better armed, however, they might have stood a chance against the army. But then it would have been an all-out battle, and with the soldiers' superior weapons, the Communards would still end up the losers.

She straightened. She couldn't give up and accept her fate, there was no room for self-pity. She banged on the door. "Hear me! I am Maria Deraismes, and I am a human being! I am a person! I have rights! You cannot silence me! Listen to me! Everyone out there, make noise! Do not be silenced by fear or tyranny! Fight for your freedom and for your lives!" Sweat poured down her face and her body shook with anger, but it felt good to shout, to hear her own voice.

When her hands were sore, she stopped banging. Had anyone heard her? Then, a moment later, other prisoners took up where she left off. The corridor came alive with a cacophony of noise. Shouts of 'I am a person' and 'I have rights' echoed. Maria smiled and struck her shackles against the metal door. It rang and clanked, joining with the rest of the clamor in a glorious melody of solidarity. No one could ignore them now. The strength of many would surely have an impact.

The din continued for some time, deafening as it was, until someone struck a heavy object against her door. She stopped and waited. Soon the other prisoners ceased, and the only sound was the ringing in her ears. She backed away a few steps.

The lock on her door clicked and the door swung inward. A silhouetted form stood in the doorway, a small lantern outstretched. "Come with me."

Should she? What if she was about to be executed? No one would even know. Who would look after Anna? Maria took a few more steps back. "Who are you? What do you want with me?"

"If you don't come willingly, I will drag you out by your hair." The man's voice was harsh, coarse, threatening.

"I will come but first tell me why I was arrested."

"You'll be told at the sentencing."

Sentencing? A lump lodged in Maria's throat. There was no trial, just a sentence? She'd already been found guilty. She stepped into the corridor and saw the other cell doors open. Men and women, some battered and some holding their heads high, were already walking down the corridor with a soldier by their side. How many prisoners? Twenty, thirty? She couldn't see them all as they stretched in an endless line down the corridor. One man had a red sash around his waist and blood stains on his shirt. The colors almost matched.

From somewhere deep inside, she summoned the last of her strength and shouted, "I demand justice!"

The soldier beside her cuffed her across the back of the head and prodded her forward. She fell in line with the other prisoners and tried to think of something encouraging to say. But what? There were no words.

One of the male prisoners ahead of her turned and lashed out at a soldier, striking him on the jaw with his shackles. Before she had time to take a breath, another soldier rushed forward and drove the butt of his rifle into the back of the prisoner's head. A sharp crack rang out, wood splintering against bone, and the prisoner fell to the ground.

"Keep moving!" shouted the soldier as he wiped the damaged butt of the rifle on the prisoner's shirt, leaving a smear of red blood.

Maria wanted to help the man, if he was still alive, and plead for mercy for everyone else, but her voice wouldn't come. All she could do was say a silent prayer for the wounded man as she passed.

They moved down the corridor to a room with a set of polished wooden double doors and were told to wait. One soldier went inside for a moment and then returned. He opened both doors wide and ushered everyone inside.

The large room, with red-veined marble floor, had no furnishings except for an ornate desk and a table strewn with papers. Seated behind the desk sat a dour-looking man in a dress military uniform that had large, round brass buttons going down the front. He was clean shaven with short white hair, round glasses halfway down his nose and medals pinned to his chest. Without looking up from a stack of papers on the desk, he waved the prisoners forward.

Maria had to work hard, breathing in slow and even breaths, to stop from fainting. A soldier pushed in front of the desk along with the other men and women. They stood together, side-by-side, await-ing their fate. She wanted to object, to argue, to say anything, but her mind couldn't grasp the words. Then, the man behind the desk looked up.

He slid his glasses further up his nose and looked at each of the prisoners, counting aloud. He cleared his throat and banged a gavel.

"Recorder, note that on Friday, the 26th of May, twenty-two Com-munard prisoners were sentenced to execution by firing squad." He banged the gavel again and went back to the papers on the desk.

Several of the prisoners began weeping, cursing and praying. How could this happen? Maria breathed in a lungful of air. How could she be sentenced to death? For what? The decision had been made without any consideration. No trial, no arguments, just a death sentence. She closed her eyes and opened them again, but she still stood in the room. It wasn't a dream.

"Sir," she said, her voice weak and breathy.

"Who speaks?" the man behind the desk looked up again.

A soldier close to Maria gave her another smack on the back of the head and stepped forward. "Chief Executive Thiers, I apologize for the outburst. These Communards still don't know their place."

Maria glared at the man behind the desk. It was Thiers himself. There he was, the man she'd traveled so far to see, casually doling out death sentences to innocent people. He was even more callous and heartless than she'd ever imagined. But if she didn't try to reason with him now, she'd lose her chance forever.

She drew in a deep breath. "*Monsieur* Thiers! You are sentencing innocents. We are not subversives. We merely wish to survive. We fight for that right. The law..."

As she expected, the soldier again cuffed her. It hurt, but she didn't care. She'd suffered much worse already. To her surprise, Thiers pushed back his chair and came around his desk. He stood before her and looked her up and down.

He took off his glasses and stroked his chin. "Are you the mouth of these traitorous vermin? Do you speak for them?"

She glanced at the soldier before continuing, "I speak for all the suffering people who are too afraid to speak for themselves."

Thiers laughed in a throaty, cruel chuckle. The man had no feelings, no sympathy, just a mocking laugh. "We all suffer here on earth. It is our lot in life. However, those who wantonly disregard the law will meet their maker a little sooner than those of us who obey the government. You will die, Communard, as a traitor to your country. I see no innocent people here before me." He turned and strode out of the room, his shiny leather boots squeaking slightly as he crossed the marble floor.

Stunned, Maria didn't know what to do next. Thiers was gone. She'd failed. "No!" She took a few steps in Thiers' direction but was stopped by an arm around her neck. The soldier tightened his grip, making it impossible to breathe. Her body stiffened and her lungs hungered for air.

The soldier let a moment before she passed out. She collapsed to her knees and gasped for air. The soldier grabbed a handful of her hair and pulled hard, jerking her head back.

He leaned down and whispered in her ear, "Your Masonic friends were all chased back to Paris where they belong. You have no one to swoop in and rescue you now. In the morning, you'll be lined up against the wall outside. I will personally put a bullet in your brain, and I will enjoy doing so."

Surely someone would come to save them all. More than anything, she wanted to be home, sitting in the garden with a cup of Anna's tea. How on earth had she come to this point? She had to find a way to stop the executions. When the soldier let go of her hair, she got to her feet as fast as she could and made a dash for the door. She didn't get far. Two other soldiers blocked her way with handguns pointed directly at her.

Chapter 35

Maria was dragged back to her cell, tossed inside, and lay sprawled on the floor. The door slammed shut and the locked clicked in place. The oppressive darkness all around was like a shroud, wrapping her in despair. She'd never see Anna or Léon again. She'd never find out what happened to Alexandre or the rest of the people. And then there was Berdine.

Where *was* Berdine? She'd been taken prisoner, yet she wasn't among the group that had been sentenced. It didn't seem likely that she'd have been sentenced at another time. So where would they have taken her? As much as Maria didn't want to think of the other alternative, she couldn't help it. Berdine might have already been executed.

She drove the thought from her mind and stood, feeling blindly for the wall. Once her fingers touched the slimy bricks, she wandered around the cell until she came to the cot. She sat on the rickety contraption and pinched her leg as hard as she could keep her mind focused.

If there was anything at all to be thankful for, it was that the Masons had been allowed to leave, except for the poor soul who'd been shot. Of course, now they would be back in Paris, among the bloodshed once again, but that was better than prison, or death by firing squad. Hopefully Anna and Léon had gone with them.

Maria touched the lumpy mattress. She'd always slept in a downy-soft bed. She'd taken the small things in life for granted, but nothing about life should ever be taken for granted. Life was truly a precious gift.

She leaned forward and rested her head in her hands and thought about her childhood. There were so many happy times. Picnics in the country, long walks through the pastures, and perhaps best of all, lively conversations around the dinner table. Such a simple and satisfying life back then.

She'd even had a pet dog, Leelee. Anna said that if she ever had a daughter, she'd name her Leelee. But Anna never did have any children. What a great mother she would have been.

"Stop living in the past, Maria," she said out loud. She closed her eyes and prayed that she'd die in her sleep so she wouldn't have to live through the terror of being riddled with bullets.

All night long she paced around the cell, sat down on the cot and prayed. She'd drifted off to sleep several times, always startled awake by a nightmare. The night dragged on endlessly until voices and sounds in the hall hinted that it must be morning.

She got off the cot and paced around the cell, stopping at the door. Her stomach clenched. More than anything, she would have liked to give Anna a goodbye kiss.

When her door opened and a streak of light shot into the room, she backed away. Instinct took over and she wanted to hide or run forward and escape the prison. The soldier motioned her out of the cell. After a moment, she realized she had my point in resisting. She'd go bravely and embrace her final minutes of life. She'd had a good life and had done her best. With any luck, the sun would shine down to greet her, to caress her and comfort her. It would be the last time she'd ever see the sun.

The rest of the prisoners were already in the corridor, lined up one behind the other. They glanced around nervously, some weeping softly, some apparently putting on a brave front like she was, their shoulders back, heads held high. When one of the soldiers blew a whistle, Maria jumped. They started off down the corridor, feet shuffling in unison. For some reason, Maria felt strong. Her legs were steady and her body felt free from illness.

They walked slowly up a flight of marble steps, the same red-veined marble as in the sentencing room, then down one corridor and another, arriving after a time at an iron gate. A rush of cool air blew through the iron slats. A soldier unlocked it and swung it open. The rusted hinges creaked loudly, breaking up the quiet morning. Now her legs trembled. A small, enclosed courtyard lay beyond the gate, with one wall splattered with red stain. Maria couldn't catch her breath and stopped walking forward until a jab in her back made her continue.

The ground in the courtyard was covered in a fine, light brown sandy soil, with no ceiling to block out the sky. But there was no sun. Dark, ominous clouds hung low, blocking any trace of light. Why couldn't she have seen the sun one last time? She took a deep, pained breath and followed the line of prisoners toward the wall.

One more time she had to try for freedom. One final time. She halted and turned to the guards behind her. Her voice cracked at first, then was strong, "Please, listen to me. We have done nothing. We did not fight. We are French citizens. Killing us is wrong and un-lawful. Let us go and stop this illegal action."

The other prisoners also stopped. A man dropped to his knees and cried out, "I am a butcher, not a soldier! I have a wife and three children!"

A very young woman with a black eye and bruised cheek sudden-ly took off across the courtyard. She'd made it about halfway when a shot rang out and she fell. The sand around her turned red. The sol-diers grabbed the rest of the prisoners, including Maria, and shoved or dragged them all to the wall. Maria resisted, but the soldier was too strong.

"Stand up straight against the wall, facing me," a soldier ordered.

Maria watched, horrified, as the company of soldiers lined up in front of her and the other prisoners and raised their rifles. Maria was in the middle. She felt a kinship to those with her. They were all dy-ing for a cause that was really common sense, not a cause at all. If her death would make a difference though, then it wouldn't be in vain. But who was to say if it would? She wanted to see Anna again, to hold her and remember the good times. She closed her eyes. She didn't want to see when the triggers were pulled.

Chapter 36

Maria's entire body shook at she leaned against the wall, waiting for the inevitable. Then she heard it. The first shot, thunderous, reverberated in the courtyard. She didn't know who'd fallen first, and she didn't want to know. Her turn would come soon enough. Then another shot rang out and another, followed by yelling and shouting. She hadn't fallen. She couldn't take it any longer and opened her eyes.

The soldiers, some with bullet wounds, lay in the dirt on their stomachs with their hands clasped at the back of their heads, and a group of commonly dressed men had them surrounded, guns aimed at the soldiers. She looked to her left and to her right. All of the prisoners were still standing.

She drew in a breath and called out shakily, "What's going on here?"

"*Mademoiselle* Deraismes?" one of the men asked.

"Yes. I'm Maria Deraismes." She stepped away from the wall.

"You must come with me right away. We don't have long before we're set upon by the rest of the army." The man pointed to three rope ladders hanging down the opposite wall.

"I don't understand. What just happened?" She could barely breathe, her heart was beating so fast.

"We positioned men on the roof overlooking the courtyard when we heard Thiers' sentence. We had to wait for the right moment when the soldiers would be focused on the prisoners."

"How did you hear the sentence? Please, I'm so confused."

"Not now, *Mademoiselle,* we must go!" He motioned to the ladders, keeping his gun aimed at the soldiers.

Some of the other men herded the anxious prisoners toward the ladders. Maria hesitated. Could it be a trick of some sort? Or was it really a rescue? She ran to the nearest ladder, her shackled wrists and skirt that kept getting in the way, making it hard to climb, but she managed, ignoring the pain as the iron shackles bit into her skin.

Even harder than the climb was getting off the ladder and onto the roof because her skirt had tangled around her legs. More men were stationed on the roof to guide the prisoners to a sturdier ladder leading from the roof to the outside of the prison. An enclosed wagon waited beneath the ladder.

No one spoke as they climbed into the wagon and sat down on a layer of hay. The man she'd spoken to hopped in and crouched near the entrance. The canopy was made of pungent oiled-leather and once everyone was inside, the man lowered a heavy leather flap. The wagon started to roll along. It felt surreal.

Maria moved near the man. "Can you tell me how you came to rescue us?"

He lifted the flap an inch, peered out and lowered the flap again. He smiled. "*Mademoiselle* we have a man on the inside who heard the sentence. Your friends are waiting for you outside Versailles."

"My friends? What friends?"

"Léon Richer, Alexandre Weill, and Victor Hugo. It was *Monsieur* Hugo who contacted us about your capture." The man shrugged casually. "I head up a small band of mercenaries. *Monsieur* Hugo pays us for information about the army and details about fighting and such."

Maria let out an exhausted breath. Leave it to Hugo to use mercenaries for research for his writings. She'd always wondered how he knew such intimate details about things. "How did *Monsieur* Hugo know I was here?"

"I will let him explain that to you." He turned away and lifted the flap again.

For some time, the wagon continued with being stopped by soldiers. It bounced over cobblestones and slid into ruts, picking up speed after a while. The people stayed quiet, leaning on one another, or staring at nothing.

A loud crack of thunder sounded, followed by rain crashing down on the wagon, heavy drops splattering and hammering on the leather canopy. Maria scooted next to the mercenary and lifted an edge of the back flap. The fresh smell of rain drifted into the wagon, and she laughed. The other prisoners stared at her as if she'd gone mad, but the mercenary laughed along with her.

"We are alive," she said above the racket. "Fill your lungs with the sweet scent of freedom!"

They soon all joined in the laughter, breathing in the fresh air that flowed over them. Before long, the wagon slowed and came to a stop. Everyone stopped laughing. Someone outside raised the leather flap all the way and Victor Hugo stood there, holding the flap himself, grinning from ear to ear, soaked to the skin.

He motioned with his head for them to get out of the wagon. "What a miserable-looking bunch of Communards I've saved from Thiers' fury." He let out a hearty guffaw. "Miserable, perhaps, but the salt of the earth."

Maria climbed out and stood beside him, rain pelting down and drenching her. "*Monsieur* Hugo, how can I ever thank you for saving these people, and me?"

"No need, *Mademoiselle*."

"But if Thiers finds out you had a hand in this—"

"He'll what? Exile me? *Merde*, I'm about to embark on another self-imposed exile anyway." He dropped the flap once everyone was out. "I have a blacksmith standing by to remove those wretched shackles."

Maria wiped the rain from her eyes. "But how did you know? How did you know we were taken prisoner?"

He said nothing but pointed across the street. Standing near a streetlamp was Berdine, dripping wet, with Léon, Anna, and Alexandre behind her.

With renewed energy, Maria hurried across the road, slipping on the wet cobbles, into the waiting arms of Anna. The embrace was the comfort of home after a long journey. Léon and Alexandre, with a white bandage around his head, joined the embrace. Rain or not, Maria didn't want to move. She had everything she needed.

Berdine squeezed in and gave Maria a kiss on the cheek. "You tried to save me and then got arrested yourself. No one has ever done anything like that before. I couldn't allow those soldiers to kill you."

"But how did you get away? I saw you taken away."

Berdine shrugged and cast her eyes down. "They just let me go. Told me to go back to Paris where I belonged. It was a miracle, Maria."

That didn't seem like Thiers to let anyone go, but who could argue with a miracle. Could a small amount of sympathy have crept into his cold heart, like it had with Daumier? If it had, there might be a little hope after all.

Maria took Berdine's hand. "I don't understand. How did *Monsieur* Hugo get involved?"

Berdine continued, "When they let me go, the guard said I should drop to my knees and thank God because no prisoners ever left with their lives. I prayed and prayed that I could do something to help other prisoners. I caught up with everyone heading back to Paris when I heard from *Monsieur* Richer that you were taken. Then, by chance, or perhaps it was fate, I found *Monsieur* Hugo. I saw *Monsieur* Hugo drinking a glass of wine at a café when we got outside of Versailles. He was concentrating on writing something. I recognized him and...I asked if he could help. He never hesitated." She raised her eyes. "I was so afraid that he couldn't do anything."

"But he did. *You* did. I don't know what to say, Berdine. How do I thank you for saving my life."

"Say you'll teach me to read."

"It will be my pleasure to teach you to read." Maria shivered against the cold rain. "I think we should get to someplace dry, don't you?"

Léon stripped off his coat and placed it over her head and shoulders. "*Monsieur* Hugo's blacksmith is waiting over there." He pointed to a rundown building that was likely once a charming inn but now looked abandoned.

"Come on, Maria, let me help you," Alexandre said in a hoarse, throaty voice.

He placed his arm around her waist and escorted her to the building. She couldn't help noticing how he breathed hard and staggered rather than walked. She reached up and touched the bandage around his head. A trace of blood had leaked through. "Alexandre, are you all right?"

He pulled her closer and helped her over the threshold, although he leaned on her for support at the same time. He let out a half-hearted laugh, "It'll take more than a bullet to stop me. I must be blessed because the bullet only grazed the side of my head."

The rest of the freed prisoners gathered inside the building near Maria, making casual conversation, but not saying too much. They appeared in shock, moving about in a half-daze. The blacksmith, a very old man with deep-set wrinkles, dark gray hair down to his shoulders and a round belly that poked out from under his coat, came over and gave the shackles around Maria's wrists a cursory examination.

He motioned her to a table. "Place your arms on the table, *Mademoiselle*."

Alexandre stuck by her side as she approached the table. He helped her lift the heavy shackles onto a small anvil and whispered in her ear, "When I heard you were arrested, I didn't want to live." He pressed against her, his warm breath tickling her cheek.

"The hardest part of prison was not knowing if you were all right," she whispered back.

The blacksmith held onto the chain between the shackles and placed a chisel on the lock of the left shackle. He struck it twice with a mallet and the lock broke. He did the same with the other, and then she was free. The shackles fell off and Alexandre gave each of her bruised wrists a kiss.

The other prisoners took their turn with the blacksmith until he'd removed all of the shackles. A man dragged the shackles into a pile where they lay like a nest of snakes. Maria turned away from the evil things. Instead, she watched the former prisoners as they slapped one another on the back or hugged and thanked the blacksmith, milled about answering questions from Hugo, and even sang a few victory songs.

She hadn't realized she'd been smiling until Léon came over and winked. "You look surprisingly cheerful, Maria."

"Relieved. We were seconds away from death, Léon. I've never experienced anything like that before. Nor do I ever want to again. But now I understand the fear and desperation that most people feel each day."

"Well, you're safe now, and these people are safe. Unfortunately, we're back in Paris again."

She nodded. "I didn't accomplish a single thing by going to Versailles. At least I don't hear any fighting. No guns or cannons. Do you think Thiers has recalled his men?"

"Not a chance. Don't be naïve. Remember, his men murdered a Freemason and Thiers himself ordered the rest of my brothers back to Paris. He doesn't seem to care about any political influences the Masons might have. Anyone with such little regard for life and reason certainly can't be trusted. We all thought us Freemasons would garner some respect." His demeanor—shoulders slumped, brow pinched—betrayed his disappointment.

"Then what's his plan? To storm into Paris again and start over? Will the barricades hold?"

Léon shook his head and sighed heavily. "Most are, but soldiers have broken through a lot of them and then they shot everyone on the other side, including children. The soldiers are growing in strength and have taken over most of the west side now. As soon as the barricades get rebuilt, they tear them down again. Thiers cares for no one, Maria."

"Oh, I know that. Have you heard any news about Louise or Dardelle? Have they been—?"

"No news. Rumor has it that Thiers has issued a bounty on Dardelle's head. He's afraid that as long as Dardelle is alive, the Commune lives on. But enough of that, you're soaking wet and shivering. You have to get dry and warm before you get sick. Hugo said we can use that wagon to go home. We have to be careful that Thiers doesn't send soldiers to your house looking for you. But there's no point staying here."

"No, I suppose not. I'll be careful." She turned and faced the other prisoners. "You should all go straight home and lock the doors. Thiers will surely attack again now that it's morning, and if he knows where you live, he might come looking. Stay out of sight."

One of the men, with narrowed eyes and a bushy mustache, shook his head adamantly. "No, *Mademoiselle*. I will not hide behind locked doors. I will not cower and wait for soldiers to drag me away again. I will stand and fight."

"Then you'll die." Maria picked up the end of the shackles. "Perhaps you should keep these as a reminder of how close you came to martyrdom."

"Just because you're too afraid to fight doesn't mean the rest of us have to surrender our souls to Thiers."

All eyes turned to Hugo as he cleared his throat and strolled around the room, his sodden boots squelching with every step. He stopped near Maria. "I am confident that one day the fight for equality will be won. However, it will not be won without bloodshed. Those who choose to fight are to be commended but cautioned not to be too hasty. That said, some of us are unable or unwilling to take up arms, but that doesn't mean we are cowards. Let me remind all of you here that we are in this fight together. We can't all be foot soldiers."

The mustached man fell quiet and looked at Maria with an expression that denoted regret for having said what he'd said. She smiled at him to let him know all was forgiven and then she turned to Hugo. "*Monsieur* Hugo, I have admired you and your work for many years, but today I have a renewed admiration."

"Admire yourself, *Mademoiselle*, for all your hard work. And make sure we win!" He laughed boisterously and headed for the door. "Well, I'm off to my latest exile on the continent. Watch behind your backs, *mes amis*."

He vanished out the door and into the downpour.

Alexandre took Maria's hand. "*Monsieur* Hugo speaks wise words. We all do our part, but you do too much."

"I do too little." She sighed. "You see how worthless I am at negotiating with Thiers. All my attempt did was get these people arrested and almost killed. I feel helpless and responsible at the same time."

"Please don't be so hard on yourself. Like Hugo said, we all do our part." He swayed slightly and gripped the end of the table.

Maria put her arm over his shoulders. His face was pale, and he seemed to have lost his *joie de vivre*. Seeing him like that, his spirit as well as his body wounded, cut her deeply. She missed the old Alexandre.

"Léon is right, Alexandre. We need to go home and rest and try to push this horror away if only for a few moments. I'll go and find Anna and Berdine."

"I'm not about to argue."

"Of course. Will you be all right?"

"I have headaches that make me dizzy. I'll sit on that old stool over there." He motioned across the room.

She gave him a kiss on the cheek and found Anna by the doorway.

Anna shot her a smile. "There you are. I can't wait to get back home. I'll never leave home again. I almost lost you, Maria."

Maria motioned to Alexandre. "You've been with him for a while, tell me the truth, is he all right?"

"We can talk about him later. Right now, we need to go home."

Léon waited outside with an umbrella and held it over them as they left the building. "Come and get in the wagon. I'll come back for Alexandre."

Maria knew that Anna's avoidance of the question about Alexandre meant it was bad news. As much as she wanted to know more, she decided not to press the issue, for the time being. Alexandre would tell her in his own time.

They went out to the wagon, crouching under the umbrella, although it hardly mattered since everyone was already soaked to the skin. They climbed in the back as the rain slowed to a gentle sprinkle. The temperature had warmed up a little, but not enough to stop Maria from shivering.

Léon returned with Alexandre and Berdine, who sat with Maria and Ann in the back, while he went up front. Without much sleep, Maria forced herself to stay awake. She wanted to see and feel everything around her, to experience every minute of life. The wagon started with a jerk and rolled along slowly.

She opened the back flap and peered out at the Parisian morning. There were only a few people wandering about, their faces serious or frightened. Gone was the Paris she knew. They passed broken barricades of wooden crates or wagons as they passed by streets and alleys. And then came the bodies. The dead lay where they'd been shot, ignored like fallen leaves on the street. Some were piled up near brick walls, their blood mixed with rain, collected into puddles between the cobblestones.

No one was safe from Thiers' wrath. Not the common man, not children, not even the Freemasons.

Berdine scooted closer. "Maria, how could this happen to so many people? Is there no mercy in this world?"

"Very little. That's why we can't give up." Maria lowered the flap. She didn't need to see any more.

When the wagon rolled into a rut, Alexandre moaned and grabbed his head. Maria glared at Anna. "He's badly hurt, isn't he? Why couldn't you tell me that?"

Alexandre crawled over to Maria. "Because, my dear, I made her promise not to tell. I didn't want you worrying about me."

She gently wrapped her arms around him, careful not to touch his bandaged head. "But you said it was only a graze."

He pulled back slightly and looked into her eyes. "It is. But when Georges Martin examined me, he said I probably have some bleeding into my brain, perhaps a fracture of my skull. The bullet may well have damaged the blood vessels." He paused. "If my brain is bruised and swells, I might die. There, now you know. And there's nothing you can do about it. So, is knowing any better than not knowing?"

Maria stared at him, unable to speak for a moment as she processed what he'd said. He couldn't die. She wouldn't allow it. "What about surgery? I've heard of surgery being done for head wounds."

Alexandre shook his head slowly. "We're in the middle of a war, Maria. Hardly the time for delicate surgery. Besides, the skilled surgeons who could do this type of work left Paris months ago."

Maria's ears rang with those stinging words. She'd gotten Alexandre back. How could this possibly be happening? "But you seem fine. You're walking and talking."

"This is why I didn't want you to know. It can happen slowly or it can happen fast." His expression darkened. "A headache is one the first sign that the brain is swelling."

The capitulation in Alexandre's voice irritated Maria. He'd never been one to give up. "No, I refuse to believe it. You only had one doctor's opinion. We'll find another doctor. Doctor Pouchard is still here. He didn't leave."

The wagon stopped and Léon called out, "Maria, Anna! We're at your house."

"Alexandre," Maria said softly, "You are planning to stay with us, aren't you?"

"I hadn't thought much about it really. But since I can't go back to Kellermeister's house, I'll be more than happy to accept your offer." He smiled. A weak smile, but a smile, nonetheless.

Berdine and Anna got out first, leaving Maria with Alexandre. She held onto him, not wanting to let go. "You go inside, and I'll see if Doctor Pouchard is home."

"I can see that trying to argue with you is a losing proposition." He smiled again and edged toward the back of the wagon. "Why don't you send Léon to find Pouchard? I'd like you to stay with me."

How could she say no? They went into the house and as she'd expected, Léon agreed to find Doctor Pouchard, but first, everyone dried off and changed clothes. The wardrobes and drawers held a mismatch of clothing, but they managed to dress appropriately.

After Léon left, Anna and Berdine set about cleaning the house and preparing a meal from whatever was left in the kitchen. The day brightened when the clouds parted to reveal the sun, although it was still somewhat cool. Not cool enough to stop Alexandre and Maria from going out to the garden.

Everything was wet, so they couldn't sit on the bench, which left strolling through the garden, arm-in-arm. The rain had chilled Maria down deep, but she didn't want to let it ruin the moment. Alexandre couldn't die. How would she live without him in her life?

They stopped walking and she gazed at the roses, shimmery droplets of water still clinging to the petals, weighing them down and forcing them toward the ground. The rain had released their perfume and filled the air with the strong aroma. She wanted it to be a perfect Saturday, lazy and slow, so she pushed all thoughts of Thiers and the Commune from her mind. The last thing she needed was an intrusion that would destroy the happiness, and her precious time with Alexandre.

Léon returned sooner than she'd expected with the bad news that Doctor Pouchard was not at home, and no one had seen him in days. Maria wanted to go and look for him, but Alexandre convinced her to stay. They all went to the kitchen and ate a thin soup made of mostly broth and herbs and a partially moldy baguette, then retired to the sitting room.

Maria sat in the old chair by the fire and warmed up. She got up again, though, when Alexandre lay down on the sofa and let out a groan. He needed a doctor. Why hadn't she insisted that Georges Martin come with them? She sat down beside him and held his hand.

As much as she tried, she couldn't stop thoughts of Thiers and the soldiers from creeping in. She'd witnessed the brutality, but the rest of the world had no idea how bad things were. No one would ever know of the mistreatment and disregard of human rights unless someone spoke up. But how? Paris had effectively been sealed off from the world. She knew the only news that got out was from Thiers. He'd have the world thinking the Communards were the ones causing the violence and bloodshed. Everyone would condemn the uprising and quash future attempts for equality. Thiers couldn't be allowed to win.

Chapter 37

Maria startled when someone knocked on the front door. Soldiers wouldn't knock, they'd break the door in. Maybe Pouchard heard they were looking for him and came back from wherever he'd gone. That didn't seem likely, but she could hope.

More knocking followed by Louise's voice, "Well, isn't anyone going to let me in?"

Anna jumped up and opened the door. "Louise!"

Maria smiled at the sight of Anna and Louise embracing and giving one another a fraternal kiss on the cheek. How far they'd come in such a short time. If only their awakening could be infectious enough to change the world.

Louise closed the door behind her and looked around. "What a wretched-looking group we have here."

"You don't look any better, Louise," Maria said with a smirk. In fact, Louise looked far worse. Her hair was tangled and going this way and that, her dress had filthy stains all over and splatters of blood, and her face was a mass of bruises and scratches.

With a shrug, Louise laughed. "We're winning, though. Once we rebuild the barricades and collect as many guns as we can from the dead soldiers, we'll be a force to be reckoned with. Thiers cannot defeat us."

"I'm not so sure." Léon got up from the sofa and stood in front of Louise. "Maria was almost killed, Alexandre was shot, and Berdine was imprisoned. Thiers has us all on the run. He has an army, Louise. What do we have? A few housemaids and shop keepers armed with brooms and rakes against an army. I don't like those odds." He returned to the sofa and flopped down. "Maria, I think I'll take Alexandre to Georges Martin's house. I can't stomach being here for another minute." He glared at Louise.

Hearing Léon with such a grim outlook only made Maria more determined to continue the fight. If they could organize the Commune Council and make an actual plan of how to protect Paris, then they might stand a chance. The Commune would work if the people stood together rather than go off on their own to fight the soldiers. Organization was the key ingredient.

Alexandre eased his body off the sofa and nodded to Léon. "Anything is better than lying here in misery. I hope your doctor friend has something to rid me of this headache."

"I'll come, too." Maria embraced Alexandre.

He kissed her cheek. "No, you stay here and recuperate from your ordeal. I'll be back as soon as the doctor gives me medicine to ease the headache. I promise."

She spoke to Léon, "Look after him."

"You know I will."

She walked with Alexandre to the door. He gave her hand quick kiss and left. She stood on the stoop and watched him walk down the front path, swaying and clutching the side of his head. It hurt too much to see him like that. She closed the door.

"Louise," Maria said, "Is Dardelle alive?"

"Of course. You don't think he'd allow himself to get captured or killed, do you? He has two rather burly guards with him at all times. Perhaps you saw them at the *Hôtel de Ville*."

Maria did remember the two men who'd whisked Dardelle away from the podium. So those were his personal guards. "But what about you? You don't have guards to protect you. Doesn't he care about that?"

"Oh, Maria, you don't understand." Louise plopped down on the sofa. "Dardelle is our leader. Without him, the people wouldn't know who to follow or who to listen to. The Commune would crumble."

"They listen to you."

"True, but I'm not their leader. We need Dardelle. He's far more charismatic than I."

There was truth in what she said. Louise reacted too much, and her undisciplined actions were too extreme to lead anyone, although she excelled at being an incredible instigator. She simply couldn't control her emotions enough to conduct a large group of Communards. But together, she and Dardelle made a formidable pair.

With Louise's arrival, all chances of ignoring unpleasant events had vanished. Maria knew it was time to jump back into protecting the Commune government against Thiers. But the only way to make it work would be to put an end to the violence.

"Louise," Maria started, "What is Dardelle's next move? I'd like to talk to him and work out a peaceful solution to—"

"Peaceful? You must be mad." Smoothing down part of her mussed hair, Louise hopped off the sofa and strolled around the room. "Do you think Thiers wants a peaceful solution? Do you think he'll withdraw his soldiers and tell them all to go home and have tea? Until Thiers lies dead by our hands, there can be no peace."

Maria wasn't sure she'd heard Louise correctly. There'd never been any talk of murdering Thiers. That certainly wasn't what the Commune was about. A twinge in Maria's stomach made her moan. Evidently it was enough to get Anna's attention. She came over and started fussing.

"All right, that's it, you need to go to bed," Anna said firmly.

Maria didn't even try to object as she usually would, because she welcomed the excuse to get away from Louise and her talk of murder. Maria sat on her bed while Anna opened the window. A soft breeze blew in, carrying with it the perfume from the garden. There had to be a way to contact Dardelle and explain to him that violence would only breed more violence. Louise knew where he was, but she wasn't likely to tell.

From the doorway of the bedroom, Louise sighed. "Sorry to interrupt, but I think I should clear up any misunderstandings between us. You're my friend, Maria, and I'd never do or say anything to upset you. Not on purpose anyway. Dardelle is planning to attack the Tuileries palace tomorrow, so if you really want to speak to him, you can meet him tonight in the Tuileries gardens by the fountain. There will be a small gathering of people who'll be helping. He's having a final briefing before the big day."

"What's he planning to do? Why does he need a final briefing?" Maria looked over at Anna and saw that she was concerned as well.

Louise winked. "It's a surprise. Meet us at the fountain around eight tonight." With that, she turned and left.

Anna shook her head. "You are absolutely not going to go out tonight."

"I am. I have to. Someone has to knock some sense into Dardelle."

Chapter 38

Maria stayed in her room for most of the day trying to think up things to say to Dardelle to get him to change his mind about attacking the palace. He was smart enough to realize that the Communard forces had to change their strategy, or Thiers would tighten his grip on Paris. Attacking the bourgeoisie by destroying the palace would only enrage Thiers. He'd send in additional troops and more people would die.

When the clock struck six, Maria went downstairs to get her coat. Léon was back and staring out the front window, drumming his fingers on the sill. The fire in the hearth had been neglected and was almost out.

"I'm glad you came back, Léon, but there's no warm fire to greet you." Maria gave his shoulder a pat. "How's Alexandre? What did Georges say?"

He didn't turn around but kept peering out the window. "Oh, ah, Georges has Alexandre resting and gave him some medicine for the pain."

"What are you looking at?" She squeezed in next to him and looked out. She saw nothing. His stiff posture and rapid breathing gave away his anxiety. "Léon? Is Alexandre really all right? Are you holding something from me?"

"What?" He looked over at her. "No, no. Alexandre's in good hands." He turned back to the window. "I shouldn't have let her go. What was I thinking?"

"Who? You shouldn't have let who go?" Maria put her hand on his cheek and turned his head toward her. "Anna? You let Anna go out?"

He shook his head. "No, no, it's Berdine. She said she had to go and check on the women she'd been helping before the Commune took effect. She said she'd only be a short time, but that was four hours ago. What have I done?"

"Where's Anna?" Maria abandoned the window and started toward the kitchen.

Léon went after her and took her hand. "She's in the back garden. Maria, what if something's happened to Berdine? I'll never forgive myself. She insisted and I didn't see the harm."

"There are soldiers patrolling around and you didn't see the harm? What's the matter with you, Léon? You're not thinking straight."

He dropped her hand and returned to the window. "I'll go after her. I know where she went."

"You'll not go anywhere. I need you to stay here with Anna. I'm going out shortly to meet with Dardelle. I'm going to turn his mind around if it's the last thing I do."

"Are you mad?" He thumped his fist on the windowsill. "Berdine's just gone missing and now you want to go out? Have you already forgotten what happened to you this morning? You were almost killed by a firing squad."

"I don't think that's something I'll soon forget, Léon. That's precisely the reason I have to talk to Dardelle. This nonsense can't go on. This is no longer a fight for equality. It's turned into a fight for power and control."

Rather than argue, they both sat down near the cold hearth and agreed that they would go together to the Tuileries and Anna would stay with one of their neighbors in case soldiers came by. As it neared seven o'clock, someone rapped on the door.

After a few more knocks came a slight whimpering sound. Someone needed help. Maria placed her hand on the knob and looked at Léon. He jumped up and shook his head, but she opened the door anyway.

Berdine stood there, looking sorrowful, her eyes red and teary. Maria motioned her inside and shut the door. "Berdine, why were you gone so long? You worried us half to death."

She didn't answer right away but kept shaking her head and clasping her hands together. Finally, she whispered, "I've done a terrible thing."

What could she possibly have done? Berdine didn't have a bad bone in her body. Maria stood back. "Come inside. What are you talking about? What's happened?"

"I've betrayed you. I've betrayed everyone. I don't deserve to live."

What could she be talking about? "Tell me what's wrong."

Berdine burst out crying. She pointed to the clock on the wall. "It's too late now. That's why they let me go."

Léon grabbed Berdine's shoulders and shook her. "Who let you go?"

"The soldiers. Thiers' soldiers," Berdine blurted.

Poor Berdine, Maria thought. She was reliving her capture in Versailles. "No, *ma chère*, we're in Paris. We're safe."

"You don't understand!" Berdine's shouted. "I told the soldiers where Dardelle would be at eight o'clock tonight. I had to. They wouldn't let me go until a little while ago so it would be too late for me to warn anyone."

Maria processed what Berdine said. "You were captured again? You can't blame yourself for that."

"Oh, Maria! You've been so kind to me, and I've betrayed you. You don't understand. I wasn't captured. I was never going to see my friends. Instead, I met the soldiers at the *Hôtel des Invalides*."

"What? Why? I don't understand why you went to meet Thiers' soldiers. How did you know about Dardelle?"

"I overheard Louise tell you when she came here. When I was in prison, Thiers said if I didn't find out where Dardelle was by the end of the day, he'd send all of his soldiers to Paris to kill everyone, including all of the children. I had no choice when I heard where he'll be." Berdine burst out in hysterical tears. "He was going to shoot the children! I'm a traitor!"

Maria had no words. Berdine was indeed a traitor in the smallest sense, but not maliciously so. She did the only thing she thought she could save innocent lives. But in doing so, she'd jeopardized the entire Commune government. And now Thiers' soldiers would find Dardelle in the Tuileries gardens and probably open fire on him and his followers.

The clock struck half past seven. Only half an hour before Dardelle would be at the fountain. Thiers likely had soldiers already positioned around the gardens, waiting. Maria paced. Léon stared off into the distance. The only sounds came from the ticking clock and Berdine's crying, although Anna had come in and did her best to comfort her.

Maria stopped pacing. With half an hour to go, she'd get the word out somehow. But she'd have to enlist help. The Masons. "Léon, listen to me. Can you get a message to as many of your Masonic brothers as you can?"

He came out of his daze. "For what reason? What can we do now?"

"We can warn as many attendees as we can. If we have a hundred men spreading the word of Thiers' plan, we can stop a lot of people going to the Tuileries, and perhaps word will get to Dardelle." Maria didn't want Berdine to feel guilty. "Berdine, Dardelle is a smart man, he probably already knows the soldiers are around."

Through her tears, Berdine mumbled, "And if he doesn't?"

"We won't think about that right now. Léon, we have to go immediately. There's no time to waste." Maria went right to the wardrobe to get her coat, but Léon got there first and placed his hand on the door.

"You're not going with me, Maria. You're staying right here with Anna and Berdine."

Maria shook her head and shoved his hand away from the wardrobe. "We can stay here and argue all night, or we can try to warn people away from the Tuileries."

After a moment of debate over who'd go and who'd stay, Maria hastily hitched her mare to the small carriage and with Léon driving, they drove straight to the Grand Orient Lodge without encountering any soldiers. Inside, a dozen Masons were discussing their next move against Thiers. Léon quickly explained about Dardelle and the Tuileries, and received an agreement that they would head off around the streets and spread the word.

Maria asked Georges about Alexandre, but he was too preoccupied to say much more than Alexandre rested comfortably. At least it wasn't bad news.

The Lodge was hot, so Maria unbuttoned her coat and fanned her face with her hand. Her stomach hurt. She felt dizzy and perspired. Now was not a good time for one of her spells. Why did she have to have such a weak body? Strength was needed, not weakness. Her whole life had been dictated by her illness. It wasn't fair.

The men slipped into their overcoats and rushed out into the night. Oh, how she wanted to be with them. If only she felt better, she could go in search of Louise. She knew several of the places Louise frequented.

Léon came over. "Maria, I really need to go and help, but I don't want to leave you alone and I don't have time to drive you back home. Do you think you'd be well enough to come along?"

Maria nodded, even though she was in no condition to go anywhere. "Don't worry about me. Let's head for the Tuileries and warn as many people who are going in that direction."

The fresh air outside eased her stomach pain a little, but the bumping and jostling of the carriage over the cobblestones made her feel sick. The sun had almost set, yet the gas lamps weren't lit, leaving the streets cloaked in darkness and shadow. The lamplighters were probably afraid to come out or had left Paris altogether. And who could really blame them?

Every once in a while, they'd pass by a lone man or woman, some with red sashes around their waists, but when Léon made an attempt to speak to them, they'd rush off. Maria knew where they were going. If they would only listen. She leaned back and closed her eyes. It had to be close to eight o'clock.

"Léon, take me to the fountain in the Tuileries."

He touched her forehead. "You're hot. I'm taking you home."

She pushed is hand away. "No, you're not. The least we can do is find Louise and get her away safely before Thiers arrests her, too."

"You're not thinking straight, Maria. If we go there, we'll be arrested as well. Do you want to go back to prison?"

She took the reins from Léon and shook them violently. The horse sped up into a steady canter. "There, now no more talk of arrest or prison. Whatever happens is meant to happen."

"Spoken like a true martyr." He took the reins back and slowed the horse to a trot.

On the right loomed the Tuileries palace, on the left the huge *Palais du Louvre* with its fabulous museum inside. How many times had she visited the Louvre? Too many times to remember. The Louvre had originally been built as a fort and then later used as a palace until Louis XIV moved court to Versailles. After that, it became a museum. If only all military forts could be turned into galleries for beauty. But now in the dark, it lay silent, a cold silhouette.

They continued past the Louvre where the trees in the Tuileries gardens were outlined against the black sky. Léon halted the carriage beneath a large weeping willow a short distance from the fountain.

He whispered, "We can wait here in the shadows. If we see Louise, I'll try to sneak around and bring her here."

Maria peered out and heard the spray of water from the fountain. Ordinarily, the gurgling and splashing of water had a calming effect, but not tonight. "I think I hear voices. Do you hear voices?"

Léon cocked his head and listened. "They're ahead, near the fountain."

Squinting, Maria made out several figures moving about near the fountain. One of them had to be Dardelle, and perhaps Louise. Maria's eyes adjusted to the dim light coming from the lamps around the Louvre. Now she could clearly see five, six, seven figures. More and more people arrived, talking quietly in indecipherable voices. She counted again. Twelve, maybe thirteen, but then more came. Why were so many people coming?

"Léon, I don't like this. There are a lot of people here. Didn't the Masons warn *anyone*?"

"I don't know. We sure didn't have any luck. What do you suppose they're all doing here? I figured it would be no more than a few of Dardelle's most trusted. We can't let them fall into Thiers' trap. I'm going to warn them that troops are coming." He got out of the carriage as a single shot rang out through the darkness.

Maria reached outside the carriage and grasped him by the sleeve. "Hurry, get back in."

More shots in rapid succession blasted from all directions. Léon hurried into the carriage. Maria saw a few people around the fountain fall, while others took off running. Following the shooting came the sound of horse hooves. Mounted soldiers rode into the gardens from the street, striking at anyone within reach with clubs or shooting those who ran. She hadn't seen any soldiers on the way, so they must have been hiding down alley ways or behind buildings.

She shook the reins and tried to get the horse to move. The mare lurched and stomped, but something stopped her moving forward. She tossed her head up and down, as if trying to break free from an unseen force. More shots rang out and then the carriage dipped down on the right.

"*Mademoiselle* Deraismes?" whispered a man's voice.

Maria turned and saw Dardelle half in the carriage, clinging to the side. "*Monsieur* Dardelle?"

"I'll explain everything once you get the carriage moving." He ducked down. "Now, please."

Léon took the reins and steered the carriage away from the gardens. Screams and curses mixed with occasional gunshots filled the air. When a soldier on foot ran past the carriage, Dardelle flung his body right across Maria and Léon. The soldier never stopped and continued on his way.

Léon shoved Dardelle. "*Mon dieu*, Dardelle, get off!" He yanked back on the reins and stopped the carriage.

Wriggling his way backward, Dardelle slipped from the carriage. "My apologies. *Merde.* How did those idiot soldiers know we were attacking the palace tonight?"

Maria managed to speak, "Tonight? Louise told me you were attacking tomorrow. I was going to meet with you tonight to try and urge you not to attack."

Dardelle glanced around. "Louise?" He let out a chuckle. "The Red Virgin of Montmartre! I suppose she wanted you to witness our great work with your own eyes."

"But I didn't come here to witness anything. Attacking the palace will create more trouble for the Commune. Don't you see that?"

Léon placed his arm around Maria's shoulder. "Because of Louise, we were placed in harm's way. Maria is ill, Dardelle. She came out tonight to put an end to this fighting between you and Thiers."

"Well, *Mademoiselle* Deraismes, take heart that we will not be attacking the palace tonight after all." With that, Dardelle ran off into the night.

The gunshots stopped and the night fell quiet again. A nervous twinge struck Maria's stomach. Dardelle's supporters and cohorts had been killed or arrested, yet Dardelle escaped once again unharmed. Only this time he didn't have his guards with him. Or perhaps they'd been killed by the soldiers. Either way, Dardelle didn't seem fazed. What sort of man runs off at the first hint of conflict, leaving his people to fend for themselves?

"Léon, take me home. There's nothing we can do here."

On the way, they saw Georges Martin walking in the direction of the Grand Orient Lodge. Léon pulled up alongside him and called out to get his attention.

Georges nodded politely and leaned in the carriage. "Léon, Maria, I didn't expect to see you. I thought you'd go straight home after we met."

Maria shook her head. "No. We went to the Tuileries."

"You did what? Does that mean Thiers didn't dispatch his soldiers after all?"

With a frown, Léon shook his head several times. "The soldiers were there, and so was Dardelle with a group of his supporters. He wasn't there to look around like we were told. He was planning to attack the palace tonight. I'm glad he was chased off."

"Yes, but people were shot." Maria winced as another pain shot through her body. "Georges, Dardelle escaped, leaving his people at the mercy of the soldiers. How can I support such a man?"

Georges studied Maria for a moment before he spoke. "It's the cause we support, not the man. I wondered why there were so many people going to the Tuileries. I ran into half a dozen. They wouldn't listen when I told them Thiers dispatched his troops to arrest Dardelle. I don't know if they thought I was lying, but they glared at me and kept going."

"At least you tried, Georges," Léon said with another shake of his head. "I'm taking Maria home, then I'll come back to the Grand Orient."

Georges nodded and continued on his way down the street. Léon clicked his tongue to get the horse moving and shook the reins to speed it up. Maria closed her eyes, thinking about the victims from tonight.

With the soldiers in the Tuileries, and Dardelle on the loose, the night had taken a dark turn. Maria thought of the dream for equality and how it now seemed fleeting, like a feather drifting aimlessly on the breeze, here one minute and gone the next. She wanted to reach up and grab the feather and bring it back to earth before it floated away permanently.

She had a nagging feeling that Dardelle's interest focused on making a fool of Thiers, no matter the cost to the people. Louise had known and worked with Dardelle for years, yet he always remained in the shadows. Until now. Could all of his work have been leading up to this moment, confronting Thiers at one of the most important symbols of tyranny; the Tuileries palace? But if that were true, he'd failed. He'd been the one attacked and chased away.

"Maria, we're here," Léon said in his soft, caring tone. "Stay there and I'll come around and help you out."

Anna stood in the doorway. Without waiting for Léon, Maria eased out of the carriage and headed to the house.

"I told you to wait for me!" Léon ran after her. "Why won't you ever listen to me?"

Maria smiled. "If I blithely listened to you, you'd think I'd gone mad."

He laughed. "Very true. But more importantly, I think Anna's cross with us. She has a very angry scowl on her face."

Anna did have a scowl, with her hands on her hips and her brow creased. Maria knew that look all too well, she'd be in for a tongue-lashing for going out.

As expected, once they were inside, Anna said what was on her mind. "I simply cannot understand the two of you. Both of you have been hurt during this siege and yet you persist in jumping back in. So tell me, did you warn everyone and save the world?"

Maria didn't have the energy to go into detail about the shooting and Dardelle, mostly because she didn't want Anna to feel vindicated. She took off her coat and hung it in the wardrobe. "Anna, you're always looking out for me, but on this occasion, your worry and concern is misplaced. We were fine. Not a soul came to the Tuileries. We came straight home. With your permission, may I retire to bed?"

The surprised and slightly disappointed look on Anna's face was worth the lie.

Anna sighed heavily. "Oh, well then, I'm glad to hear you didn't run into any trouble. Go right up to bed and I'll bring you a hot cup of broth. Léon, you're welcome to stay on the sofa. Berdine's in the guest room."

He shook his head and winked at Maria, acknowledging their shared secret about the Tuileries. "I have to stop by the Grand Orient Lodge, Anna. But thank you for your kindness. Oh, Maria, I'll drop by tomorrow afternoon so we can discuss an article about Dardelle and the Commune."

Maria winked back and went up the stairs before Anna could say anymore. Writing about the imprisonment of the innocent people and how Dardelle seemingly placed his followers in danger while always protecting himself would be a good idea. The people should know the type of man they believed in. She lay down without undressing, sinking slowly into the mattress. At that moment, there was nothing wrong in the world.

Chapter 39

Rain tumbled down heavily during the night, with brilliant flashes of lightning and crashes of thunder keeping Maria from sleeping very well. As a little girl in the country, thunderstorms were a source of enjoyment. She and Anna would each try to guess when the next rumble of thunder would occur and then laugh and giggle when they got it wrong. That was then. Now, an uneasiness hung in the air, a tingling sensation that made her nervous.

She lay under the covers for a time, worried about Alexandre and hoping Georges was tending to him. Such a kind and intelligent man as Alexandre couldn't die. She hadn't even told him exactly how she felt about him.

When she heard Anna or Berdine moving about, she got up and slipped into one of the few day dresses she hadn't donated and went downstairs. A roaring fire blazed and the faint smell of baking bread wafted from the kitchen. Her stomach growled.

"Anna," she called, nearing the kitchen.

Anna peeked out of the kitchen. "Oh, dear, I was hoping you'd be able to sleep in. I started a fire. Did the storm keep you awake, too?"

Maria nodded and sat at the kitchen table. A few plain scones were piled on a small tray. She picked one up and breathed in the delicious scent. "Did you make these this morning?" The scone was warm, but not hot. "You must have been up early."

"I couldn't sleep. I did the best I could with what we have left. We're out of currants and spices, so these are little more than flour, yeast, and the last of the butter and sugar. We've no jam left either. We desperately need supplies. What's the Commune Council doing about bringing food and clothing into Paris?"

"Nothing from what I can tell. Not a thing has improved since the Council took over. We'll all starve soon. I want to see if I can meet with the Council to discuss the lack of supplies. If they make a plea to Thiers, maybe he'll allow some food shipments in." Maria tore off a piece of the scone and nibbled on it. Bland, but she wasn't about to say that to Anna. At least they still had a bit of food. "Where's Berdine?"

With a silly smirk, Anna shrugged. "I'm not supposed to say."

"What are you talking about? Where is she?" Maria stood, hands on hips. "Anna, answer me."

"Oh, it's nothing bad. She had sense enough to stay in last night. It's supposed to be a surprise for you."

"What is?"

"She's up in her room...learning to read." Anna motioned to the chair. "Sit back down and eat your scone."

Maria couldn't help but smile. Berdine meant what she said about learning to read. Anna must have spent some time explaining the basics to her. No surprise there since Anna had the patience of a teacher. Once she could read, there'd be no stopping Berdine's desire to learn. Maria wanted to go up and see her, but as Anna said, Berdine wanted it to be a surprise.

After finishing the dry scone and the rest of the tea, Maria sat by the fire in the sitting room to warm up. The rain continued pounding on the roof, creating a rhythm that made her drowsy. She forced herself to stay awake and wished it would be a normal Sunday morning when they'd spend time visiting with friends and relaxing over a leisurely lunch, but nothing was normal. The prickly sensation she'd felt before hung on. Something was about to happen.

A log in the fireplace popped and sparks shot out. She jumped up to stamp out any embers, but the screen stopped the sparks from landing on the carpet. She wasn't usually so nervous. What had made her like that? Something about last night. Something Dardelle said.

He'd assured her that he wouldn't attack the palace. No, that wasn't quite right. He said he wouldn't attack the palace that night.

He never said he'd given up the plan entirely. If he carried out his plan, Thiers would be enraged and send more soldiers into the city.

"Anna! I'm going to Léon's."

"No, you're not," Anna said from the kitchen doorway. "It's cold and raining. You can wait until the weather clears and then go out."

"I feel better, and the fresh air will do me good. I need to talk with Léon."

Anna wiped her hands on her apron. "Then I'll come with you."

"And leave Berdine here by herself? I don't think she should be alone. She's probably still shaken from dealing with the soldiers." Maria slowly edged toward the front door.

"Well," Anna paused, "All right then. But don't you be long. I think we might have some turnips and carrots in the garden that I can boil into a stew."

"I thought all of the vegetables were gone." Maria could imagine a vegetable stew, thick and savory, simmering on the stove top. Their small vegetable garden never produced very much, but anything would be welcome at this point.

"They might not be ready to pick yet, but they'll still make a decent stew."

"Then I'll definitely be back for supper. You could turn an old shoe into a tasty meal."

"Well after today, an old shoe is what we'll be having unless we can get more supplies." Anna waved Maria away. "Go on then, but stay as dry and warm as you can."

"I will." With that, Maria put on her coat, grabbed an umbrella from the stand by the door, and stepped outside. She sniffed the air, fresh from the rain. The dirt, with its heavy, earthy scent and the wet flowers with their faint perfume filling the air was delightful.

She didn't want to take the carriage because the mare had been exhibiting signs of a lame foreleg, limping and stumbling every now and then. The sixteen-year-old mare hadn't been in the best of health because of the poor-quality food she'd been receiving. How sad that even the animals of Paris suffered. The whole city was in a disastrous state.

Even with the umbrella, Maria became soaked from the driving rain. Wet or not, she enjoyed being outside. Throughout her life, she'd had a kinship with the natural world, especially when things weren't going well. She could retreat to the garden or take a walk in the park to escape the trouble of the world and clear her head. Although now that the Commune showed signs of failure and Thiers' troops sporadically attacked the city, escape from the world became harder and harder.

After an inordinate amount of time dodging puddles and the occasional water splash from a passing carriage, she arrived at Léon's house and knocked on the door. Once she asked his opinion about Dardelle, she'd ask him to take her to Georges so she could visit with Alexandre. She knocked on the door again.

Léon opened it wide and ushered her inside. "What are you doing out on a day like this?"

No point responded to that question. "Listen, Léon, I think Dardelle plans to attack the palace." She folded the umbrella and slipped it into a stand by the door. "If he does, he'll enrage Thiers."

"We definitely think alike, because I noticed how he neglected to say that he'd never attack the palace." He shut the door.

"Exactly. So what do we do?" She took off her wet coat and slung it over an old cane-back chair. "I also need to look in on Alexandre while I'm out."

"I knew you would." Léon motioned to a chair. "Sit down and I'll show you my latest work. We can visit Georges and Alexandre later."

"You've been writing? How did you find the time? I haven't picked up a pen since Versailles."

"I spent a little time early this morning. This blasted storm kept me awake most of the night." He picked up a piece of paper from the desk. "Let me know what you think."

She read through his article carefully. In only a page, he'd managed to capture the horror of the trip to Versailles. But for full effect, it needed enhancing so the world would truly see how the Communards and innocent citizens were treated. "It's good, although—"

"You'd add in more details to evoke sympathy and understanding."

She smiled. "You can always read what's on my mind. Before I take pen in hand, though, I'd like to see Alexandre to put my worried mind to rest."

He laughed and took the paper back. "Then I suppose my hard work will have to wait. I can't get the paper published right now anyway. My office is too close to the west side where soldiers scurry about like a mob of rats in the sewers."

"I know. What if the soldiers have broken into your office and destroyed your equipment?"

"I don't want to think of that. It's taken me a lifetime to buy that new printing press. Do you want to warm up before we head off to Georges' house? I have a pot of hot tea in the kitchen."

"No." Maria motioned to the door. "I want to go now." She'd waited long enough to visit Alexandre.

"Come out the back way. I've already hitched my horse to my carriage. I'd planned on driving over to your house later on in the day."

Maria grabbed her umbrella and went with Léon to the stable where they climbed into the carriage. He drove the covered carriage to the street, although with the rain so unrelenting, the small cover did little to keep them dry and Maria shivered. She couldn't wait to see Alexandre and hoped Georges had good news about his injury. The thought of holding his hand again warmed her inside. If Alexandre did indeed need surgery to save his life, then she'd find a way to get him out of Paris.

Driving through the streets toward Georges' house felt like passing through a cemetery. Paris—cold, wet, and dark with no signs of life anywhere—had died. The slick cobblestone roadway and tree branches bent from the weight of the rain pressing down on them added to the gloomy sensation. She tried to stop shivering but couldn't. It wasn't only the cold, but that deep down feeling of dread that hung over her.

Léon slowed the carriage near Georges' house. Before they had the chance to stop completely, Georges opened the door and dashed down the path to them.

He nodded a quick greeting. "Well, good day. I was about to send word to you, Maria, that I took Alexandre to another doctor, Dr. Goudie. He's a good friend of mine, a Mason, and has treated a lot of head wounds. I thought Alexandre should see a specialist."

"Why? What's happened to him?" She asked as all sorts of images of Alexandre writhing in agony flashed in her mind.

"Oh, please don't worry, Maria. He's doing fine, it's just that head wounds can turn out for the worst if not monitored by a specialist. It's only a precaution. Léon, you know where Goudie lives, don't you?"

Léon thought for a moment. "I think so. I haven't been to his house in quite a while though. He's a couple of streets over, isn't he? Small house with the rose garden out front?"

"That's the one." Georges dipped his head politely to Maria and ran back into his house.

Léon shook the reins and continued down the street. Before long, they stopped in front of Goudie's house, a modest place made of red brick with two chimneys, one at either end of the house, yet neither one produced smoke. It had to be near freezing inside. That certainly wasn't a good atmosphere for Alexandre to be in.

Léon climbed from the carriage and raised a large umbrella before helping her out. She put up her own umbrella so he could use his own to stay dry, and followed him to the door. A man— slightly built with a long, hooked nose, and eyes set a bit too close together—answered. With his brow pinched and his eyes flitting around, he didn't look like a physician, but more like someone guilty and afraid.

Léon smiled politely. "*Bonjour.* You must be Frederick. I believe we met a year or so ago. We've come to see Doctor Goudie's new patient, Alexandre Weill."

So the man wasn't the doctor after all. A servant or butler perhaps. Maria looked past Frederick and saw the house cloaked in darkness. No warmth came from inside. This was no place for Alexandre. "What's happened?" she asked softly.

Frederick waved them inside and shut the door behind them. He mumbled, "They came and took Doctor Goudie in the middle of the night." He shook his head and threw up his arms. "They barged in and took him! Armed soldiers, in a physician's home. None of us are safe!"

"What!" Léon rushed forward and ran from room to room.

Maria followed after him, finding each room empty. One room, the examination room, had papers strewn about, books and medical instruments tossed onto the floor. "Léon, what happened? Where's Alexandre?"

"I don't know. Why would soldiers take Goudie? He isn't even actively involved in the Commune." Léon went back to Frederick. "Where did they take him? What did they say? Did they take Alexandre Weill as well?"

Frederick nodded and began fussing around with a dusting rag, sweeping it over the nearest furniture. "Such a mess, such a mess. It'll take me all day to clean up."

Maria's breath hitched in her throat. To think soldiers would take a sick patient away from his doctor was unconscionable. "What do we do now, Léon? We have to find Alexandre."

"And Goudie. The Freemasons will consider this a personal attack against the Masons. At least I do. Goudie's a high-ranking Mason. I'd bet that's the reason they took him. Thiers might be trying to locate members of the Brotherhood, round them up because of their involvement in supporting the Commune."

Maria found it hard to concentrate on except Alexandre, but she did remember what Berdine said. "Léon, the *Hôtel des Invalides*. That's where Berdine said she went to meet the soldiers. I'm sure that's where they'd take them. It must be their headquarters."

"I think you're right."

"We have to go there and try to get them freed."

Léon objected, "But how? Thiers has the west side secured. If we try to cross over the Seine, we'll run into soldiers and get captured. I'm not going to let anything happen to you again."

"Léon, please, we've got to try. If you don't come with me, I'll go on my own."

"All right, all right. But at the first sign of trouble, I'm turning around." He called out to Frederick, who'd wandered off down the hall, "We're leaving now! Will you be all right here by yourself? Frederick?"

When no response came, Maria and Léon hurried to the carriage. Léon shook the reins hard and turned the carriage around toward the Seine, a fair distance from Goudie's house. Even though the horse trotted quickly, it took too long getting to the end of the street. Maria leaned forward, silently urging the horse on.

The rain finally eased and the clouds thinned, allowing a trace of brightness to break through. Without the constant hammering of the rain, Maria's thoughts drifted to how the eerie silence pervaded the city. She almost wished for the time before the Commune when music and people moving about filled the streets. There was no going back, though, and now Thiers ached to crush Dardelle and the Commune. Dardelle would do everything in his power to stop Thiers. While she also wanted Thiers gone, the constant battles meant there'd be no winners.

That feeling she'd had all day had to have been because Alexandre was taken prisoner, and the Commune would soon be destroyed by Thiers. A street marker ahead said they were almost to the *rue de Rivoli*, which meant they'd be at the Tuileries soon. From there they could cross the Seine at one of the more distant bridges, not too close to the *Hôtel des Invalides*, perhaps the *Pont du Carrousel* at the eastern end of the Tuileries. That is if soldiers weren't blocking the way.

"Léon, what if we can't get across the Seine this time? We got across before because the soldiers hadn't occupied the city. But now..." Maria leaned back.

He pulled on the reins and slowed the horse. "I don't know. If I had some money, I could bribe the soldiers to let us across."

"I don't have anything either. But I'm still willing to try to cross if you are."

He nodded and continued onto *rue de Rivoli*. As they neared the Tuileries palace on their right, Maria smelled an acrid odor hanging in the air. The closer they got, the stronger the smell, sharp and stinging her eyes. What was it? Burning oil? Then she saw smoke pluming upward from the palace itself, filling the sky. The odor became stronger. Léon steered the horse to the far side of the street and stopped.

"The palace is on fire," Léon said in a stunned voice.

"Dardelle. He's condemned us all." Maria watched for a moment as the blaze grew, engulfing fully half of the palace. Flames of red shot skyward and smoke billowed from the windows.

It wouldn't be long before the soldiers crossed from the west bank to the Tuileries. They'd swarm into the east side of Paris in a furious mass, shooting and killing everyone they saw. Maria turned away. Dardelle undoubtedly relied on inciting the soldiers and force the people who'd all but given up the fight to again join the battle. But perhaps some good could come from Dardelle's actions. The palace symbolized the monarchy and by destroying it, he'd made a point that nobody could ignore.

Maria thought for a second. The fire might work to their advantage. "Léon, if Thiers' men cross over the river, the bridges will be open. We can cross then."

"I doubt any of the bridges will be completely unguarded."

"I won't give up. Not when we're this close." Her stomach hurt from the smoke, yet not so bad she'd give up. She would do anything if it meant the difference between finding Alexandre or abandoning him.

They drove down the *rue de Rivoli* and turned left down a street leading to the *Pont du Carrousel*. Shouts and the thunderous sound of countless horse hooves on the cobblestones rang out. The army had arrived on the east bank and were heading toward them.

Immediately, Léon turned the carriage around and headed back toward the *rue de Rivoli*. "Maria, keep an eye out behind us." He spurred the horse on with an urgent shake of the reins.

Maria twisted around in her seat and saw a line of foot soldiers, fully armed, their uniforms dark blue, and their knee-high boots polished glossy black. Bayoneted rifles were carried in the ready position at the soldiers' sides, barrels pointing up to the sky. What a truly horrifying image to behold, one that would be burned in her memory, like the attack at the *Hôtel de Ville*.

The soldiers must have noticed the carriage, because a whistle blew and they charged, with their rifles now pointed forward. Maria gasped. "Léon, they're coming!"

"I'm not deaf, Maria, I can hear them." He shouted at the horse and continued to whip the reins up and down.

Before long, they were right back at the burning palace. Communards had seemingly come out of nowhere and were rushing about, dancing in the streets in front of the palace, cheering, and waving red flags and banners. Léon pulled the carriage off the main street and stopped. They were now trapped between Dardelle's followers and the merciless soldiers.

Soldiers began to fan out as they poured onto the *rue de Rivoli*, surrounding the palace and forming a large circle around the Communards.

"Hold on tight, I'm getting us out of here." He got the horse moving again, but before they got far, a small contingent of soldiers blocked their way with rifles lowered and pointed forward. Léon mumbled softly, "Forgive me, Maria."

"I'm here willingly. There's nothing to be forgiven." Maria looked up at the dark, smoky sky. Ash fell like snow, filtering down over the Louvre and the Tuileries gardens, covering everything in a gray shroud.

Expecting to be arrested any minute, Maria waited. Léon dropped the reins and placed his hands in his lap. But nothing happened. The soldiers advanced a few more steps, then unexpectedly raised their rifles again to the carry position and turned around. They marched away, back toward the palace.

Maria let out a long exhale. "I thought they had us. I suppose they decided two people in a carriage weren't as important as the burning palace."

Without a word, Léon took hold of the reins and maneuvered the carriage to the *rue de Rivoli* but headed away from the trouble this time. Maria turned in her seat and saw more and more soldiers filling the streets. Communards faced the soldiers, waving their banners and flags, shouting and mocking, daring the soldiers to fire their weapons.

"Léon, we should go back and help them."

"And what would we do? We were fortunate to get away from the soldiers with our lives."

"But if those soldiers let us go, perhaps others will be sympathetic—"

"Two of those soldiers are members at my Lodge, Maria. They only let us go because I'm the master of the lodge. We were lucky. I'm not willing to rely on future luck. Dardelle knew what he was doing by burning the palace. He has to deal with the consequences."

"But he's taking innocent people with him."

"Don't you think I know that! They are with him willingly. Remember that."

She wanted to say something, to offer a word to let him know she understood how he felt, but no words would come. As the carriage rolled along, putting more distance between them and the conflagration, clouds gathered and a crash of thunder boomed overhead, followed shortly by a downpour. At least the rain would douse the fire. But it wouldn't stop the soldiers.

When they were almost to the *Hôtel de Ville*, with the palace out of view, Louise, bareback on a black horse, rode by clutching a pole with a bright red flag secured at the top. She smiled at Maria, shouted *liberty!* and galloped away.

"Take me home, Léon. I want to be home. Louise won't be coming back this time." The end of the Commune would come quickly, and with it, the end of hope for a new Paris.

Chapter 40

Maria hated driving away from the burning Tuileries palace, leaving the people to fend for themselves, but what choice did she have? Outnumbered and unarmed, they didn't stand a chance. As Léon steered the carriage through the streets, the rain eased off, allowing the heavy odor of blood to fill the air. He managed to stay ahead of the soldiers, who had quickly crossed the Seine in multitudes and set about rounding up anyone on the street.

Soldiers scattered everywhere behind them, cracking the butts of their rifles over the heads of resisters or firing directly into gatherings of people. Maria couldn't stand to watch any longer and turned, staring straight ahead.

Soldiers rushed past the carriage, too preoccupied to bother stopping it. Each time they did, Maria held her breath, certain she was about to die. Léon neared her house where Anna stood on the front stoop, staring forlornly into the distance. Even seeing Anna safe didn't fill the empty place in Maria's heart that only Alexandre could fill. He'd become a casualty of the Commune, and there was nothing she could do to help him.

Léon pulled up in front of the house and waited while Maria got out. He handed her the umbrella, but she refused. She wanted the drizzle to wash away the scent of death that clung to her. She plodded up the path to Anna's waiting arms.

Anna wiped away particles of ash that clung to Maria's face. "Thank God you're all right. We heard that the palace is on fire and that the Commune is all but finished." She pointed in the direction of the Tuileries. "There's smoke everywhere. The city is on fire."

While Maria knew the Commune had died along with innocent people, hearing Anna say the words made it sink in. The people had made a simple request for equality. They wanted equal rights and opportunities. Was that so much to ask? Why was Thiers so threatened by social change? He must be afraid of sharing power with women and the lower-classes.

She turned and waved to Léon. A spreading plume of smoke rose in the distance. She went inside and took off her coat, letting it fall to the ground. "I feel sick, Anna."

"Sit down and let me get you some of your tea."

Maria gently pushed her away. "No, no, not physically sick. It's my soul that aches. I feel so helpless. So hopeless. What can we do now?"

Anna shook her head. "Find another way to continue the fight."

Maria nodded, happy to hear Anna wasn't ready to give up. A small fire burned in the fireplace, not enough to heat the house though. It no longer felt like home. Maria slumped onto the sofa, her eyes drifting over the room. "Where's Berdine?"

"Oh, she should be home any time. She left a while ago to help the doctors at Saint-Sulpice."

"Saint-Sulpice?" Maria hadn't thought of Saint-Sulpice in years. She'd visited it only once before with Papa. Why would Berdine go there?

Anna continued, "Yes, you remember, the seminary is a hospital. Berdine helps by washing the linens."

"Oh, yes, I do remember that."

Saint-Sulpice was a beautiful church, with a golden pulpit and enormous pipe organ. Papa took her to see the Gnomon, an old device tracking the sun, which the priests used to determine the exact date of the equinoxes and solstices.

Maria drifted back to her childhood. "Anna, can you remember when Papa said science was vital to understanding the world. He took us to Saint-Sulpice to show us the Gnomon and gave us a lesson about the lens in the stained-glass window. If I'm not mistaken, there's a line made up of brass running along the floor."

"That's right. He told us how the sun would shine through the lens and cast light on the brass line. Wasn't it used to determine the correct date for Easter?"

"I think so." Maria sighed. "Those were happy times. The Gnomon doesn't matter now though, does it? If I could go back to those days when we had no worries and were busy learning about everything, I would."

"Well, Berdine is there and can look upon the Gnomon as often as she pleases. Let's tell her all about it when she returns."

"We should...wait." Maria had an awful thought. "Anna, Saint-Sulpice is on the west bank. Thiers has the west bank."

Anna's face blanched. Maria stood up and paced around the room. If Berdine had already crossed the Seine, she might be safe. But if she remained at the seminary, she'd be in danger if the soldiers raided the church.

The clock on the wall chimed four times. If Thiers' entire army had been brought over to the Tuileries palace, Berdine wouldn't stand a chance.

"I should have stopped her," Anna cried. "I wasn't thinking. I know where Saint-Sulpice is. Why didn't I stop her?"

Maria hugged Anna tightly and whispered, "We're all frazzled and not thinking straight. And it's what Berdine wanted to do. I'm sure she's fine. She'll stay in the seminary with the patients until it's safe to come out." Hopefully she sounded confident and none of her doubt came through. Anna certainly didn't need any more tension heaped upon her.

"Do you think so? Do you really think she's all right? What if the soldiers catch her again and want more information about Dardelle? She knows nothing."

Maria stared out the front window. "I doubt the soldiers would know she's at the seminary."

Although it continued to rain, smoke filled the sky, and sodden ash covered the path and the trees. Paris now looked like an entry way into hell. Every now and then, a bedraggled person ran past the house, shielding their eyes from the ashy rain. What were they running from? The soldiers? The fire? The immorality of the government? She wanted to join them, to run and not stop until she reached a place where everyone had the right to live in peace.

"I think I'll go lie down." Maria started for the stairs, but a loud commotion outside made her stop and go back to the window. A large group of people passed by the house. Their clothes were tattered and bloodied, some were limping, some were being supported by others. Two large men with dirty bandages wrapped around their heads pulled a wooden vegetable cart behind them, its rickety wooden wheels squealing with each turn.

They stopped and one of the men with the cart shouted, "*Mademoiselle* Deraismes! Is this the home of *Mademoiselle* Deraismes?"

Maria flung open the door and dashed out into the rain. "I'm Maria Deraismes."

The man motioned her forward. Maria ran down the path. A sheet was draped over the cart. A feeling of dread washed over her. Was it Alexandre under the sheet? Why hadn't she insisted that Léon try to cross the Seine to the *Hôtel des Invalides*? They could have made it if they'd only tried. Now Alexandre might lie dead in an old merchant's cart. She wanted to scream, to cry out, but her throat tightened too much to let any sound out. She'd never forgive herself. Never.

She stepped onto the road and stared at the sheet. It had once been white but now a layer of sooty smudge covered it. "Please..." Her voice came out in a choked whisper. But she couldn't bring herself to say anything more.

The men carefully lifted half of the sheet, holding it aloft so the rain wouldn't fall inside the cart. Maria held her breath and moved closer. She closed her eyes and remembered Alexandre, full of life. His quick wit, his insightful writing. She'd treasure their friendship until the day she died. Opening her eyes, she looked down and let out her breath.

She had a brief sense of relief that it wasn't Alexandre, but it quickly vanished when her eyes fell upon Berdine. Her beautiful face, now splattered with blood, and her blue cotton blouse stained red. Her eyes were closed, but she wasn't dead. Her chest rose and fell in short bursts.

"Berdine," Maria said softly.

Berdine's eyes fluttered and opened. "*Mademoiselle...Maria...*"

Maria turned to the men. "What happened? Who did this?"

"Soldiers. They came into the hospital and went through, shooting the patients one by one. The nurses, bless their souls, stood in front of their patients, but the soldiers shot them as well. Shot each woman in the head." The man averted his eyes and shook his head sadly. "They even shot the doctors. When they'd finished, they realized there were still helpers around. Janitors, and us cooks, it didn't matter. We got out, but Berdine received a shot in the back as she ran. She said to bring her here."

Maria crawled half into the small wagon and smoothed Berdine's hair. "I should have been there with you, Berdine. I'm so very sorry for leaving you alone."

With a pale hand, Berdine reached out and grasped Maria's dress. "You saved me, Maria." She drew in a deep, painful breath. "My...coat pocket."

Maria felt around Berdine's coat and reached into a large pocket. She pulled out Hugo's *Les Miserables*. "Is this what you wanted?"

Berdine nodded, her eyes closing slightly. "Tell *Monsieur* Hugo...that I was only...able to read the first two pages."

Wiping a tear, Maria leaned down and kissed Berdine's cheek. "When you're better, you can finish it."

"I don't think I'll get better. But it's all right, I'm a free woman, Maria. You freed me from insignificance. I am someone. If I can read…so can every woman. Don't stop…" Berdine coughed and groaned. "Don't stop fighting until all women are free. Educate them, Maria." She coughed again, harder this time, and closed her eyes. One final labored breath, and then she was gone.

"Maria," Anna's whispered.

Maria noticed Anna helping to hold up the covering. "Oh, Anna."

Maria gave Berdine a final kiss on the forehead and backed out of the cart. She stood in the gentle rain and looked around. Sodden ash and half-burned papers drifted down from the sky, sticking to the wet cobbles and lodging in between tree branches. Most of the people had scattered, limping away down the street.

Anna let go of the cover and took Maria's hand. "Don't mourn her, celebrate her life. You made a difference to her."

"How?" Maria pulled away. "How did I make a difference? She's dead. It didn't matter to the soldiers if she could read a book or not." Her mind reeled.

One of the men tapped Maria on the shoulder. "*Mademoiselle*, I knew Berdine. You gave her hope. That's how you freed her. She meant you gave her hope."

What good was it to give someone hope only to have them die at the hands of an unjust government? Hope meant nothing unless actualized. The Latin phrase *acta non verba* floated into Maria's head. Action, not words. Hadn't she done the opposite? She'd spent her entire adult life writing and making speeches about equality and human rights, but what had she really done? Others, like Louise and Dardelle, did the real work. They were with the people, fighting, literally, for their beliefs and a better world.

"Maria," Anna said softly, "We should go back inside. They'll take care of Berdine."

The men with the cart nodded and carefully replaced the cover, then continued pulling the cart. It rolled along, giving off a tired squeak with each turn of the wheels. A crushing sadness made her entire body leaden.

The rain stopped, leaving everything dripping. Maria looked down and realized she had the book. The rain ruined it, yet she couldn't bring herself to throw it away. Instead, she clutched it to her chest and walked slowly up the path to the house. Ash and burned papers still floated from the sky.

She half stumbled up the stairs to her bedroom, her sanctuary, and closed the door. The daguerreotype of her parents stood as a reminder of happier times. If only she could be a carefree child again, enjoying the innocence of youth, where there was no killing and no worries, only play. But she wasn't a child, and Paris was not a playground. The streets were awash with blood.

A sharp piercing pain in her stomach made her cry out. Her insides felt twisted. She dropped to her knees and crawled to the bed, but didn't have the strength to climb onto the mattress. She lay on her side, curled up in agony with her eyes squeezed shut.

The door opened and the floor creaked under muffled footsteps. It had to be Anna, yet all sound evaporated into nothingness. She could no longer feel any pain. Could this be what it was like to die? If death ended in a quiet peace, she'd welcome it. Or would she? There still wasn't equality and peace in France. She'd have to fight against the hands of death, to struggle out from their grip. She had to live.

Chapter 41

Maria opened her eyes to bright sunshine. She'd been lying on the floor of her bedroom, but now she lay in her bed. The gray clouds vanished and the sun shone in through the window. Hopefully a new day would bring an end to the violence.

She threw the covers off and stood on shaky legs. Anna must have dressed her in her nightgown. The wooden floor felt warm on her feet, in fact, the entire room was warm from the sun pouring in.

Maria stopped at the window and took in cloudless blue sky. No smoke or ash fell. A man on a bicycle rode by nonchalantly. He didn't look afraid at all. Perhaps he was one of Thiers' men. But he didn't wear a soldier's uniform.

She sat in a chair beside the window and rested her head in her hands, remembering Berdine.

The door opened and Anna came in with a bowl and a towel on a tray.

"Maria? You're awake. How are you feeling?"

"A little sleepy." She swallowed to coat her dry throat and continued, "When I'm up to it, I want to send a message to the soldier in charge at the *Hôtel des Invalides*. I must find out about Alexandre."

Anna put the tray down on the desk and sat on the edge of the bed. "Maria, you've been unconscious for a week. It's Sunday the 28th. Thiers has firm control of Paris and all the prisoners at the *Hôtel des Invalides* were..." she paused and looked down at the ground. "The prisoners were either exiled or...executed."

Maria struggled to understand what Anna said. "Stop lying to me, Anna. I know you don't want me getting involved further with Thiers, but I have to. I can't rest until I know what's happened to Alexandre."

"I'm not lying. Léon spent the last two days trying to get a list of the prisoners and their fate, but it's like he's talking to a lamppost. He did hear, though, that Louise is due to stand trial next week. But there's no news of anyone else."

"Stop it! I haven't been lying here for a week, and you know it." Maria stood, slightly nauseous. "It's just my stomach again. And now that I've had a good night's sleep, I can—"

"You were near death, Maria. The doctor had no faith that you'd ever wake up again. You've been lying there a step away from meeting Mother and Father in the next world. You have indeed been unconscious for almost a week. Why would I lie about that?"

Maria stared back out the window. The streets were cleaned not only of the ash, but all the papers that were strewn about. "You are telling me the truth, aren't you? But what of the Tuileries Palace? What about Dardelle and the Communards? Where is everyone?" She turned to face Anna.

"Well, like I said, they captured Louise, but not Dardelle. You should feel lucky that you weren't awake to witness the horror of the past week. Soldiers killed anyone on the street, especially anyone near the remaining barricades. They killed women and children. Lined them up against a wall and shot them, or so I heard." Anna wiped away a stream of tears. "I closed up the doors and windows and hid inside like a frightened child."

"I don't believe it. Even Thiers wouldn't do a thing like that."

"No? Do you remember that large blue and white house on the *rue de Rosiers*? The one with the black wrought iron fence around it? Well, Thiers' men used that as a holding area to bring Communards for execution. They rounded up everyone and then lined them up against a wall and shot them. Those who weren't murdered set fire to every building on the *rue de Rivoli*. They burned the Ministry of Finance, banks, even the Tuileries gardens. But it didn't stop the soldiers. Nothing stopped the soldiers."

"How many were killed?"

"There's no exact tally, but Léon estimates well over 20,000." Anna wiped her eyes again.

"What?" Maria couldn't breathe. She gasped for air, finally opening the window and leaning out for fresh air. "That can't be right. Fewer than that died in the revolution."

"I know. They didn't even give the dead proper burials. They dumped them into a ditch, one on top of the other, like garbage. This isn't the Paris we grew up in, Maria."

After another deep inhalation, Maria shut the window, blocking out the city. "And the rest of the world? Have they done nothing?"

"No. They considered the Commune to be a threat to their own governments and they all supported Thiers." Anna went to Maria and felt her forehead. "You're warm. Get back in bed and I'll bring you something to eat."

"How can I eat?"

"There's food again in Paris now that Thiers won. It's a ploy to make the people believe he's the best one to govern."

"No, Anna, I can't fill my stomach when our brothers and sisters were murdered, and Paris has been thrust back a hundred years by the bourgeoisie. I don't think I'll ever pick up a fork again. I'd rather starve."

Anna motioned to the bed. "Get in bed and we'll talk about you martyring yourself later. Léon should be here soon. Even during the fighting, he came. He comes by every day about this time to check on you."

Maria shook her head and breathed in and out for a few seconds. "Do you think they killed Alexandre? Would they have killed him for no reason?" Maria crawled into bed and curled up on her side. "Was I dreaming, or was I told that all of the patients at Saint-Sulpice were killed?"

Anna pulled up the covers and tucked them in. "Unfortunately, it wasn't a dream. Let's try to put the past behind us. You're terribly ill and shouldn't be worrying about anything except getting better."

Not worrying? Maria could do nothing but worry about the fate of Paris and her people, and of course Alexandre. Her heart was empty, a hollow shell. Had everything been for nothing? Surely the rest of the world would condemn the deaths of 20,000 people, even if they disagreed with the Commune.

"Anna! Anna!" Léon shouted from downstairs.

"Up here, Léon! Maria's awake!" Anna shouted back.

His footsteps thumped up the stairs and he rushed into the room. "Maria!" He bounded to the bed and knelt, giving her a hard kiss on the cheek. "Tell me I'm not imagining it. Tell me you're really, truly awake and well."

Maria scooted up in bed. "I'm awake. But I wish I'd woken from a terrible nightmare. Anna told me about Thiers' rampage. How could this happen?"

He got up and dragged a chair to the bedside. "It's criminal," he said. "But perhaps I can cheer you up a little."

"How? I don't think I'll ever smile again."

"Alexandre Weill lives." Léon drew in a deep breath and took Maria's hand. "Remember my friend, Doctor Goudie, who cared for Alexandre? And remember how I said the Freemasons would consider Doctor Goudie's abduction as an attack on them personally? Well, they did...we did. We marched, two hundred men strong, to the *Hôtel des Invalides* and demanded their release. Not one soldier stopped us the entire way. I don't know why. Maybe they figured the fighting was all but over and there was no point in harassing us. But whatever the reason, we got Goudie and Alexandre spared from execution."

Maria sat up. "Where is he? Alexandre, I mean."

"Wait, wait, don't get too excited. They were exiled along with Louise and a group of other Communards."

Maria slumped back onto the pillows. At least exile wasn't death. "They're safe though. So where were they exiled?"

"The island of New Caledonia." Léon pulled a crumpled sheet of paper from his pocket and straightened it. "I'm working on an article about the trial and exile. You won't believe how cowardly Thiers was. To find Louise, he put her mother in prison and had her beaten every day. Once Louise found out, she surrendered. And you want to know what Louise said at her trial?" He glanced at the paper and read, "Since it seems that any heart which beats for liberty has the right only to a small amount of lead, I demand my share. If you are not cowards, kill me." He folded the paper and slipped it back into his pocket. "She even yelled 'long live the Commune', and that if they didn't kill her, she'd avenge the martyrs. How she managed to live and be exiled is a mystery to me."

"Not to me." Maria closed her eyes and saw the image of Louise, red sash around her waist and fire in her eyes. Whether it was bravery or foolhardiness, Louise was the strongest woman Maria had ever met. "It's simple, Léon, they didn't want to make a martyr *of her*. Much better to exile her on a faraway island than to leave her memory forever stamped on Paris."

"I suppose you're right. Anyway, we're petitioning to get Goudie and Alexandre released from exile as they did nothing wrong."

Maria squeezed Léon's hand. "And what of Alexandre's injury? Now he'll never get treatment." Even if Alexandre was resigned to dying, it hurt to think that he'd die on a lonely island in the Pacific Ocean so far from France.

With a sly smile, Léon leaned in close. "Goudie got a message to me before they were shipped out. The cold and dampness of the cell they were in somehow kept the swelling of Alexandre's brain down and he seems to have recovered well. He's still plagued with headaches, but he made it a week without any further trouble."

"You couldn't tell me that sooner?" A heavy weight lifted. "All right, so where do we go from here? We should organize a banquet, a public meeting to discuss in open forum the ramifications of Thiers' government."

Léon stared at her and shook his head. "Not so fast, *mon amie*. There are curfews and restrictions governing gatherings and meetings. No more than two people are allowed to gather openly. Be patient. Things will settle soon. Besides, from what the doctor says, you'll need plenty of rest. He said you're malnourished and weak."

"Doctor Pouchard?"

"No. No one's seen him. Rumor has it he managed to escape to England where he has relatives."

"Oh." Maria would miss Pouchard. He understood her and her illness. She didn't particularly trust anyone else.

"Georges is too busy to devote to your round-the-clock care, so he recommended a colleague of his."

All caught up with the happenings over the past week, Maria rested and chatted through the day about the tragedy of the Commune and where Dardelle could be. When it grew dark. Anna lit lamps and brought up a tray of roast capon, fresh sliced baguette with strawberry jam, and a pot of chamomile and lemon tea. As they ate, the conversation came around to issues of equality and state-sponsored education for all citizens.

Maria thought of Berdine and how she'd taught herself to read, which gave her hope that she could one day climb out of the trap that poverty put her in. Poor Berdine. She gave her life helping others. Her memory should not be lost. No woman should suffer as she had. Liberty could only be obtained through equality.

The hour grew late. Léon left and Anna went to bed, but too many thoughts ran through Maria's head for her to sleep. As Léon said, they'd have to wait a while to begin hosting banquets and speeches, but as soon as the time was right, she'd push ahead, continuing where she left off. She sat down at her desk, kissed the daguerreotype of her parents and with pen in hand, began jotting down the events of the Commune while it was all still fresh in her mind.

Chapter 42

1873, Paris

The two years that followed the massacre of the Commune saw Paris brought into a time of peace, although Thiers' conservative government continued to create a rift between the monarchists and the remaining supporters of equality. To his credit, Thiers managed to oversee the complete withdrawal of German troops from Paris and paid off the war debt to Germany, but his popularity suffered regardless and by May, he resigned his presidency. The new Provisional President, Patrice MacMahon, a duke, and the leader of the Versailles troops during the Commune, replaced Thiers.

In late September, Maria sat in her garden with Hubertine Auclert, Léon's new secretary and a very outspoken young feminist not unlike Louise. Hubertine provided good company and had excellent insights about the new government, yet she leaned toward using violence rather than a benign expression of protest. This irritated Léon and several times he'd threatened to fire her.

Maria pulled her coat collar up when a chill set in and took a sip of the tea. "So, Hubertine, what news do you have of Louise? I've heard there's now a plague of typhus on New Caledonia." She had an inkling of what New Caledonia was like from a brief letter she'd received from Alexandre almost six months ago but wanted to know more.

He'd been released from his exile, thanks to the Freemasons' persistent petitioning, but he'd gone to nearby Australia to live, rather than return to France. The letter had been apologetic and kind yet lacking in the sweetness and emotion she would have expected. Alexandre wrote that he was well, although thin and feeling older than his years, but healthy enough. It tore at Maria that not once did he beg her to sail to Australia or tell her that he missed her. He'd changed and started a new life without her. But try as she might, she couldn't forget him.

Hubertine removed a knitted cap from her head and shook out her shoulder-length hair. "It's a haven for disease, Maria. But I've confidence that one day soon Louise will be back amongst us."

"I hope you're right." Maria finished the tea and glanced up at the sky. It might rain or snow. The cloud cover became a darker gray and the crispness in the air led her to believe snow more likely.

Hubertine excused herself after finishing her tea and scone, leaving Maria alone with her thoughts. She got up and wandered around the garden. Not much had really changed over the years. Women were still repressed and couldn't find decent employment, poverty still raged through the city and anyone publicly denouncing MacMahon found themselves arrested.

How depressing to see such little change. So many died hoping they'd make a difference, and while many people honored their sacrifice, the government still favored the wealthy. To make matters worse, her stomach ailment had her spending most days at home, resting and feeling useless.

When the weather made it too uncomfortable to stay outside any longer, she went in and sat down at the kitchen table idly picking at a piece of bread.

"Maria," Anna said from the doorway, "Léon's carriage and driver are outside waiting for you."

"Oh, dear, I'd completely forgotten about the meeting." She stood and headed for the front door.

Anna followed after her. "Why must you continue to hold meetings? If MacMahon's spies catch the scent, they'll burst in like a pack of hungry wolves and arrest you all."

"It's in the Grand Orient Lodge. Even MacMahon wouldn't try to interfere with a Masonic meeting."

"A Masonic meeting? You can't attend a—"

"It's not really a Masonic meeting, Anna. That's our subterfuge." The Masons were willing to sponsor their buildings for meetings and discussions on equality, yet they still steadfastly refused to admit women into the Order.

To Maria, it was hypocritical of them to speak about equal rights and treatment of women and then turn around and deny them entry. Thankfully, a growing number and men, and women, thought the same way as she did. Both Léon and Georges Martin had talked of making a formal petition to the Grand Orient to initiate women as a unified stand against misogynistic and prejudicial views. She gladly supported them.

She grabbed her coin purse off the table by the door and hurried out. Léon waited on the street with his large Phaeton carriage, his driver nodding to her as she approached. Léon put on new wheels recently and had the interior reupholstered, but it still looked as old and ugly as it always had. She didn't mind, though, because it made her feel more like one of the ordinary working-class people, her people. Léon would never waste money buying a new carriage like so many of the bourgeoisie did for the sole purpose of showing off their wealth. That was one of the reasons she loved him and treasured his friendship.

Once in the Phaeton, she watched people strolling by, their gait not as lively as it once had been, or at least it seemed that way to her. The wealthy, however, didn't seem fazed at all. To them, the Commune had never existed. They might not have been affected, but she'd lost hundreds of friends during the fighting.

At a crossroads, the driver stopped the Phaeton to allow another carriage to go by. Right away, a swarm of needy people rushed into the street, their dirty and calloused hands reaching in, begging Maria for money. She didn't hesitate and opened her purse, dropping a franc into each grateful palm. Léon always handed out coins as well. The coins were never enough, though.

When the purse emptied, she apologized, "I'm sorry, that's all I have."

The driver continued down the street. She stared straight ahead, not wanting to see the desperate faces. Paris remained under the strangle hold of a callous government who cared little for the poor.

Arriving at the Grand Orient, she climbed out of the Phaeton, causing its springs to groan and creak as she moved. A few snowflakes drifted down, so she hurried inside with Léon, pulling her collar up and keeping her head down so no one on the street would notice a woman entering the Lodge. She didn't like sneaking about, but drawing attention to herself or anyone else would be worse.

Léon found Georges Martin in the foyer. Georges, always looking more formal than Léon, wore a silk top hat, black full-length jacket, and shiny black shoes. His appearance, and his demeanor, commanded authority, while in truth he was as approachable and friendly as Léon. She felt a connection with Georges, an instant fraternal bond. She enjoyed being around him, not like how it was with Alexandre, but a more professional relationship.

Léon took her coat as she unbuttoned it. He hung it on a coat tree and motioned toward the meeting hall. "According to Georges, we have about fifty people here today. Not as many as I'd hoped, but still, fifty isn't so bad."

Maria smiled. "It only takes one person to put things right. One person could restore Paris if he wanted to."

Removing his hat, Georges sighed. "You're talking about MacMahon. That man's as much a menace as Thiers."

"Hopefully not." Maria moved into the hall with Léon at her side. "Oh, Léon, I spoke with Hubertine today."

"And did she tell you how she wants to find Dardelle and burn down everything along the *rue de Rivoli* again?"

Maria stopped at the Lodge entrance. "What? I hope you're making a joke." The chairs were situated in a circle, not facing the lectern, and about half of the seats were filled. She recognized many of the men, but there were a few she hadn't seen before. "Léon, are these all men you trust?"

"Explicitly. Not all are Masons, though. That man over there wearing the white woolen scarf, he was a soldier in Thiers' army. They imprisoned him for a year because he refused to shoot a group of children during the Commune. These are good people, Maria."

"So long as you vouch for them, I'll consider them my friends as well." She found a chair near a red-faced and rather rotund bald man and sat down.

Léon and Georges walked into the center of the circle and waited until all eyes were on them. Being involved with secretive discussions, although dangerous, were exciting and she'd never considered not attending. It made her feel like she was doing something for the people of France.

Georges spoke first, "It pleases me to see so many of our dear friends here this afternoon." He pointed to Maria. "I'm sure you all know *Mademoiselle* Maria Deraismes. The first motion I would like to put forth is that we open these meetings to all women as well as men. It seems hypocrisy not to do so."

The men nodded which made Léon smile broadly and wink at Maria. After Georges' opening, the meeting ensued, ranging from topics of open education for all adults and children, the elimination of government sanctioned prostitution, and better, safer, affordable housing for the poor. The lively discussion that followed ended with a loose plan about how to approach the government with a petition.

What a shame Anna wasn't there to hear it. Or Hubertine. Of course, Hubertine would likely declare that militant tactics were needed to make a point, not petitions or protests. After the meeting dispersed and the attendees went their separate ways, Léon and Georges took Maria aside.

Georges glanced at Léon, then turned his attention to Maria. "We would like to make you a proposition."

"What sort of proposition?" She looked over at Léon, who gave no indication of what Georges was talking about.

Georges continued, "We are attempting a coup of sorts."

Léon interjected, "Oh, for heaven's sake, Georges. We're pulling together all the Lodges who agree with us that women should be included in Masonry. We want you to be the first woman initiated."

She stood, speechless. "Why me?" She'd waited so long to hear that the Freemasons were changing their age-old tradition of men only. Finally, progress was at hand. Once a male-dominated group like the Freemasons relinquished their gender bias, it would surely have an effect, like ripples in a pond, spreading out in all directions.

"Why not you? For you to be initiated will make a statement, an impact, that France, no, that the world can't ignore. This will be one barrier broken that'll lead to many others. So, what do you say?" Léon grasped her hand.

She squeezed his hand. "Of course. How can I refuse?"

"Hold on, Léon." Georges held up his hand. "Maria, nothing is set in stone yet. We've only started discussing this in open Lodge. It may take a while yet."

Maria shrugged. She didn't care about waiting so long as it happened. "Just remember, I'm not getting any younger, so don't take too long."

They chatted for a few more minutes as everyone dispersed, then Léon locked up the Lodge. He climbed into the Phaeton with Maria while Georges took his own carriage home. After dropping off Maria, Léon waved goodbye and headed off. Maria stood for a moment on the footpath near the road and breathed in the air, sweetly perfumed from vines of jasmine climbing up the lamppost. The snow had stopped, leaving a thin dusting on the leaves and cobblestones.

Could Paris be on the brink of reaching equality after all? She looked up at the full moon breaking through the scattered clouds. She'd dreamed of becoming a Freemason for years. To think that one day soon she might don the apron of a Mason, like Papa. She hurried up the path, excited to tell Anna the news. Nothing was going to stop the speeding train of equality. Nothing.

Chapter 43

1878, Paris

For five long years Maria, Léon, and Georges kept up the fight to permit women into Freemasonry as a united front for equality. Five years out of her life and still the Grand Orient steadfastly refused to alter their prejudicial tradition. She stood across the street from the Lodge building and shifted her feet. With a sigh, she popped another powdery peppermint into her mouth. Even though Anna insisted that peppermint would ease her stomachache, it never did a thing but coat her tongue with thick minty powder. Yet she ate them anyway, always hoping they'd help.

Maria waited outside the Lodge for Georges, fanning her face in the heat. He took too long. The meeting had ended more than twenty minutes ago. Georges said he'd come right out and let her know of the latest verdict to amend the charter to allow women. She had a bad feeling in the pit of her stomach that the answer would once again be 'no', but held onto the possibility that it could be 'yes' this time. How could they keep refusing?

Finally, Georges stepped out of the building and waved to her. His face was not the face of a man who'd won a victory. He walked slowly across the street and shook his head. "Stubborn, that's what they are. Old men who won't listen to reason. Half of them are monarchists who still believe women should be chained to the home like slaves."

"At least you tried. Again." Maria motioned to her carriage a short distance away. "Why don't you come home with me and Anna can make us a nice lunch." More disappointing news, but she held in her heart that the old men of the Lodges wouldn't always be around. The younger set tended to embrace equality. Maybe it was simply a matter of timing.

"I'd love to join you for lunch, but I have another engagement. I have to go to Le Pecq."

"What's in Le Pecq?" Maria had never been to the small town west of Paris. She'd heard it was a lovely place, but somehow never managed to visit. "Going away for a holiday?" She loved to tease Georges because he made a point of saying how he would one day go off on holiday and not come back until Paris was governed fairly. As long as she'd known him, he'd stayed in Paris.

"Hardly. There's a Masonic Lodge there that I've been communicating with."

"And? Are you going to keep me in suspense? Are you to be initiated into a new Lodge?" Maria felt a stab of envy that he could be initiated, yet she still could not.

"I'm not ready for that yet, *mon amie*. Not until women are allowed in. I'll say this, though, this Lodge is made up of free-thinking men. In fact, their Lodge is named *Les Libres Penseurs*."

What a perfect name for such a Lodge, Maria thought wistfully. The Free Thinkers. Now she'd have to visit Le Pecq. "Then I shall bid you adieu. But do promise me you and your wife will drop by for afternoon tea one day soon."

He tipped his hat with a wink and a smile. "You have my promise. Oh, I almost forgot, my wife would love to have your sister's recipe for currant jam."

"Of course."

Georges walked Maria to her carriage and helped her inside, then headed off to his own carriage. She sat for a moment to collect her thoughts. A Lodge who named themselves free thinkers might influence other Lodges. Maybe things were finally moving in the right direction. With true equality in a Masonic Lodge, the scales would certainly tip in favor of feminism.

She untied the reins and started the old mare moving, grateful that Anna had put up the carriage's canopy. Although even in the shade she still felt flushed and hot. How could it be so warm when it wasn't even summer yet? She'd never liked the heat. On the hottest days when she was young, she'd sit in the shade under a tree and sketch landscapes of rolling hills dotted with fluffy sheep or draw imaginary scenes from fairy tales.

Now she had no time to sketch, she had too much to do. She'd been working with Léon to organize the largest meeting ever to discuss women's rights, which took up a sizable amount of each day. Léon dubbed it the first International Congress on Women's Rights.

She picked up a fan from the seat and waved it near her face. It helped some, but not enough. Why hadn't she worn her thinner day dress? She'd have to change as soon as she got home or risk heat stroke.

She stopped the carriage at a crossroads and waited while a small group of nuns walked by at a brisk pace. At least joining a nunnery was considered a respected vocation for a woman. One of the few. The absurdity irritated her, women had to resort to a life of religion as an honorable occupation outside the home. Working women stood on the far ends of the scale of decency. One end held a pious life while the other resulted in a life of squalor as a prostitute or scullery maid. Woman had no choices in between.

But with the Congress, change would come. Attendance would consist of women from all over the world, bringing with them fresh ideas about how to change their governments. Maria felt energized to be alive in such an exciting time. She pulled on the reins and stopped the carriage outside her house, behind a coal-black horse with a shabby red blanket on its back. No saddle, just a blanket in Communard-red. Right away she knew it belonged to Hubertine.

After securing the reins to a post, Maria went inside and found Hubertine pacing back and forth in front of the sofa. She turned, her brow slightly pinched and her eyes glaring.

"Maria, how could you disallow women's political rights on the Congress agenda?"

As Maria feared, Hubertine would make a fuss over the Congress agenda. Hubertine was too young and rash to realize that the subject of politics would incite anger rather than a serious discussion about education, divorce, and paternal responsibility for children. Both Maria and Léon agreed not to bring up political equality at the Congress. Political discussions were better saved for another time.

Maria closed the door. "Hubertine, how nice to see you again." She moved to the sofa and sat. "Won't you sit?"

With hands on hips, Hubertine shook her head. "How can you hold a women's rights conference without bringing up the subject of suffrage?"

"This isn't the venue for that. Our priority is to provide an equal education for women. Once women have well-paying positions, are protected in divorce issues, and receive compensatory money from the fathers of their children, then we can press forward with suffrage. You know this. One step at a time. This is precisely what Léon has been writing about for months. Have you not been paying attention?"

"Of course I have. Every day at work I hear Léon talking about school and college and how women shouldn't be excluded. But I honestly thought you'd put voting on the agenda."

"Well, we're not. There will be plenty of other opportunities to discuss voting."

"What are women without the vote?" Hubertine spun around and headed for the door. Without turning around, she mumbled, "Equality should not be obtained piecemeal."

Maria started to say that change would have to come piecemeal if it was to come at all, but Hubertine left before she had the chance. Hubertine mimicked Louise in her hot-headedness. They both wanted everything all at once. Too much too soon would overwhelm the policy makers and cause denial of everything.

"Anna!" Maria called out.

From upstairs, Anna replied, "Up here."

"Have we anything cold to drink?"

Anna came to the top of the staircase. "I've made some lemon and ginger water. It's chilling in the ice box. Oh, any news from the Masons?"

"The usual."

"Sorry. One day women will don the apron. I know they will."

"So do I. But it's frustrating. Georges went to Pecq to visit with the Free Thinkers."

Anna came all the way down the stairs. "Who are they? And did Hubertine leave already?"

"Yes, she left in a huff. The Free Thinkers are a Lodge. I have a feeling our cause rests with them. Why is it so blasted hot outside?" Maria followed Anna into the kitchen.

Ann snickered. "I don't know, but I'm enjoying it."

"Well, it's too hot for my liking."

Anna brought out two glasses from the cupboard. "It's all because you're heating up Paris with the Congress. It'll overshadow the Exposition."

"I don't want it to overshadow the Exposition, but it will co-incide with it. Just think, Anna, all nations coming together to see progress at the Exposition, and to see progress in feminism." Maria smiled at the idea. Two major events both happening together. It wasn't by coincidence that Léon suggested summertime for the Congress.

Anna and Maria sipped on the sugary lemon and ginger water and chatted about the Commune, feminism, and Masonic lore. The esoteric aspect of Masonry was especially intriguing, although Maria only knew some of the symbolism. Even though Léon was like a brother, he wouldn't divulge the meaning of the symbols or anything at all about the rituals, insisting that she'd find out when she was initiated. That increased her curiosity even more, and Léon knew it.

The next few months passed quickly, with the weather staying unseasonably warm, but Maria hadn't time to bemoan the heat. She busied herself preparing for the Congress. Attendees were scheduled to come from Holland, Russia, and even the United States of America. The excitement caught up with her and she'd been resting in bed for a few days with her usual stomach problems, tended to by Anna with her constantly changing potions and concoctions. But nothing really worked.

Maria woke up on the day of the Congress weak, but otherwise healthy. A few clouds scattered across the sky and a light breeze blew through the trees. Any relief from the relentless heat helped. The Congress started at ten in the morning with her giving the opening greeting, and she was ready. She dressed in her nicest, but somewhat plain dress because she wanted to avoid looking too bourgeoisie.

After securing her hair into a chignon and fastening a locket with a photo of her parents' around her neck, she went down for some breakfast. She sat and watched Anna fussing around flipping crepes and baking scones. Everything Anna did was with love and that made Maria never feel alone. Even after receiving word that Alexandre had married an Australian woman, Anna provided wise words and warm hugs.

Anna placed food on the table and wiped her hands on her apron. "I have to run upstairs and fix my hair, but then I'll be right back to join you."

"You look fine."

"What, with flour on my face and my hair a mess? I can't attend the Congress like this."

"Yes, all right, go and make yourself beautiful." Maria checked the kitchen pendulum clock. Plenty of time before they had to leave.

Léon said he'd stop by at nine with his Phaeton carriage to pick them up. The last time she'd spoken to him, he seemed more nervous than she did about the Congress.

After eating some of the jam-filled crepes and nibbling on a currant scone, Maria strolled to the front of the house and looked through the window. A carriage went by and then another. Small groups of people walked by dressed in finery, the women carrying parasols or fancy silk fans. They were going to the Exposition, or perhaps some were heading to the Congress across the street from the Exposition where they'd leased a banquet hall for the occasion.

Anna came down looking lovely as usual. Maria followed her back to the kitchen and sat with her while she ate her breakfast. There wasn't much conversation, but when Maria felt a sharp pain in her stomach and groaned out loud, Anna jumped up.

"That's it, you're getting a cup of medicinal tea, the one you hate, and a handful of peppermints." Anna took the canister of bitter tea from the shelf and placed a scoop in the silver tea infuser ball, then placed it in a pot of hot water. "Here, eat the peppermints first." She placed a handful of white peppermints on the table.

"Oh, Anna, I'll be fine. It's my nerves. Or maybe your cooking."

Anna frowned. "There's nothing wrong with my cooking. Eat the peppermints or I'll force them down your throat."

Reluctantly, Maria chewed up half of the peppermints and washed them down with water. When the tea had steeped, she sipped the nasty tasting brew. Before she finished it, the front door opened, and Léon called out.

Anna pointed to the cup of tea. "Finish that. I'll go see to him."

As soon as Anna left the kitchen, Maria poured the tea into a potted fern on the counter. She didn't need to finish it. Once the Congress started, she'd be fine.

"Maria!" Léon said joyfully from the doorway of the kitchen. "You look incredibly well, except for that white powder around your mouth. What is that?"

Maria wiped her mouth. "Peppermint powder. Anna insisted."

"That sounds like Anna. Well, are you ready?" He made a sweeping motion with his arm. "My carriage awaits the Deraismes sisters."

Being in the presence of Léon and his exuberant mood lifted Maria's spirits as well. Her nervousness faded, replaced with excitement. Even Anna let down her guard as sisterly protector as she got into the carriage, glancing around at the people strolling by, completely oblivious to Maria.

They drove through the streets, among the throngs of people now crowding the foot paths and roadways. Léon maneuvered the Phaeton to a side street near to the banquet hall and secured the reins. He drew in a deep breath. "Are you feeling well?"

Maria nodded. "I am. I need to find *Madame* Mozzoni before anything else."

"Who's that?" Anna asked, stepping from the carriage. "I don't think you mentioned her before."

"I think I did. She's a lady from Italy. She'll be making the opening address after I make the official greeting. I've never met her, but I understand she's a rather stout woman with white hair."

"I'll keep out an eye for her." Léon pointed to the building. "You two go ahead and go inside. Oh, Maria, I have a satchel with stationary and a sign-in form." He reached into the back of the Phaeton and pulled out a black leather satchel. "Can you take this inside?"

Anna took the satchel. "Aren't you coming in?"

He shook his head. "I'll wait out here so the attendees will know where to go."

Maria could read Léon's like an open book. He had something on his mind. The banquet hall was clearly marked, so there wasn't any need to guide people. She knew he wanted to stand guard in case the misogynists would try to stage a protest. But that wasn't likely to happen. Daumier and his followers had kept to themselves for years, concentrating more on their caricatures or writing about the politics of the government. They'd all but given up on their outspoken rants on feminism.

She left Léon and went into the hall with Anna, where stood a table and lectern at the front of the hall, with rows and rows of wooden chairs set up, filling the room. If everyone attended who replied, they would have around 200 people. She counted the chairs, 15 rows with 15 chairs in each row. More than enough to seat everyone.

A nice cross breeze coming in through the open windows on both sides cooled the hall. While Anna strolled around, Maria sat in the back row where it would be difficult to see the lectern once all of the other seats were filled. The seats couldn't be moved to allow everyone to have a view of the lectern, but hopefully those in the back wouldn't care and understand that words spoken were more important than seeing the speaker.

"*Mademoiselle* Deraismes?" came a soft-spoken voice from the doorway.

Maria turned and saw a woman who fit Anna-Maria Mozzoni's description perfectly. The woman, short and round with grayish-white hair piled on top of her head in a circular bun, approached. She wore small eyeglasses and a smile that lit up her face.

"You must be *Madame* Mozzoni." Maria gave her a kiss on both cheeks.

"*Sì.* I apologize if my French isn't so well."

"Do not worry about it at all. We have representatives from all over the world coming, some who understand French and some who don't. We will have translators for those who need them. Would you like to sit down at the speaker's table for a moment and collect your thoughts?" Maria instantly liked Anna-Maria. Her manor was gracious and unassuming, but something else about her teased Maria. She couldn't quite place it until she thought of her name. "*Madame*, your name, Anna-Maria, is quite coincidental. My name is Maria and my sister's name is Anna."

Madame Mozzoni laughed a light, carefree laugh. "I hadn't realized that. The Fates must have had a hand in me coming here."

Maria agreed. She escorted *Madame* Mozzoni to the speaker's table near the lectern and sat with her while Anna dashed around straightening the chairs that didn't need straightening. After a brief chat about the issues to be discussed, Maria and *Madame* Mozzoni stood at the entrance of the hall to greet visitors as they arrived.

As soon as Maria stepped out of the building, she saw Léon heading her way, followed by a man, head down, in a hat and gray overcoat. The weather was far too warm to be wearing a coat, and the way the man hid his face meant he didn't want to be recognized.

When they were close, the man looked up. Victor Hugo smiled, and Maria smiled back. She hadn't seen him in years, not since he'd worked in the Senate alongside Georges Martin. Georges was a popular senator, but Hugo was not. After failing to sway the other senators to his side on several issues, Hugo went into seclusion to concentrate on writing again.

"*Mademoiselle* Deraismes," he said quietly, "I hope my presence here isn't a hindrance to your worthy conference."

"Never." Maria ushered him inside and motioned to *Madame* Mozzoni. "This is Anna-Maria Mozzoni. She—"

"Yes, yes, she is giving the opening address. I've seen a copy of the agenda." Hugo glanced at Léon.

"We can't hide anything from you, can we?" Maria smiled again.

"No, you can't. Not when I have Léon feeding me information. I've also been privy to the list of attendees. Very impressive. We'll talk later." He nodded and followed Léon to the front row of seats.

As more and more people, men and women in equal numbers, came into the hall and milled about, Maria felt overwhelmed, a strange feeling since she'd spoken in front of crowds many times. A few minutes before ten, she sat with Anna on a bench outside the hall to regain her composure.

"Anna, this is the most important conference in my lifetime. I'm afraid something will happen. What if Daumier or his cohorts storm into the hall? What if MacMahon decides he doesn't want the Congress in Paris?"

"Oh, Maria, you can come up with a hundred bad scenarios, but why not concentrate on the good that we'll accomplish over the next two weeks."

"I'll try."

They went back into the hall. The chairs filled and soft voices echoed in the room. Maria's stomach fluttered a bit, but she thought of Anna's words, calmed down, and headed to the lectern, passing Victor Hugo and Léon on the way. *Madame* Mozzoni already had her seat at the speaker's table and gave Maria a nod and a smile.

Once behind the podium, Maria drew in a deep breath and looked out over the crowd. She instantly recognized a few Masons. And almost lost among the people was Hubertine, dressed in a bland brown dress with a conspicuous red scarf holding her hair in a bun. Regardless of anyone's beliefs, they'd all come together for this one conference. The diversity of attendees made a fabulous mix. There'd be such a difference in point of view and insight, exactly what feminism needed.

The clock struck ten and the audience quieted.

Maria motioned with a sweep of her arm to all the attendees. "I see before me a dedicated group of humanity. Over the next two weeks, we will discuss issues of education, legislature, morality, history, and how women fit into the economy. These five topics are central to our struggle for equality. Welcome, my brothers and sisters, to the first International Congress on Women's Rights."

Chapter 44

Christmas, 1881

For three and a half years after the success of the Congress of Women's Rights, Maria and Léon pushed the government to accept women's issues, but each time MacMahon refused to make any concessions. Maria sat on the marble bench in the rear garden shivering, watching the pure white snow fall from the dark gray sky.

She blinked some flakes off her eyelashes and lifted a parasol over her head. The cold air refreshed her and she enjoyed a bit of time to herself. She knew that Anna would soon find out she wasn't by the fire where she was supposed to be. In two days, it would already be Christmas and not much had changed.

Last year Hubertine waged a revolt against taxes, saying if women were not to be represented by the government, then they should not pay taxes. Her revolt fell on deaf ears, and she grew sullener than ever. Hubertine's increasingly violent attitude had caused a huge rift between her and Léon, but Maria, against Léon's advice, wrote a few essays for Hubertine's paper *La Citoyenne*, the citizen.

She worked with Hubertine because she felt helpless and needed to do something. The only good to come from the women's rights conference was that the government had reluctantly set up a system of secondary education for girls and discussed a law to permit a woman to divorce her husband. But that was it. Hardly enough to get too excited about.

The whole idea of equality was slowly disappearing. Paris had returned to a bustling metropolis, full of life and color, yet wasn't progressing forward. The old revolutionary chant of liberty, equality, fraternity faded away.

Maria stamped her feet to stay warm and watched the snow dust the dormant rose bushes. Even though her stomach had been bothering her more than usual and her new doctor insisted she stop all writing and speaking engagements, she refused to do as he said. She'd been working in secret on a book about the Commune and the callous injustice done to the Communards, depicting in graphic detail the cruelty and senseless murder. The chapter about the murder at Saint-Sulpice and Berdine's death proved too difficult, though, and caused her to put the manuscript away. She'd go back to it later.

Every time she remembered Berdine, she remembered her clearly, begging on the street corner the first time they'd met. In such a short time, Berdine had regained her self-worth, although it did her no good. She'd died at the hands of injustice.

"Maria?" Anna called from the back door. "Are you in the garden?"

"I am."

"Then get back inside right now." Anna plodded over to the bench. "What are you doing sitting in the snow?"

"I needed some fresh air, that's all." Maria got up and held the parasol over Anna. "I'm feeling a touch of melancholy today."

They walked back inside to the warmth of the kitchen.

Anna shook the snow off the parasol into the sink. "It's the season. It's cold and your stomach always hurts more in the cold."

"But it's almost Christmas. I usually love Christmas. I have this relentless realization that we've hardly made any progress at all and I'm getting too old to keep pace with the younger feminists. I don't want to retire from public speaking and have Hubertine or Louise be recognized as the leaders for equality. Their methods aren't what I stand for, they're too extreme and off-putting. They'll undo everything that we've worked for."

Anna set the parasol on the counter and sat. "Louise is dedicated. How could she undo anything?"

In an instant Maria regretted saying what she had said. For years now Anna had defended Louise's actions. Even during Louise's imprisonment and exile, Anna managed to write to her offering to help in any way she could. Theirs was an odd friendship, but a strong one. A friendship that Maria knew she shouldn't judge.

She unbuttoned her coat and took Anna's hand in hers. "I didn't mean anything by that. You know how I feel about their tactics. They don't understand that to get the government to embrace change is through the legislature, not violence and threats."

Anna squeezed Maria's hand. "So you say. Has the government listened? Has MacMahon suddenly changed his mind about declaring all women full citizens of France?" Without waiting for an answer, Anna continued, "No, he's done nothing. Women still have fewer rights than men. Unless we do something drastic, it'll always be that way."

"Maria! Anna!" Léon's shouted from the foyer.

"We'll talk about this later, Anna." Maria didn't want to hear any more from her sister and hurried away, finding Léon in the foyer brushing snow off the shoulders of his woolen overcoat.

"There you are," he said with a flat expression. "You won't believe what I heard."

"Tell me and I'll be the judge whether or not I believe it." Maria motioned to the sofa in the sitting room.

She sat, but Léon remained standing. "Now, I don't want you to get upset."

"Are you going to play, Léon? I'm not in the mood for game playing."

Léon drew in a deep breath and blurted, "Alexandre is back in France."

She hadn't thought of Alexandre for months, trying hard to block him from her mind. And now he'd returned. The news hit her like a hammer to the gut. "How do you know he's here?" was all she could say.

"Perhaps I should sit." Léon took off his coat and draped it over the end of the sofa and sat next to her. He gazed into her eyes for a moment before continuing, "He sent me a telegraph from Lyon. He's written a series of essays about his imprisonment on New Caledonia and his life in Australia."

"Oh." Maria looked away. She'd thought for a moment that he came back to see her. "And his wife? Did he bring his wife to parade around in front of me?" She knew she sounded jealous and regretted saying anything at all, but she couldn't take the words back. They hung in the air, dripping with venom. She looked back at Léon.

He shook his head. "I think he came alone. Maria, he never meant to hurt you. I know he didn't. I'm sure he wanted to block out the evil and start a new life. He's not a young man and hasn't a lifetime left."

Maria jumped up. "And I'm not a young woman anymore. He always told me he never intended to marry, that he valued friendship above the legality of marriage. He and I believed the same thing, or so I thought. I never needed a husband to make me whole, but apparently he needed a wife."

"He did hurt you, didn't he? Would you have married him if he'd asked?"

She didn't even have to think about the answer. "No. You know how I feel. I've always thought of marriage as a form of indentured servitude for the female half and my mind hasn't changed. No one will hold dominion over me. Don't you understand? When he took a wife, his ideals changed. Mine haven't. I thought he and I had a bond, a connection of the minds."

"Give him a chance. I don't think he's changed all that much. He'll arrive in Paris the day after tomorrow."

What? It hadn't occurred to her that he'd come to Paris. What would she say to him? They couldn't pick up where they'd left off. Too much had come between them. The truth was, he'd chosen another woman over her, and it stung. As much as she didn't want to get married, it would have been nice to have been asked, just once.

But he never asked her to come to Australia and he never offered to come back to Paris so they could be together.

Without another word, she hurried upstairs and lay down on her bed. Perhaps she and Anna could go to the country and stay there until Alexandre left. But wasn't that running away from the problem instead of dealing with it? It still hurt, though. How could she face him with so much hurt in her heart? She sat up and slipped off her damp coat. Why did life have to be so complicated? Her time would be better spent focusing on the next senate meeting. She'd been collaborating with Georges Martin on the topic of state-sanctioned prostitution.

La politique de la bréche, the strategy of the breach, is what the fight for equality had been dubbed She, Léon, and Georges agreed that the way to gain footing was to chip away, piece by piece, at the stubborn brick wall of misogynism, to breach its walls. Anna didn't understand and still insisted that Hubertine and Louise's forceful and violent methods would work far better.

Maria sighed and rubbed her tired eyes. She should visit Georges again soon because she had much to learn from him. He never stayed still, always had several irons in the fire. He'd had several mysterious visits to Pecq over the years, yet he never disclosed very much about his journey. He'd been initiated, passed to the second degree and raised as a Master Mason about three years ago. Léon also remained closed-mouthed, leading Maria to guess they were involved with Masonic business that they couldn't discuss with a non-Mason. She knew in her heart that it had to do with the Free Thinkers Lodge.

"Maria, please come back down!" Léon called.

"I'm tired. I'm going to rest for a while," she shouted back. "I'll see you tomorrow."

She stared up at the ceiling. She didn't want to think about Alexandre. She didn't want to remember the way his hand felt in hers or how they used to sit in the garden together, talking of politics and how to prune roses in the autumn so they'd bloom full in the spring. Humorously conspiring about how they'd take over the government and declare everyone a citizen. No, she didn't want to be reminded of those times. What good would come of stirring up old dead embers that had been extinguished long ago?

After a minute, Maria heard the front door close. She'd apologize to Léon tomorrow for being rude. She lay there for a while, but then decided she shouldn't mope about. She picked up the daguerreotype of her parents and gave her mother's photo a kiss.

"Oh, *Maman*, I wish you were here. I feel so lost. I don't know where I'm going these days. Why haven't I had any luck in changing things? At least Hubertine and Louise get attention. I do nothing but write, and I don't even do that very often anymore. And I still have nightmares about the prison in Versailles. I can't help thinking that if I'd died, I would have been recognized as a martyr for women's rights. But I didn't want to die, and I still don't. I'm getting old and I don't want to die without accomplishing anything."

"Maria!" Anna shouted from downstairs.

Maria replaced the daguerreotype. "I have to do something, *Maman*. Something big. Something that will get people talking again about equality. But what can I do?"

"Maria! Georges Martin is here to see you."

Georges Martin? What a coincidence, she'd been thinking about him. Did Georges and Léon come together? She glanced in the full-length mirror and smoothed her mussed hair. There were a few strands of gray. She went downstairs and saw Georges standing in the foyer holding his hat.

"Good morning, Maria," he said softly.

"I wasn't expecting to see you today, Georges. Won't you sit down?" She motioned to the sitting room, but he stayed where he was.

"I dropped by to ask you a serious question."

"What sort of question?"

"What is your honest opinion of the Masonic Order?" Georges kept his eyes on her.

She didn't know what to say. Her mind still reeled from the news about Alexandre. And besides, Georges already knew her opinion of the Masons. "I'm not so sure I understand, Georges."

"I need to hear from your lips what you think of the Masonic Order." He raised an eyebrow. "Just say whatever comes to you."

She thought for a moment. Papa had been a Mason, and she trusted the Order, having dealt with them in one fashion or another for years, but she'd never really given any thought to her opinion of them. "I believe that it's as much a woman's place to stand in the Lodge as it is to stand beside all men as equals. From what you and Léon have told me, the Masonic Lodge is perhaps the only true institution of equality. Léon said that all outer status or position in society isn't recognized in the Lodge. No one is rich or poor behind the closed door. So, I suppose then, I consider that fact the most important aspect of Masonry. My opinion of Masonry, therefore, is that the organization is an important part of society because it promotes equality, charity, and morality. Is that an acceptable answer?"

Georges smiled and placed his hat back on his head. "There is no right or wrong answer, Maria. Well, I have to be running off now."

"What? You just got here. Did you see Léon? He left a moment ago. Do you mean to tell me that you came all the way here to ask me one question?"

"No, no, I'm on my way to conduct some business. Your house was on the way. And I saw Léon as he left." He nodded and left without another word.

Maria stood near the door for a moment. Her house was never on the way to anywhere. He was up to something. Léon had to be involved as well. Georges used the Masonry question as a ruse. The two of them had to be plotting a way to get her to meet with Alexandre.

But she wouldn't. She didn't want to see him. She'd moved on without him.

Chapter 45

On Christmas Eve, Maria and Anna spent the morning decorating a small spruce tree Georges had dropped off the day before. Although Maria had her suspicions that he and Léon were planning something, she did her best to push it from her mind and enjoy the day. Unbridled curiosity, as her mother had been fond of saying, should not overpower one's mind.

After securing a silver star on top of the tree, she sat with Anna and had some brandy and sugar pastries. The lovely tree, with garlands of holly and small candles fixed to the outer branches, glowed. It wasn't a fancy or huge tree compared to the Christmas trees they had when they were young, but it still made the house feel festive, especially with the evergreen scent filling the room.

"Anna, do you remember when we were children and how we'd stare at the tree for hours, dreaming of Christmas morning?"

"How could I forget? Mother would tell us to go to bed about a dozen times." Anna laughed.

"Those were good times, weren't they? Uncomplicated times." If only life could be uncomplicated now, with no worries about old friends returning from Australia.

Anna reached her arm around Maria's shoulders. "You're thinking of Alexandre, aren't you?"

Maria didn't want to think about him, but she couldn't help it. According to what Léon said, Alexandre should be in Paris by now. It would be nice to see him again, just to say hello. Nothing more than hello.

With a slow shake of her head, Maria said softly, "I'm not thinking of him. I was thinking about the great things we can accomplish in the new year."

"Liar." Anna gave Maria a kiss on the cheek. "I'm going to make us some lunch." She called out on her way to the kitchen, "I believe Alexandre is staying with Léon."

Maria suspected as much. She did need to go and see Léon about a conference in January, and if she happened to run into Alexandre, well, then she'd have the opportunity to wish him well without it appearing like she went there specifically to see him. "Anna! I'm going to visit Léon. About a business matter."

She slipped on her coat and gloves and headed out. The sun shone, melting the thin layer of snow that covered the ground, making everything wet. Even with the chilled air, the day was perfect for a walk. As she strolled, she went over what she'd say to Alexandre. She'd love to tell him how he hurt her, made her feel like she wasn't important enough to be in his life, but she'd never do that. She'd keep the conversation light and casual, avoiding any talk of emotions and pain.

She passed by several children playing in the snow drifts, taking turns pulling each other in a sled. She stopped to watch for a few minutes when she heard someone call her name. "Maria! Maria!"

She turned and saw Louise and Hubertine hurrying toward her, both with bright red sashes tied around their waists. It had been a while since she'd seen either of them, but it appeared they were still promoting themselves as active Communards. Now that she thought about it, she'd only seen Louise once, right after she was released from prison on New Caledonia.

Louise embraced Maria and kissed her on both cheeks. "Oh, Maria, it's so nice to see you again. Where are you off to?"

"Léon's house." Maria nodded to Hubertine. "And where are you two going?"

Hubertine spoke, "A rally. We were going to your house to invite you. You really should come, Maria. Someone you know will be there." She winked.

Who could she be speaking of? Not Léon. He was adamantly against anything Hubertine did, and Georges wouldn't attend. "Who are you talking about?"

Lowering her voice to a whisper, Louise said, "Dardelle. That bastard Thiers thought he killed Dardelle, but he was wrong. He hid far away from France. Now he's back to lead the people again."

Maria had no intention of going to any rally, let alone one with Dardelle leading the rabble. Louise and Hubertine were so dedicated, but their way wasn't Maria's way. "Louise, I can't support Dardelle. You know that. His reckless acts got innocent people killed at Montmartre. He left us all there to die while he scurried away like a rat. Then he tricked me into going to the Tuileries and later burned the palace. I work for changes in legislature, legal changes. I don't support name-calling or violence. Remember, I've seen the outcome of violent tactics. Meeting violence with violence only causes death and destruction. That's not the way to accomplish anything. There are always reasonable, peaceful solutions."

"*Merde*!" Hubertine threw her arms up in the air. "You sound just like Léon."

"I take that as a compliment." Maria pointed down the street. "I really do have to be going. Standing here in the cold is no good for me."

Louise nodded and took Hubertine's hand, leading her away. "All right, Maria, go on your way. But while we have our differences, I will always consider you my friend. And even though Hubertine is angry, she is your friend, too. We're all on the same side of justice, you know."

"*Adieu*, Louise." Maria turned and continued down the street without looking back. Getting into a debate with either Hubertine or Louise would only create turmoil, and she didn't want any additional turmoil in her life right now. Seeing Alexandre again would be enough.

After a few more minutes of walking, she warmed up and allowed herself to enjoy the sun blanketing her. She passed by two little boys playing with a puppy on the footpath, trying to make it roll over. It didn't, and they giggled. Hearing carefree children's laughter made her smile. They smiled back and resumed their attempted training of the puppy.

When she arrived at Léon's house, she stopped. There in the window stood Alexandre. She recognized him right away. He wasn't looking out, but stood sideways with a cup in his hand. He always enjoyed a cup of *café au lait*. Her legs trembled and her palms were damp through her gloves. She took a deep breath and knocked on the door.

Léon opened the door. "Ah! Maria, my love. Happy Christmas Eve! What brings you out on a chilly day like this? I told you I'd visit after Christmas." He ushered her inside.

"I've been confined at home with Anna far too long. Her constant mothering drives me mad."

He smiled and shut the door. "Well, I can understand that." He lowered his voice, "You do know that Alexandre is here, don't you?"

"I do. But I haven't come to see him. I thought we could discuss January's conference."

"It's not until the end of January, but if you want to discuss it, then I suppose we should discuss it."

"Is that Maria Deraismes I hear?" Alexandre asked.

Maria trembled even more hearing his voice. Why was it that of all the things she'd lived through, the mere sound of his voice made her tremble? It wasn't fair. She didn't love him anymore...at least she'd tried to convince herself of that. But she knew the truth. She wanted to see him, to hold him, to talk like they used to. Forget the past, and live in the present. He stood in the next room, without his wife. Perhaps for today they could be as they were.

He came into the foyer looking older, his hair almost entirely gray, and his body slightly stooped, but it was Alexandre nonetheless. His presence hadn't changed. When he smiled, the life instantly flowed back into his face. Through his thinning hair, she saw the two-inch scar from his bullet wound.

"Maria," he said almost reverently, "It's so wonderful to see you again."

What should she say? That she'd missed him, that she was angry that he'd moved away and married? A simple greeting would be best. "Hello, Alexandre."

"I wasn't certain you'd want to see me again after so long. I'm an old man now with wrinkles and creases marring my complexion. But I see you haven't changed so much, you're still as radiant as ever."

Compliments? He tossed out compliments. What sort of married man compliments another woman so blatantly? She shook her head slightly. "I've changed. So, have you left your wife in Australia while you travel the world? She must be a very understanding woman." Why did she say that? Now he'd know of her jealousy.

"You haven't heard, then. My wife died a year ago. She made me promise to return to France to continue writing. I couldn't seem to write much in Australia. She said I never belonged there and that France was my muse." He paused and took Maria's hand in his. "But France isn't my muse, Maria."

His warm touch invited her in, brought back a flush of desire that she'd long suppressed. Why did he have to come back? She looked over at Léon, his face a blank canvas. He wasn't about to help her make any decisions about Alexandre.

Gently, she pulled her hand away. "I've come to see Léon, Alexandre. Would you please excuse us for a moment?" She motioned for Léon to follow her into his study.

Once inside the study, Léon closed the door. "All right, what's going on? You and I both know you didn't come here to see me.

He's a wreck without you, Maria. He confided in me that he never stopped thinking of you."

"Really?" Maria paced around the study, shoving a chair out of the way as she circled. "So was he thinking of me when he bedded down each night with his wife? And now that she's dead, he thinks he can come back here and resume where he left off?"

"I've never seen you like this. You need to talk to him about your feelings, not to me." He pointed to the door. "Talk to him."

How could she sit and talk with Alexandre when simply being in the same room with him hurt so much? "Perhaps later. I don't think I'm ready."

"Then why did you come here? It wasn't to discuss a meeting in January. I know that much."

"I'd better go. Anna will wonder where I am." She gave Léon a gentle kiss on each cheek and rushed through the house to the front door. She paused when Alexandre called out.

"Maria, you're not leaving, are you?" he asked.

She didn't turn but opened the door. "I have an important engagement to attend to, but I'll come around after Christmas, if you'll still be here then." She stepped outside and walked quickly down the path to the street.

She didn't look back to see if Alexandre watched from the window but kept walking. She needed time to sort out her feelings before discussing anything with him. But how much time? She hadn't seen him in years and yet her love for him still burned as strong as before. Wasn't time supposed to heal old wounds?

Chapter 46

January 1882

Christmas came and went peacefully, although Alexandre stayed at the back of Maria's thoughts. She delayed another visit to see Alexandre. Now, the middle of the month, she reconsidered. She missed him, and there'd be no harm in talking. She had to clear the air between them, or she'd never be able to continue without thinking of him every day.

She gazed out her bedroom window at the ice-covered tree branches and shivered. For the past couple of days, she'd been slightly unwell and restless, not her stomach so much as a general feeling of malaise, as if her entire body wanted nothing more than rest. Her head ached and her limbs were stiff and sore. She craved springtime so she could smell the fragrant flowers and see the red-breasted robins pulling at worms in the soil. She sighed and turned away from the window.

Anna came in looking confused. "Georges Martin is here to see you."

"Georges? What does he want? Did you tell him I'm feeling a bit sickly?"

"I did, and he insisted that you come downstairs. Let me tell him to come back another day."

Maria shook her head. "Tell him I'll be down in a moment. He wouldn't come here unless it was something important." She got up and slipped on a dressing gown over her day dress, put on her house shoes, and went downstairs.

When Georges saw her, he smiled. "Maria, I'm so very sorry to take you out of your sick bed, but there's a matter that requires your immediate attention."

"What sort of matter? I've already spoken to Léon about the conference in a few weeks."

"This isn't anything to do with the conference. I need you to come with me right now."

Did she hear correctly? He wanted her to go outside in the frozen air? "Georges, really, I'm not up to a carriage ride at the moment."

"You have to come," he persisted, then lowered his voice, "It's important, very important. I can't say anything more."

The hint of mystery teased at her, but wasn't sure she should go out. "Perhaps tomorrow—"

"No, now. I assure you, you won't be disappointed. Besides, you have a healthy glow to your cheeks. I don't think you're as ill as you think. Remember, I'm a doctor. I'll see to it that you're kept warm."

Anna shook her head and stood beside Maria. "She can't go with you, Georges. She needs to rest in bed. The doctor said—"

"I'm a doctor and I said I'd look after her. I have warm blankets in my carriage." Georges took Maria's hand. "Go and get dressed warmly, we have to leave right away."

"To where?" Maria's curiosity piqued. "What's so important? Tell me or I won't go with you."

"Léon said you'd insist on knowing."

"Léon? So he's in on this mystery?" She glanced at Anna. "Anna, why don't you make me some of my tea. It'll be all right."

Anna nodded. "I'll make your tea, but only if you promise you won't go."

Georges spoke up, "She has to come with me, Anna."

Before Anna could object, Maria held up a hand. "Don't worry. Let me talk to Georges in private."

Without a word, Anna spun around and stomped to the kitchen. Georges let out a stifled laugh. "Looks like I've made your sister cross with me."

"Oh, don't mind Anna. It's me you have to worry about." Maria smirked. "Why won't you tell me where you want me to go? If it's to see Alexandre, I've planned to go and see him later on."

"No, not that. A hint. I'll give you a hint. We're going to Pecq."

Maria smiled. "Now was that so hard? I'll hurry and change into some traveling clothes." She hastened up the stairs to her room.

Pecq? She knew right away that a trip to Pecq meant it had something to do with the Free Thinkers Lodge. Could it be that they were going to discuss initiating women? How exciting that she'd been invited.

Georges called after her, "With the roads as slippery as they are, it'll take us a couple hours to get to Pecq."

Although she still didn't feel at her best, she was not about to let her stomach ruin her chances of meeting the Masons of Pecq. Slipping out of her thin day dress, she put on her favorite brown heavy woolen dress. She loved how the white trim on the shoulders looked like snow had drifted down and settled there. She grabbed her gloves and proceeded downstairs, only to find Anna standing with her hands on her hips.

"Where do you think you're going? I have the tea steeping."

"I won't be long." Maria glanced at Georges.

He already had her coat in his hands. "Don't fret, Anna, I'll take good care of her. Why don't you put some tea in a cup and Maria can drink it on the way."

Anna frowned, but went back to the kitchen, returning a moment later with a steaming cup in her hand. "Don't spill it, it's hot. I only filled it half-way so it won't slosh out."

Maria took the cup. "I won't be long, Anna."

George took the cup and helped Maria into her coat. Once she had it buttoned, she took the cup and gave Anna a kiss on the cheek. She followed Georges to the waiting carriage. He took the reins and moved the carriage down the street slowly so the dual horses wouldn't slip on the ice. Unfortunately, the tea did slosh around and spilled onto Maria's gloves. The partially open carriage let the cold air chill her, so she drank as much of the hot tea as she could to keep warm, then tipped the rest onto the street and put the cup on the floor.

What a thrill to think they'd soon be in Pecq talking about the equality of Freemasonry, or so she hoped. She'd never been privy to Masonic discussions outside of having them sponsor her speeches, and whatever George or Léon told her. But this would be an actual meeting with the Masons. What an honor it would be to sit in council with them. A little advance notice would have been nice so she could have prepared a speech, although she'd become good at thinking on her feet.

"Georges, what exactly are we going to discuss? Is this an open-Lodge meeting? I thought the uninitiated couldn't attend Lodge once it's been officially opened. Does this mean they are willing to consider initiating women? Am I to make my case in an open meeting?"

"So many questions." He smiled. "We can talk about anything, other than what the meeting is for."

"That's not fair! Why the secrecy? Is the Lodge in danger if anyone finds out a woman is coming? Is that it?"

"Anything other than what the meeting is for."

"Oh, for heaven's sake, Georges. Fine. This has certainly been a stretch of foul weather, hasn't it?"

Georges laughed. "Yes, indeed. I cannot wait until spring arrives."

"Nor can I."

The conversation ended. Georges concentrated on the road and Maria looked out at the frozen city. They continued to roll through the quiet streets with hardly another word between them. By the time they finally approached the small town of Pecq, Maria was chilled to the bone and shivering. Other than being cold, she felt well. The tea must have helped to settle her stomach.

They turned off the main street and onto a narrow lane bordered on both sides by brick buildings that were old and weathered. As Georges pulled up in front of a small two-story building that had a faded red façade, a man rushed out in shirt sleeves and waved for Georges to hurry.

"Where are we, Georges?" Maria asked. The streets were deserted and the heavy gray clouds seemed to muffle all sound. It had an eerie ambiance.

"*Les Libres Penseurs.*" Georges winked and helped her from the carriage. "Careful, it's icy. The Lodge should have already been called to order. They're waiting for you."

Maria stepped onto the footpath, her legs shaking so much that she almost collapsed. "Called to order? Am I really allowed into open Lodge?" She followed Georges up the path toward the building. "You could have told me that before when I first asked. What should I say?"

Just short of the front door, Georges stopped walking and looked at Maria. "Stop worrying. My dear friend, you are about to be the first woman initiated into this Lodge, and it warms my heart to be here with you on this historic occasion. Now, come with me and I'll help you get prepared."

She didn't know what to say. So much ran through her mind. When had they decided to initiate her? Were other Lodges in agreement or was it only *Les Libres Penseurs?* And what did Georges mean by 'get prepared'.

They went inside and the man in shirt sleeves locked the door behind them and then disappeared down a hallway. Georges led her to a small, dark room, and told her to sit down on a brocade chair. The room was warm, and the windows were covered in black fabric.

There was a small table beside the chair with a single candle burning next to a human skull. A human skull?

"Maria, I hope you aren't cross that I had to whisk you away like this, but an initiation is traditionally done in secret. Especially since no other Lodge in France will initiate a woman. This is a sensitive undertaking, and a very serious one. In the wardrobe over there," he pointed to a narrow wardrobe across from the chair, "is a robe for you to slip over your dress. Remove your shoes and any valuables, such as money or jewelry you might have on you and let me know when you're ready. You are to enter the Lodge without valuables or anything to denote social standing. I'll be right outside. But take a moment to sit quietly and reflect on your life up to this point."

She nodded and he left. There she sat, alone in the dim, flickering light, staring at the ghostly skull. It seemed like a dream. Was she really about to become an initiate Freemason, an entered apprentice? Did the skull represent a sort of symbolic death of her old life, where she'd be reborn into a new life as a Freemason?

She would join the Free Thinkers, the men who believed in true equality. They were putting their beliefs into action. *Acta non verba.* Léon always said that inside the Lodge, a person's religion, politics, or social standing meant nothing. Perhaps a Masonic Lodge was the only place where a man and a woman could stand together in harmony, sharing masculine and feminine energies.

The skull's empty eye sockets drew her in. *Maman's* words came back once again. Everyone is the same under the skin. Now it all made sense. Skin simply covered up the truth that all people come from the same stock; strip away all outer coverings and you can't tell one person from another.

She leaned closer and touched the skull with her fingertips. She'd come so far in her lifetime and lived through some awful times. But there were also plenty of joyous times with friends, and of course Anna. The candle sent little fingers of shadows over the skull, almost animating it. It didn't seem like a frightening thing, but maybe a reminder that death waits for everyone. Was that why the skull sat in the room? Maria thought for a minute. It could be a lesson showing that each person should make their life count. Had she made her life count? Over the years, had she done all that she could to help others? Was there more she could do?

After a moment more of reflection, Maria opened the wardrobe and took out the solitary black robe. She got out of her coat and shoes and slipped the robe over her head. It bunched around the floor at her feet. She wasn't wearing any jewelry and any money she had was in her coat pocket, so she lifted the bottom of the robe and knocked on the door.

"Georges, I'm ready."

The door opened and Georges ushered her out into the hall. He circled around her, as if sizing her up. "Put this on." He handed her a blindfold.

She looked at Georges. "Is this really necessary? Why must I be blindfolded?"

"Wear the blindfold or you'll not enter the Lodge. You are blinded by ignorance and the mundane world. Until you are properly initiated, you are not able to see the light of truth." His voice was stern, authoritative. Not at all like his normal tone. He'd turned into a different person. He took the blindfold and wrapped it around her eyes, securing it tightly. She felt him place something around her neck, like a noose. He didn't tighten it too much, but she felt it trail down her back.

Her chest tightened and she couldn't breathe. "Georges," she whispered. "I'm not sure—"

"Take my hand and follow me. I'm your guide."

He took her hand in his. She trusted him. She walked slowly beside him and held the flowing robe up with her free hand so she wouldn't trip. Then, they stopped.

Someone knocked on a door. Was it Georges or the man in the shirt sleeves? A door creaked open, and a deep voice boomed, "Who have you there?"

Maria could barely hear the response because the blood pounded in her ears, but it sounded like Georges said her name. After more questions and answers that were equally hard to understand, they moved forward, presumably through the door to the Lodge. Absolute silence greeted her. She had no conception of what lay inside. Was it a large room where men stared at her or was it another small room like the one with the skull? She'd crossed the threshold leading to another world, a world she knew nothing about.

Her entire body shook now, but Georges still gripped her hand firmly. She was told to kneel, which she did. Georges released her hand. Something sharp pressed against her chest. What was it? A voice said the dagger at her breast was to be a prick to her conscience that she should never reveal any of the Masonic secrets. She stayed perfectly still, vulnerable in the hands of strangers, yet she somehow didn't fear them. She drew in a deep breath and listened as she was asked if she wanted to proceed or retreat back to the outer world.

Without hesitation, she replied, "I wish to proceed."

Georges took her hand again and told her to stand. As disorienting as it was to be blindfolded, having Georges by her side reassured her. She'd soon be an entered apprentice Freemason and forever joined with Georges and all other Masons. She sensed Papa beside her, smiling and welcoming her.

Georges told her to walk with him to circumnavigate the Lodge. Her gait wasn't steady, and her feet were like lead, making her shuffle rather than walk. Through her stocking feet she felt carpet, which muffled the sound of Georges' footsteps as he walked next to her. She drew in a deep breath and squeezed Georges' hand. Her new life had begun.

Chapter 47

Once the initiation finished and she'd sworn a sacred oath, the Lodge master removed the blindfold and a noose from around her neck and tied a pure white lambskin apron around her waist. It symbolized, he said, the innocence and purity of the initiate.

She looked around and saw many faces that she recognized. She smiled when she saw Léon seated near a podium situated at the east end of the Lodge. He winked and dabbed his eyes with a handkerchief. She blinked away a tear of her own.

The meeting closed and Georges escorted back to the dark room to change. This time, however, the fabric didn't cover the window, and a lamp burned brightly. She removed the robe, put on her shoes, and found everyone gathered in the foyer. They all shook her hand and congratulated her.

Léon approached and embraced her. "So now you're a Freemason, Maria. You carry the light of Freemasonry with you, like a torch in the night, to guide yourself and to help all of humanity. It's a responsibility. One that I know you will cherish as we all do. Congratulations, my brother."

Maria knew the term 'brother' wasn't a gender-specific title, but simply signified a fraternal bond, one that she was now part of. "Léon, I don't know what to say. This was unexpected. I'd hoped for so long that a woman would be initiated, but I never imagined it would be me."

"Who else could it be?" He laughed. "Oh, and we have a tradition after each meeting. Wine, bread, and cheese." He clasped her hand and took her to a dining hall with a large table containing bottles of wine, wheels of cheese, and baguettes.

As the men filtered into the dining room, she tried to count them, but lost track after thirty. So many men had come to welcome her into the Brotherhood.

After toasting and chatting for a time, the group finally disbanded, and Georges drove her home. On the way, everything looked different, like a veil had been lifted from her eyes and she saw the world clearly for the first time. The Brotherhood created a bond where people helped and cared for one another. That's what the Commune tried to do, but the concept wasn't carried out effectively. She placed her hand on a leather case that Léon gave her where her white apron lay. What an honor, a privilege, to be included into the Masonic Order.

The carriage jolted to a stop. "Maria," Georges said softly, "I am immensely proud to be your brother and your friend. We cannot let the momentum of this day slow. We must continue initiating women."

Maria noticed they'd already made it to her house. "Of course. Thank you, Georges. I really mean it. I feel so..."

"Words aren't necessary. Humanity is finally progressing. This one act will allow equality to flow from the Lodges to the outer world. You know, I never understood why my mother, the woman who gave me life, was less of a citizen than I, just because she'd been born female."

"That will change now, Georges."

Maria stepped from the carriage, flashed him a smile, and walked up the path. Anna opened the door and ushered her inside where she had a warm fire going.

"Where have you been, Maria? You said you wouldn't be long, and it's been half the day. Where were you?"

"Anna, come and sit with me." She sat on the sofa and waited until Anna sat, too. "You won't believe what's happened."

She explained as much about the trip to Pecq as she could to Anna, who sat with her mouth agape, especially when Maria showed her the apron. She gently removed it from the case and placed it across

Anna's lap. While Anna couldn't be told anything about the actual initiation, Maria did her best to describe the excitement she'd felt.

Anna ran her hand over the apron. "I can't believe it. You're a Freemason. What's it like?"

"I do feel different somehow. I can't explain it, but I feel changed. You know, when I stood in that Lodge, surrounded by all those men, I wasn't a woman, I was equal. No defined by sex. I've waited my whole life to feel like that."

"I envy you." Anna sighed and placed the apron back in the case. "You've done it. You've breached the walls holding us back."

"That apron is for all of the women in every country. Georges told me that we have to keep pushing forward. This is only the beginning."

They sat for some time, dreaming up ways to spread the word that women were permitted to join the Freemasons as an example of equality. When the sun went down, a knock on the door interrupted their discussion.

Maria stood and stretched. "Now who can that be at this hour?" She answered the door and there on the stoop bathed in the last of the dusk sun stood Alexandre.

His eyes focused on hers and she couldn't look away. What was he doing, showing up without notice? She wanted to be angry with him, but she wasn't. His expression and sad eyes gave off a forlorn look, as if he would break down at any moment. Her heart wouldn't allow her to be angry.

He glanced over at Anna. "Excuse me, Anna, but I need to speak to Maria alone," he said softly, his voice cracking slightly on the last word.

"Oh, ah..." Anna hesitated, "I'll go and put on a pot of coffee." She got off the sofa and went to the kitchen.

Alexandre stepped inside and shut the door and removed his hat. Maria motioned him to sit on the sofa. He sat at the far end, his eyes staring down at his feet "Maria, I know I hurt you. That was never my intention, I swear to you. But I find I cannot live without you. I can't go on without seeing your face or hearing your voice. I crave our discussions and debates and the closeness we once shared. I love you, Maria, and if you'll accept my proposal, I should like very much to marry you."

Marry? He proposed marriage knowing full well that she had no desire to marry. "Why are you asking me to marry you?"

"I just told you."

"No, you didn't. You know how I feel about the institution of marriage. Did you expect me to change my opinion simply because you asked me?" She hoped she didn't sound too harsh. She truly didn't want to be married. Independence was far more appealing. Although she loved him, she didn't need a ceremony and document to prove her love.

Alexandre finally looked up and gazed into her eyes. "I thought that was what you wanted. You seemed...upset or jealous that I'd married."

She had been jealous, just a little, but deep down, she knew she never would have accepted his proposal back then, or now. "The past is the past, Alexandre. We can't change the past, but we can change the future. As much as I'm loathed to admit it, I was jealous, and maybe I still am...a bit. You chose another woman over me, shutting me out without so much as a reason. Why didn't you come back to Paris? You have no idea how much I wanted you to come back."

He paused for a moment before speaking, "I wanted a new beginning. When they released me from prison, all I wanted to do was forget the past. Forget the things that led to imprisonment. But I never forgot you."

Maria took his hand in hers. "We should never forget the past and must learn from it. It's the past that has brought us to this point. We're here now, together. Isn't that what matters?"

"It is. You are a special woman, Maria. I dreamed of returning and seeing you again. So where do we go from here?"

"I know my path now." Maria pointed to the apron case on the table beside the sofa.

"And what is your path?" He picked up the case and looked inside. "Is that what I think it is? What's happened?"

"I'm no longer a solitary woman fighting against inequality, Alexandre, I'm a Freemason with an army of free thinkers at my back to support me and nurture my spirit. When I pass through the Lodge doors, I stand as an equal. I am free from tyranny, repression, and prejudice. The government might not consider women as equals, but the Lodge does."

"And where does that leave me? Leave us?" He gave her hand a tender squeeze.

"We move forward. I have my path set before me and now you have to find yours. You'll always be in my heart, but my aspirations are now broadened beyond you and me. I have to spread the word that women can indeed be equal, if they are willing to take the first step. This is a steppingstone, and it'll lead to legislation declaring women full citizens, I can feel it. We're on the cusp of a new world, Alexandre."

"Then I'll help. I'll resume my writing." He let go of her hand and put the apron case back on the table. "I want to be in your life. Perhaps I was being selfish by thinking I could have you for myself. I think it's best if I stay close to you from now on, helping you in whatever capacity I can. Together, we will let the world know that women and men can work together as one. We will be lifelong friends in this fight."

Maria smiled. She edged toward him and wrapped her arms around his neck in a warm and familiar embrace. She'd never stop loving him, whether they were together or far apart.

Throughout all of her life, her friends had taught her valuable lessons. Louise and Hubertine were the epitome of strength and passion, while Léon and Georges were persistent, dedicated, and open-minded. Even the despicable Daumier had a little compassion that surfaced when it was needed most. Then there was Anna, dear sweet Anna, with her protective and caring soul. And last, Alexandre. He embodied love. With all of these qualities, Maria knew she'd grown to be a better person. And wasn't that the point of life? To grow and learn and love?

She had purpose again. After the downfall of the Commune, she'd lost her way, but now a beacon guided her through the darkness of ignorance, the beacon of equality that Freemasonry brought. She would carry that beacon proudly into the world so all women and men could share the light together, no one better than the other, but as equals.

End

Don't miss out!

Visit the website below and you can sign up to receive emails whenever Sofia Diana Gabel publishes a new book. There's no charge and no obligation.

https://books2read.com/r/B-A-GPBBB-JDYTG

BOOKS 2 READ

Connecting independent readers to independent writers.

About the Author

Born in Sydney, Australia, Sofia Diana Gabel is a multi-genre author now living in the Pacific Northwest. Her published works include novels, novellas, and stand-alone short stories as well as inclusions in anthologies. She holds two bachelor's degrees, and a master's degree in archaeology, with additional coursework in creative writing. In addition to writing, she loves hiking forest and coastal trails, hanging out with family, and traveling as much as possible. She's a wanderer at heart and finds it hard to settle in one place for long. And why should she? There are so many places to explore!

Read more at sofiadianagabel.com.